First Step

KEITH BRADY

ISBN: 978-1-7636653-1-6

For friends and family.
And imagination.
And life.

CONTENTS

ACKNOWLEDGMENTS

I am greatly indebted to those who encouraged me to write in various forms. My soccer teammates from KPSC and walking footy at Pittwater put up with multiple poems over the years.
My family offered encouragement and critical appraisal as they worked through the first rough drafts. I want to express my sincere thanks to my wife Janet and children Geoff and Bron for their excellent feedback. I also want to thank my sister Michelle for her excellent editing, which made the story much more professional than it would have been.

Chapter 1

Dr. James Kentley, a renowned physicist, frowned at the display, his lips tight and his nose wrinkled in concentration. His lab coat stirred as he swayed, a sign of his restless mind. The laboratory was silent and still, a stark contrast to the storm of thoughts in his head.

A man stuck his head in the lab door and looked around. "Coffee, James?" He received no response. Blinking, he moved closer. "James? You okay?"

James jerked as his concentration shattered. "Uh?" He turned and looked at the man, confusion in his eyes. "Oh! Liam. Sorry mate, I was thinking."

Liam smiled. "No problem. I came to see if anyone wanted a coffee. I'm heading to the cafe."

James ran a hand through his dark, unkempt hair. "No thanks, Liam." He frowned and looked back at the screen. "I've had enough for the moment."

Liam looked at the display and back at James. "Let me know if you need anything." James didn't answer Liam's offer; he had turned back to the display, forehead lined in concentration.

Liam quietly closed the lab's door as he left.

James realigned the target and double-checked the power settings before re-running the test. Same result. He frowned as he worked through the results, thumbs tapping the bench. Closing his eyes, he visualised the accelerator firing electrons at the target and smashing into the protons and neutrons. He frowned as he pictured smaller particles exploding like shrapnel, their movement creating a kaleidoscope of varying fields. His logic gates required customised fine-tuning to interface with external hardware and maximise performance. He'd achieved what he needed for the job, but a new batch of targets had thrown up an odd result - a gap in a particle's trail. This anomaly, a particle's momentary disappearance, was irritating and challenging. He scratched his head at the incongruity of a particle coming and going. He could feel an idea scratching around but couldn't pull it out.

James's natural curiosity and determination nagged at him to find a solution. Though not directly related to his current project, this anomaly had become a puzzle he couldn't ignore. He chuckled as he recognised this compulsive element of his personality. It had previously landed him in strife with his supervisor and professor while researching his thesis at the university. At his graduation, his professor gave him a wry smile and suggested the corporate world and James would have an interesting time. Not surprisingly, the professor was right.

James had worked with three technology companies in the space of five years. In each, he had a conflict with management. Two firms focused on short-term revenue at the expense of product quality, staff and marketplace reputation. In contrast, James focused on the quality of the product and the opportunities presented for long-term results for the company and its clients. The third company conducted business in a manner James could only interpret as unethical. He took his concerns to his manager. As a result, he was made redundant shortly afterwards.

The Australian corporate culture may have been less cut-throat than other countries, but James still worried about his fit in the corporate world. He talked about the issue with the few people he trusted, and after one clarifying discussion with Harry Barnes, a friend from his university days, James decided to go solo. He created his own technology consulting company called 'JK Miniaturisation'. The change suited him, and he quickly built a reputation as a problem solver focusing on miniaturisation and robotics. One of his more significant developments, the J-Gate, involved miniaturised linear accelerators for computing applications where high performance was critical. Built on his original university thesis, the J-Gate used variations in power and electric fields to facilitate super-fast processing of simple calculations.

The J-Gate's reputation had landed James a contract with AI4U, an up-and-coming Australian company specialising in bespoke artificial intelligence systems. For security reasons, AI4U required James to work in their offices in Redfern, south of Sydney's CBD. AI4U's central laboratory in the basement had become James's home away from home.

James had prepared another variation on his tests when his Project Manager, Scott Willis, entered the lab. "James, how are those chips coming along?"

James groaned. Interactions with Scott had a way of ending in pointless conflict. He sat back from the display and smiled. "And 'Hello' to you too, Scott." Scott, oblivious to the dig, looked confused. James shook his head before grinning and looking at Scott. "I'm progressing ahead of schedule. The testing has worked out better than expected, and the J-Gates and processor connectors are ready for final assembly by your engineers." James leaned forward, eyes opened in invitation. "I'm about to run another test on the strange track. Would you like...".

Scott interrupted. "Shit James! This processing enhancement for the demo with Martyn Analytics has to be finished by the end of the month! We can't muck around!" He went a bit red around the cheeks and continued. "If you can't do the job properly, I'll finish it myself! Get me? I can't afford for AI4U to miss out on this deal."

James raised his hands in surrender. "Okay, okay, Scott. Don't burst a valve! Everything's done except checking the final build when the engineers sign off, and reviewing the documentation. It's just that this..."

"I don't want to hear about your anomaly! Get the checks and documentation done and on my desk by the end of next week! No excuses!"

"But they're not due till..."

"I don't care when they're due! End of next week. Get the job done!" With that, Scott stormed out of the lab.

James shrugged. He didn't understand Scott's aversion to discussion and closed mind to new knowledge. He looked at the lab's closed door and his brow furrowed. AI4U's engineers planned to complete the final build before the middle of the following week, three weeks ahead of schedule. James smiled to himself, happy to be self-employed and able to escape bosses who took a lot of the joy and sense of achievement out of work!

James sent the components to engineering late Friday afternoon. The gates' design had proven to increase the speed of AI4U's artificial intelligence engine by a factor of three. Martyn Analytics had grown to be one of Europe's largest data analytics companies, and a share of their business would be worth billions to AI4U.

* * *

Early on Saturday morning, James was still frustrated with Scott's attitude, a distraction affecting his ongoing consideration of the enigma he'd encountered with the gap in the particle trail. He shook his head, but his mind kept circling the question. Deciding to try a change of scenery, he drove to the coast for a walk and headed to Long Reef, one of his favourites. Rather than taking his usual route to 'Longie' headland, he turned north and headed along the beach. Clouds had built during the morning, and rain threatened, which kept most people at home. It suited his mood, and he was glad when the rain started.

He made his way up the coarse gold sand and onto the concrete apron at the rock pool at Collaroy. Down the other side, he waded through thick weed washed in with the surf. As he looked north towards Narrabeen, a mob of silver gulls began squabbling over a tasty morsel, and he chuckled at their antics. Seagulls doing what seagulls do got his thinking back on track. He had to focus on the basics-chunk the problem down and build the solution one piece at a time. He turned back towards his car with a simple action plan and laughed at himself for his muddled thinking.

James drove home, showered, and put on dry clothes before eating a tuna, mayo, and gherkin sandwich for lunch. He made his way into AI4U and quickly organised his work area for a series of tests, which he decided would be a decent foundation for his thinking and further experimentation. He started with the target that caused the anomaly to confirm the trails with gaps. He switched to another target from the same batch, and the test showed the same particle trails, but these remained unbroken. Repeating the tests with another two of the same batch of targets gave the same result: unbroken trails.

James scratched the back of his neck and frowned as he spoke aloud. "There's something about this particular target. Something in its structure causes the particles to behave differently and cause the gap in the trail." He placed the offending target under a magnifier but couldn't see anything obvious. He magnified and made copies of both targets and put them side by side on a viewer. Comparing the images, he couldn't see any noticeable differences and decided to give the targets to a specialist materials expert for a complete physical analysis. The materials used in the target consisted of precise amounts of tungsten, carbon, and bronze, which formed a monochrome grey alloy. As he turned to shut off the screen, he noticed a difference in the colour of the samples out of the corner of his eye. The targets should be identical, but the one producing the anomaly seemed to have a slight tinge. He frowned at the screen, but whatever he'd seen had gone. He shook his head, and his eyes darkened in determination.

James turned off the equipment he'd been using and started to secure the lab. He placed the two target samples in sealed containers and put them in his pocket. His efforts came to a surprised halt when the door slammed open, and Scott entered, arms waving around his head while he shouted about trespass and security.

James noticed a couple of security guards accompanying Scott, so he half-raised his hands to calm the situation. "Scott! What's the matter with you, mate?"

Scott stepped close and shouted. "What are you doing here? It's out of hours. You shouldn't be here!"

James looked at him and the security guards. "What are you talking about? I've been in after-hours often over the last six months. There's never been an issue. It's a good quiet time to concentrate and get work done." The guards nodded their agreement.

"I don't care about the past!" shouted Scott. "What have you been doing here today?"

James's eyes darkened as his brow furrowed. "Looking into the anomaly with the J-Gate and ... "

Scott pushed his palm close to James's face. "Stop right there! Is your anomaly authorised work? Is your anomaly work I have scheduled you to do? Is your anomaly anything to do with the Martyn project?"

James looked gobsmacked at Scott's emotional state. "Well, no. Not as such."

Scott turned to the security guards. "See! Get him out of here." He looked back at James. "Your contract is terminated! Don't bother coming back. I'll have HR send you anything personal from your desk!"

Horrified by this turn of events, James tried to reason with Scott. "Scott, hang on a tick. I've finished the wafers. They'll be with the engineers on Friday afternoon. What's your problem here?"

Scott turned with a sneer. "I know about the engineers, but you've been a pain in my arse since you joined the project. You go off on tangents and have no respect for my authority. You've undermined me with the whole team!"

James spread his hands. "I'm sorry you feel that way. It wasn't my intention to undermine you. I've always delivered my work on time, on budget and in good order."

Scott pushed past the guards. "It's not always about doing the job right; it's about how you do it." With that enigmatic comment, he left, and the guards escorted James to his car.

Chapter 2

Five men, each representing a pivotal role in the operations of WestProtect, chatted quietly as they sipped on drinks and waited for the sixth member of their group. These were the leadership of WestProtect, an American-based, non-government organisation dedicated to Western society's success and ongoing freedom. WestProtect presented itself to the public as a conservative think-tank funded by wealthy individuals, corporations, and other groups with similar goals of 'small' government, low taxes, and the freedom to do what they wanted without intervention.

The dining table in the centre of the room looked fantastic, displaying the finest china, silver, and crystal glassware meticulously laid by the property's staff. The dining room, a place of high-level discussions and strategic planning, formed an integral part of the sprawling property owned by WestProtect outside of Millington, West Virginia. Waiters stood at the room's perimeter, watching the men like hawks, ready to meet any need; the staff's movement and timing were carefully orchestrated to ensure complete confidentiality during the event.

A flurry of activity announced the arrival of Thomas Artur Sheridan. Thomas ordered a scotch. "Apologies for my being delayed..." He accepted his glass from the waiter and tasted the drink while waiting for the server to return to his position, out of hearing. "Ah! That's a nice drop!" He smiled and held his glass in a toast to his friends. "A delay well worthwhile, though. The UK has agreed with the idea and will be more, shall we say, obliging when they meet with the Secretary of State." They clinked glasses and signalled for refills as Thomas added more detail about his recent meeting.

When the drinks arrived, Ainsley van den Favel, WestProtect's chairman, looked around in expectation. "Let's get started, shall we?" He received gestures of agreement and called the head waiter. "We're ready to start, thank you." The waiter nodded. "Yes, sir!" as he signalled for the remaining staff to exit the room.

Once the room had cleared, Ainsley turned to his left and raised an eyebrow in question. Emanuel Thorpe, Head of Martial Response and Security, checked the room before drawing what looked like a remote control from his inner jacket pocket. Emanuel activated the device, a security scanner that swept the room and surrounding area for signs of electronic activity that could point to a potential security breach. Satisfied, he adjusted the scanner's mode to sense human sound; apart from their breathing, nothing registered. He put the device into watch mode and returned it to his pocket. "We're clear."

Ainsley smiled. "Excellent!"

Ainsley surveyed the others. "Welcome! It has been a while since our last get-together, and a lot has happened. Let's enjoy the starter before getting on to business." A faint ping sounded, and the men quietened. Ten seconds later, doors opened, and staff efficiently delivered a bowl of soup to each man before disappearing again. The talk quietened as the men enjoyed their first course, although there were occasional murmurs of appreciation for the complex flavour of the starter.

Again, a soft ping announced the waiters' arrival. They cleared the table and served a second course, this time of fish. They replenished wine and other beverages, and after a last look, the waiters left the room.

Emanuel checked his security scanner and indicated to Ainsley the meeting could proceed.

Ainsley lifted his chin and smiled. He relished his position as the head of WestProtect and his influence with the five men at the table. He turned to Braydon Dempsey, WestProtect's Head of Finance. "Braydon?"

Braydon smiled like a cat with cream-covered whiskers. His report, concise and to the point, gave insight into the performance of several initiatives, both long- and short-term. He was exceptionally pleased with their positioning in response to Europe's troubles. "The war between Russia and Ukraine continues to deliver the inflation we need to get a rise in interest rates. I expect employment to rise again in the short term before falling off in the following ten to twelve months. This will increase wages but at a rate less than inflation." He raised his eyebrows. "This continued pressure on the population will keep them focused on themselves and agitated against our adversaries." He lifted his chin. "Central banks will buy back the money they printed during the pandemic and, previously, the GFC. The buyback will put upward pressure on interest rates, which will be blamed on inflation." He smiled. "Our combined wealth will increase strongly during the upcoming year, and I expect we will enter a time of more stable politics once buybacks end and interest rates ease."

Shortly after Braydon finished, the ping sounded, and the plates were cleared. The head waiter called his staff to serve the main course. Each meal was prepared according to the men's preferences, and a sommelier followed the meals, serving fresh wines to match the food. She placed more wine on a sideboard before she left the room. With serving complete, the head waiter checked with Ainsley to ensure nothing remained to be done as the doors would remain locked for ninety minutes. Ainsley nodded his satisfaction and signalled for the man to leave. Once again, Emanuel ensured the room's security before the main course started.

Ainsley called for briefings from Elias Donovan, who handled US Domestic Affairs, followed by Thomas Sheridan on Foreign Affairs. When they had finished, Ainsley stood, eyes dark. "As you all know, we're financially sound. The countries we are interested in are doing what we need them to both here and overseas." His eyebrows lowered as he went on. "Technology, however, is not our strong suit. As a result, our security is at risk." He lifted his chin and looked towards Darius Robins, Head of Communications and Technology. "I have spoken with Darius about the problem and had several group discussions with your staff and external advisors. The recent developments in technology threaten to leave us behind. This situation affects all of us in one way or another, and we become more vulnerable as days go by." His jaw tightened, and he took a moment to ease the emotion. "Vulnerability to artificial intelligence is fast becoming a real threat. Technology can be used to influence people through analysis of their beliefs, priorities, and politics. Newer developments can achieve this faster and better than we can; It can influence money markets, interest rates, bitcoin prices, and other investments to our loss." His lips tightened. "There is also work being done that can be detrimental to security by cracking codes and intercepting communications." He ran his eyes over his leadership group. "Technology must be our number one priority until we either invent or acquire capabilities closer to the leading edge of AI, nanotechnology, drones, robotics, and quantum computing."

Ainsley turned to Darius. "Anything to add?"

Darius, the big-boned, loud and boisterous CEO of a privately funded Silicon Valley enterprise, looked sombre; he had none of his usual energy and charisma. "We provide cloud services and big data analytics - artificial intelligence is disruptive and has the potential to make or break us." His eyes narrowed. "We've built a team to focus on AI from people within the group and supplemented them with a selection of 'experts' from outside." He frowned as he looked around the group. "I say 'experts' because the landscape changes so quickly. Every day, there is a new startup, a new library of language models, a new funding round, and a new failure." His frown deepened. "As a going concern, we can't hope to keep pace with the mainstream, let alone the leading edge." He shook his head slowly. "I've stated this previously: I don't believe a startup of our own will do any better than what we're doing right now." He glanced towards Braydon and shrugged. "I believe a startup with the right publicity could gain financially if one of the bigger technology firms makes an offer." He shook his head. "The payback for the risks tells me it's not worth trying the strategy. We should develop the best solutions to meet our objectives and invest in the best people we can find. Then, we keep upgrading."

Ainsley nodded, and his eyes crinkled in frustration. "I agree with Darius. The feeding frenzy generated by AI reminds me of the dotcom boom and bust, and we need to steer clear of the churn." He scowled and shook his head as he turned to Emanuel.

Emanuel Thorpe set aside the remains of his grilled brown trout and addressed the table. "Besides Darius's team, we have a research centre in Colorado focused on security and weapons. They make good progress but have not created anything offering a significant advantage. We trail technology firms and foreign countries in two areas - AI and nanotechnology. We can't take our eye off the new development in nanotechnology, which is increasingly important, especially in surveillance and, closely related, robotics." He frowned and gave a shake of his head. "Artificial intelligence is a soft spot for everybody, not only us. Whoever cracks AI will gain a huge advantage because the AI's algorithms will build capabilities exponentially. I can't stress this enough."

The men chatted after they finished their main meals as fifteen to twenty minutes had been scheduled for ad-hoc discussion. During this time, Thomas Sheridan took the opportunity to speak with Ainsley and Emanuel. Thomas had recently returned from a five-week relationship trip, visiting the various WestProtect groups in other countries. "Emanuel, I've been thinking about your suggestion to be on the lookout for AI opportunities. An active member in Australia, Harper Caldwell, heads an AI firm called AI4U; he told me about his company's products at a function last month."

Emanuel's brow furrowed, and he nodded. "I know of AI4U. If I recall correctly, they build AI engines for data analytics."

"That's right." Thomas smiled and cocked his head. "Their main thrust involves using data from social media and other mass activity sites to provide a customer with the ability to target messaging and product information to the public. Their experience covers solutions for political campaigns, online advertising click-through rates, and simple online shopping results."

Thomas shrugged and tilted his head. "They're not breaking any revenue records, but their solution's reputation is growing."

Emanuel nodded. "They sound interesting." He pursed his lips. Can you look into their personnel and expertise areas? Perhaps talk with this Caldwell fellow. Where does he see himself in a few years? Can we make better use of him in WestProtect? Let's see if we can motivate him to push for technical breakthroughs to assist us."

Ainsley pursed his lips. "It wouldn't help Darius unless there's specific IP (intellectual property) or people they can get hold of, but the Colorado effort could use fresh ideas if AI4U gets onto something solid." He cocked his head. "Worth looking into, Thomas."

Sheridan nodded, and their conversation moved on to other topics until interrupted by the ping signalling a course change.

* * *

The morning following the dinner, Thomas called his senior associate in Australia, Robert Hickey-Roche, on their secure line. "Roche, how are you?"

Robert Hickey-Roche preferred to be addressed as 'Roche', his grandmother's surname, as she had been the central figure in his early life and taught him much about their family's place in society. She also introduced him to the people who would guide him through business and politics. "Hello, Thomas. It's good to hear from you." He chuckled. Have you decided to join our Australasian summit conference after all?"

Thomas laughed. "No, Roche, I'll leave the summit in your experienced hands."

Roche snorted. "You simply don't want to come to the frontier. Let your hair down! Come and see how we Aussies get the job done - we may surprise you!"

They laughed at the familiar banter until Thomas broached the reason for his call. "I do need something from you, Roche. We had our leadership lunch yesterday. The dominant theme was a real urgency to come to grips with artificial intelligence research and applications. I mentioned AI4U was starting to get competitive results, and Ainsley suggested we look into anything of potential benefit to us."

Roche nodded, his interest piqued. "Yes, they have been doing good business recently. They appear to have assembled an excellent team that's gelling well and innovating. I'll talk with Harper Caldwell and see what he has to say. He's giving a short presentation at the conference, so he's keen."

Thomas thanked Hickey-Roche and made a note in his diary to catch up with him after the Australasian summit.

At the same time, Roche made a note to have lunch with Harper over the next few days.

Chapter 3

Monday morning came by, and James called Scott at AI4U to see if the situation had stabilised over the weekend.

Scott answered abruptly. "Kently, you're off the books here. Don't call again!" And he hung up.

James didn't get a chance to say a word. He looked at his phone and shook his head. He couldn't figure out why he continually had these issues. He did the work, he did it well, and he did it at a fair price. What was the problem?

James found that being outdoors in a natural environment helped his thinking, so he decided to drive to Long Reef and walk in the seaside air. He sometimes considered getting himself a corporate mentor for advice, but he didn't know anyone from the corporate sector he trusted enough to talk to. In the past, the only advice he'd ever been given was to toe the line' or, 'If you want to get ahead, you have to conform'. He hadn't been prepared to do either, which often meant leaving his employer and finding somewhere where he could work effectively.

Reaching the Long Reef lookout, James looked out to sea and narrowed his eyes as he enjoyed the tangy air. The sun shone brightly, and an easterly breeze blew with enough strength to support a couple of paragliders stalking the cliff. Hearing a high-pitched sound, James looked behind him and upwards as his ears tuned in to the direction of the noise. One of the paragliders had a radio hanging off the bar. James shook his head and laughed at the absurdity of taking a radio with you when flying in the wind.

He walked westwards on the Dee Why side of the golf course, mindful of golfers preparing to tee off for the par four parallel with the track. He'd never heard of anyone getting hit, but the possibility always loomed. Coming to the narrow wooden bridge over a creek about halfway back to the main road, he jumped onto the beach. He kept an eye open for cuttlebones, which often washed onto the sand. If he found any, he collected them for Bob, a local bird breeder James had talked with on occasion. James appreciated Bob's down-to-earth, straightforward, honest take on most subjects. He also played walking football with his friends from England. Bob bred canaries and finches and mentioned they loved cuttlebones, so James kept a bag in the car for when they happened on each other.

He strolled along the high water mark and picked up a couple of smaller cuttlebones, their whiteness stark against the dark, dry seaweed and pale sand. As he walked, his mind went over his options, but the anomaly and the situation at AI4U kept tripping over each other. He was no closer to a solution when he returned to his car after his walk. James passed by a rubbish bin and dropped in the junk he'd collected while on the beach. He'd been so focused on his problem that he hadn't noticed when he picked up bits of plastic and trash left behind by the public. He put the cuttlebones in their bag and returned home to continue his internal struggle.

Later in the day, James continued to mull over his problem. He needed to discover the difference between the composite target samples and look further into what the difference meant. The more he thought about it, the more a potential solution came to mind - Harry Barnes, one of the few people James had clicked with at university and had consistently helped James when needed. They had shared technical interests and, more importantly to James, shared a distrust of corporations, the government, and people's motivations in general.

Harry had been working on a Doctor of Computer Engineering; his thesis covered architectural considerations in constructing quantum computers. Harry had completed his doctorate, and the university, impressed with his ideas, referred the work to their futures board for introduction to venture capitalists interested in helping graduates develop their ideas into products. In the five years since he'd started up, Harry had been successful enough to exercise an escape clause and buy out the VC's stake. The VCs had made way more profit than expected and told Harry they'd be happy to invest in future developments if the opportunity arose.

James gave Harry a call and explained the situation. The following day, they found a quiet corner in a convenient pub in the city. Harry listened to James as he related his experiences at AI4U and expressed his amazement at Scott's attitude. As Harry put it, "I can understand the pieces Scott put together, and there's a kind of logic to his way of thinking." He raised his eyebrows and continued. "But I can't fathom anyone thinking that way!" He shook his head and frowned. "What if your strange results turn out to be a game changer or disruptive? He's extremely shortsighted!"

James picked up his glass for a toast. "Well, here's to new beginnings! Again!" They had a laugh, clinked glasses, and finished their Coopers. Harry checked the time. "I've another hour before a meeting at four. Let's have a coffee and talk about the future."

They relocated to a cafe not far away and ordered coffee. Harry sat back in his chair. "Okay, James, tell me what you think you have and what you need to make it happen."

James spent a half hour talking through the miniaturisation work he'd been doing for AI4U's AI system and the appearance of the anomaly in the cloud chamber. "I have a theory on what the gap in the trails represents, but I need to do more experiments to figure out the process." He went on to describe the slight colour difference between the composite targets. "I'll need to check the molecular makeup of the two composites and find out what's different. Once I know that, I can begin collecting data on why the difference has an impact."

Harry nodded. "So, a fair bit of lab work and data collection, eh?"

James shrugged. "Nothing comes without hard work."

Harry raised his eyes. "Okay. Tell me about this theory you have about the gap in the particle trail."

James lowered his eyes and chewed on the inside of his lip. This was the moment his idea came into the light of day. If correct, this would be a discovery that could change the world. James looked Harry in the eye. "I believe the gap is time."

Harry looked surprised and confused. "Time?"

"Yes, time!" James took another deep breath and punched the idea out. "The gap is caused by the movement of the Earth in space while the particle has been physically relocated back in time. When the particle returns to the present, the present has moved. It's almost instantaneous, but not quite."

James remained silent and waited while Harry chewed through the idea.

James watched Harry's expression and saw him come to the point of the logical follow-up question. "What causes the particle to move back in time?"

James laughed out loud. "You're a quick bugger, aren't you?" He lifted his head. "That's why I need to do the research. I think the strange composite generates a second synthetic particle, and its field interacts with the first particle's field, causing the anomaly. The interaction of the fields results in the decay of the second particle until it has been exhausted. The field collapses, and the first particle returns to the present."

James shrugged. "It's the only scenario that fits what happens. I need to identify the second particle, create it in a controlled fashion, and then test my theory about the interaction of the fields."

Harry was silent again as he mulled over James's revelations. Finally, he looked at James. "Holy Shit! If you are right, it'll be the biggest game changer since the wheel." He frowned. "What's your plan? Where will you do the lab work?"

James countered with raised eyes and a cheeky grin. "I had considered checking with the university to see if I could get time there." He shrugged. "Or the government, though I hate to suggest them given the way they're loose with public money, not to mention their ever-strengthening ties with the USA."

Harry was shaking his head. "No, James, you can't take this to the university or the government. It's too big! Imagine what would happen if they treated something significant like they had everything else?" He snorted and laughed. "You have to find another way to develop it."

James shrugged his shoulders and smiled. "There isn't anyone else who has the resources. Harry, I need a lab, and I will also need smart people. It won't be cheap."

Harry frowned. "Look, James, come and join me at SplitQC. I have the people you need and the space to set up a lab. The company has done well over the last few years, so I have enough cash in reserves to invest in your research." He leaned forward. "If you're right, the discovery will herald a new and unexpected technology. Its applications could change our civilisation."

James considered Harry's open offer but baulked at joining the company, even though he trusted Harry implicitly. "Harry, that's a great offer, but I can't join the company." He shook his head. "You know me. I have to maintain my independence." He looked Harry in the eye. "Is there another way you can help me?"

Harry sighed and grinned. "Consider it done. I'll set you up with a lab and provide you with the people you need. You'll have no contractual or moral obligation to repay me. No strings." He smiled. "Will that work for you?"

James sat back, astonished. "You'll do that? You'll trust me to that extent?"

Harry smiled back. "James, there's nobody I trust more! It's like you said: I know you, mate." He paused and smiled at James. "And you know me."

* * *

With the Martyn Analytics team seen off, Harper Caldwell, CEO of AI4U, and his Chief Information Officer, Hugh Barton, discussed the demonstration in Harper's office. Harper grinned, eyes glinting. "That went extremely well. The new AI hardware performed beyond expectations. I'm sure the speed clinched the deal in the end."

Hugh had been the CIO at AI4U for just two years. He considered Harper a friend and professional colleague, having previously worked with him at various public companies. Harper, himself, had been brought into AI4U after an extensive international search for '*The type of Chief Executive who could lead the business through the turbulence of a changing world.*' The board expected Harper would sharpen profits, cut waste and procure emerging winners. He had a history of success in creating shareholder value, but some commentators viewed his methods as mercenary and short-term. One strategy he often used was to get staff off the balance sheet by making them redundant during a reorganisation and then hiring the good ones back in as contractors. Harper and Hugh had enjoyed particular success with savings in information technology departments.

Hugh's smile mirrored Harper's delight. Both were basking in the shared success of the AI hardware project, a significant milestone in their professional journey. "Yes, a great result. We dedicated substantial attention and focus to miniaturising key elements, a crucial step in enhancing processing speeds."

Harper's eyes focused on the distance as he considered his strategy. "Your bloke Scott Willis project managed the hardware upgrades, didn't he?"

"Yes. I brought Scott in from my previous gig. We're of like mind in the way we approach getting results."

Harper's eyes sharpened with strategic intent as he considered the next move. "Given our significant impact with Martyn Analytics, I'm confident our AI hardware will outperform GPUs (graphics processing units). I propose a meeting with the three of us. By capitalising on the improvements we've already made, we can position ourselves for a larger share of the market and increased profits."

Hugh tilted his head in agreement. "If we couple our existing software design with an even better in-house hardware design, we'll be hard to beat for many years."

Harper leaned forward, eyes narrowed. "Arrange the meeting for Monday, after lunch, say half past two. Have Scott Willis there and anyone else who may have useful input."

Hugh made a note on his phone and nodded. "I will do that, Harper." He put his phone away and relaxed in his chair. "Do you have any plans for the weekend?"

Harper smiled. "WestProtect's having their biannual Australasian summit conference in the Robertson Valley."

Hugh shook his head and shivered. "Brr. Too cold for me at this time of year."

Harper laughed out loud. "Not for us, Hugh. We'll have roaring fires, good food and plenty of interesting discussion on the future." He caught Hugh's eye. You should join us. The think tank is always interested in new talent. You'd fit right in!"

It was Hugh's turn to chuckle. "You've asked me often enough over the years, Harper. I'm not ready to tell the world how to live yet, but give me a year, and I may change my mind."

Harper stood. "Well, I better get going. I'll see you next week."

"You too, Harper. Enjoy the conference."

Chapter 4

WestProtect's Australasian event garnered strong support; there wasn't an empty seat in the auditorium as the guest speaker prepared for the keynote presentation.

The keynote speaker, a former Australian Prime Minister, started his address softly. "WestProtect's mission is to provide leadership and insight into the development and protection of our Christian values, our democratic society, our rules-based approach and our economic system that rewards effort and innovation." He looked out over the group and spoke with more force. "That society, my friends, is in mortal danger!"

He raised his arm, index finger pointing to the roof, "Firstly, our two-party system of politics has been infiltrated by a woke rabble of independents who spout questionable science about climate change to slow industry. They undermine our governments through exaggerated claims of corruption and nepotism. They want to 'give' people benefits from revenue we, you and I, have had to work hard for!"

He looked at his hand, and a second finger joined the first, "Woke progressives in coffee shops subvert the laws and policies put in place to protect us from harm and protect our industries from threat. Loopholes are created to facilitate the arrival of terrorists to our shores and illegals to our welfare system. These same people continue to chip away at previous governments' funding policies to divert revenue into socialist ambitions without any consideration of the lives they wreck on the way."

He scowled as he raised a third finger. "And, worst of all, suggesting those of us who accumulate wealth through dint of hard work, our blood, sweat and tears..", a pause, "...should hand over our wealth to bludgers through tax reform and changes to economic levers such as subsidies and quotas."

The keynote continued in this vein, with the speaker referring to WestProtect's research, the Western way of life and the dignity of work, amongst other themes. The speech made a powerful statement, encapsulating the frustration and anger experienced by the group's members in the face of global change. Those members consist of captains of industry, church and politics. All successful in industries as broad in scope as media, high tech, mining, armaments, pharmaceuticals and consulting. They also had representation from the Christian church, including Roman Catholicism, the Church of England, and Evangelical Protestantism. To a man, they encountered the changes happening within their nations. Indeed, due to populist uprisings, two nearby countries were not represented.

Those present listened and pondered.

At the end of the speech, the speaker shook his head and sighed. "My friends, we live in challenging times. We must bite the bullet, take the socialist snake by the neck and strangle it into submission." He looked out over the audience, his face etched in determination. "I don't know how we can achieve what we must to save our way of life, but technology will be a crucial element in this conflict. Make this summit the foundation stone of our strategy for moving forward."

He raised his arm again, this time with a closed fist. "No one can succeed if not us! Be strong! Find answers! With God's help, we will prevail!"

The attendees rose, clapped, and cheered. They were all strong, successful people. They would find a way.

Harper Caldwell's break-out session on Artificial Intelligence attracted a packed audience. Comfortable on the stage, he smiled as he walked and talked. "AI will be a disruptive technology. We approach the day when AI interactions with humans will seem natural." He held up a hand and chuckled. "Not conscious interactions! We're a long way from anything we could call consciousness. What I mean is, within a defined perspective, the AI may 'appear' to have consciousness because it can analyse, innovate and build new algorithms based on learned events. It will simply be an extremely sophisticated piece of programming."

One of the attendees, Mandy Malone, raised her hand with a question. Mandy lived outside of Washington, DC, and worked with Thomas Sheridan. Harper smiled and acknowledged her. "Yes, Mandy?"

"Thanks, Harper. Tom Sheridan wanted me to get your views on when you believe artificial intelligence and, to a degree, quantum computing will combine to be useful. In a targeted way?"

Harper pursed his lips before answering. "That's a good question. We seem to have been on the cusp of a breakthrough for a decade but can't quite get over the line." He raised his head and frowned. "We're on the verge. I can almost taste it." There were a few chuckles at this, and Harper smiled and shook his head. "Most recently, we've introduced quantum computing-based logic systems into parts of the AI's processing sub-systems. These improvements significantly increase the processing power and, in turn, its learning capability." He held his thumb and index finger one to the other, almost touching. "We're this close! It won't be long before we break through the frontier, and when we do, everything will change!"

Mandy cocked her head, "Change everything? How do you mean?"

Harper smiled. "We've recently won a contract with Martyn Analytics for an AI to process data relating to people's 'footprint' on the internet. The AI will look at the places they go, their searches, the products they buy, and so on. It's a massive amount of data. An AI analyses the data so any 'individual' can be targeted to receive information in a form to which the 'individual' will respond positively. Or negatively, for that matter." He sighed. "Development of the AI took months of work across multiple disciplines. And that's regardless of the library we have already developed as a core for AI processes in general." His eyes narrowed as he considered the future. "When we crack that processing frontier, an AI will do that work without human intervention. We'll tell the AI what we want to achieve, and the AI itself will build the processes and algorithms required to access data and produce the result."

"What if the AI decides to kill off humanity?"

Harper didn't see who asked the question but laughed. "The AI can't 'decide' to do anything outside of the instructions it has been given. It doesn't have free will to make those kinds of decisions." He looked at his audience. "AIs are purpose-built for specific tasks. The AI I mention can push conservative ideas tailored to an individual's values in advertising and information they access online. The AI analyses the individual's interactions with the internet and social media to determine those ideas." Harper shrugged.

"Not only will we save time and get to more people, but we'll give those people a better opportunity to be exposed to 'right thinking'. The key aspect of the AIs we're building now is their algorithms. By monitoring results over time, the AIs can improve their algorithms to get a better result."

He raised a hand. "Let's leave it there for the time being."

It was a valuable summit for Harper. He made strong connections to one or two conservative politicians in Australia and the USA while raising his standing among the members.

Chapter 5

Harry quickly organised access for James to use an empty warehouse-cum-factory owned by SplitQC in Tumbi Umbi, north of Sydney. He even sent over a bench-size linear accelerator his engineers had used for their research.

Within a few days, James had rented a house in Long Jetty and moved his files and lab equipment into the vacant warehouse. When the lab equipment was organised, James quickly reproduced the tests he'd made at AI4U. He called Harry to give him the news and ask about having the composite targets analysed by an expert.

Harry volunteered the services of one of his best materials scientists, who had recently finished a significant project. "I know she'd be happy to help out. Her last project was conducted under pressure, and yours will give her something new to look at, which will help her rebalance." He sighed. "It's great to have good people, but sometimes this work can get intense and focused."

James smiled to himself. "I know just what you mean, mate. When can she get here?"

"I'll give her a call and outline the situation. She lives in an apartment on the harbour so she can get there anytime. Her name is Imogen Matthews. I'll get her to give you a call."

James's phone rang an hour later. "Hello?"

"Oh, hello. This is Imogen Matthews. Harry Barnes asked me to give you a call."

"Right! Hi Imogen. Did Harry give you any information on what I'm doing here?"

Imogen snorted. "Sorry about that! I don't usually snort to strangers!"

"No problem. I'm known for snorting on occasion. I assume he didn't give you a lot of detail?"

Imogen laughed this time. "That's an understatement! He said you had something I'd find extremely interesting and that he wanted me to help you out. That was it! He said he had to go and I should check my email."

James shook his head. "It may not be interesting at all, but it is a puzzle, so that's a plus."

"Well, I need a break, so I'm happy to have a look. I have the address of the lab you've set up but don't know much about Tumbi Umbi... what sort of a name is that anyway?"

James laughed. "I Googled it! It's an aboriginal word meaning 'tall trees' or 'raging water'. There's not much of either of those around that I can see, but it's a nice area up here on the Coast."

"Hmm... I like the sound of indigenous words; they have a poetic ring."

James laughed again. "They sure do. Look, have you picked somewhere to stay?"

"Not yet. Can you recommend anywhere?"

"Nothing specific. I've heard the Shady Bay Motel is nice. I'd offer the second bedroom at my place, but it's a two-bedroom, one-bathroom place and probably a bit of a squeeze for strangers."

Imogen chuckled. "I'll stick with Google and, perhaps, the Shady Bay."

James laughed. "Good Choice! When do you expect to get here?"

"How about the day after tomorrow? Give me time to sort out a few loose ends."

"Sounds great. I look forward to meeting you and working with you. Thanks for taking the chance!"

"Chance is my second name! After the last year or so, I'm open to anything to relax!"

"Okay then. See you in a couple of days."

James sat back. He felt positive after speaking with Imogen on the phone. He'd never found it easy to work with someone new, but Harry's recommendation was worth its weight in gold. That, plus the fact that Imogen sounded easygoing, confident and level-headed, went a long way to putting James at ease.

The following morning, after a restless night, James decided to take it easy. Regardless of how he had thought the evening before, he was still nervous about trusting someone else with his research and ideas. He was cynical of most people's motivations and had trust levels of zero after being burned professionally on a couple of occasions.

He followed a coffee with bathroom necessities and a shower. Feeling refreshed, he cooked himself a basil and cheese omelette, which he quickly ate before driving to Tuggerah Lake.

The tension he had felt slowly dissipated as he looked over the glassy water. Feeling recharged in spirit, he walked to the lakeside track at Tumbi Umbi Creek, turned east and started walking. The weed growing at the lake's edge gave the air an earthy tang, which he found pleasant. He'd heard that you could catch prawns in the weed but had not seen anyone doing so. Perhaps it was only on nights with a full moon or something like that.

The lake was quiet and peaceful. Being shallow, it was free of fishermen and sailboards except in the far distance. Bird life was the one thing it did have plenty of, and James stopped occasionally to watch the numerous black swans, pelicans and cormorants. Egrets and herons fished at the edges, while ducks favoured the creeks and shaded areas. Along the track were plenty of corellas making a racket in the she-oaks. Their screeching was sometimes joined by lorikeets, rosellas and sulphur-crested cockatoos adding to the symphony. Magpies strutted in the grassy areas hunting for beetles and worms while noisy miners 'peep peeped' at anyone getting close to their territory.

James enjoyed the birds. He especially liked the pelicans as they flew low to the water, graceful despite their size, wings almost motionless as they glided to their new fishing spot. He found his unease slowly falling away and stopped for another coffee and light lunch before heading home, where he looked forward to a quiet afternoon and barbecued salmon for dinner.

After an early night, James woke refreshed and looked forward to meeting and working with Imogen. Somewhere in the past day, he'd reconciled himself to give her the benefit of the doubt on the back of Harry's trust.

Chapter 6

Scott had a smile on his face and felt pumped as he walked into the meeting. He saw this as an excellent opportunity to move up in the ranks, as he'd not had many chances to talk with his CEO.

His boss, Hugh Barton, waved him over before turning to Harper Caldwell. "This is Scott Willis, Harper. He's our Project Manager for the Martyn Analytics bid and was responsible for the new AI hardware configuration."

Harper shook Scott's hand. "Excellent work, Scott. I look forward to hearing more about it." He leaned in towards Scott and said, in a more inclusive tone, "I believe this is important work, Scott. I expect we'll be working closer together in the future."

Scott's eyes widened with surprise and pleasure. "Of course, Sir. I'll look forward to it."

Harper smiled. "Just Harper, please, Scott, no need for formality amongst friends."

Before Scott could comment, Harper pointed to the front of the room. "Why don't you give me an overview of what you've done and how you did it? That'll give me a better grounding for my ideas."

Scott walked to the front of the room and presented an overview as requested. He outlined the key elements in the new configuration and drilled into the faster communications interface and the use of wafers to miniaturise quantum logic processes. When he finished, he looked at Harper. "Any questions?"

Harper referred to his notes before turning back to Scott. "You mentioned the software guys had to redevelop the interfaces to the new hardware?"

"Er... Yes, that's correct."

"So, we'll need to iterate the product version to indicate the upgrade?"

Scott looked over at Hugh. "I believe so. That's the process, isn't it, Hugh?"

Hugh took the baton and responded. "Yes, the product guys will roll out a new version. By rights, If we plan to keep the new hardware architecture, we should release a new version series."

Harper raised a finger. "That's what I thought, except perhaps a new product release would serve us better." He paused and looked at his notes. "Scott, tell me more about the quantum elements. We're a software house delivering custom AI applications. How can these hardware components help us further?"

Scott shrugged. "The components form a quantum computing-based preprocessor for simpler, more common processes used by the AI. It's a hybrid solution; classical computing for complex processes integrates with quantum computing for mundane processes. The result is a significant improvement in overall performance.

Harper nodded. "Is it conceivable that we could join the race to develop a fully functioning Quantum Computer rather than a hybrid?"

"Yes. We could create a team with that goal in mind."

Harper turned to Hugh. "Hugh, what about using these quantum elements for the AI's more complex processes?"

Hugh nodded. "Expanding the scope does have potential. We'd need to leverage James's J-Gate wafer technology, but since our implementation is the first real proof of concept, I'm sure he'd get behind the development."

Harper looked up with a frown. "James? Who is James?"

Hugh shrugged a shoulder. "One of our contractors. We met him at the technology show in Hannover and decided he had good ideas. He joined Scott's group about a year ago to engineer those ideas into something we could use." Hugh raised his eyebrows. "That resulted in the wafer technology we're using."

Harper considered the new information for a moment before looking at his watch. "A contractor, eh? Can I have a look at his contract? I assume we have the standard NDA (Non-Disclosure Agreement) and the like?"

Hugh looked at Scott, who returned a frown and shrugged.

Hugh tilted his head, a question in his eyes, before he turned back to Harper, "I'll get a copy of the contract to you this afternoon?"

"Good," said Harper, "It will be worthwhile getting together with James and seeing what he thinks about more focused and longer-term work." He looked at his watch again. "I have to head out for another meeting. Let's continue this in the next day or so. I look forward to meeting this James..?"

Scott swallowed. "Kentley, James Kentley."

"James Kentley," Harper repeated as he left the room.

"That went well, Scott. Good Job!"

Scott looked a little pale as he turned towards Hugh. "I hope so, Hugh."

Hugh frowned. "Why's that?" He noticed Scott's pallor had turned noticeably pale. "What's wrong, Scott?"

Scott remained silent for a moment as he considered his predicament. He looked at Hugh and sighed. "I fired Kentley a few weeks ago."

"You what!? Fired him? Why on earth did you fire him?"

Scott shook his head. "The bugger just wouldn't respect me! He kept working on activities outside the job's specifications."

Hugh's brow furrowed over his eyes. "Scott! We've talked about this before. Just because someone doesn't kowtow to every one of your whims doesn't mean they're not doing their job!"

Scott remained silent.

"Shit! Where is he now? Can you get a hold of him?"

"I don't know Hugh. I'll give him a call."

"You'd better get him back here!" Hugh paused a moment. "What were these activities you took exception to?"

Scott shook his head. "Something to do with particle trails in the cloud chamber." He frowned. "Whatever it was, he was fixated on finding out what it was rather than working on his assigned tasks."

Hugh turned. "But he still got the job done!"

"Yeah, he got the job done, but I didn't like his attitude."

As Hugh went through the door, he said, "You better find him, Scott, and you'd better get him back here! Harper has set his sights on something, and it looks like Kentley figures big in that plan." He turned to go but stopped and caught Scott's eye. "The contract is standard?"

Scott frowned and shifted his feet. "No, it wasn't."

Hugh squeezed out. "What was different, Scott?"

"He maintained ownership of his IP and any improvements he made while working with us."

Hugh took a breath, and Scott quickly continued. "But he licensed AI4U to use his solutions within the scope of AI4U's products at no cost!"

Hugh growled and shook his head as he started towards his office. Without turning, he called, "Make this right, Scott! Make it right!"

* * *

James opened the lab at eight in the morning and ensured it was ready for his visitor. At half past eight, he heard a "Hello?" and opened the office door. James wasn't sure what he was expecting Imogen to be like but he certainly wasn't expecting the person ringing the bell. She was young, around his age, her hair was blonde and short, and she dressed casually in jeans and a burgundy tee with a stitched motif of a cat curled up and sleeping on the left shoulder.

"Oh! Hi. Imogen?"

Imogen smiled a yard wide. "That's me! You must be James. Great to meet you!" She held out her hand and shook James's vigorously.

James smiled in relief but wasn't sure why. Imogen's friendly, relaxed manner seemed so natural that James couldn't help but be at ease himself. He smiled back at her and held the door wide. "Come on in, and I'll bring you up to speed."

They sat at a large table James had found leaning on the wall at the back of the office. That and four chairs made up what he'd dubbed the Conference Room. An hour and a brewed coffee later, he'd told Imogen about the odd results from the two supposedly identical targets. He didn't go into theories about time but did say their task was to determine what caused the anomaly and, if possible, why it was happening. "We need to analyse the composition of the targets and find out what's causing the synthetic particles in the first place. Once we work that out, we can look into the anomaly and see if it's worth further research."

James sat back while Imogen, the key to their investigation, reviewed her notes and muttered under her breath. "I've worked on a few projects using different techniques to develop high-speed metals for drilling and grinding applications as well as tungsten, brass, carbon and mercury-based alloys for medical accelerators such as X-rays." She turned a page. "I need to analyse both samples and reproduce them to be sure the percentages are right. I can then begin to vary fractions and power input until we get the same results you have seen in your tests."

She looked at James, frowned and shook her head. "There's no magic bullet for this. It could take time and be onerous." She smiled. "You never know; we could get lucky and crack it the first time!" She waggled her eyebrows, and James cracked up laughing.

"That's just what I expect, Imogen. A lot of frustrating, hard work, but I'm happy to take the lotto win if it comes around!"

They reviewed the equipment James had already set up in the warehouse and discussed what else they may need.

Imogen made a list and emailed Harry asking for equipment from her lab. "He'll have it all delivered by lunchtime tomorrow," her brow furrowed in thought. It'll take a day or so to get it all set up and calibrated, so I'll be ready to start my analysis the day after tomorrow."

James smiled appreciatively. "That's great news, Imogen." He frowned, "I want to get moving on this." He shrugged and shook his head. "I can't explain why, but I feel like a kid on the verge of something big."

This time, Imogen laughed. "Step by step is the best way, James. Do the work, do it smart, and the results will come!"

James smiled. "Too true, Imogen, too true." He relaxed and changed tack. "Where did you end up with your accommodation?"

Imogen smiled. "Shady Bay had a lovely room available, and I got a great rate, so I'll see how it goes." She looked around the warehouse area, "Well, I'll get started. I have some of the equipment I need in the car." She pointed to a good-sized workbench on the far side of the factory. "Is that bench okay to use? It's a good size for my gear."

"No problem. All my electronics are on the bench over by the office wall. Do you need a hand with your gear?"

She smiled. "Sure, thanks."

With that, they set up her instruments on the bench. James checked that the power was sufficient and left Imogen to calibrate her instruments. After a few hours of tinkering, Imogen was ready to make initial baseline tests with the composite material.

"Can I get you a sandwich for lunch?"

Imogen grinned as her stomach made it known it was ready for food, "I am a touch hungry."

James laughed. "Great timing! There's a cafe down the road, and they make a great salad sandwich."

"Do they have seats?"

James nodded. "Yes, they do." He shrugged, "There's also a park with picnic tables by the lake if you like."

Imogen's eyes lit up. "Let's go! I do like the water."

Their sandwich was finished after half an hour spent talking about various birds, floods and weed. The hit of the outing was a white spoonbill sharing the lake's edge with a white egret. They were both keen to get to work, but they left the picnic table and birds with some reluctance.

They spent the afternoon familiarising themselves with the equipment and samples, with Imogen cataloguing everything as they worked through the various materials and James's findings. By late afternoon, they'd reviewed the power settings and calibration of his bench equipment.

"That's all of it," said James as he checked the time. "Let's knock off for the day and start testing in earnest tomorrow morning."

"It's good to have that done and, yes, a fresh start in the morning will be perfect." She looked at James, head slightly to the side. "How about you join me for dinner? Give us a chance to get to know each other."

James considered the steak he had defrosted and smiled. "Sure. That's a great idea."

Imogen smiled, eyes twinkling, "See you at Shady's restaurant at seven?"

"I'll be there."

When James arrived home, he checked the steak and replaced it in the freezer.

* * *

Scott wasn't happy about getting James Kentley to return, but he had no choice. He scrolled through his contacts and called.

James answered after a few rings. "Hi Scott, James here!"

"James. Thank goodness I got you."

"Look, Scott, I'm pretty busy here. What do you want?"

Scott looked at his phone. He was surprised. It'd only been a few weeks since he'd sacked him, and he'd expected Kentley to be happy to take a call. "Oh, alright." Scott took a breath and looked like he'd sucked a lemon. "Look, I'm sorry for being an ass! Can you come into the office? I'll reinstate the contract."

Scott gritted his teeth and waited a few more seconds before adding. "At a higher rate?"

There was silence for a while, and Scott thought he had him, but Kentley declined. "No, Scott, I don't want to work with you any longer."

Scott grimaced, his eyes clouded in fear. He tried to sound upbeat. "But James, surely we can talk about it? The wafers worked well, and we can help you improve on them. We can also look into the other thing you wanted to check out?"

There was a longer pause, and Scott crossed his fingers. "Look, Scott, I am not interested. I'm working on my research now and making good progress."

Scott slumped and swallowed. Brow creased as he racked his brain for another angle. "Shit James! This may make or break me! Can't you get off your high horse and.."

The silence was deafening. Kentley had hung up on him. "What a bastard! He could have, at least, listened!"

Chapter 7

James walked into the restaurant not long before seven. Imogen sat at a table on the back wall and waved an arm to get his attention. James smiled and waved back as he made his way over.

Imogen smiled and pointed to the opposite chair. "Hi, James. Sit and relax!"

A waitress asked James if he'd like a drink. He checked Imogen had something and ordered himself a light beer. James smiled. "So, Imogen, how is the room? Settled in?"

She shrugged. "It's fine. Quieter than a lot of places I've stayed over the years." She looked across at him. "You've only been here for a few weeks as well. Haven't you?"

"Yes. I moved two weeks ago when Harry made the warehouse available."

"Where in Sydney do you live normally?"

"I have a house in Chatswood."

"A house?"

James shrugged. "It was left to me by my parents."

Imogen frowned. "Left to you?"

James shrugged, "They died three years ago in a car accident. The brakes failed."

James saw that Imogen was concerned she'd brought the memory back, and he held out a hand. "Don't worry. I came to terms with their loss quickly. I miss them, of course, but it was an accident. The accident took my parents, but the years of life they did get were worthwhile." He smiled. "They wouldn't trade a minute of it."

Imogen nodded. "I understand. I'm glad you see things realistically; life can be a terrible burden if you take its ups and downs personally."

James cocked his head and raised an eyebrow in question. "You sound like you've been through a bit yourself?"

Imogen lifted her head as the waitress served James his beer and then waited while they selected their meals from the menu. After the waitress left with their order, Imogen lifted her wine and held it out. James clinked glasses. "Cheers!" They had a drink, and both sat back quietly for a moment.

Imogen raised her eyes. "How old are you, James?"

He frowned momentarily. "Thirty-two. Why?"

She smiled. "I'm thirty." She paused for a few seconds before continuing. "My father was a publican." She chuckled. "A real publican! He owned and ran a pub in a country town in Victoria."

James raised his eyes, but Imogen continued before he could say anything. "He never made a lot of money, but he certainly got to know many people in the town and the surrounding countryside." She stopped for a sip of wine. "He met my mother not long after he bought the pub. She was a salesperson for cleaning products, believe it or not! Brushes, mops, brooms and the like. Anyway, they hit it off straight away. It was unbelievable. He was a big bloke at six foot five, and she was a foot shorter and half his width."

Her eyes looked into the distance as she remembered. "His hair was fair and thin. He kept it short, like a soldier might. Mum's was black as night and long and wavy. And shiny!" She paused again, "Chalk and cheese! But they snapped together like magnets and, like magnets, had an attraction for the people living in the area." She chuckled, "It wasn't long before they had to add another bar and lounge to the pub. Dad was always having his ear bent by someone or other telling a story, wrangling a problem, or simply looking for advice."

She sipped her wine, "The ladies, too, would talk with Mum about fashion, their men, their kids and the local teachers. It's what happens in country pubs, I guess." She drained her glass and caught the eye of the waitress. She signalled for another and continued her tale.

"Mum died not long after I turned seventeen. She was cleaning out the gutters before the bushfire season started and fell off the ladder." Imogen's face saddened. "Dad was devastated. His world went from something rich and beautiful one day to an arid wasteland. Hopeless. Meaningless." She took a breath. "I didn't know what had happened or why it had happened or how to react. React to my father. React to the people who came offering sympathy. React to my feelings of loss. Dad never recovered. He ran the pub for another year, but it slowly declined. Fortunately, Dad saw the writing on the wall and sold."

James's lips and mouth tightened as he listened attentively.

She sighed and went on. "We moved to Melbourne. Dad bought a three-bedroom house in an unloved suburb on the bay. He was in and out of work for a few years. He suffered from depression and couldn't settle." Imogen looked at James. "He tried to get help because he knew something was wrong. 'Wrong in the head!' He used to say." Imogen shook herself. "Despite all the hard times, he never used the money from the pub after he'd bought the house."

She smiled. "He made sure I worked hard at school and afterwards used the savings to put me through university. My graduation was one of the few times I saw a smile on his face after Mum. He died two years after I graduated." She smiled wistfully. "He was so proud of me and relieved when I landed a good job at CSIRO. I sometimes think he stayed alive until I was on my feet." She looked at James again, a smile on her face. "Once I was set, he let go of life to return to mum."

James reached over as tears formed in Imogen's eyes, but she lifted her hand, "No, I'm okay. I was remembering when I found him dead in his bedroom." She smiled again, "He was lying flat on his back with his arms crossed on his chest and a big smile on his face." She chuckled. "It was the weirdest sight, but I'm sure he was happy at the end!"

With that, Imogen held up her glass for a toast and spoke. "To our Mums and Dads!"

James joined the toast with an enigmatic look on his face. He thought he may have met a kindred spirit. They were both orphans making their way. Regardless of anything else, he sensed he could trust Imogen and that she felt the same about him. Trust was a stranger to James. He had few close friends and was not one to keep in touch. Those friendships he did have, though, were strong and resilient. In many ways, James kept himself to himself and his work.

Their talk flowed freely as the evening progressed. Imogen was a bright and interesting conversationalist. She had a passion for her work, similar to James's. She insisted it was simply because she loved the elements. "They're building blocks of life! How could I not get joy from working with and understanding them better."

When James talked about his research into miniaturisation, robotics and putting a linear accelerator onto a silicon wafer, she shook her head and laughed. "You work with the building blocks of my building blocks! I could never get interested in the quantum level. I did try, though." She shrugged. "I'm able to get my hands on the elements. I can touch them, poke them, mix them. Understand them!"

James laughed in turn. "Well, that's something for sure." He grinned. "If I'm brutally honest, I don't understand quantum physics in any real sense." He frowned, "I know how to apply the effects and get an expected response." James chuckled. "If you ask me about the Higgs Bosun or bottom quarks, I'd be in deep water!"

Unlike James, Imogen was interested in other people and how they lived. She had spent time travelling through Asia and Europe, mostly alone. James shook his head. "I'm too interested in my research. I don't desire to go anywhere else unless it's to learn more about miniaturisation, robotics, nanotech and quantum potential." He smiled and laughed. "But you sure make it sound like it could be fun."

They finished their meals and sat quietly to relax for a few minutes. The waitress cleared away the dishes and asked if they wanted dessert. Neither wanted more food, but they ordered tea. When the tea arrived, Imogen looked at James with a smile in her eye. "James, do you recall when you talked about what you were looking for this morning?" James nodded, and Imogen went on. "Were you holding something back?"

James chuckled and smiled. "I thought I'd got away with that."

Imogen waved a hand as if to say he didn't have to tell her unless he wanted to, but James shrugged it away. "It's okay. I can't keep it to myself. Anyway, it may be nothing at all."

She nodded and sat quietly while he worked out how to explain his thinking. James caught Imogen's eye. "The composite target we use in the silicon wafer is supposed to give off short wavelength particles, much like those used in x-rays."

Imogen nodded, and James went on. "The composite we are using does exactly what I expect, but it also generates a short-lived, unknown particle. This type of particle is referred to as an exotic or synthetic particle. It doesn't interfere with the wafer's performance, so I've left it as an interesting subject for later research."

Imogen's eyes narrowed in interest. "Go on."

James chuckled. "Well, I tested a new batch of the composites, and everything was the same. We had the particles we wanted, and I also noted the synthetic ones." He gave a puzzled frown. "The trouble is, the synthetic tracks in the cloud chamber have a gap."

Imogen frowned. "A gap?"

James nodded. "A gap!" His eyes narrowed. "The only way I can explain the gap is if the particle disappears or ceases to exist for an instant and then reappears. I can only explain the effect if the particle moves backward in time."

Imogen looked at James with a sparkle in her eye and cocked her head. "So, your theory is that it's a time machine?"

James laughed out loud in relief when she hadn't run out the door. "No, not a time machine as such. What I think is happening is that the new composite fires off a second synthetic we don't see." He held up a finger. "As soon as it is created, its field reacts with the field of the first particle and their combined field is responsible for the move in time. When the second synthetic is exhausted, its field collapses, and the first particle returns to the present!" He shrugged. "Simple!"

Imogen looked at him, mouth agape, and started to laugh. James laughed with her, and it took a few seconds before they eventually calmed down. "If I am right, it will be an amazing discovery." James smiled and raised his eyes. "But the chances of a discovery like that are billions to one. All I want to do is work out what's happening."

Imogen nodded and looked serious. "And I will be happy to help." They clinked tea cups and finished their tea. Imogen sighed. "Thanks for trusting me, James."

James looked her in the eye, smiled and shook her hand. He was relieved he had someone he felt comfortable with to share his work. He felt something else but couldn't define exactly what it was. Excitement? Optimism?

He shook the feeling off. "Thanks for dinner, Imogen. It's been great getting to know you better." He smiled and took a deep breath. "We've got a lot to do, so I'll get back home. See you in the morning."

Chapter 8

Scott returned to his desk to consider his options. There had to be a way to retrieve the situation. He knew James couldn't do anything without resources, so he must have gone somewhere. Scott called his favourite recruiter.

A voice answered after two rings, "FastTech Personnel. This is Kelly."

Scott smiled. "Hi Kelly, it's Scott Wallis from AI4U. Is Lily in the office?"

"Hey Scott, good to hear from you. Hang on, and I'll see if she's free."

Scott waited less than a minute before hearing a click, followed by Lily's warm tone. She also had a smile in her voice. "Hi Scott, long time no hire! What's happening?"

"Oh, Lil, it's good to talk to a friendly voice! I have a problem!"

Lily's interest was piqued. "What's happened, Scott? How can I help?"

Scott's voice went an octave lower. "I can't talk over the phone; can we get together for lunch? Say one thirty at Humboldt?"

Lily checked the time and her calendar and sighed. "Sure, Scott. I'll meet you there. I have to run and sort a few things out."

"Thanks, Lil, I owe you one!"

"You bet you do!" Said Lily as she hung up.

Scott checked the time. He had an hour and a half before meeting Lily. He knew he had to tell Hugh but couldn't bring himself to make the call. Thoughts swirled in his mind, from his rise in status with Harper to his potential fall. Somehow, he needed to blame Kentley for the whole mess.

He called Hugh. "Yes, Scott?"

"Hugh, we need to talk. There's a problem."

"What problem?"

"Kentley's not coming back. He's already back into research. What I want to know is who he is with and for how long they have been together."

* * *

Scott walked into Hugh's office.

Hugh was on the phone and held up a finger to indicate he wouldn't be long. "Yes, Harper. Sure, Harper, I'll make sure it's sorted out."

"Uh Huh... yes... will do."

He looked towards Scott and sighed. "Okay, Harper. Scott's here now, so I'll... "

He rolled his eyes and shook his head. "I'm sure it's not that bad, Harper."

Scott could hear Harper shouting on the phone and then there was silence.

Hugh looked at his phone and pointed to his meeting table. "He's not happy, that's for sure."

"We're in the shit, Scott. Well, at least you are! I may be able to climb out if I'm lucky!"

Scott cocked his head and asked. "Kentley?"

"Of course it's Kentley! He is the key man on the wafer development?"

Scott nodded. "Yes, but..."

"No buts! He was the key resource and.." his voice climbed. "...AND his contract had modified Terms and Conditions that mean we don't own the Intellectual Property on our own bloody hardware!"

Scott looked at the table. "It didn't seem so bad at the time. He gave us free use of the module for..."

Hugh held up his hand, palm out. "But WE can't develop the chip! WE CAN'T make improvements or have patents!" He paused for breath. "We can't do anything until we reverse-engineer the bloody wafers and try to understand what bloody Kentley's done so we can do it again slightly bloody differently!"

Hugh shook his head. "The CEO has reamed me all ways." He looked Scott in the eye. "I trusted you to be able to handle this job. It wasn't all that bloody difficult," he shouted. "WAS IT?"

Scott mumbled and shrugged. "I'm sorry, Hugh, things got a bit out of control. I didn't know Harper was going to decide to build his own damn hardware!"

Hugh sagged. "It's nothing to do with what Harper wants. It's simply that we stick to the rules. You know how important Terms and Conditions are to us." He grimaced and looked sidewise at Scott. "And the NDA." He looked back at Scott. "You did get the NDA signed, didn't you?"

Scott nodded. "Yes, of course! It's in Kentley's HR file."

Hugh frowned. "Huh! Harper told me he couldn't find the paperwork in the file."

Scott shrugged. "I took it over to the..." He cocked his head. "Hold on. I have it in my top drawer. I planned to take it to HR but got interrupted. It was a while ago now!"

Hugh stood. "Go and get it now. I don't want any more cock-ups!"

Scott left Hugh's office and walked along the corridor to his own. As he neared his office, a secretary tried to get his attention for a bundle of papers she held. He pushed past with a grunted "Later!" and slammed his door as he entered.

He sat, opened the file drawer and pulled out the Martyn Analytics admin folder. After shuffling through the file twice, he slapped the folder onto his desk. "Shit! Where did I put the bloody NDA?"

Despite being a poor manager of people, Scott had enough experience to sit back and calm his emotions. He closed his eyes and tried to recall what he'd done with the NDA paperwork. He'd handled the document too long ago and had forgotten so he decided to go through his desk from top to bottom in an orderly fashion.

He found the papers after fifteen minutes of searching. During that time, Hugh had called twice to ask when he was returning.

After a quick check to be sure the NDA was signed and dated correctly, Scott returned to Hugh's office.

Hugh glared as Scott entered his office, paper in hand. "I almost sent security to help you!" He looked at the document in Scott's hand. "Is that it?"

Scott nodded. "Yes..." and stepped backwards quickly as Hugh snatched the NDA from his hand.

Hugh sat and started to go through the document. He noticed a handwritten addition to the disclosure clause, read the text and swore. "Shit!"

Scott frowned. "What?"

Hugh pointed to the change, which mirrored the changes in the employment contract. Anything James invented or discovered through his work would not be included in the definition of Confidential Information. "We have no legal avenue to get Kentley back."

Hugh looked at Scott and shook his head as he picked up his office phone. He pressed the '0'. After a moment, "Please send two officers to my office."

Scott's face took on a comical, surprised look. "Hugh? What's that?"

"I'm sorry, Scott. Harper was crystal clear with me just now. We can't take the risk of having you in the company."

Scott pleaded. "But, Hugh, I can make this right."

There was a knock on the office door. "Come in," ordered Hugh. "You may escort Mr. Willis from the premises. No detours to his office or other areas of the business." He looked at Scott as the security men moved to flank him for the walk out of the building. "Scott, I'll have HR send on the contents of your office later today. Good Luck to you."

Scott was escorted to the front desk without another word. Before leaving the building, his access credentials were cancelled.

* * *

After their dinner, Imogen and James were already feeling relaxed while they worked. Imogen began with a preliminary analysis of the targets' composition. After some time and the occasional expletive or grunt of dismay, she made her way to James's bench with a frown.

He looked at her and noticed her expression. "What's the problem?"

Imogen shook her head. "I don't know!" She shrugged her shoulders. "The alloys are identical as far as I can tell with the equipment I'm using now."

James was about to object, but Imogen held a hand to forestall him. "With the equipment I have, I can break down the main elements in the composition, but there must be contamination that is too small to register." She shook her head and checked her watch. "The spectroscope will clarify the situation."

James cocked his head. "Spectroscope? Aren't they big?"

She laughed. "Technology improves all the time, as your linear accelerator wafers testify. The spectroscope I'm getting is a portable version. It weighs under twenty kilograms and combines microscopy and spectroscopy. I have one included in the list I sent to Harry."

They talked about the analyser, its capabilities and materials science in general until they were interrupted by a shout from the front door. It was the courier with Imogen's equipment. James raised the roller shutter, and the driver reversed the van into the warehouse.

After unloading, Imogen focused on unpacking and calibrating the new equipment. When she was ready, she set up the analyser with the first composite and spent an hour looking at different angles and saving relevant images. She then swapped in the second sample and did the same.

It was getting late in the day when she waved James over. She smiled and pointed at the display. "Look there."

On the screen were two images with charts that looked identical to James's untrained eye.

Imogen pointed at a spot on the second image. "There is a difference. It's tiny, but it's consistent. If I had to guess, I'd say there was a contamination issue when the composites were made."

James nodded and smiled. "Can you tell what the contamination is? Is there some way to gauge its impact on my tests?"

Imogen shrugged. "Sure. But it'll take time."

* * *

Lily was about to leave the restaurant when Scott finally arrived. He was over half an hour late, and Lily wasn't one to waste her time.

"I'm sorry, Lil."

"Are you alright, Scott? What happened? You look terrible!"

Scott sat and slumped. "I've been let go, Lil. Fired! I'm buggered now. I'll never get another job!"

Lily waved over a waiter and ordered Scott a cold beer. She was unsure how to handle the situation, but Scott had been a good source of revenue for a few years, so she felt partially obliged to hear him out. "What happened?"

Scott spilled out his version of events. He cast himself as doing the right thing and Kentley as the villain.

At the end of the sorry tale and their lunch, Lily stood and looked at Scott with a frown. "Scott, from my perspective, you've messed up. You've not operated per AI4U's standard procedures with their contracts, and you've not been reasonable with your management of James Kentley." She put her bag over her shoulder and closed her discussion with, "Don't bother calling me again."

Scott looked at his plate and wondered if she was right.

Chapter 9

Harper entered the Harry Noble Reserve and found a shady spot under a tree. He was out of place in his tailored suit and polished shoes but didn't attract the attention of 'ordinary' people as they chatted and laughed while their dogs ran around, tongues lolling. His ex-wife, Darcy, had wanted a dog before their divorce. She'd said it may bring them closer together since he didn't want to be weighed down with kids. He laughed to himself. "Kids and dogs. Who's got time for kids and dogs!"

He waited.

Mohamed "Mo" Banks joined him a short while later. Mo was an unusual man. He was of average height and slim, but his arms, legs and face seemed triple-jointed. He played soccer, and his opponents were often dazzled as his body moved one way and his legs moved another. They would suddenly find themselves dispossessed of the ball and see Mo heading towards the goal with a cheeky smile and a swagger.

He stuck out a hand. "Hi, Mr. Caldwell. It's good to see you again." That was the other thing about Mo; he was always polite and formal.

Caldwell grimaced. "Good to see you, Mo. Though I wasn't expecting to need your services again so soon."

Mo shrugged. "That's how it goes sometimes, Mr. Caldwell. How can I help?"

Mo's business services were distinctly shady - much like the tree they stood under. Mo was also expensive. He styled himself as running a Private Investigation service. It was not a registered business, and he didn't have an Australian Business Number. He was well-known, however. He and his team were experts at finding people and things, extracting information, hacking communications networks and break-and-enter. Despite the volume of work Mo's enterprise undertook, Mo kept himself removed from the action, leaving underlings to take any punishment if caught.

Harper growled. "Mo, I'm not sure what the problem is." He shrugged before continuing. "I've stumbled onto an opportunity, but one of my staff has cocked things up."

Mo shrugged and remained silent.

Harper frowned. "We had a contractor develop hardware for us, which works exceedingly well. In addition, he looks to have stumbled onto another possibility that may be profitable." He broke eye contact with Mo as a dog ran into the trees twenty metres away.

Mo cocked his head in surprise. "But you'd have a contract to protect your investment in any IP. Wouldn't you?"

Harper shook his head and sighed. "That's where my staffer cocked up. The contractor retained the rights to any new IP he discovered." He took a breath and locked eyes with Mo again.

Mo squinted. "That would hurt! What do you think I can do for you?"

Harper's face darkened. "What I want you to do is two things. First, get me whatever information you can on the contractor, James Kentley. I want to know his designs for the work he did for AI4U. Second, I want to know what he stumbled on. It may be nothing, but I sense it's got a lot of potential." He pulled an envelope from his jacket pocket and handed it to Mo, "Here's what we know about Kentley regarding address, contacts and technical background. If I get more, I'll pass it on to you."

Mo took the envelope. "I'll get my team onto it and get back to you as soon as I have something concrete. My fees will be the same as usual, and I'll need five grand up front."

Harper pulled another envelope from his pocket. "Here's fifteen to get you started. This is important to me, and I'm looking for quick answers."

Mo's eyebrows rose. "Mr Caldwell, you have our attention. I'll get back to you with an update in a week."

With that, they shook hands and went their separate ways.

* * *

Mo walked to a local cafe, ordered a coffee at the counter and found a spot away from distraction. While waiting for his coffee, he started a secure messaging app and sent a note to Pearl O'Reilly. Pearl, a hacker, lived on the outskirts of Dublin in Ireland. They had met in Ireland four years previously. Mo had been trying to identify a corporate spy stealing software from an Australian FinTech firm. Mo had been referred to Pearl when he needed someone to help find any traces of the theft online. She proved to be a brilliant hacker and found the traces Mo required to identify the spy. Mo and Pearl shared an ambivalence to law and order and had worked together on various projects in the years since. Pearl had developed the messaging app for herself and a few friends. His note read, "Hi Pearl, James Kentley ex AI4U. Need current location or trail and anything on research and employment projects."

He sent the text as his coffee arrived and leaned back to consider Harper's job. Pearl would get back to him when she had something. In the meantime, he needed feet on the pavement to see what could be found locally.

He called Lowen Wall, one of his 'investigators', "Yep?"

"Hi, Lowie, you busy?"

"G'day Mo. I'm finishing the Jansen job today and plan to get onto Broadbill tomorrow. It looks messy!"

Mo frowned. "Bugger! I need to find a bloke. It's important."

Lowen sighed loudly. "Well, I guess I can squeeze it ..."

At that moment, Mo's phone showed a purple-coloured message arriving. "That was quick! Hang on, Lowie. I've just got a message that might help." He switched to Pearl's message app and read the text, "Kentley using Credit Card. A place called Tumbi Umbi? He's been there for at least a few weeks. His home address is in Chatswood, so he may be visiting someone. I will advise more later."

Mo switched back to Lowen, "Okay, Lowie, we've got a start at least. The bloke I'm after is in Tumbi Umbi, possibly as a visitor since he lives in Chatswood."

"Tumbi Umbi?" asked Lowen, "Where the hell's that?"

Mo laughed. "I just looked it up, and it's on the Central Coast. Bottom of Tuggerah Lake."

Lowen was silent for a few seconds. "Look Mo, I can't get there myself, but I know a bloke who lives in Woy Woy. He's done a few low-key jobs for me before. I'll get him onto tracking this bloke, sifting his bins, that kind of thing."

Mo considered the idea and, in the end, had nobody else to call on. "You trust this bloke?"

Lowen laughed. "His name's Bernie Ong. Yeah, I trust him. We go way back." He paused a moment and then continued. "He's a pensioner! Fit and wiry, with Chinese and European blood, which comes in handy sometimes. He's one of those people nobody notices!" He laughed out loud. And he's always happy to add cash to his pension!"

Mo nodded to himself. "Okay, mate, get him onto it. The person I'm after is James Kentley. He's your basic office worker, so he'll not be trying to cover his tracks. That's how I know he's in Tumbi Umbi. I'll send you a picture and whatever else I know in a few minutes."

"Sounds straightforward, Mo. Will advise. See you later."

Mo zipped a package with photos of Kentley and the places he'd used his credit card in and around Tumbi Umbi and emailed Lowen. After his coffee, Mo walked to the station and picked up a train to Central. He was going to Chatswood to see what he could find at Kentley's house.

* * *

Imogen tapped James on the shoulder. Her smile told all, and James knew in his gut that she had found the answer.

Imogen pointed to a bump on the spectroscope's detail graphs. "See that small bump there?"

James nodded. There was a tiny indication of something registering in the analysis of the second sample, whereas there was none in the first. "What is it?"

Imogen tapped the screen. "That's Chlorine! The count is tiny; it's a minor part of the composite. But it isn't in the first sample. If I had to guess, I'd say it's a contaminant rather than an intentional part of the structure, but I'll need to test it to be sure."

"That's great news! It must be what is causing the second synthetic. Chlorine! I wonder how it got there?" James stepped back to let Imogen get on with her investigation.

When Imogen noticed James waiting, she laughed. "Give me time! It'll take an hour or two!"

James chuckled and shook his head. "Okay. I'll get back to work! But that's fantastic, Imogen! I can hardly believe that we're getting close at last!"

A short while later, Imogen shouted, "Ha!"

James dropped what he was doing and almost ran to her bench. "What have you found?"

She grinned at him. "Nothing earth-shattering, but I now know the chlorine is part of the composite and not on the surface!" She turned back to her notes on her laptop and made the appropriate entries. "Now we can start testing to find the exact composite mix that will generate the second synthetic."

James ducked his head. "Inside? Inside the composite? I thought it would be on the surface from tap water, salt, or something stupid like that."

Imogen shrugged. "I would have been surprised if it had been a surface contaminant as it would have been washed away or worn over time." She shook her head. "I have no idea how it got there, but it's part of the composite's structure. If I had to guess, chlorine was introduced during the initial working of the alloy. Hard to say, as there are a couple of ways to make something like your targets."

James shrugged. "It doesn't matter how it happened, to be honest, the key's in replicating the effect." He smiled and nodded thanks before returning to his bench, where he was refining the miniaturised linear accelerators.

* * *

Mo walked towards Bales Park in Chatswood. When he arrived, he sat on a bench to get a feel for the place and the movement of people in the area. Compared to the bustle of the Chatswood shopping and business district, it was quiet and peaceful.

Mo proceeded across the park, his gaze fixed on Kentley's home. The surroundings were devoid of people, with trees on the median strip and tall shrubs along the fence line providing a natural screen for the front of the house. He navigated the driveway and circled the back of the building, meticulously checking for security measures. To his surprise, there were none. Taking advantage of the better screening, he returned to the front door.

The door had a deadbolt and lockable handset. Mo shrugged, pulled on plastic gloves, and tried the handset, but it was locked as expected. Reaching into his inside pocket, he took out a soft leather roll from which he selected the appropriate tools. He twisted and jiggled and the door was unlocked and open in seconds. He smiled as he entered the house. It was one of those strange quirks of human behaviour that many people installed deadlocks and didn't use them.

Mo went through the house carefully. There wasn't a lot there, which Mo found unusual. There were a couple of framed photos on the lounge room wall. They looked old, perhaps his parents. There was no desk, computer, or obvious work area. He did find a few handwritten notes with diagrams on a shelf in the kitchen. They made no sense to him, but he took pictures with his phone.

While the visit was a bust for information, Mo did gain insight into Kentley's character. He didn't seem to have a girlfriend or many casual friends, and he probably spent his time at work or thinking about his work. Harper Caldwell's interest and the results of this visit also piqued Mo's interest.

Mo checked the area before exiting the house and locking the door. He removed his gloves, carefully replaced them in his pocket and headed back to the bench in the park. The area felt calm, and after a few minutes, he walked to the train station and returned home.

* * *

Mo's phone buzzed as he entered his apartment. Looking, he saw another message from Pearl via her app. Additional information on Kentley includes his work and research history over the last ten years and verifies his current link with SplitQC and its founder, Harry Barnes. There was no employment contract, so she assumed the relationship was informal. Pearl's report also listed academic papers that gave additional insight into James's research. It included superconductors and linear accelerator decision gates used with miniaturisation techniques and robotics.

Chapter 10

Imogen pushed her chair back and rubbed her tired eyes. "I'm done!" she shook her head slowly. I need a change to freshen my brain! Do you have any ideas?"

They'd both been working long and intense hours, and the fatigue was starting to impact their concentration and attention to detail. James scratched the back of his head. "I agree; it's time for a circuit breaker."

Imogen raised her eyes. "Ever been in a kayak?"

"A kayak? No. I've never thought of it before!"

She laughed. "Neither have I, but they have a tandem at the motel for guests. It doesn't get a lot of use."

James looked a bit uncertain but masked his doubts. "That sounds like just the thing! Er, how do we get the kayak into the water?"

Imogen chuckled. "The Shady Bay has a boat ramp to the creek, so we just carry it down and drop it in. Nothing easier!"

James shook his head, his eyes uncertain. "What time do you want to get going?"

"How about you join me for breakfast at the motel, and we can head out afterwards?"

"Sounds like a plan. I'll check my insurance?"

"What?"

"Nothing. Just talking to myself!" James smiled bravely. "I'll see you in the morning."

* * *

The kayak was a basic sit-on model from a specialist warehouse in Wyong. At thirty kilograms, it wasn't too difficult to handle, and once they got the hang of getting on and off, the vessel was stable and easy to paddle. Once in the 'yak' as the motel called it, James looked over his shoulder, "Left or right?"

"Let's go left to the lake," said Imogen. So, left to the lake is where they went.

They didn't talk much while paddling, preferring to enjoy the quiet and bird life. Imogen pointed to the She-oaks lining the creek ahead, where a sea eagle perched on a branch. It was either resting or had a beady eye looking for a tasty mullet. There were a lot of cormorant nests as well. The cormorants were quite skittish and would fly off if the kayak got too close to their tree or the paddlers looked at them directly. Judging by the full bellies of the cormorants flying in from the lake, they were good fishers. On returning from the lake, they landed on a sunny branch or rock and spread their wings to dry as they digested their catch. There were many 'shags on rocks' as the saying goes.

They paddled to the creek's opening and into the lake. Off the entry point was a small island occupied by a large population of cormorants perched in the branches of the trees. James noticed the all-black cormorants were together as a group and, on another set of trees, the ones with variations of black and white. He thought it could be a type of family affiliation and pointed it out to Imogen. She shook her head and shrugged. Like James, Imogen wasn't up with bird life on the lake.

They floated in the shallows and looked at what must have been close to a hundred birds when they suddenly took flight and headed in all directions. They kept to their groups despite their urgency. James looked around and saw a large sea eagle swoop in and land on a perch at the end of the island. After a few minutes, the initial panic must have settled as cormorants started to fly back to the trees. James noted half of them must have gone to safer roosts.

Another species that caught both of their attention was the pelican. They watched as the large birds splashed in the shallows, presumably to clean their feathers, or fished the slightly deeper water or sat contentedly on the grassy verges of the island. Pelicans are beautiful birds, graceful in flight despite their size. While hunting, they hunch their heads onto their back to hide their head from the prey and swim through the weeds in the shallows. Suddenly, they launch their head into the water, necks extended and mouths open. After a few seconds, the head lifts, water streaming out of a closed mouth; the bill lifts skyward and is given an occasional shake as the water empties. A final shake is needed to position the 'catch' and, what must be a satisfied swallow, sees the meal complete. The hunt resumes.

One of the funniest things they saw was a fishing pelican accompanied by three young cormorants. Wherever the pelican went, the little cormorants stayed with it. The kayakers weren't sure if the pelican was happy to have the company, but Imogen laughed as they watched the situation. James thought the young cormorants may have trusted the pelican's experience to find fish, while Imogen reckoned they hoped for a mullet that had been stunned by the pelican's feeding. Either way, it looked cute!

After an energetic couple of hours, they paddled back to the motel. A gardener helped them put the 'yak' on its rack, where they hosed it clean for the next customer. After thanking the gardener for the advice and help, they returned to the motel for a light lunch and discussed the sights they'd seen. The change of pace helped them relax and recharge their batteries.

The view from the Shady Bay restaurant's balcony took in much of Tuggerah Lake and part of where they'd paddled. James looked out to the far shoreline and breathed deeply. "It's a nice spot up here, isn't it."

Imogen smiled back. "It certainly is. I've always gone farther afield for holidays... it seems we have a jewel closer to home."

James laughed. "Well, I'm positive we'll get more opportunities to explore further in the next few months." He rolled a shoulder. "I wonder if they have motors for these 'yaks'?"

Imogen grinned and shook her head. She enjoyed James's company and wondered if their friendship could lead to something more profound in the future.

* * *

Bernie Ong was a simple bloke who, in the main, went unnoticed. He wore shorts and thongs in the summer, tracksuit pants in the winter, and matching runners from the cheaper stores. His fashion rules amounted to just one: 'clashing tops and bottoms'. After talking with Lowen Wall, he hopped on the train to Tuggerah and a bus from there to Tumbi Umbi.

He had a battered-looking fold-up shopping cart, which he dragged behind him as he walked from the bus stop to the industrial park. He went through a familiar routine of shuffling to the warehouse units one by one and searching through the rubbish bins at the side of the buildings. He began with the yellow-lidded recycling bin and pulled out plastic bottles and aluminium cans, one at a time. He placed a can carefully on the pavement and stomped to flatten it. Then he'd bend to pick up the newly flattened treasure and put it carefully into his trolley. Anyone noticing him saw a down-on-their-luck old guy collecting cans for cash. Most people ignored him or, if interested, would watch him for a while, judge him harmless and leave him to it.

When he'd extracted as much as possible from the recycling, Bernie moved on to the general rubbish bin to see if any cans had slipped in by mistake. If he found one, he'd follow the same process as before. This continued until he was happy he'd cleared that unit. Then he moved on to the next.

He got to Kentley's unit and proceeded in the same fashion. However, he kept an eye open for any paperwork that may interest Lowen. He was particularly interested in anything with letterhead or a business name, receipts, and delivery dockets. He also watched for handwritten notes or computer printouts. Bernie had worked in the offices of various companies until he had a meltdown at fifty-five, so he knew the type of information Lowen was after. Pickings were slim, but he found a duplicate of a courier's docket in the rubbish bin. It included both pickup and delivery addresses and was recent. Bernie smiled. He moved on to the next unit before returning to the bus stop to start the journey home.

When he arrived home, he called Lowen and told him the news: "The delivery only referred to boxes, so I don't know what it was, but the total weight was over twenty-five kilos, so reasonably heavy."

He waited while Lowen made a note, then nodded as Lowen asked for more. "The pickup address is in Macquarie Park, and the company is listed as SplitQC Pty Ltd."

He nodded as Lowen asked him to check the bins every couple of days but keep it low-key. Bernie smiled when Lowen said he'd send him an extra couple of hundred bucks for the good work.

* * *

James and Imogen's testing continued solidly with an occasional kayak diversion. It was a hard slog, and both hit the wall at various times. At such moments, they tallied a new failure and hoped that they would eventually crack the secret. Imogen even mentioned Edison's nine hundred and ninety-nine failures as the numbers of their tests mounted.

James constantly looked for ways to use technology to speed up their efforts. He found an open-source image recognition program and modified it to compare Imogen's test results against a baseline. The result would identify differences. The software wasn't perfect, but it made the task less tedious and saved time.

The breakthrough came as a surprise one afternoon. Imogen had set up another composite variation in the test area and started the accelerator. The tests had progressed through almost ten per cent of the power variables when the computer sounded an alert.

Imogen's voice was excited as she called James over to the bench. "I think we've found it!" she exclaimed, her face shining with the thrill of a potential breakthrough.

They waited impatiently for the final test to be completed. Once done, Imogen displayed the results summary, which listed the results sorted by power variation index. Two entries were highlighted.

She clicked on the first. "BINGO!"

The image they looked at had been filtered using James's software, so all the known tracks had been removed. They were left with the particle tracks they had been searching for.

James smiled broadly. "We have tracks! That must be the second synthetic! You've done it!"

With the successful isolation of the second synthetic particle, James and Imogen felt a surge of triumph. They now knew the composition of the new target and the precise power needed to generate the field. As they looked at each other, a shared sense of accomplishment prompted them to break into a spontaneous celebration dance.

Their celebrations ended awkwardly when they realised they were holding onto each other. Regardless, they looked at each other and smiled. They had work to do, but there was something else to work out when time allowed.

Little did they know that time would become a very precious commodity indeed.

With the hard work done, it came down to repetition and patience. They finished with three targets whose composition was almost identical. They referred to the composites as A, B and C. Composite A was the original composite James had used at AI4U. It generated the first synthetic with unbroken trails. Composite B was the new offshoot from the contaminated composite that created the second synthetic particle. Last of all was Composite C, which combined elements of A and B to produce a similar result to the original contaminated composite but with a gap. They'd made a significant step forward but still had to determine how and why the particle fields interacted. Imogen's experience and insights were proving priceless.

James called Harry to make sure the factory would remain available for a while longer.

Harry was enthusiastic. "James! No problem, mate. The building is yours for as long as you need it."

James expressed his gratitude, and Harry reaffirmed his support. "Imogen says that what you're doing looks very exciting."

James laughed and agreed. "She's great! I don't think I'd have got close to understanding what was going on without her!"

Harry laughed out loud. "All my staff are stars, James! See you later!" With that, he hung up.

James put the phone down and shook his head, thinking that Harry was very different from most CEOs.

Chapter 11

Marty Elliot sighed as he locked the shipping container. It had been another long day dealing with suppliers who couldn't supply, builders who couldn't build and debtors who couldn't pay. He looked to the heavens and shook his head. "Why do I bother?" He looked as though he was going to ask more but, in the end, shook his head again and started walking towards his car.

Marty wasn't religious, but he had a bet each way now and then. "Just in case!" he whispered as he turned onto the main road into town.

The pub wasn't crowded, and he found one of his preferred tables at the back with a view of the other patrons. He wasn't from a military background by any means, but he did like to keep an eye on the activity and people around him when he could. He took his first mouthful of the schooner of New he'd ordered at the bar. A smile beamed on his face. Marty's smile could light up a room; this one was no different. "Ah..." He sighed, "That's bloody beautiful!" He took a second mouthful before putting the beer on a coaster and picking up his phone to check for messages. He frowned when he didn't see one from Hoshi. Hoshi had promised Marty that he'd have the prefab pricing a week ago after saying there had been trouble with the sales guy and a supply problem out of India. But, despite all that, he'd told Marty that he would get a price ASAP! Still nothing! "How can I get these bloody houses built if I can't get the walls!" He shook his head again, had another drink and sat back in the chair.

It had been a hard five years. Marty smiled; it was closer to twenty years if he was honest with himself. That's how long ago it had been since he'd started the idea to provide cheap housing. His memory glossed over the New Zealand trial builds that hadn't gotten off the ground, and he skipped over the failed Japanese construction company. There were other things he managed to skip over as well; there were always plenty of things that didn't go right. Sometimes, it was as though fate was against him. Not that he believed in that stuff. He looked heavenwards, just in case, and had another drink of beer.

His latest shot at housing had kicked off in Australia some five years ago when he asked the Queensland Government to give him some land to build on. They'd declined when he couldn't provide proof or documentation of ever building anything. His desire wasn't enough. He'd got the same story in New South Wales, so he was now looking for a backer to provide the land for a proof-of-concept dwelling.

"Marty!" The call roused him from his rehash of his memory banks, and he looked over to the bar. It was Bernie Ong, an old work colleague from when he was having a go at a 'normal' nine-to-five job.

Marty held up his now empty glass and mouthed "New".

He hadn't seen Bernie for a couple of years, but they shared the odd text now and then. Bernie had always been in regular nine-to-five work, mainly sales, but some project work as well. Over the years, Marty has given subtle hints to Bernie that he could invest in Marty's housing ideas, but to no effect. Either Bernie didn't understand the oblique references or didn't want to get involved. Marty shrugged to himself. It wasn't surprising Bernie wouldn't get involved because he'd been there when the dotcom crash saw Marty's self-managed super go up in smoke.

"Hey Marty! How're they hangin', mate?" asked Bernie as he sat down and put the beers on coasters.

Marty smiled, and his face lit up. "Great, Bernie! Everything's going well." He lifted his beer and held it out for a toast. "Cheers!" They had a drink, and Marty cocked his head. "How's it going with you, mate?"

Bernie smiled. "All good. The grandkids are great, so the kids are great, and that means the missus is great!" He smiled at his wit and had a good swallow. "Even got a bit of cash work to top up the pension!"

Marty smiled; he'd always liked Bernie. Bernie was easygoing, and Marty could trust him not to betray any of the confidences Marty shared now and then. Bernie was the only 'straight' person Marty had ever talked with about his other life.

Since Marty didn't offer, Bernie asked. "What are you doing here, mate? How's business?" Bernie waggled his eyebrows when asking the latter.

"Not too bad. Heading south of Camden in a couple of days to look at some land for the housing."

Bernie frowned. "The housing? How's that going, mate? It's been a bit of a bugger to get going? Is the Government helping yet?"

That's Bernie, always with the questions. That is probably why he was a reasonable sales guy. Marty shook his head. "It's a hard slog, Bernie. I'll crack it, though, if this meeting goes okay."

Bernie nodded. He'd heard it before. "What about the 'other' side?" He asked, with an emphasis on the 'other'.

"Oh, it's going okay. I've had to talk with a few people, and I'm storing stuff at home again."

Bernie pursed his lips. "That's a bugger, mate!" Bernie knew Marty had tried to put himself at a distance from the 'business' because the cops were getting close, but you can't trust anyone these days! One of the people he'd handed some of the business over to skimmed a bit for himself and ended up selling light pounds. Marty had to get help to sort the bloke out. He got his stuff back, and the bloke had moved to Adelaide, but it slowed everything down.

Bernie had asked him why he didn't chuck the whole game away. Marty had tried to explain. "Bernie, there are two worlds. Normal people have normal lives in one, and there is excitement and deals in the other. I'm sort of playing in both!"

Bernie hadn't understood the buzz of living on the edge, but that was okay.

They chatted about this and that for a while, and Marty's ears perked up when Bernie talked about his extra funds. "It's cash only, mate.

Under the table." Bernie smiled, "You'd be proud of me!" Then he laughed, and Marty got up for a few more beers.

When he returned, they decided to have something to eat and looked at the menu.

Bernie frowned in thought and then decided. "I'm going for the burger and chips." He put on a sad face and ended with a grin. "The wheat will give me indigestion, but it's worth it now and then!"

That wasn't strictly true. If Bernie were true to form, he'd wake in the middle of the night with raging heartburn. He'd have to get up, have a couple of antacids, add a pillow, and try to sleep on his back, hoping gravity kept the acid down where it was manageable.

Marty chuckled. Bernie always complained about his wheat allergy, but he always had wheat. Go figure!

Marty continued their earlier conversation when they'd placed their order. "Now, Bernie, what's this cash work you've got? Do you get much out of it?"

Bernie looked around to make sure they were out of earshot. "I can't let Centrelink get wind of it, or they may bugger up my pension!"

They both looked around again. Satisfied, Bernie continued. "It's nothing. I had a call from a bloke who gives me cash for odd jobs now and then. He said ..." Bernie looked over his shoulder again and recounted his call with Lowen.

"He asked me if I had time to make a couple of bucks on the side." He shook his head as though it was unbelievable. "I'm a bloody pensioner! I've always got time and am always interested in extra cash!" He shook his head again. "Anyway, he said it wasn't illegal and would be easy." His nose wrinkled, "It does require going through bins, though!"

Marty smiled. "Bins? You checking if someone's playing around or something?"

Bernie looked aghast. "No, nothing like that!" He looked around again before leaning closer to Marty, "It's looking for leads into what a business is doing in a warehouse in Tumbi Umbi."

Marty frowned. "Drugs?"

Bernie shook his head. "I don't think so." He shrugged, "I don't think the bloke who asked me knows what it is either. I'm looking for paperwork, documentation, and any office scraps. Anything to give them an idea of what the business is doing and who else is involved." He chuckled. "Pretty airy-fairy thinking about it now, but he's already paid me six hundred bucks for a week's worth of bin trolling."

Marty nodded appreciatively, "Sounds good to me. Have you found anything?"

Bernie shrugged. "I don't know for sure. He was happy when I told him about a delivery the other day. This afternoon, I found a spreadsheet in the recycling, which I'll be sending him tomorrow."

"Can I have a look at it, Bernie? Just interested to see."

"Sure, mate, it's right here." With that, Bernie pulled a backpack from the top of his shopping trolley and riffled through scraps of paper until he smiled. "Here's the printout. I hope it's useful to him."

Marty looked at the page. There was enough detail for him to recognise a checklist of ingredients or something similar. Most had handwritten crosses in the end column, but a few had ticks. He asked Bernie, "Do you know what company owns the place?"

"No. But a delivery has been made from a company in Macquarie Park called SplitQC."

Marty grunted appreciatively, "I've heard of them; they're a technology firm. I wonder what's going on."

Marty couldn't let an opportunity go begging, so he asked Bernie about Lowen, who had organised him to do the job. "Lowen Wall's his name. I've known him on and off for a few years. He's a decent bloke who works with some PI firm. He occasionally asks me to do simple jobs like go through bins." He looked quizzical, "What's your idea on this? I'm surprised you're interested."

Marty shrugged, doubtful himself. "I don't know, Bernie. Something is going on, and you know me. I would like to know what's happening on the off-chance I can use it." He frowned. "I've heard of this Lowan Wall bloke before as well. I can't pin him, though." He shook his head. "I'll have to think about it."

Bernie gave a shaky smile. "You're not going to wreck my little job, are you?"

Marty smiled and shook his head. "No way, Bernie! Don't worry about it. Another beer?"

Later that evening, Marty recalled that Wall was part of Mo Bank's team. That was enough to spur him to get online and learn more about SplitQC and its founder, Harry Barnes. Barnes seemed smart. He was into computers and had a successful company engaged in research and development into quantum computing. The company had a couple of standing contracts with Australia's Department of Defence, and over a few short years, Barnes had built a small but effective team.

Marty couldn't find anything obvious about the warehouse in Tumbi Umbi or what it was being used for.

When looking at the spreadsheet printout, Marty noticed a series of chemical notations, including W, B, C and Hg. He knew that 'W' was the symbol for Tungsten, and B and C were Boron and Carbon. He didn't recognise Hg, so he looked it up - Mercury. He went back to the SplitQC staff page and scrolled through the bios again, but nothing stood out.

Marty frowned. He'd just have to go and have a look for himself.

* * *

James and Imogen planned a series of tests to see how the two sets of synthetic particles interacted. They designed the tests to determine which sequence the composites had to be fired, for how long and with what amount of energy. The result of research may be glamorous, but the reality comes down to rigorous testing and consistent results, which you repeat until all variations have been trialled or you get a breakthrough. It took time for them to understand what was happening and how to use it, but in the end, it was relatively simple.

Once they knew what was happening with the particles and fields associated with the composition of the targets, James could take the experiment out of the bench-mounted linear accelerator and build an experimental test module in his miniaturised world. He made a simple construct using two wafers for Composite A and two for Composite B. He only planned to use one each but added a second for redundancy. He wired the wafers into a simple control circuit. They ran diagnostics and executed a simple test without encountering any problems.

James called Harry for a Zoom meeting so they could give him an update and discuss their next steps.

After sharing their findings, Harry's eyes lit up with intrigue and excitement. "So, if I understand this correctly, we have two generators. Each one produces a stream of particles that generate an electromagnetic field, but their interaction goes beyond that. When these fields converge, they lead to a cessation of motion in the spatial dimensions of the spacetime continuum?"

James nodded, and Harry went on. "A side effect of the interaction is that all matter inside the field, including the streams of particles themselves, gets forced into the time dimension?"

James nodded again, leaving Harry to continue verbalising his understanding. "And... since we are already in the present, the matter can only go backwards into the past?"

James shook his head. "That's not exactly right. There is no path into the past as such."

Harry waved his hand. "Sorry, it's the terminology I used." He smiled and frowned. "It appears to 'Step' back in time."

James smiled and nodded encouragement. "And when the second generator stops generating a stream of particles and, therefore, its field, the particles from the first generator return to the present. Or 'Step return' to the present!"

James chuckled and smiled. "That's just about spot on, Harry."

"What if the first generator stops generating?"

James looked serious but chuckled again. "That's what I like about you, Harry! You don't miss possibilities! Our tests show that both fields are required to Step back. If either is removed, the Step field collapses, and the contained matter returns to the present."

They talked for a few minutes to clarify a couple of points before James continued. "The next logical step is to see what we can do with these fields. Can we move, or 'Step', objects back and forth? How big an object can be Stepped? Can we see what the environment is like back in time?" He shrugged. "There are a lot of questions, and we need to get a start on answering them."

Harry nodded. "What do you need?" James let out a breath and smiled. "I wasn't sure if you'd agree to back me more... I haven't shown much return for the help so far."

Harry shook his head. "James, I know it may result in a dead end, but nothing has ever been achieved without a risk of failure. What you're doing is exploring; to my mind, exploration is a key gain from our evolution as a species. Not just an exploration of the physical world, by moving around and touching things, but the exploration of our reality through thought, ideas and imagination." He grinned, "Then, turning those ideas into something we can touch and see. That, in turn, sparks more exploration."

Harry was silent for a moment, his eyes hooded in thought. James could see the passion being banked and replaced with determination. "Whatever you need, James. I don't have infinite resources, but whatever I can spare, you can have."

James looked at Harry and cocked his head, "I don't need much in the way of money, Harry. What I do need is help with artificial intelligence."

Chapter 12

James met with Harry and one of his quantum computing specialists, Jeroen Bos. Jerry, as he was known, had completed his PhD at Oxford and specialised in AI development. He had led Harry's AI team for three years. Jerry had significantly increased SplitQC's productivity by using AI to control their trials of quantum hardware variations. The AI used the results to interpolate new algorithms for itself and, subsequently, improve processes for the quantum computer process.

Jerry's eyes danced as he held out a hand. "It's great to meet you, James. Harry's filled me in on your miniaturisation work, which I see as one of the keys to enhanced AI performance. I look forward to learning more about your work in the area." He rubbed his closely shaved head with a hand and smiled. "I'm also fascinated by what Harry's told me of your silicon wafer-based linear accelerators." He shook his head. "That may have enormous implications in increasing the scope of AI resourcing and power usage."

They started to talk more about AI and miniaturisation when Harry interrupted. "Enough chat for now! Let's get you two onto developing this AI!" He pointed. "James, give us a rundown of what you've found so far. I didn't even try to explain it to Jerry, and I could do with a recap myself anyway."

James laughed. "It is hard to get your head around, even for me!" He gave them a reasonable overview of the research and their assumptions. "So, what we have is two field generators. The first creates a field that, for our purposes, has the potential to Step back in time. The second produces a field that does nothing on its own but will activate the potential when the two fields interact. I am starting to label them as Potential and Activator to differentiate them. When the second, the Activator, stops projecting its field, the Activation stops and the Potential returns to the present."

James shrugged and looked at Jerry. "That's it, Jerry. Ultimately, it's a straightforward process once you know the target composition that creates the particles and the interaction between the different particle's fields." He grinned and looked sheepish. "I don't think this whole effect would have been found except by accident. I got lucky and had the opportunity to find out what was happening."

Jerry looked at James. "I'm amazed and impressed regardless of how you found this. Tell me, how can I help?"

James's eyes darkened. "I want to work with something inside the Potential field, but the times I'm working with are nanoseconds; I can't physically react fast enough to gauge timing, quantities and the like. It's okay for the experimentation we've been doing in the lab, but anything that Steps back will need to take a capability for logic back with it."

Jerry nodded. "Have you got some idea of what capabilities you'll need?"

"I need an AI. One I can connect to multiple Potentials and multiple Activators. It has to accept voice commands to change various parameters and start or stop field generators to achieve a test result. And, then, record the results and analyse the data to learn."

Jerry smiled. "Now, that sounds like an excellent project. I have an inkling mass will be an important factor, so I'll begin with that in mind, and your miniature linear accelerators, of course."

Harry shook his head and smiled. "Before you get too engrossed, Jerry, drop what you're doing and head to Tumbi Umbi. I'll get Alice to book you into the Shady Bay motel."

Jerry grinned and nodded; the multiple AI projects excited him, and he was keen to get on with their design. "I'll be there tomorrow afternoon." He shook James's hand. "I look forward to working with you, James."

James smiled back. "Me too, Jerry!"

* * *

James and Jerry, with input from Imogen, designed the AI architecture from scratch and incorporated the wafer accelerators James had enhanced for AI4U and proprietary quantum computing processes developed at SplitQC. Their new understanding and technology were also incorporated into the baseline language models the new AIs would use to communicate. One of the critical processes they wanted to include in the AI's model was the ability to learn, analyse and improve its algorithms when the opportunity arose.

James's satisfaction was evident once the language model was finalised and tested. He was eager to include what he referred to as fundamental principles: "If we're dispatching an artifact to another time or place, we must ensure it doesn't repeat our mistakes."

Harry, Imogen, and Jerry found James's reasoning sound and playfully dubbed it the Asimov Robot Principal. It was a straightforward yet profound concept: The AI models would be guided by a comprehensive codex - a commitment to life, free will, and responsible automation.

Once the models were complete, Jerry coded the initial focus for the Step AI to control subtle changes to the field generators and Step timing and prioritise learning from experience as testing progressed.

With the help of SplitQC experts, they pushed through many issues associated with interfaces, overheating, learning algorithms and many other problems. It took time, but they built a working beta artificial intelligence named "Quinn" to bring together 'Quantum' and 'Linear Accelerator'.

During this time, James and Imogen built and tested a simple module to test the Step process. It consisted of potential and activator generators attached to a 556 dual timer plus a lightweight power supply. Testing of the module couldn't be confirmed because a Step was instantaneous. They took heart from the fact they hadn't had a burnout. James expanded the circuit to incorporate a programmable Raspberry controller with WiFi. With this setup, they could interface Quinn to the module, and Quinn could handle the tests with precision.

The big day arrived when they could test the complete package. To help, they used a high-speed camera that would catch anything happening to the test module itself.

Since Jerry had the lion's share of Quinn's development, he got the honours to kick off the initial test. They had done so much preliminary work and testing they had no doubt everything would work as expected. James grinned towards Imogen, who gave him an encouraging nod before he turned to Jerry with a smile. "Mr Bos, you have the helm."

Jerry lifted his head and confidently said, "Quinn, I'm Ready for the setup of the Step Test."

"Step Test Setup Ready."

"Quinn, Set Potential at standard output."

"Potential Output Set."

"Quinn, Set Activate output at standard output and Set Activate Timing at Standard plus one second."

"Activate Output Set. Activate Timing Set."

"Quinn, Execute Step Test."

"Step Test starting in Five.. Four.. Three.. Two.. One.. Mark."

"Test complete", said Quinn without any discernible pause.

James played back the high-speed recording and saw the proof. The test module disappeared for around a thousandth of a second.

Jerry's eyes goggled. "Bloody hell! Did you see that?"

James raised a fist. "Yes! I knew it!" He looked at Jerry and considered the result for a moment. "I figured we'd have a longer Step. Let's lift the Activators output by one K."

Jerry nodded. "Quinn, adjust Activate Output to one thousand times standard and re-run Step test."

"Activate adjusted to one thousand times standard. Step test starting in Five.. Four.. Three.. Two.. One.. Mark."

This time, they saw the module disappear with their own eyes. It reappeared a second later.

James looked at Jerry, "One more run."

"Quinn, Set Activate Timing for Standard plus ten seconds."

"Activate Timing set."

"Quinn, Execute Step test."

"Step Test starting in Five.. Four.. Three.. Two.. One.. Mark."

The test module disappeared; ten seconds later, it reappeared as the computer pinged and the AI reported, "Step test Complete."

* * *

The rain that had come down all day came down a little harder. A pale orange glow surrounded the sodium lights installed at the back of the units, but they were far from prying eyes on a cold, wet night in June.

Marty made his way along one side of the building and around to the rear. On this wall were doors to the back of the warehouse and an external storage room, but it was the three windows Marty was interested in. Two were toilet windows, which he could use if necessary, but he'd prefer the larger third window if possible. All the windows were secured with an aluminium screen screwed to the exterior.

The building was relatively old, and Marty, relying on wear and tear and human nature, wasn't disappointed. He levered up an edge of the screen and worked his way around the screws until he had enough leverage to manhandle it off. When his hand slipped, and he skinned a knuckle, he went back to patiently jimmying until the screen fell to the ground. Well hidden at the rear, he had no concern that anyone would notice him, and the rain covered any sounds he made. He tried the window, and, with a bit of a shake, it slid open. He smiled. Human nature often puts trust in windows covered by security screens.

The top of the garbage bins, neatly arranged along the wall on the side of the building, came to a foot or so below the window sill. Marty quickly wheeled one into position and leveraged himself into the building. Turning on a torch, he entered the warehouse and looked for anything to help him determine what the building was being used for. A solid timber bench on the wall to his left carried various tools and instruments. He didn't recognise anything except a soldering station. He took a picture with his phone and collected samples of residue that looked like grit on an otherwise clean surface. He checked the waste bins but found nothing except an empty food container. There were no files he could see, not even a computer. There was a whiteboard that was wiped clean. He was about to move into the office area but realised the whiteboard had two sides. He flipped the back over and saw it was also wiped, though there were some residual markings. He took another photo and returned the whiteboard to its original position.

On the wall adjacent to the roller shutter was another bench. This one was steel rather than timber, and he could tell it had been used for spot welding but not how recently. A long machine resembling a lathe was set at one end of the bench, and other bits and pieces were strewn about. He took another picture and checked the bin for useful waste but came up empty-handed. He frowned as he entered the office space; it looked like it was hardly ever used. There was a small mezzanine area, but it was vacant.

He went downstairs to double-check he'd covered everything and noticed a corner with a stack of empty boxes. He shrugged at the probable waste of time and energy but pulled the boxes into a line with their labelling visible and took another photo.

After replacing the boxes, he checked the toilets and storage room. Finding nothing of interest in them, he returned to the open window, climbed out into the rain and shut it securely. After wrestling the security frame back into place and pushing the bin around the corner, he gave the area a last check before returning home.

Chapter 13

Marty woke early the next day and went through his morning rituals, finishing with two eggs on toast and a black plunger coffee. He scrolled through his emails as he sipped the hot brew. Nothing was urgent or noteworthy, so he shifted to the photos he'd snapped at the warehouse. His nose wrinkled. Apart from looking scientific, they made no impression, and he couldn't make head nor tail of them.

He sat back, eyes scrunched as he considered what, if anything, to do. He almost deleted the lot but shook his head and grunted to himself. "I need more information." Swiping to his contacts, he set the search term to 'science' and was surprised when names started listing. Marty's greatest asset was information. He maintained a network of ideas, possibilities and people. Reading the notes he'd made when he'd entered these contacts, he smiled when he came to one Dorian Johnstone. He'd met Dorian at a technology trade show at Rosehill Racecourse a few years previously. Dorian was a service technician with a science instruments company, and he may be able to tell him what he was looking at.

He pressed the call button, and the phone answered on the first ring: "Dorian's phone, Edwin speaking."

"Oh. Hi Edwin, I'm after Dorian. Is he about?"

"He's not far away. Hang on a tick, and I'll try to find him. What's your name?"

"I'm Marty Elliott. We met..."

"Hang on!" Edwin cut Marty off and left him to wait. A few minutes later, a new voice came on the line. "Hello? I'm Dorian. Do I know you?"

Marty chuckled. "Only if you have an excellent memory, Dorian! My name is Marty Elliott, and we met a few years back at a SciTech show in Rosehill. We had a chat and swapped business cards but were passing boats."

"Hmm.. my memory isn't that good, to be honest. What can I do for you?"

Marty laughed. "My memory isn't that good either, mate! I'd be lost without notes and technology!"

Dorian snorted. "Tell me about it! I don't think I have a brain anymore. So, why are you calling me now?"

Marty took a breath. "I'm doing some.... call it research, for a friend. I have some photos of equipment I don't recognise, and I was hoping you'd look and see if you can identify what they are."

Dorian shrugged to himself. "That should be okay. Send them to my email, and I'll check them out."

Marty's eyes rose. "Crikey! Thanks, Dorian. I was expecting to have to convince you!"

Dorian laughed. "I've not got anything pressing for a few days. I'm on light duties because of a respiratory bug, and they don't want to wear me out, so I'm catching up on new tech and manuals. All the boring stuff. At least this will be a little different!" He coughed as he finished talking, followed by a groan.

Marty sounded undecided. "Are you sure you're up to it? I don't want to make you worse!"

Dorian chuckled at the same time as damping on another tickle. "You should have heard me yesterday! Today, I'm almost cured!"

"Well, okay, and thanks, Dorian. It'll be a big help to me. I'll send the pictures to the email on your card. It hasn't changed in the last three years, has it?"

"No mate, nothing changes around here!"

Marty laughed. "Well, make sure you save my details. I'm a bit of a generalist and can, perhaps, give you a hand some time."

They ended the call. Marty zipped the photos and sent them off.

* * *

A few hours later, he received a call back from Dorian. "Hey Dorian, Marty here."

"Hi, Marty. I'm sorry it took longer than expected, but the whiteboard images took me a while to work out."

"Oh, okay. I'm surprised it was interesting at all."

Dorian sniffed, "It may not have been except for the other items. In case you don't know the science behind them, I've written an overview to help you know what the instruments are and what they do. In a nutshell, you have a linear accelerator and a cloud chamber which..."

Marty interrupted, surprised, "Linear Accelerator? Aren't they used to smash atoms and things together?"

"Yes. That's right! The cloud chamber is a tool to see the particles produced when you smash the others together."

"Isn't that dangerous?"

"Not at all, Marty. These small units don't go nearly as fast as, for example, the LHC in Cern."

"LHC?"

"Large Hadron Collider. It spins particles around a circle of magnets and smashes them into targets like gold foil to see what happens. Anyway, no! It's no more dangerous than an x-ray, which is simply another type of linear accelerator."

"Okay, I'll take your word for it. What else?"

"Well, the accelerator is a general-purpose unit used for research. But, the interesting thing was the whiteboard."

"The whiteboard? You're kidding me!"

"Nope, The whiteboard had been used to rough out a design for a miniature accelerator. I checked in with a mate in Taiwan who is up with this technology. He told me all but one of the drawings looked like the silicon chips used for quantum computers. He called them wafers."

"Above my pay grade." sighed Marty.

Dorian laughed, "Mine too, mate, but there's more!"

"More?"

"Yes. There was one drawing that was a bit different. He said it looked less like a wafer and more like a miniaturised LINAC. That's Linear Accelerator."

"Miniature Linear Accelerator... on a chip like a computer chip?"

"That's about it. I'm pretty excited by the whole idea! Where did you find this? Who's doing the work? It would be amazing if someone cracked that capability. Who knows where it may lead!"

Marty scratched his head. "Okay. Wow! You've got me excited." He paused a moment. "Look, I can't tell you where or who, as it's a client's brief that I'm working on. But thanks for your help. Once I see where it goes, I may be able to tell you more."

"No worries, Marty, keep me in mind. I'm glad to help more if you need it!"

"Okay, thanks again. Oh! Don't forget to put me in your contact list. Happy to help you out if you need it in the future."

"Sure will, Marty. Thanks"

* * *

Marty was in a quandary. He had stumbled onto some information and didn't know what to do with it. One thing he knew for sure was that it looked like it could be dangerous if it got into the wrong hands. That, plus he couldn't see any way to make something out of it for himself using the right hands, made his decision for him.

He frowned before dialling a number from memory. He waited through the recorded information until it finally asked him to record a message. "Leigh, Marty."

The following morning, Marty got a call back from Leigh Buchanan, an officer in the AFP (Australian Federal Police). "Hi Marty, how're things going? Are you keeping out of trouble?"

"Hi, Leigh. Always out of trouble, mate, you know me!"

Leigh laughed. "That'll be the day! What's up?"

"Mate, I've stumbled onto something and don't know what it is. Thought I'd give you a call and see if AFP needs to know."

Leigh snorted. "Something you can't handle, eh? Must be interesting."

"It may be nothing, but I've looked into it as much as possible, and I've got a feeling it's important."

"Is it something we need to meet about, or can we talk about it?"

"I'd prefer to keep it off the airwaves if possible; you never know these days!"

"Okay. Hang on." There was silence for a few minutes, then, "I've got time later today. Where are you?"

"Up in the Central Coast. Let's meet at the Two Creeks Cafe at Killarney Vale. It's private and not far from what's got me worked up."

"Okay, Marty, See you at five!"

* * *

Leigh waited at a table at the back of the cafe, where he had a good view of the area. Seeing Leigh had a takeaway coffee on the table, Marty ordered one himself. Leigh smiled. "Hi, Marty. Good to see you're still kicking, mate!"

Marty grimaced. "Likewise! I'm not sure which of us is the more fortunate!"

Leigh laughed. "I always think I'm doing okay if I wake to a new day these days!"

Marty nodded. "I have to agree with that! Dealing with the bloody Government is enough to send me into cardiac arrest!"

"Are you still trying to get the affordable housing thing going?"

Marty raised his eyes, and his mouth quirked.

Leigh's eyes skyrocketed, "You're crazy, mate! It's been years!" He shook his head, "They'll never give you the land, and they'll only work with big corporations! Give it up, mate!"

Marty grimaced and shook his head. "I'll get them to come over to my way of thinking. Affordable housing is a problem they need to fix."

Leigh held out his hand, "I know, I know. It's just that they won't fix it... and, if they do, they'll give the contract to their friends."

He saw Marty wasn't going to budge, "Ah well! Keep at it, then. At least it keeps you out of real trouble!"

Marty smiled and nodded, "That it does!"

Marty's coffee arrived, and he pointed to the door, "Let's get out in the air." They walked silently until they reached the walking track at the southern end of Tuggerah Lake.

Leigh looked sideways. "So, what's this situation you've come across?"

Marty took a sip of his coffee, looked across at Leigh and frowned as he spoke. "As I told you on the phone, I'm not sure. I ran into an old friend doing a bit of cash work for a mate of his. This mate of his works with Mohamed Banks."

Leigh looked interested at the mention of Mohamed but didn't interrupt.

Marty shrugged. "I asked what he was doing, and he said it involved skimming bins for information." Marty sighed. "I recognised a company involved and thought I'd look into it more myself." He raised his eyes and shrugged. "So, I popped into the premises of interest and looked around."

Leigh raised his eyes at that but held his silence. He knew Marty walked a fine line, but he also knew Marty wasn't the type of criminal he was interested in.

Marty knew what Leigh was thinking and smiled. "The place was bare except for machines I didn't recognise. On first impression, I thought it may be a drug lab, but the equipment was nothing like I'd seen before, and they had no security systems."

Marty waited for an elderly couple to pass them in the opposite direction and continued. "I looked closer at the machinery and noted the supplier of one was a scientific instrument company."

Leigh looked at Marty, wondering where the conversation was going. "Go on."

Marty sighed and shook his head. "I sent pictures I'd taken to a contact with scientific equipment experience, and he identified a linear accelerator."

Leigh interrupted. "Linear Accelerator? Like science fiction?"

Marty laughed. "Not science fiction, but, yes, a linear accelerator, cloud chamber and all."

Leigh shook his head and frowned. "I'm not sure why you are interested; it's not your usual hustle. What's got you so involved?"

Marty cocked his head and smiled. "I'm not quite done yet. One of my pictures was of diagrams on a whiteboard. My contact had to dig but told me they looked like miniaturisation plans for a linear accelerator."

He scratched his head and looked for a bin to chuck his cup. "The way the warehouse is being used looks ad hoc, but inside, cutting-edge physics research and design are going on."

Marty's nose wrinkled as he caught Leigh's eye, "Mo Banks is looking for information about what's happening at the warehouse, probably for a client. And, the company SplitQC is involved."

Marty raised his brows and shook his head. "Put it all together, and I reckon something's going on that's either dodgy or dangerous! Neither option attracts me, and I figure you should know about it rather than others I know."

Leigh scratched his head and considered the information Marty had given him. "I think you've stumbled onto something, Marty, that's for sure."

Marty shrugged. "There are too many odd factors, and it just doesn't feel right."

Leigh smiled and chuckled. "SplitQC is a company I know about as they have contracts with the DoD (Department of Defence). That plus bloody Mo Banks sets my alarm bells ringing regardless of this being a warehouse in Tumbi Umbi." He pondered for a moment, then looked at Marty. "I'll get a report together and send it to the boss. Let's see what he makes of it."

Marty nodded. "Right then. Thanks. I'll get going."

Leigh took hold of Marty's shoulder. "Are you going to be around for a while? I may need you."

Marty grunted. "I'll be at my place back in Berkeley Vale. I need to head north sometime next month to see how the kids and missus are getting on, but I'll be here for at least the next few weeks."

Leigh chuckled. He'd never really understood Marty's family life and wasn't sure he wanted to know. "Okay, mate. Thanks for the tip, and good luck!"

Marty's head gave a slight shake. "Cheers, Leigh."

Chapter 14

James had Harry join them at Tumbi to test the larger test module and ushered him into the test area. Imogen smiled at James's evident excitement about the upcoming session and slipped a grin towards Jerry, who smiled and shook his head.

Once Harry was settled, James looked at his colleagues and noticed their cheesy grins. He cocked his head and shrugged. "What? What did I do?"

Jerry smiled and shrugged. "Nothing, mate. Just happy to see you're enjoying your work."

James looked at Harry, who was also smiling and laughed. "Well, I am excited!" His eyes glittered. "Let's do this!"

Turning to Harry, James indicated the test area. "We've been using small masses in previous tests, but this is a step up to half a kilo." Sitting on the test bed was a clear box. Inside were various electronic components, including wires to each face of the box where something was attached to the inner surface. "Because of the size of the module, we have placed multiple field generators on the flat surfaces." He frowned as he mentally visualised the shaping of the field and shook his head when he realised he'd gone off on a tangent. "Sorry. Just thinking about the multiple fields." He shrugged an apology towards Harry. "When multiple generators are used, the field shapes itself to the module, whereas a single field generates a sphere of particles." His eyes glazed again momentarily, but he lifted his chin. "That's for another time." He turned back to the module. "The other interesting change in this setup is we've included a camera to take pictures of the conditions when the module is Stepped back."

Harry looked impressed. "Sounds like a great step forward if you'll excuse the pun."

James rolled his eyes and shook his head. "Been done before!" He laughed and turned back to Imogen and Jerry. "Okay! Let's get this started. Quinn, Set parameters for Test Alpha-two-four."

"Alpha-two-four Parameters Set"

James turned to Harry. "The test is designated Alpha-two-four. It's the fourth in a series of tests we've used to trial different fits of generators onto a cube-shaped mass. This test consists of a five-minute Step and includes the camera being rotated through three sixty degrees."

Harry nodded understanding, and James continued with Quinn. "Quinn, Execute Test Alpha-two-four"

"Alpha-two-four starting in Five.. Four.. Three.. Two.. One.. Mark. Countdown timer started."

A display by the test area initiated a counter at five minutes and started counting down by tenths of a second.

There was nothing to do but wait; the four watchers were silent. All were nervous, even though James and Jerry were confident of a successful result. The only real unknown was what the camera would show if it worked. James looked at the display; the countdown was just over two minutes. He felt his anticipation rise as the timer eventually raced down to zero.

Quinn chimed in with, "Test Alpha-two-four Complete."

The module was back and looked as though it had never been away. Jerry smiled. "Quinn, check all test module systems and physical attributes."

"All test module systems are fully functional."

"All physical attributes are within normal ranges."

The four approached the module. While James opened the cover, Jerry retrieved and connected the camera interface cable before asking Quinn to download the pictures. They pulled chairs around a large monitor, and Jerry displayed the first image.

Although they had no expectations, James was both excited at having pictures and disappointed as they were nothing like Hubble's. He'd expected galaxies and nebulae. Instead, there was a lot of haze, with areas brighter than others.

Jerry, however, had a massive smile on his face. "This is fantastic!" He looked at the other three and noticed their questioning eyes. "Don't you understand? This is the last part of the inflation after the big bang! This is the time just before the universe begins to expand and form the clusters of dust that become the galaxies."

It slowly dawned on James that the module had Stepped back in time as far as it could go. They were looking at images of the universe as it was over thirteen billion years ago, well before it had become the way we know it today. He turned to Harry. "We need to keep this well under wraps for the time being. I think it's bigger than we realise right now."

Harry nodded. "I agree. Until we know more, we must keep this discovery to ourselves ." Harry looked at the images scrolling across the screen with a strange look. "What if we can move a bit back there?"

Jerry jerked his head. "What?"

"I said, what if we can move the module a bit when it's back in time? Will the module come back, or will it go somewhere else?"

Imogen looked stunned. "Oh dear! Let's find out!"

The three men looked at Imogen, wondering what she had in mind. She explained, "If we add a small bottle of compressed air and a control for the valve, we should be able to move the module."

James was thinking as she spoke. "We'd have to have two nozzles. One to move and one to stop." He frowned. "No! Blast it! We'll have to plan and test the best way. We'll need to be able to get back to where we started, and we'll need flexibility to do that." The wheels were spinning, and he nodded to himself. "We'll also need to get Quinn loaded with data on air pressure, vectors, and mapping."

James and Imogen laughed with excitement. Imogen pointed to one of the 3D printers, "It'll take a bit of searching for designs, but I don't see any reason why we shouldn't be able to test a move inside a day or two."

James looked over to Jerry. "What do you think, Jerry?"

Before Jerry could answer, Harry held up his phone, which was bleating a message. "I'll leave you to it. I need to get back to the office." He smiled. "Keep going!"

They saw Harry off and spent the following few hours brainstorming ideas and reviewing 3D printer designs.

* * *

Mo and Lowen sat at a picnic table in a park on Tuggerah Lake. It was late afternoon, and the lake was smooth as a mirror. Fifty metres away, there was a kids' playground, but apart from that, they were alone. Both men ignored the colour of the evening sky and the movement of birds heading off to their evening roost.

Mo got straight to business. "Okay, Lowie, what have you got?"

Lowen swiped to a note app on his phone. "He's rented a house in Long Jetty. I talked to the estate agent; the lease is month-by-month and is being paid by SplitQC. Kentley's working out of a warehouse-cum-factory unit in Tumbi Umbi." He shrugged. "By the look of it, he's using the space rather than running a business. The unit is owned outright by SplitQC and has been unused for some time." Lowen looked across at Mo. "The unit had been used to store electronics equipment until SplitQC expanded their head office in Macquarie Park."

Once again, Lowen checked to see if Mo had any questions before continuing his report. "Kentley has two people working with him.

There's a SplitQC tech named Imogen Matthews. She's a materials scientist." Lowen shrugged and continued. "She is staying at a nearby motel. I assume she's only here for the short term." He looked at Mo. "They were recently joined by another expert, a computer nerd named Jeroen Bos. He's staying at the same motel in a different room."

He checked his notes. "They work long hours and, in my experience, are the most intensely focused people I've seen in a long time. All three get to the unit early, work long hours, and don't notice much of what's happening around them." He cocked his head. "That said, Kentley and the woman occasionally take a kayak out for a morning paddle. My theory is it's to let off steam." He looked again at Mo. "I don't believe there is any romantic connection between them."

Mo grunted. "Good work. Anything else?"

Lowen shook his head. "Nothing. All I can suggest is we get surveillance inside the warehouse."

Mo nodded. "I agree. Let's get over there. I want to have a look at the layout."

After a quiet drive around the unit complex, they parked outside a local cafe. Mo turned to Lowen. "It doesn't look secure. What do you reckon?"

"I agree. I saw no security alarms. The industrial complex has a patrol that drives around occasionally during the day, and at night, they have a scheduled round where they walk through the complex and check the odd door and window. Apart from that, it's an open book."

Mo nodded and pursed his lips. "Okay, let's get ears and eyes inside."

That night, once the area was quiet, they went to the back of the unit, where Mo picked the door's lock. They placed stealth microphones in the office and warehouse, and a camera was set up to view the workbenches in the warehouse area. Mo connected the devices to a WiFi router, gave them a group name and set the device to connect to the internet. The setup had enough power for three days of operation and should be able to provide Mo with further answers.

Chapter 15

The morning briefing ended, and Jackson Dunne, head of AFP's Organised Crime Squad in NSW, waved Leigh Buchanan and his partner Callie Stubbs over. "Leigh, I've read your report about Tumbi Umbi and agree we should look into this further."

Leigh nodded before he shook his head and sighed. "There's something off, for sure. No idea what, though!"

He looked at Callie and back at Jackson, who went on. "I want you to head to SplitQC and talk with the boss, Harry Barnes." He raised his eyebrows. Harry is expecting you this morning at ten thirty and is happy to hear what you say, given that they work with DoD."

Leigh looked across to Callie and shrugged. "We're on it!"

* * *

Leigh and Callie were ushered into SplitQC's boardroom, where Harry Barnes finished silencing his phone. Harry looked up and smiled. "Hi, I'm Harry Barnes. Nice to meet you."

Leigh shook hands. "Leigh Buchanan, thanks for the time."

Harry turned to Callie, who also shook Harry's hand in greeting. "Callie Stubbs. Good to meet you too, Sir."

Harry chuckled. "No need for 'Sir' around here. Call me Harry." He indicated the chairs, "Sit. Be comfortable. Can I get you a coffee? Tea?"

Callie smiled. "I'd kill for a coffee, to be honest."

Harry turned to Leigh, "How about you?"

"Sure. Coffee sounds great!"

Harry walked over to the wet area and poured three cups of coffee before looking over and asking. "Milk? Sugar?"

"Black for me, thanks," said Callie while Leigh opted for milk.

Harry brought the mugs to the table and set them on coasters before sipping his. He waited for the others to have a chance to taste theirs before speaking. "I understand you are concerned about the research I'm supporting on the Coast. I'm happy to help however I can, but I'm not sure what the trouble is?"

Leigh nodded and stood. "Do you mind if I walk around a bit? It helps me think."

Harry laughed. "Of course. Let me know if you want anything like a whiteboard or projector."

Leigh smiled. "First of all, thanks for taking the time to talk with us!"

Harry's eyes narrowed. "Security is important to me, as is our work with the Government. My calendar is cleared until I'm happy and you're happy we don't have a situation to worry about."

Leigh frowned and nodded. "Okay. As you are aware, Callie and I are with the Federal Police. In general, our operational focus is on organised crime." He shrugged. "Drugs, guns, terrorists and the like. We also develop technology to give us an edge and to protect Australia's critical capabilities."

Leigh looked at Harry. "Callie and I are generalists. Callie knows a bit about technology, and I know a bit about criminals. Between us, we don't get lost!"

Leigh paused for another sip of coffee. "This situation came out of the blue. One of my informal contacts called and told me he'd come across something odd he thought I should know about." Leigh smiled. "My informant is a sort of criminal, sort of do-gooder. He's a bit like a spider in a web." Leigh shrugged. "He has a lot of contacts and hears about what others need in addition to possible opportunities to make a profit. He profits when the people he helps profit and when he sells for a profit." Leigh's chin lifted. "Sometimes he hears about things he's not comfortable with. When that happens, he'll let someone like me know about it. Things like bad drugs, guns, extremists, organ theft!" He gave his head a shake. "Anyway, he got wind of something going on at Tumbi Umbi and decided to have a look for himself."

Harry cocked his head. "Have a look? What do you mean 'Have a look!'?"

Leigh waggled his eyes and grinned. "Just that! He broke into your unit and 'had a look'."

Harry was agog. "He broke in? And he had a look? What about security?"

Leigh and Callie laughed at Harry's surprise. "That's why we're here, Harry. Security at the unit doesn't exist. If you want it to be secure, you'll need to get someone onto it."

Harry shook his head. "My fault! I didn't think of it; I'm sure James wouldn't have. He's more focused on his work than who's looking!" Harry sighed. I'll get it attended to. Please, go on."

Leigh looked to Callie. "We'll help with your security if you don't mind." It wasn't a question, and Harry remained quiet while Callie made a note.

Leigh went on. "What my contact found set off red flags for him. Number one is that a certain Mohamed Banks is looking at the unit. Mohamed thinks he's smart, but he's a criminal. He pretends to tread the fine line between what's legal and what isn't, but he's usually well over on the wrong side of the divide. He's also known for involvement in industrial espionage - spying rather than prevention." He lifted his head. "Whenever we hear about something involving Mo, we flag it as interesting and look into it."

Harry nodded understanding, albeit with a question in his eyes.

Leigh went on. "My informant was also uneasy about the kind of work being conducted at Tumbi Umbi." He held up a hand to stop Harry's question and pulled a page of note paper from his pocket. "He's listed some equipment he came across. A linear accelerator? A cloud chamber? Spectroscope? A Ball Mill? Two 3D printers, metallurgical powders and other bibs and bobs too numerous to mention." He looked at Harry again before continuing. "Plus... plus what look like design drawings for, and I quote, 'a miniaturised linear accelerator in a silicon wafer'!"

Harry looked stunned. "Your 'informer' got all that information from a single break-in to the warehouse in Tumbi?"

Leigh nodded, and Harry sighed. "Well then! I surely had better beef up security at the warehouse." Harry smiled, "And I wouldn't mind a number for this informant of yours! He or she is bloody well connected!"

At that, Callie laughed out loud. "That's for sure! He surprised me with this lot. He knows nothing about technology like this!"

Harry took a breath. "So, what do you need from me?"

Leigh looked at Callie and waved for her to continue. "Can we start with what's being worked on in the warehouse?"

Harry grimaced. "I'll tell you what I can. Some things are speculative, and I won't mention them unless I think they are important. Will that suffice for the moment?"

Callie looked to Leigh, who shrugged. "Okay, let's start with that and see where we get."

Harry nodded. "It started when a university mate called for help. His employer terminated his contract early because he'd looked into an anomaly he'd come across in the miniaturisation work he'd been doing for them. Now I know James, James Kentley, very well. He's never dodged his work and is self-driven and independent. James told me he thought the project manager had felt undermined by James's independence and, in the end, he fired him."

Harry checked that Callie and Leigh had no questions before proceeding. "James doesn't trust people easily; he came to me reluctantly. But we go way back, and he felt he could talk to me."

Harry went to the fridge and pulled out three bottles of water. He gave one each to Leigh and Callie before opening his and having a long swallow. "The company he'd been working for was AI4U; They build tailored artificial intelligence solutions for different business applications. Their solutions can range from analysing social media sites to big data reporting to analysis of a company's products based on feedback on their websites."

Harry again checked that Leigh and Callie were with him before continuing. "James was improving AI4U's hardware by incorporating his miniaturised J-Gate technology. A key component of James's technology is a novel processing gate based on the movement of particles through a linear accelerator etched into a silicon wafer."

Leigh looked lost, but Callie was hanging in by the skin of her teeth and nodded. Harry continued. "Well, he successfully improved their performance by two to three hundred per cent. It was a factor that, in the end, landed the deal they were working on." Harry shrugged. "That should have been reason enough for a bonus, but James was fired before the final presentation and winning of the deal."

He had another sip of water. "His old boss tried to get him to come back, but James had already spoken to me, and I'd offered the warehouse at Tumbi and resources to continue his research."

Callie looked puzzled. "Sorry, I must have missed something. What research?"

Harry chuckled. "Probably the way I'm telling the story. While testing the linear accelerator setup at AI4U, James noticed something odd. Without getting too detailed, some of the particles disappeared and reappeared. He noticed this as a break in their trails in the cloud chamber."

Harry took another drink of water and looked again at Callie and Leigh. "James had ideas about what was causing the anomaly, and SplitQC is helping him find answers. It's too early to tell, but the results may be good for our work on quantum computing, or another opportunity may open up."

Callie raised a finger. "Is he making progress?"

Harry nodded. "It appears so. They've worked out the elements and are now looking into what they can do with them."

Leigh cocked his head. "Without telling me what, is there any chance that it could be weaponised or have a military use?"

Harry looked at the table and then back at Leigh, lips compressed. "It's possible. Unlikely, but possible."

He looked back to the table, thinking of his conversation with James earlier that morning. "I spoke with James this morning. They've had a breakthrough that may lead to useful technologies. There could be military uses for it." He held up a finger, "But, and it's a big but, there's still a lot of R&D needed to advance further."

Leigh lifted his head, eyes narrowed. "In that case, security is even more important. I'll talk with Jacko and see what he thinks, but we may come and look the site over."

Harry's lips were tight as he considered the implications.

Leigh looked at Callie and motioned towards the exit. As they stood and gathered their things, Leigh nodded to Harry. "Thanks for filling us in, Harry. I know it's difficult when you need to protect your IP, but we're on the same side."

Harry nodded, "I will. I will also sort out the security at the warehouse - not just physical but communications and digital."

Callie nodded. "If you need help, we have good resources you may not get otherwise."

Harry made a note. "I'll ask Codie to review what we need to do. If he needs to get in touch, he will."

Leigh's head lifted in interest. "Codie Maxwell?" Harry nodded, and Leigh smiled, "Codie Maxwell. I remember now! He joined you guys when he returned from the Middle East. He's a top bloke and a great asset for you."

Harry grinned. "He can be dour at times, but I think we have a very good head of security."

Leigh chuckled. "Well, give him my best. Tell him I'll come and do some extra stress testing. Just to be sure!"

Harry shook their hands and led them to the lifts. When they were gone, he called Codie for a meeting.

While Harry called Codie, Leigh made a call of his own. "Hi, Leigh. What's happening?"

"Marty, I need your help for a day or two."

"Okay, but you'll owe me one! What do you need?"

Leigh laughed. "I think I'm still in credit, you bloody crook! This may help level things, though." He took a breath. "That mob out at Tumbi Umbi?"

Marty stretched out a "Yeah?"

"Well, something is going on, and I'm not sure what. I've talked to SplitQC, and they're getting their security squared away at the warehouse but can't watch everywhere yet."

"Uh-huh."

Leigh chuckled softly. "Well, they don't go anywhere apart from the warehouse and the motel. For security reasons, I can't get our people onto it quickly, so can you keep an eye on the motel for me? Just for a day or two while they get security sorted out?"

Marty laughed. "Is that all? Sure mate. I'll get on it right now."

Leigh laughed, "Thanks, Marty."

Marty chuckled to himself. He was sometimes lucky and sometimes unlucky, but he looked like he was in a purple patch at the moment. Smiling, he got organised, locked up, and made his way to Shady Bay.

Once he checked in, he ordered a cool beer and settled into a comfortable chair in the lounge, which offered a good view of people coming and going.

* * *

The question of movement whilst Stepped back had the three scientists excited.

James and Imogen quickly agreed on a spherical design for the test module and selected two basic formats.

Jerry, meanwhile, was concerned about handling the complexity of aligning movement vectors with the star map coordinates.

Their final design was spherical and incorporated a network of nozzles connected to a compressed air supply. After discussing various configurations for the air nozzles, they agreed on something resembling prickle circulation stimulation balls.

Using a 3D printer to produce the two hemispheres of the sphere was vital to having such a seemingly complex solution work effectively. Each hemisphere incorporated air ducts and component bays.

Jerry had underlying doubts and joined James and Imogen to discuss his concerns. "I don't like not having any control when the module is Stepped back. It's a bit like leaving the doors to your house open when you're heading off for a week's holiday." He frowned. "We rely on a timing circuit and assume the module will travel in a straight line. What if we're not where we need to be? What if the assumption is wrong?"

Imogen cocked her head and shrugged. "True, but what can we do? We don't have a way to communicate. Perhaps we should set up a module big enough for us to go along!"

James laughed at Imogen's joke and noticed Jerry wasn't joining in. "What?" asked James, smiling, "It wasn't funny?"

Jerry looked at Imogen with wide eyes. "No. It's a great idea!"

James held his palms out. "Well? What? Out with it!"

Jerry grinned from ear to ear, "We can't go! At least not yet. But Quinn can go!" James frowned as Jerry continued. "Not the full Quinn, but a smaller copy." He frowned. "A Quinlet!" Jerry laughed. "Yes! A Quinlet. A piece of Quinn with enough programming to handle situations autonomously while Stepped."

He clapped James on the back, "I think I can get Quinn to do the actual work of creating the Quinlet."

Jerry disappeared and hunkered down at a table he'd set up in the warehouse where he could think without James and Imogen's constant chatter. He surfaced an hour later, tired but with a smile on his face. "Done! Quinn can now program a Quinlet on a separate CPU interfaced with the control module via an alternate input." He rolled the tension out of his shoulders. "What it means is Quinn can cover various scenarios and possible responses to them." His mouth quirked, and he shrugged. "The main scenario I am interested in is what to do if the module is not in the correct location for the return Step. Knowing where that location is and having the processes to get there is critical. If we can't do that, we'll lose modules like water through a sieve."

Imogen made the final adjustments to the module design to replace the timer circuit with a Quinlet. She looked at James and Jerry and smiled as she started the 3D printers. "Here goes."

Chapter 16

They had no idea how the first movement test would go. There were many possible outcomes, from losing the module to blowing up or nothing happening and anything in between. The first thing they needed to work out was the interval of time that should be used for the move.

They had no idea what distance the module would move or what would happen when it stopped in a different position and returned to the present. They'd discussed the idea amongst themselves and Harry, and their best guess was that the module would return to the present but in a different spatial location. Where that location ended up was unknown without prior data. It could be on Harry's office chair, at the bottom of Sydney Harbour or in Andromeda.

Given they didn't even know the rate of movement based on the compressed air pressure in the air cylinders, they asked Quinn if its data on mass and distance Stepped could be extrapolated to help determine a reasonable time interval. Quinn replied, "Unable to infer an unknown from an unrelated dataset."

They opted to expel half of one per cent of the tank's air in any direction. Then follow with the same amount in the opposite direction. This procedure should bring the module to a standstill in a different place. Once in the new location, Quinlet would record that location in the three-dimensional reference database and compare the new location to the starting point. It would then reverse the movement and check if it was back in its original position. If not in the original position, it was to record the location for later review and make adjustments until the correct position was reached. Once in position, it would return to the present.

Imogen summarised. "If the test is successful, we'll know if the module moves due to a volume of air at a certain pressure, and we may be able to calculate how far it moves." She shrugged and smiled. "That is if it moves at all, of course. With that information, we can work out what to try next."

"Sounds fair to me." James said, "Let's get it done."

Jerry gave the order. "Quinn, load Step Test Bravo-three-six."

"Step Test Bravo-three-six Loaded."

"Quinn, Execute Test Bravo-three-six."

"Bravo-three-six starting in Five.. Four.. Three.. Two.. One.. Mark."

Just under thirty seconds later, the test module reappeared. It was in the same position it was in when the test started.

"Test Bravo-three-six Complete."

Jerry raised his eyes and smiled. "Quinn, Provide a summary of Test Bravo-three-six."

"Test Bravo-three-six summary: Test module Stepped; Air expelled from Nozzle one, ninety for three seconds. Air expelled from Nozzle one, negative ninety for three seconds; three-dimensional positioning showed different spatial coordinates; Air expelled from Nozzle one, negative ninety for three seconds; Air expelled from Nozzle one, ninety for three seconds; Test module at rest at original coordinates; Activator ends; Test module returns; All movement and location data saved; All test module systems fully functional; All physical attributes within normal ranges."

James chuckled and looked at Imogen before addressing the AI, "Quinn, how far did the Test module move spatially?"

"Distance travelled was 3.3982 centimetres."

"Hmm.. thanks Quinn. It would appear that the module travels in a straight line and reverses along the same line. Jerry, do we still have the simple test modules we used earlier?"

"Sure. They're in the storage room."

"Could you get one with a camera, timer and compressed air? I want to Step the module back, move a shorter distance and return to the present. I want to see where it lands when it returns to the present!"

As Jerry turned to head towards the storeroom, James's smile grew. "Then I want to bring it back here!"

It took a couple of hours to prepare the test module and set up the test profile, Bravo-three-seven, for Quinn to execute. It was set to Step back and, hopefully, move the module one micrometre. Then, it would return to its space in the present. Once there, it would record the GPS location and take a picture before immediately Stepping back, relocating to the starting baseline and then Stepping back to the present.

When they were ready, James said. "Quinn, load Step Test Bravo-three-seven."

"Step Test Bravo-three-seven Loaded."

"Quinn, Execute Test Bravo-three-seven."

"Bravo-three-seven starting in Five.. Four.. Three.. Two.. One.. Mark."

A few seconds later, the test module reappeared. Once again, it was in the same position as when the test started.

"Test Bravo-three-six Complete."

James looked at Jerry and Imogen and shook his head in amazement and surprise. He was heard to say to no one in particular. "I was expecting to see it in here somewhere. I wonder where it went? Quinn, where did the module go?"

"GPS indicates Shellbrook in Canada."

"Shellbrook? Never heard of it! Quinn, did we get any pictures?"

An image flashed up on the main display. It looked like a railway yard. Leaves from a bush in front of the image made it more difficult to make out details. There was an orange building that could be used for grain storage.

Jerry squinted. "There's a word on the end. I think it says 'Pioneer'. Perhaps cement storage? By the look of the image, the module is on the ground in a scrubby area."

James laughed. "Canada! Can you believe it!" Jerry and James looked at each other and suddenly started dancing around together and whooping with excitement. Imogen, who was back at her bench, looked, looked up.

James grinned and waved her over. "We've been to Canada! This is the most significant discovery since the wheel!

After they calmed down, James grinned, "We can build a few more of these and get Quinn mapping the Earth as a start!" He bit his lip, "And we'd better bring Harry up to date! He wouldn't want to miss this news!"

James's phone rang before he could hit the call button. "Harry, Hi. I was about to call you!"

Harry interrupted. "Hi, James. I can't talk right now, but I want you to consider that security may be compromised."

"Compromised? Okay."

Harry went on, "I'll get it fixed first thing. In the meantime, if you're talking about what you're doing, it'd be best to go outside the warehouse, just in case."

James frowned at the phone and the others. "Okay, Harry, will do."

James stood. "Let's pop outside for a moment." Once away from the building, James relayed Harry's directions. They talked about what may be happening, but there was no point speculating.

James frowned. "Let's get back to what we were talking about before we came outside."

They agreed and walked down the driveway while James outlined his idea. "So, I was thinking of a fleet of drones, purpose-built for mapping and exploration. At least as far as we can with the compressed air." He shrugged. "If we can go to Canada, we should be able to go anywhere in the world." His face looked determined, "In fact, we should be able to go anywhere in the galaxy in time."

Jerry's eyes widened, "Bloody hell!"

Imogen's mouth opened, and when she realised she was gaping, she shut it with a snap.

James laughed. "That's exactly what I thought! The biggest expense will be the cost of drones that get destroyed if they relocate in an ocean or other obstacle."

Jerry waved his hand in disagreement, "Not if Quinn controls the movements and is hooked into a topographic database. That way, it can remain above sea level and ground level." He thought for a moment and added. "We could even hook into real-time air and sea movements to avoid accidents."

James grinned, "That's what I'm after. If we can get Quinn mapping in the background, it should be able to get enough data to set up algorithms to land a drone anywhere on the planet!"

James looked at his two friends and said, "That's a big result. A lot of good could come of it, but also a lot of bad."

Imogen nodded in agreement. "Knowledge of this cannot spread beyond ourselves and Harry. It's too dangerous."

While they couldn't automate the production of the field generators, they did make good use of the 3D printers. Imogen suggested they modify the module's design to incorporate sealing clips that could be activated electronically when they wanted to open the module and replace the compressed air container. They manually fitted the compressed air, field generation chips, power supply and Quinlet into prebuilt slots before the sphere was sealed.

Quinn tested the individual system elements and launched a simple Step back and return test to ensure the drone worked under Step conditions.

When they were ready, they set the completed drones on a piece of cardboard labelled "The Launchpad" and set Quinn to work.

The drones disappeared and reappeared at intervals according to whatever plan Quinn had worked out with its algorithms. If something happened to a drone, Quinn would log the event and pick a spare from the "Spares". Imogen or James would build new drones once they got to five spares. Interestingly, they never had to make more drones. Two were logged as lost, one after Stepping back and the second in transit to its 'new' present. They could only assume a failure in the device but couldn't verify that was the case. What amazed the three of them was the apparent safety of the Step process.

Chapter 17

Harry had called James within an hour of Leigh and Callie leaving. He'd then briefed Codie on the situation, and they arranged to drive to Tumbi first thing the following day. Codie had also arranged for one of his security staff to grab a van and bring relevant equipment to the warehouse.

James was pacing outside the warehouse as Harry and Codie arrived. Harry looked strained, so James ushered them inside without any preamble. "Go through to the office. I have coffee waiting."

Jerry and Imogen stood when their boss walked in. Harry looked their way, "Sit. Relax. We'll sort this out one way or another."

Once settled, Harry introduced Codie to James and started to talk. Codie stopped him quickly with a shake of a finger. "Let's keep ourselves to ourselves for the moment. I suggest we go outside."

Harry berated himself, "What was I thinking! Of course." He took his coffee and motioned to the door.

Once outside and away from the warehouse, Harry gave a quick overview of the situation outlined by the AFP. "So, if we include the AFP, we have two parties interested in the work here." He tapped the side of his cup nervously. "Depending on what they know and how well they keep secrets, there may be more."

He looked at James, worried he'd breached his confidence. "James, I had to tell the AFP about your research."

James frowned and gave Harry a shrug. "Don't let it bother you, Harry, I understand. You were in a tight spot, and we'll have more issues like this in the future. I'll trust the people you trust."

Harry smiled and relaxed as James continued, "Besides, they haven't learned much because we haven't either!"

Codie raised a hand and, again, cautioned them. "I suggest we keep quiet about anything important until we sweep the warehouse and set up decent security." He looked at his watch, "My team should be here any minute, so we won't have to wait long." He looked at Harry, "Perhaps a brief tour of the premises?"

Harry agreed. "Good thought, Codie. Let's get at it."

They started on the outside, and it didn't take long for Codie to find the loose security grille on the window by the toilets. He took it off and placed it on the ground without comment. James looked at the grille and frowned. He looked up and saw Codie smiling at him. Before James could say anything, Codie put a finger to his lips, shook his head slightly and mouthed, "Later." James sighed and nodded, as did the others. They remained silent as they continued their inspection of the building.

The van arrived not long after they'd finished outside. The driver spoke to Codie while the passenger went to the back of the vehicle, opened the doors and pulled out what looked like a metal detector. Codie introduced them as Matt and Mary and asked the others to remain outside while they checked the warehouse.

While Codie and his crew were checking inside, the others waited quietly, occasionally looking at the door when they heard muffled talk from the warehouse. There was a sharp shout of "Matt" at one stage, but they had no idea what was happening inside.

After a short time, Codie waved and motioned the others back into the building. He gathered them into a group in the warehouse by the lab bench and pointed to various electronic items at one end. "These two are microphones. This one is a camera. They use WiFi to connect to a router and, from there, to the internet."

James shrugged. "But how...?"

Codie shook his head and smiled. "The security here is non-existent! It was simple for them to install these devices without being seen or heard."

James sagged. He felt deflated by his ignorance and the danger his lack of foresight had placed them in.

Codie nodded understanding. "Don't worry about it now; you weren't to know." He smiled. "But now you know, there won't be an excuse if it happens again!"

James shrugged and shook his head as Codie went on. "The batteries in these last a few days and were still powered up, so they were probably only installed in the last day or so," he shrugged. "Unless they've had a chance to swap in fresh batteries."

James put his hands on his head. "Shit! What have we said while they were listening?"

Jerry and Imogen had a quick chat, and Jerry offered. "Apart from our daily discussion of what to trial and setting up experiments, they've probably got the idea that we have an AI we use for tests, and we've been to Canada."

James grimaced, "And the drones.. mapping.." He shook his head, "Anywhere on the planet!" James felt twisted inside, "If these people know these things, we're probably in danger here."

Codie had been listening in while James was talking with Jerry and Imogen. He cocked his head. "Why are you so concerned? Surely, there's no danger for you here if the security is set up properly."

James looked at him and turned to include Harry. "These people know we have created a device that can be sent to a spot anywhere in the world."

Harry frowned, trying to see what James was getting at. James grimaced. "Can't you see? The device could contain drugs, poison, or a bomb! Anything!"

Codie got it first, "Bloody hell! You're right. If the wrong people get their hands on this, there's no limit to the damage they could do!"

James gave a short nod, "Yeah, you are partly right, but you still don't get it! Even if the 'right' people get their hands on a capability like this, how long would it be before President Zhu or a US Presidential candidate died in mysterious circumstances?" James got a bit wild-eyed, "Or valuables stolen, or information, or photos taken?"

They were silent as James's eyes went flat. "With this device, you could go anywhere and do anything."

Harry frowned. "We need to pack this up and get back to Macquarie Park. We'll be safe there."

Codie shook his head. "Not necessarily. They know about the connection with SplitQC and would have eyes on all our facilities. Leaving may seem like a smart move, but, in the end, we'd have to spread security too thinly." He paused a moment. "No. We'll be better off staying where we can concentrate resources. We can increase our electronic security and supplement that with boots on the ground."

James nodded in agreement. "We'll have to get moving with the testing. If we can find answers, we may be able to hide them well enough to give us time to decide what to do with the technology."

Harry looked up suddenly, "Bugger! What about the AFP? How much should we tell them?"

James's eyebrows shot up in surprise. "Nothing beyond what they already know! We can't trust anyone with this, especially organisations like the police! Bloody hell, with their criminal and political connections! If they find out what we've got so far, we'll have all sorts of people breathing down our necks! Once anyone with an eye for cash knows, we'll all be stuffed!"

Codie nodded. "I agree with you, James. The fewer people who know what's going on, the better." He rubbed his chin. "I'll handle the AFP. The people we're dealing with are straight, and they'll keep knowledge of us within their department." He smiled. "Who knows, we may be able to enlist their help to rattle Mohamed Banks and see who he's talking to."

Harry nodded slowly, "We'll keep operations based here. Codie will stiffen security and have people on-site twenty-four hours a day." He licked his lips, "I'm thinking you should all move into the warehouse rather than using external accommodation."

Codie nodded his agreement. "Good idea. I'll have portable beds and linen brought with the men." He pressed a button on his walkie-talkie and murmured instructions to Mary.

Jerry tapped Imogen on the shoulder. "We can head to the motel now and grab our gear if you like. It's probably safe enough for the next few hours."

Imogen nodded and turned to Codie. "What do you think, Codie? Will we need an escort?"

Codie frowned, "It's probably okay, but I'll send Matt as your driver. Be quick, though."

* * *

Mo was in the Shady Bay restaurant checking messages when his phone buzzed. He'd decided to stay on the Coast for a day or two and had booked into the same motel the SplitQC people were using. The message had a purple background, and he immediately knew it had been sent from the surveillance system at the warehouse unit.

He looked at the message and frowned. The system had been disconnected! He swore and pulled up the last download. It clearly showed someone with a detector scanning the warehouse. "The buggers! They've got themselves a security boost, eh?" He thought for a moment and smiled. He had enough information for Harper. His eyes narrowed. The modules that could go anywhere had piqued his interest; if he could get his hands on them, he'd be able to ask a high price.

He called Lowen and told him to get back to the motel. "We've got a problem we need to tend to."

When Lowen returned, Mo gave him instructions. "Lowie, I need you to keep an eye on the motel's entrance. When the woman from the warehouse arrives, let me know and follow her to her room."

Lowen was puzzled but nodded as Mo continued, "They've found the surveillance we set up, and I need a bargaining chip."

Lowen nodded understanding, and Mo went on. "I'll be inside her room. When she enters, I want you to follow on a few seconds later and help me if needed."

Mo smiled. "If all goes well, we'll get her back to Sydney and see what and who she knows!"

Lowen frowned and looked at his watch. "It's not half twelve yet. They'll be a good five hours, at least, before they come back here."

Mo shook his head. "I don't want to take a chance." He hooked his head towards the restaurant reception area. "Grab us takeaway sandwiches and water. We should have time to eat something."

Chapter 18

Imogen walked up the corridor and unlocked the door to her room. She pushed on the door, and when it started to open, it suddenly opened fully, and she lost her balance. "What the.." was as far as she got before a sharp pain exploded on the back of her head, and all went black.

Meanwhile, Jerry went to his room on the upper floor and quickly packed his bag. He gave the room a final look and took the lift to the lobby to wait for Imogen. Nobody else was about, and a car was leaving the car park. Otherwise, all was quiet.

Jerry took his bag to the car and placed it in the trunk. He walked to the driver's window, and Matt asked, "Where's Imogen?"

Jerry shrugged and smiled, "Not down yet, but she shouldn't be long."

They waited another five minutes. Matt started to feel unsettled, so he called Imogen on the phone. When it rang out, he headed to her room on the second floor and found the door ajar. He knocked lightly. "Imogen? We need to get going." When nobody answered, he carefully entered the room where Imogen's belongings were untouched. It was as though she hadn't been there at all.

Matt immediately called Codie and told him what had happened.

Codie asked. "Did you see anything?"

"No. Nothing untoward. A couple of cars left around five minutes after we arrived, but it's been quiet since then."

Codie growled. "Bugger! I bet one of the cars had Imogen! Get back here ASAP!"

Matt hopped into the car. "On my way!"

* * *

Marty noticed the strangers enter the motel in the afternoon. He wouldn't have thought anything of them except they seemed a bit on edge, and one wore a cap that he kept low on his face. The one with the cap went upstairs in the lift, presumably to his room. The other returned to his car in the car park, where he reclined the seat and leaned back. An hour or so later, Marty spotted the two workers from the warehouse entering the motel. They entered the lift, talking in hushed tones and appeared focused on something important. The stranger who had been in the car followed them into the lobby and took the fire stairs to the accommodation area.

Marty thought. "Bugger it! I can't follow everyone!"

It took him a couple of minutes, but, in the end, he decided to stay on the ground floor and look at the fire stairs. He opened the door to the fire stairs a fraction and heard nothing. Opening it wider, he scanned the area. A flight of stairs was to his left, and a short corridor continued straight to an Exit that opened at the side of the building. He heard a muffled scuffle from above and quickly closed the door again. He left the entry area and returned to his car, where he could see both the main entry and the side door. The bloke who had followed the workers in and then gone up the fire stairs came back out the main entry. He was alone. After a quick scan of the area, he returned to his car and drove to the side entry, where he got out of his vehicle. He looked around before knocking lightly on the door. The door opened, and Marty saw the man with the cap holding the woman from the warehouse. The second man helped with the woman, and they dumped her into the back of the car. The men got into the car and drove off.

Marty waited a short while to let them get a start and followed. Some fifteen minutes later, his phone buzzed. "Marty here."

An agitated Leigh asked. "Marty, where are you?"

Marty chuckled. "I thought you'd call sometime soon! I'm on the freeway heading to Sydney."

Leigh sighed. "Tell me you have the woman."

"I don't have her myself, but I am following the car that does have her, as well as the two tough guys who snatched her!"

"Thank the stars for that, mate! Let me know once they get where they're going, and we'll see about getting her back."

Marty smiled. "No problem, Leigh. Hey, what's her name?"

"Imogen Matthews. The bloke she works with is Jerry Bos."

"Okay, Leigh, thanks. I'll let you know when they stop."

* * *

Codie's face said it all. He looked pale and was biting at his lip. His brow furrowed deeper the closer he got to where Harry and James discussed the bugs, security and safety. Harry noticed him first and stopped talking mid-word.

James frowned and turned. He saw Codie's expression, and his stomach fell. "What's happened?"

Codie winced. "I'm sorry, James, Harry. Imogen's been abducted!"

Harry and James looked up in shock, "What? How?"

Codie shook his head, "I don't know enough yet, but Matt and Jerry will be here shortly, and I have a call to make."

As Codie walked to the side to make his call, Harry and James looked at each other, horrified at this unexpected situation.

Codie came back as Matt and Jerry ran in. Matt looked across at Codie. "I'm sorry, Codie. I don't know what happened!"

James almost ran over to Matt and shouted. "What bloody happened? What the hell are you doing? What's happened to her?"

Codie pulled James's hands away from Matt's arms. "James! Stop. This won't help. We must keep our composure, or we won't get through this. We knew we had to beef up security, and we have." He released James as he calmed. "James. Things happen! We do our best, but there's always a possibility that something we can't predict will happen." He softened his tone. "I know how you feel about Imogen. We'll get her back. I promise."

James took a deep breath. "How can you promise, Codie? How?"

Codie's brows pulled together as he held eye contact, "Because we will get her back. I've just spoken with the AFP, and they have the situation in hand." He nodded to James, "They are already aware of the situation and are working as we speak to get her back."

James rubbed his eyes. "How can they know? It's only just happened!"

Codie smiled and shook his head. "Leigh is a good operator. He had a man at the motel in case. That's why we know what we know." He shrugged, "They're the only viable option we have available, and they're good at what they do."

Codie looked grim but confident. "Let me worry about Imogen - I'll get her back. Meanwhile, you have work to do, and this situation can't change your focus. Security here will be hardened. Your work must continue. We have to get out of here." He looked at James. "Imogen will be here as soon as we can get her back. I'll keep you posted."

James felt his insides churn but knew worrying wouldn't help. All they could do was get on with their research and experimentation and trust Imogen would be okay.

Chapter 19

Imogen grunted as she lost her footing on the kerb. The people hustling her along kept her from falling, but she'd have bruises where their fingers dug into her arms. She sucked air into her lungs, but the stale air inside the hood they'd put over her head didn't give her enough oxygen. Her heart was beating like a jackhammer and seemed to intensify with each sucked-in breath.

She was shoved through a door, which slammed shut behind her and pushed against a wall.

"Where do you want her?"

"In the spare room down the hall. There's a couple of chairs and tape."

"Hood?"

"Keep it on, but loosen the ties once she's taped to the chair."

Imogen's heart had slowed to the speed of an eggbeater, and she sucked in enough air to gasp out, "Who are you? What are you doing?"

Her head snapped back as she was slapped through the bag. "Shut up!"

She was roughly jerked by the arm and shoved forward. A door opened, and after standing for a moment, she was pushed onto a chair. She had the absurd thought that she was lucky she hadn't drunk much water that morning. She snorted at the notion and was told to shut up again as the man taped her arms and legs to the chair. The last thing he did before closing the door and leaving her was to loosen the hood ties.

Imogen's lungs were happy to get the fresher air and put it to work. She could feel her fear and uncertainty slowly calm to a level she could cope with. She realised that her kidnapping wasn't a random event and had to be connected to James and his research. She winced as the hood rubbed against the back of her head and made her aware of the ache at the back of her skull. She grunted. "Bastards!" She frowned and thought as the pain stilled.

* * *

Marty called Leigh once he was sure of where Imogen was being held. He'd followed the car over the Sydney Harbour Bridge and around to a house on Glebe Point Road. It was a two-story terrace with an iron grille fence and a jacaranda on the front verge.

Leigh answered. "Hi, Marty. What have you got?"

"I'm parked down the road from a terrace in Glebe." He gave Leigh the address. "They took her in there about half an hour ago. Since then, nothing. No lights. No sound."

Leigh sighed. "Hang in there. I'll get back to you shortly."

"Righto." and Marty hung up.

* * *

Surprisingly, Quinn signalled the completion of the mapping process.

James turned to Jerry, a puzzled look on his face. "That can't be right, can it?"

Jerry looked unsure as well. "I'll check the logs."

He displayed the logs on a screen and scrolled through them. "Nope! It all looks fine."

He shrugged and raised his brows. "Quinn, Analysis of the mapping process."

"Drone mapping analysis executing."

"Drone mapping analysis complete."

"Quinn, list execution summary of drone mapping analysis."

"Summary follows:"

"Algorithm One, Five percent in 03:15:06"

"Algorithm Two, Twelve percent in 01:46:00"

"Algorithm Three, Twelve per cent in 00:05:48"

"Algorithm Four, Seventy-One percent in 00:09:36"

"List complete."

Jerry's voice was filled with awe. "Quinn is an exceptional AI. It completed the task in a remarkably short time and generated new, highly efficient algorithms as it gained data. Amazing!"

James was stunned by the result. "That's brilliant! Let's test it." He grabbed some tape, looked around for a likely spot on the floor and used the tape to make an 'X'. Jerry marked the location of the 'X' on a schematic digitally available to Quinn.

He then said, "Quinn, load Step Test Bravo-eight-zero."

"Step Test Bravo-eight-zero Loaded."

"Quinn, Execute Test Bravo-eight-zero."

"Bravo-eight-zero starting in Five.. Four.. Three.. Two.. One.. Mark."

The test module appeared on the floor on top of the 'X'.

"Test Bravo-eight-zero Complete."

James and Jerry looked at each other and smiled delightedly. James suggested. "Let's do one more test but a bit further away."

Jerry's curiosity was piqued. "I'm intrigued. Where are you thinking of?"

James chuckled and Googled a list of live-stream webcams. He looked at them briefly and selected one: "Right there! Near the Temple Bar in Dublin." He watched the feed for a moment. How about going to the left of the door of that restaurant? It's in the camera view and is closed, so there's not much chance of the module being noticed there."

Jerry had a look and scratched his head. "Hmm.. okay. Quinn, manual coordinate select for Test Bravo-eight-zero."

"Bravo-eight-zero manual coordinate select ready."

"Quinn, find Temple Bar, Dublin."

"Coordinates located."

Once Quinn accessed the coordinates, a Google Maps view was displayed on the screen. An 'X' appeared on the road marked in front of the Temple Bar.

"Quinn, switch to street view."

"Quinn, rotate the view ninety degrees."

Jerry smiled and nodded. "Excellent, that's perfect." He clicked the cursor on the pavement, and an 'X' appeared.

"Quinn, Set Bravo-eight-zero manual coordinate."

"Bravo-eight-zero Coordinate set."

Jerry looked at James and crossed his fingers. "Quinn, Execute Test Bravo-eight-zero"

Two pairs of eyes were glued to the screen as Quinn cycled through the test. Suddenly, the test module disappeared from the floor and, shortly afterwards, appeared in the video feed. It was perfectly placed, exactly where Jerry had indicated on the map."

Jerry quickly said, "Quinn, return the test module to Home."

"Test module returned to Home."

The pair high-fived, and Jerry's eyes glazed over, "That was amazing! We can send anything, anywhere in the world!"

James's mood came back to earth quickly. "I wish Imogen were here to see this; she'd be over the moon!"

Jerry smiled stoically. "When she gets back, she will surely be in for a surprise!"

Chapter 20

Imogen's heart started beating harder as she heard footsteps approach and the door opening. A chair was drawn up in front of her, and someone sat.

"Now, let's see what we've got here."

Imogen waited for the hood to be removed, but the man started asking questions.

"What do you know about James Kentley? What's he working on?"

Imogen shook her head. "James? Why do you want to know about James? Why am I here?"

Her head snapped to the side, and the pain seared where she'd been hit. The man said. "This can be as painful as you want it to be. No questions, only answers. What do you know of Kentley and his research?"

Imogen knew this wasn't a time to fight. She relaxed her head and shoulders in a submissive gesture and sighed. "I don't know James well. I've only known him for a few weeks."

"What about his research?"

"He's trying to understand something he found with particles in a linac."

"Linac? What's that?"

"A linear accelerator. It pulses a beam.."

"I know what it does. What about his work at AI4U?"

"I didn't know him then, but that's where he found this thing he's trying to understand."

"Who was he really working for?"

Imogen was surprised by the question. "What? I don't know what you're talking about. He has his own company and works for himself."

"What about the materials he stole?"

"What are you talking about? What materials?"

"What do you do?"

"I'm helping with alloys for his experiments. I'm a materials analyst."

"What materials did he provide you with?"

"Targets. Things for his research."

"Where did he get these materials?"

"I don't know. I expect they came from AI4U when he left."

"Materials he stole. What about the miniaturisation?"

"Miniaturisation? What about it?"

"Is that what you're doing at Tumbi Umbi?"

"Miniaturisation? No. Well, not that I'm aware of."

The man paused and muttered that he'd have to talk with Kentley in person. Then he started on a different tack: "What's this thing you call a module?"

The question confirmed Imogen's deduction that these people were the ones who had bugged the warehouse. The knowledge strengthened her determination to be careful about what she told them. "The module? It's just a case we made to do experiments to test ideas."

"How did the module go to Canada?"

"You know about Canada?" She slumped her shoulders in defeat. "It was one of the few experiments that worked. The module was relocated to Canada."

"I see. And this module relocated because of something Kentley found at AI4U."

"I don't know for sure, but I think so."

"Tell me more about the module and this anomaly."

Imogen sighed. "I told you the module is a case, a container, and we use it to put an experiment together."

"And the anomaly? What is that about?"

"The anomaly is what the experiments are for. We're trying to work out what the anomaly is."

"Okay. What are these experiments you put in the module?"

"There's a combination of computer chips, timer circuits and other electronics I don't know much about."

"So, why are you involved?"

"I'm a materials scientist. I helped work out what alloy caused the anomaly."

"Alloy. For the accelerator... the linac?"

"Yes."

"How do you fit a linear accelerator into the module case?"

"James developed a miniaturised linac that we use in the module."

"Miniaturised when he was at AI4U?"

"I don't think so. I'm pretty sure he started it at university a few years ago. Why?"

"Did the module that went to Canada use a miniature linac?"

"Yes. That was one of the components."

"What did the experiment do?"

"What did it do? What do you mean? It went to Canada."

She didn't feel the slap coming, but once again, it sent flashes of pain into her head and brain. "Don't get smart. What did the experiment module do? How did it work?"

Imogen took a breath to calm herself and lifted her head defiantly. "The linac fires electrons at a target, which generates a field."

"Target?"

"Yes."

"What is the target?"

"It's an alloy of metals. Some use gold foil, but these use tungsten mainly."

"Hmm. Okay, what about this field it generates?"

"When the electrons hit the target, they smash into particles and break them into smaller particles. How much do you know about quantum physics?"

"Just keep it simple."

"Okay. The smaller particles can generate a field, like a magnetic field, as they move. They don't last long."

"And it's this field that sent the module to Canada?"

"That's right." Imogen sensed the questions were coming to an end. She was happy she hadn't given much away.

The man paused. "How does this generated field send something to Canada? The Step, I think you call it."

Imogen bit the inside of her lip as she considered her answer. "The Step is a step back in the time dimension. I don't understand it too well."

"Time dimension? Like the Tardis?"

Imogen shrugged, "The what?"

"The Tardis... Dr. Who." Seeing Imogen shake her head under the hood, Mo moved on. "What about this Quinn person? Who's that?"

Imogen smiled to herself. "Quinn is the name of a program we use to do the test calculations. Using Quinn is much faster than working them out on paper each time."

"Quinn is a computer program?"

"Yes."

There was a pause for five seconds. "Why were you and your colleague at the motel?"

Imogen was happy to answer this one. "They were fixing our security. We're moving into the warehouse to make protecting us from people like you easier."

Imogen heard the chair scrape and the door close. She turned her head towards the door, "What about me? Can I go?" There was no answer as the footsteps receded.

* * *

It was close to two in the morning when Leigh called Marty. "We're fifteen minutes away. Any changes?"

Marty shook his head. "None I'm aware of, but I nodded off for an hour around midnight. Their car is still where it was parked, so I'd say nothing's changed."

"Let's hope so!" said Leigh. "We'll be there shortly."

Leigh arrived with four other men dressed in dark clothing without visible AFP insignia.

He explained the plan to Marty, "Two of us will go in through the front and two at the back at the same time. We should be able to go silent, but given it's one of Mo's places, the security may mean we have to use force."

He looked hard at Marty, "You shouldn't need to be involved. Just keep an eye open and keep your head down."

Marty nodded, "No worries mate. I'm not a bloody hero!"

Leigh and his men checked their comms gear before making their way silently to the front and back doors. Unfortunately, Leigh was right about Mo's possibly having tough security. In the end, it was better than Leigh had expected.

* * *

Mo was sitting on the banks of Sydney Harbour, watching the fireworks. A particularly noisy buzzing fire wheel bearing down on him woke him with a start. He realised the movement sensor at the rear of the house had detected something, and the silent alarm by the bed was going off. He quickly rose and dressed before shaking Lowen awake and retrieving batons. "Someone's going to try to get in shortly. If we're to get away, we need to leave the woman. I've got everything I can from her anyway."

Lowen whispered, "We'll go out through the roof?"

Mo listened for a moment. "Yes. Follow me."

They made their way quietly upstairs and through a concealed door that opened into a small space, giving access to a ladder mounted on the wall. They climbed the short ladder into the roof space just as metal rams smashed through the front and back doors.

* * *

Amid the noise of the men clearing rooms, Mo and Lowen exited onto the roof and climbed down the side of the house. Mo twisted a panel on the fence to the adjoining property, and they slipped through.

Mo held his finger to his lips as he replaced the panel. "We'll split up here. You go out the back of this place into the lane and go home. I'll hold here for a while and see if I can find out what happened and who's involved."

Lowen nodded and quietly made his way out the back. Mo, however, moved to the front of the house, where he could see the street.

After a short while, four men came out of the house with the woman. They looked up and down the street while the woman was settled into the back seat of a van. Mo was none the wiser as the vehicle drove off.

Mo waited for a half hour before deciding he was in the clear.

Focused on what had happened, he pulled out his phone and called Caldwell. "Harper, we need to meet... Tomorrow morning? Sure... nine-thirty at Sunnies. Done."

* * *

Imogen stretched her arms and legs periodically for what seemed like hours. She heard the faint murmur of voices elsewhere in the house, but nobody came to check on her. She occasionally dozed and had weird dreams that, fortunately, dissipated when she stirred.

She was awake when she heard loud noises, crashing and shouts. She jerked upright when someone bashed the door of the room open and shouted, "Clear!" before yelling out the door, "She's in here!" She heard a snick before the hood lifted off her head, and she saw a man in black reaching for her arm with a knife. He noticed her open eyes and stood back a step. "Federal Police, ma'am." He looked from her eyes to her arms and held out the knife. "I'll cut away the tape, ma'am?"

Imogen was at a loss for words and nodded. She watched wide-eyed as the man sliced the tape. She didn't feel the few hairs on her arm pull out as she peeled her arm from the tape. She repeated the process with her other arm as the man cut her legs free and put his knife away.

The hours had robbed her muscles of strength, and she lost her balance as she stood. As she tottered, the man put a steadying hand on her shoulder, and she turned to him with a small smile. "Thanks. How did you find me?"

The man's eyes smiled as he helped Imogen to the door and looked down the corridor. "Leigh will answer your questions, ma'am. Let's get you out of here first."

Another man joined them. "I'm Leigh Buchanan, AFP." He grinned with relief. "It's good to meet you, Imogen."

Imogen felt her face crumple as she let the tension and fear wash out of her tired body. She reached out to Leigh, who held her as the welling of emotion slowly subsided. Then, she lifted her head and smiled. "Thank you. Thanks to all of you for helping get me out of here."

Leigh grinned. "Just doing our job. Let's get you back to HQ."

* * *

Marty waited till Mo had left before calling Leigh.

"Marty, Hi. How did you get on?"

Marty laughed. "I'm amazed you could predict all that, Leigh. How'd you know?"

Leigh snorted. "Not rocket science, Marty. Mo's not stupid. If we had to break in, he'd have known we were there beforehand. It's a risk but one we were up for. I called you to get out of sight and watch the adjacent properties. What happened?"

Marty sighed. "I only saw Mo. I assume the other bloke went out the back lane. We got lucky, though."

"How's that?"

"Mo's arranged to meet someone called Harper tomorrow morning. Nine-thirty at Sunnies." Marty shook his head. "Unfortunately, Mo may recognise me from the motel, so I'll need to keep my distance."

Leigh agreed. "I'll get there myself and see what they're up to." He paused. "Marty, I need a favour. Can you take Imogen Matthews back to the warehouse at Tumbi?"

Marty nodded. "No problem. Where will I pick her up?"

"We'll need to check her out and be sure she's okay physically. After that, a debrief. I'd say she'll be ready to go late tomorrow or, perhaps, the morning after?"

Marty rubbed his eyes. "That's okay. Do you have a cot I can use? I'd prefer not to overnight in the car if I can help it."

"Hang on." Marty could hear Leigh murmuring in the background. "Come by Goulburn Street, and we'll fix you up. I'll be sorting out the Sunnies setup, so I won't see you until later in the morning."

Marty chuckled. "I'll be there. Thanks."

"My thanks to you, Marty. Are you sure you don't want a job?"

Marty snorted as he closed off the call and headed to AFP's offices for a well-deserved sleep.

* * *

Imogen was helped out of the van and into an elevator. Leigh looked at her with concern. "Sorry about all that. How are you feeling?"

Imogen shook her head and bared her teeth as her head throbbed. She gently massaged the back of her head and looked at Leigh. "If I wasn't so tired and if my head didn't hurt so much, I'd be very bloody angry at the idiots who ambushed me!" She gave him a small smile. "I'm okay. Nothing a rest won't fix."

The lift stopped, and they exited into a lobby with a couple of meeting rooms to the side and a corridor leading further into the building. They entered one of the rooms, and Imogen was happy to sit at the conference table.

Leigh's eyes winced in sympathy as he watched Imogen gently rub the back of her head. "We know who took you, and we'll arrest him and his buddy when we've got the full picture of who else is involved." He smiled. "I can't let you talk with him, but I'll pass on a message if you like."

Imogen looked at Leigh and chuckled. "No. There's no point." She smiled. "Just knowing you're going to catch him is enough payback for me."

Leigh returned the smile. "Our medic will be in shortly to check your head and help with the pain." He cocked his head in question. "Would it be alright with you if my colleague asked you a few questions before you catch some sleep?"

Imogen nodded in agreement, and Leigh opened the door for the medic. As the medic prepped his equipment, Leigh caught Imogen's eye. "My colleague, Callie, will be with you in a few minutes."

Imogen felt much better after the medic gave her painkillers for her headache. The conference room was plain but did have a water cooler with hot and cold water. She was looking for tea when the door opened, and two women entered.

Imogen looked at them, eyebrows raised in question. "Tea?" One of the women went to a cupboard where she grabbed a couple of boxes of different teas. "I'm Callie Stubbs. You don't know me, but my partner, Leigh, and I spoke to your boss, Harry Barnes, a few days ago about possible security issues."

Imogen poured hot water over a Lemon and Ginger tea bag and jiggled it in her cup. "Harry and Codie mentioned the AFP when they checked our security and found bugs in the warehouse. I thought they planned to keep quiet about the situation; Something about not trusting too many people."

Callie's face turned sour. "It's not such a stupid idea. We're a big, bureaucratic organisation, and anyone can be bribed if enough is offered." She shrugged. "Be that as it may, here we are! We had someone watching the motel while we were getting organised. It was fortunate he was able to follow you to Glebe." She grinned. "I bet the buggers who took you got a shock when we came along!"

Imogen shrugged. "I never even got to see them! I got a whack on the head, and when I woke, they'd put a bag over my head and trussed me like a chicken!"

Callie chuckled. "I'm sorry you had to go through it; I'm sure it wasn't pleasant!"

"The biggest thing for me was the fear of having no idea what was happening. I'm used to having some control over things, but this was like being tossed around in a storm, and I couldn't touch the sides!"

Callie smiled. "This is my colleague, Shari Gilmour. Shari's our resident expert on all things Mohamed Banks!"

Imogen frowned. "Mohamed Banks?"

Shari smiled, "He's one of the characters I keep close tabs on. I sift through communications and look for any activity involving corporate or government espionage." She shrugged. "He's the one who kidnapped you."

Imogen's eyes widened. "Why would someone involved in..." Realisation came quickly. "He's the one who bugged us!" She thought for a moment. "But, how would he have known about James's research?"

Shari nodded. "Score one for you!" She knew Imogen was tired after her ordeal and gave her a sympathetic smile. "Look, are you okay to tell us about what happened while it's fresh in your mind? I know you're tired."

Imogen yawned and shook her head. "It's okay. I am tired, but I did doze on their bloody chair, and I'm a bit tense from the rescue." She felt the back of her head and winced. "I also need the pain meds your medic gave me to kick in a bit more!"

Shari and Callie exchanged a look, and Shari turned back to Imogen. "Okay, it shouldn't take long." She took a breath. "Have you heard of Harper Caldwell or AI4U?"

Imogen shrugged. "James worked for AI4U before he got in touch with Harry. AI4U fired him!"

"That's right. AI4U, or rather, Harper Caldwell, their CEO, now wants the technology you've discovered."

Imogen nodded. "Okay, I see the connection." She looked around and shrugged, "How can I help you?"

Shari sighed, "You probably can't, but I want to ask you about your interactions with Mo. What questions did he ask? What were his reactions like? Did he involve anybody else? That sort of thing."

Imogen nodded. "Okay. Where do you want me to start?"

"How about from when you regained consciousness? Were you still in the car, or were you in the house?"

"I came to when they took me from the car. I think they must have slapped my cheeks to wake me." She felt her cheek as she remembered the sting. "They half dragged me into what sounded like an empty room and taped me to a chair." She chuckled to herself. "I remember thinking it was good that I hadn't had any water for a while. Silly, I know!" She got serious again, "I still had the bag over my head, so I was unable to see who asked me the questions, but he spoke well and didn't have an accent of any sort."

Shari nodded. "That sounds like Mo. Go on."

"He seemed fixated on James's research. He mentioned AI4U and James's work there and asked what I knew about it. It took me a while to convince him I knew nothing about James's miniaturisation work at AI4U or anywhere else." She shook her head. "Once convinced of that, he began to ask me about what we were doing. What was the module, and what did it have to do with Canada? I realised then he knew more than I originally supposed he had, so I decided to tell him what he already knew, in as few words as possible."

She paused for a few seconds before continuing. "He asked if the test module was connected to the anomaly James found at AI4U. I told him that it was. Then, he was interested in the module and what it did. I told him it was a bit of equipment we used to test different scientific theories. He seemed to believe that was significant. I don't know why."

Shari interrupted. "Mo knows nothing about science, so he was probably going off bits and pieces he'd picked up from the surveillance and Caldwell."

Imogen frowned. "Well, he got quite pushy about the module, and when I hedged around, he slapped me. He told me he knew about Canada and Quinn, and I should be truthful if I wanted to live." She smiled. "I'm a realist. He knew what he'd mentioned and would piece things together in time anyway, so I told him. I told him the linear accelerator made things move and that Quinn was a computer program we used for calculations. He was very excited when I mentioned that Canada was our first successful experiment."

Shari asked, "Anything else?"

"I didn't offer anything else, and he didn't push for anything else. He left me in the chair, and there I remained until your people rescued me."

Callie stepped forward. "Imogen, I assume that Quinn, experiments and Canada are on the list of things Codie didn't want us to know?"

Imogen compressed her lips and nodded. "Can you give us a rundown so we can do our jobs?"

Imogen considered the request and nodded in agreement. "In essence, the technology is used to 'Step' a module into the past. While Stepped, it is possible to move spatially. We don't know why we can. We use compressed air controlled by an artificial intelligence called Quinn. When located where we want it, the module is returned to the present in its new location, such as Canada. Before I was mugged, we were looking at using our AI to map the Earth. When that's done, we should be able to Step anywhere on the planet within seconds."

Imogen's eyes drooped tiredly, and she shrugged. "That's it! At the moment, we can move a small module around the planet and local space. We believe the technology will work on larger objects and greater distances, but, at this stage, we can't do that."

Callie and Shari's mouths opened, and their eyes widened as Imogen told them what had been discovered. Once Imogen finished, it took a few seconds for them to snap out of it.

Callie said, "That's unbelievable! No wonder you want to keep it quiet." She thought for a moment. "Look, we want to keep an eye on Mohamed Banks for a while to see if he has any other connections to this. Once we're done with him, we'll arrest him for the kidnapping and put him behind bars for a few years. Is that okay with you?"

Imogen nodded. "Whatever you need to do is okay with me. I certainly don't want him getting close to me again. Next time, I'll kick him where it hurts the most!"

Callie smiled her agreement. "Let's leave it at that for now, then. We have someone coming to take you back to the Coast when we're finished with any more questions we may have. Why don't you try to get a bit of sleep?"

"A wash and a sleep would be well received. Where do I go?"

Callie waved to Shari. "Shari will take you to a bedroom with en suite. It's all made up and ready. Someone will wake you at around half past seven. It's only a few hours, but it'll take the edge off."

Imogen was asleep ten minutes later.

Chapter 21

Harper Caldwell sat at a table on the back wall in Sunnies Cafe, waiting for Mo. Apart from a young woman jiving to her ear pods and the wait staff, the place was empty. It was nine thirty-eight, Mo was late, and Harper was getting rattled. He checked his phone for messages, and when he looked up, Mo walked towards him.

Harper scowled. "Jesus, Mo! Where have you been?"

Mo sat across from Harper. "Take it easy, Mr Caldwell. I drove over, and there were roadworks. One of the trucks backed into a hole and got stuck. Took them a while to get it sorted."

Harper shook his head. "Shit! Bloody country's going to the dogs! We need to return to some good old work ethic values, if you ask me!"

Mo frowned. "This is beyond my pay grade, Mr. Caldwell. I do the best I can, however it is."

Harper looked at Mo, gaze sharp. "What have you got for me, Mo?"

Mo waited as his coffee arrived and took a moment to add sugar while the waiter moved off. He looked around the cafe and noticed the girl listening to music and browsing her phone. Glancing in her direction, he raised an eyebrow at Harper.

Harper looked at her. "She was here when I arrived, finishing off breakfast. She's had toast, juice and, more recently, a coffee." Harper looked to the ceiling. "Wish I had her appetite!"

Mo chuckled. "I don't know; you seem to do okay, Mr Caldwell."

Harper remained silent.

Mo got serious and pulled a few pages of notes from his pocket. "First thing is Kentley himself. He's hooked up with a company called SplitQC."

Harper cocked his head. "SplitQC? Harry Barnes?"

Mo nodded. "That's the one. He's not an employee. By the look of it, this Harry Barnes is bankrolling Kentley's research. He's got a place, and a couple of technical scientists are helping him."

Harper interrupted again. "Research! Did you get any more on that?"

Mo looked at Harper. "I'll get to that, but one thing interesting about Kentley—at least I found it interesting—is that he doesn't have any attachments to people. There's nothing to indicate family, close friends or the like. He's focused on his work, and I think that's all he has."

Mo took a breath. "As far as work, all I found in his house were these notes and drawings." Mo handed Harper a copy of what he'd found at Kentley's house. "Needless to say, I couldn't make head nor tail of them. Perhaps you'll have better luck."

Harper looked at the pictures and had no idea either. He put them to the side. "I'll get my people to look at them. What about his research?"

Mo straightened. "Now, that was more interesting! Barnes has given him the use of a warehouse in Tumbi Umbi."

"Tumbi What?"

Mo chuckled. "Tumbi Umbi. It's on the Central Coast, southern end of Tuggerah Lake."

Harper's face soured. "Bloody boondocks! What's he doing there?"

Mo shrugged. "I don't think the location was the reason for being there. I think it's where Barnes had a space Kentley could use." Mo looked back to his notes and pulled out more photos. "These are photos of the equipment he's using for his experiments. Once again, I don't know what they do or how they work."

Harper pointed to a rack of spiky balls. "What the hell are those?"

Mo looked at Harper. "I don't know for sure. They made them not long after I recorded this conversation." With that, he clicked on an audio file on his phone.

"Quinn, load Step Test Bravo-three-seven."

"Step Test Bravo-three-seven Loaded."

"Quinn, Execute Test Bravo-three-seven."

"Bravo-three-seven starting in Five.. Four.. Three.. Two.. One.. Mark."

"Test Bravo-three-six Complete."

"I was expecting to see it in here somewhere. I wonder where it went? Quinn, where did the module go?"

"GPS indicates Shellbrook in Canada."

"Shellbrook? Never heard of it!"

"Quinn, did we get any pictures?"

"There's a word on the end. I think it says Pioneer. Perhaps cement storage? By the look of things, the module is on the ground in a scrubby area."

"Canada! Can you believe it!"

Sounds of cheering...

"We'd better bring Harry up to date! He wouldn't want to miss this!"

The audio finished, and Harper was silent. Mo looked at him and noticed he was very pale. "Are you okay, Mr. Caldwell?" He reached across and shook Harper by the shoulder. "Mr. Caldwell?"

Harper came to himself and shook Mo off, asking. "Anything else?"

Mo looked abashed. "Well, yes and no." Harper glared, so Mo continued. "They found my surveillance equipment, so I invited one of the scientists to tell me what was going on first-hand." Mo shrugged. "Let's say Ms. Imogen Matthews helped with our enquiries."

Harper frowned, confused. "What did she say?"

Mo tongued his teeth and cocked his head. "She was quite forthcoming. Her job is to help Kentley work out what was in the 'target' material in their tests. She said they discovered what was happening and could replicate the effect." Mo paused and looked uncertain. "She said they went back in time!"

Harper was confused. "Back in time? A time machine?"

Mo shook his head. "It's not a time machine, but the module thing. She said the module went back in time, and they moved it. Then it came back somewhere else."

Harper scratched his eyebrow. "That doesn't make sense!"

Mo shrugged. "It's what she told me. She said it went to Canada, just like the recording says." Mo added. "She also said they were beefing up security and moving into the warehouse full-time. That was why she returned to the motel to pick up her bags."

"Shit!" said Harper. "How the hell am I going to get my hands on this gear?"

Mo shook his head, "I can't help with that anymore, Mr. Caldwell. The security they are putting in place looks pretty strong to me. I think their security bloke is ex-military."

Harper stood. "I have to go. Thank you, Mohamed. You've done well. I'll take it from here." Harper took Mo's documents and photographs and returned to AI4U.

Mo sat back in the chair, wondering what he'd got himself into. He shook his head; he wanted to know more about this time machine.

When he got to his car, he called Lowen. "Lowen, I want to set up a team to get into the warehouse at Tumbi Umbi. Can you pick three or four capable lads and meet me in two hours?"

"No problem, Mo. Where do you want to meet?"

Mo thought for a moment. "How about the cafe across from the Star in Redfern?"

"Okay, Mo, see you there."

Some two hours later, Mo was discussing his plan with Lowen and four men they'd worked with on various operations in the past. They were thugs who hired themselves out for a price but were good at their work.

After reviewing the plan several times, they ironed out a few details and agreed it would work.

Mo reiterated, "Lowen will have a van ready in the car park later this afternoon. We'll park the van out of sight and approach the estate on foot. Once we get to the warehouse, I'll take one of you and wait outside to pick up any runners. Lowen and you three go in the front and sort out their security. Then we'll see what all the excitement is about their technology."

He handed each of the four men an envelope. "Half now, half when we're done. Okay?"

There were no questions. "Good. Get yourselves set and meet us at the van at three."

* * *

A car drove in and parked by the office. The driver got out and opened the passenger door to help Imogen out. James and Jerry rushed and fussed to help and guide her inside. Codie joined the driver and talked with him quietly before leading him into the office.

They helped Imogen to a chair, but she shooed them away with her hands. "I'm alright! Stop fussing!" She did look alright, to be honest. She had a bruised cheek, some scratching on her hands and a bruise on her left bicep. She'd also had a knock to the back of her head and winced as she rubbed the spot lightly.

James asked. "Do you want paracetamol?"

She smiled and nodded. "That's probably a good idea. My head hurts like hell!"

Matt and Jerry joined them as James passed over the pills and a bottle of water.

Matt looked like a sorry puppy as he asked for forgiveness.

Imogen frowned. "What could you have done? They attacked me as soon as I walked into my room!" She smiled. "It's ended okay, so don't worry about it. We'll all be more careful in the future."

Matt looked relieved and promised to do better next time before heading back outside.

Jerry told Imogen his side of the encounter, which wasn't much. Jerry nudged James in the ribs. "She looks okay, James. Certainly, none the worse for the experience."

James nodded and frowned darkly. "I want to know who took her and why!" He looked across to where Codie stood talking with the stranger. Codie, noticing the glance, waved them over. "James, Jerry, this is Marty Elliot. He's the chap who followed Imogen's kidnappers and helped the AFP get her free."

Marty was of average height, a little overweight, greying to white, and sporting a magnificent moustache and goatee. Under the moustache was a wide, welcoming smile accompanied by merrily smiling blue eyes that twinkled. Marty held their gaze and held out his hand. "Hi. It's good to meet you."

They shook hands, and James was sincerely grateful. "Thanks for looking after Imogen, Marty. We've missed her and were worried despite the AFP saying they had everything under control!"

Marty bent his head, "Just glad I could help and not too much harm was done." Marty explained he'd done nothing special except driving a bit and keeping a low profile. "A low profile is my forte! It keeps me out of sight and, mostly, out of mind!"

He gave them a huge smile. "I'll be getting along if that suits you folks; I have a million things to catch up on!" He held out a card to James.

James looked at the card and then glanced quizzically at Marty. "Solutions Expert?"

Marty smiled. "Yeah, that's what I do."

James cocked his head. "Any particular specialty area?"

Marty laughed. A high-pitched, happy laugh. "Nothing in particular. If you have a problem, I'll probably be able to help sort it out or put you in touch with someone who can."

James looked from Marty's smile to Codie's frown and decided to leave things at that. "Well, it's good to know you. Thanks again for looking out for Imogen!"

Marty looked James in the eye, and James saw a keen intelligence there. Marty nodded. "It was my pleasure, she's a smart lady!" He looked to the side, then back at James. "Remember. Call me if you need anything. I have a feeling we'll meet again!" With that, he waved a general goodbye and left.

James turned to Codie. "Who was he, Codie? How did he get involved?"

Codie chuckled. "Marty's a good guy. I've heard him described as a spider in the middle of a web of information." Codie shrugged, "He doesn't put much store in the law. Says it lets too many people down." He reflected a moment. "Marty judges things his way. If he likes you, he helps you. If he doesn't like you, then odd little things go wrong."

James frowned and squinted in question. "Then how did he get involved with this?"

Codie laughed. "Marty and Jacko Dunne at the AFP go back a long way. That relationship rubbed off on Leigh Buchanan and prompted him to ask Marty to help by watching the motel until we fixed our security." Codie smiled. "Luckily, he did in the end, or we'd have had no way of finding Imogen."

They looked toward Imogen and saw her talking animatedly with Jerry.

James looked thoughtful as he thanked Codie and went to join his friends.

Imogen smiled. "Jerry's been bringing me up to date. It's amazing to hear what's gone on while I was away. I can't believe you sent a module to Dublin!"

James's eyes caught Imogen's, and his brows came together. "It is amazing, and because of that, we're in greater danger than ever." He leaned forward and smiled. "But I know what we have to do."

Chapter 22

Harper called Hugh as soon as he got to his desk. When Hugh arrived, Harper rounded on him. "Damn you, Hugh! Why didn't you keep a closer eye on that bloody idiot?"

Hugh took a step back. He knew Harper's temper could be wild. "Harper, cool down. It's only the oddness of the situation that has caused the problem. Things like this can't be predicted!"

Harper waved his arms around. "But, sacking bloody Kentley! That bastard's found something. Something he got wind of here!"

Harper sneered and clenched his jaw. "I want to know everything that happened. Everything the bastard touched. Everything he used." He thought for a moment. "I want what he did for our Martyn Analytics AI pulled to pieces and analysed." He looked at Hugh. "And I want it done NOW! No bloody pussy footing around. Drop everything else and get onto it. I want a progress report in an hour!"

Hugh started to talk, but Harper drowned him out. "NOW! Get out there, find it, get back! Simple."

Hugh left without a backward glance. He went immediately to the lab used by James Kentley and called the lab assistant over. "Has anything been touched at Kentley's workbench yet?"

The assistant shook his head. "Not yet. We were..."

Hugh turned away. "Good! Let's go there first and have a chat."

James's workbench was in a laboratory in the basement at AI4U's head office. The room had space for a half dozen areas that could be configured for different activities. Amongst other instruments on James's bench were a linear accelerator with a cloud chamber, a company computer and other bits and pieces of unknown purpose.

Hugh called over two technicians in the lab when he arrived. "Do you know what Kentley was working on over here?"

One of them nodded. "Yes, Mr. Barton, he was working on customising his logic gate for the Martyn Analytics project."

Hugh smiled, "Call me Hugh." He cocked his head. "How did you know that?"

The tech looked concerned. "Sorry, Mr. Barton. He told me, and I helped out occasionally. I didn't think it was a secret or anything."

Hugh saw that he'd frightened the man. "No, no, no, don't worry about that. You're not in any strife. I want to know what Kentley was working on. It may open up another opportunity if we're lucky." Hugh smiled. "What's your name?"

"Phil Stamford, Sir"

Hugh ignored the 'Sir'. "Phil, tell me all you know about Kentley's work here."

Phil looked from Hugh to his colleagues and back again. "Well, it's not much, but I'll do my best." When Hugh nodded encouragement, he went on. "He asked me to help set up the linac once or twice when he was switching components."

Hugh held out a hand. "linac? And, what components?"

Phil pointed at one of the machines. "Linear Accelerator. Often referred to as a 'LINAC' for short." He shrugged and continued. "The components differed. Mostly the targets, but sometimes he'd switch out the laser or adjust positioning."

The assistant looked at Hugh. "The targets. He talked about them a lot recently. I believe he had an issue with one?"

Phil looked at Hugh to make sure he should answer and, when Hugh nodded, spoke up. "I think the target was his most important item. He needed to get it just right so the particles would behave correctly in the miniature version." He chuckled. "He was confused when one gave him a problem; he muttered that it should be the same and wondered if he'd set the equipment incorrectly."

Hugh latched onto that. "Did he say what the issue was?"

Phil nodded. "Yes. He showed me the particle tracks! It was strange, but I don't think he ever worked it out!"

"When you say 'strange', what do you mean?"

Phil thought back. "The tracks were off to one side. Normally, they appeared as solid tracks and lasted a short time. The ones he was worried about weren't solid; they had a gap."

The assistant turned to Hugh. "That's right. He mentioned the gap to me when he was mucking about with it. He was extremely interested in it."

Hugh turned his attention back to Phil. "Do you know where he kept these targets?"

Phil pointed to a cupboard against the wall between two of the benches. "His stocks were on the left-hand side in the storage cupboard. He may also have had some on his bench or drawers, but I don't know."

Hugh smiled. "Thank you, Phil. I'll come and ask if we need any more information."

Hugh and the assistant opened the storage cupboard and pulled out a sealed tray with unused targets. The assistant went to the workbench and checked the shelf underneath. He noticed a photo of particle tracks, which he took to Hugh. Hugh had a look and walked across to Phil. "Are these the tracks?"

Phil grinned and pointed to the unbroken lines at the lower left of the photo. "That's them!" He nodded. "The others he showed me had a gap about a fifth back from where they end."

He returned the picture, and Hugh thanked him as he returned to James's bench. They found nothing else of interest, but he did notice a target amongst waste in a box on one side. He picked it out and gave it to the lab assistant. "Get these tested using the same setup Kentley used? I'll get Jenny Worland to give you a hand. Get a start on it now and make sure the first two tests use one of these unused targets and that one from the waste bin."

He looked at his watch, "Get back to me in half an hour, and we'll update Harper."

The assistant took the targets from Hugh and scooted.

* * *

One hour after leaving Harper's office, Hugh was back.

Harper motioned him to close the door. "What have you got for me?"

Hugh handed over a sheet of paper. "So far, we've retrieved and tested about half the targets Kentley used. All give the same result where extra particles are emitted from the target. However, the particle tracks remain unbroken, so they're not the anomaly that Kentley was looking at."

Harper frowned and shook his head. "That's it? That's all we've got?"

Hugh sighed. "It's a bit like chasing shadows. I talked with another technician who works in the lab used by Kentley. He says Kentley was interested in the anomaly he came across. He said Kentley thought he may have made an error setting up a test, but he reproduced the result multiple times."

Harper nodded, "If the result was unexpected and the setup was correct, what else had changed?"

"I believe it was the target. Somehow, the structure of the target was altered, perhaps an impurity. Whatever it was, it resulted in the anomaly that got Kentley excited."

Harper scrunched his face. "Why? Why did he get worked up? What was he thinking?" He looked at Hugh. "And, where is the altered target?"

Hugh shrugged, "We can't find any sign of it. All I can suggest is that he had it with him when escorted from the premises."

"The bastard's a thief!" Harper shouted, "We can have him arrested!"

Hugh shook his head. "I'm not sure we have anything to go on. There's no proof of anything being stolen, and we chuck these things in the trash once they're finished anyway!"

Harper growled. "I'll keep it in mind, though! Bastard!" He clenched his fists. "How can we find what caused the anomaly?"

Hugh dropped his gaze and looked back at Harper. "I talked with the lab assistant, and he may have given me an idea."

Harper turned to Hugh with a scowl on his face, "You let Scott stuff this whole thing up, so I'd appreciate it if you came up with something to help get us out of the shit!"

Hugh winced. "I've worked with these kinds of projects in the past, and some general understanding of the technologies rubs off and sticks."

Harper nodded, and Hugh continued his thought. "If you work on the assumption the gap in the trail is a by-product of whatever happened." He frowned. "Then you consider their surprised comments about Canada." Hugh looked closely at Harper. "Well, it's possible their experiment was to see where the module went when placed under some condition imposed by the anomaly." He sighed and shook his head. "It's possibly a long shot, but I'd say the anomaly allowed them to move the module instantly to Canada."

Harper shook his head. "I don't get what you're talking about. Sounds like.."

"Hang on!" interrupted Hugh. "If you go back to the gap in the cloud trail, the particle trail is the clue! The particle doesn't cease to exist; it simply goes somewhere and returns! Do you see?"

Harper remained puzzled. Hugh put his hands wide to the sides. "Shit! It's obvious to me now! The particle can't move in space; there is no trail of it doing so. Where can the particle go?" Harper looked at him blankly. "Time! It can only go back in time! Once it's there, something happens with the anomaly and the particle comes back to the present and continues on its merry way! It explains it all!"

Harper started to nod. "The Canada event was an experiment to see where it went when it went back.."

"No!" said Hugh. "Canada was an experiment to see if they could move it while it was already back in time! That's why they were so surprised and excited!"

Harper's face twisted, "We have to get our hands on that tech! Can you imagine what it's worth? We could." He stopped short. "We have to get it!" Harper looked at his watch. "I'm out for the afternoon. Hugh, think about this and try to come up with some ideas. I'll do the same, and we can compare notes later."

With that, Harper grabbed his keys and phone and left the building.

Chapter 23

James was jittery.

Imogen's kidnapping had been the catalyst that brought the reality of their situation bubbling up his spine as fear and blooming in his mind as a combination of concern and determination that was almost black and white in its clarity.

He asked Imogen, Harry and Jerry to join him in the office and opened up to them. "I'm extremely concerned about our situation here."

Harry started to talk, but James held him off by waving his hand. "Not concerned, bad word! I'm scared out of my wits by our situation! We now know we have a disruptive technology, and people are after it. As I see the situation, we have two choices. First, we capitulate and go into hiding. The probable outcome is the government takes over the research and development, and we disappear somewhere." He waved his hands to keep the others from interrupting, "Or, choice two, we accelerate the research and give ourselves a third option."

Before they could say anything, his eyes narrowed, and he continued. "The Step process is safe, reproducible and targeted. We can send the module wherever we want to go on Earth." He took a breath to steady himself and ploughed on. "We have to go for the next two stages, and I believe we can achieve them quickly enough to give us time to work out how to handle this new tech."

James looked at his colleagues. This was the first time he'd known what had to be done and how to do it. He was nervous and excited at the same time. This was the first time he'd taken on the role of a leader, and he was ready to step up to the challenge.

Harry looked at him oddly but shrugged his shoulders. His expression turned serious. "Okay, what are these stages you refer to?"

James laid out his plan. "First, we build or obtain a module that will carry people. The more people, the better, but at least two."

Imogen raised her head and nodded. "A manned module is the next logical step."

James smiled, and his eyes sparkled; it would be interesting to see how they reacted to the next stage. "The second stage, which we'll begin immediately, is to get Quinn mapping the Step characteristics of larger masses and further movements while Stepped."

Harry cocked his head, and Jerry frowned. James could see they didn't get it. He stood tall and, with a steady voice, said. "We are going to find a planet."

He watched it sink in, and his eyes narrowed. "And, when we find one we can live on", he lifted his head, "we are going to move the research there!"

Imogen's face lit up. She put her hand on James's forearm. "We can do it. I'm sure."

Harry's jaw dropped while he processed what James had said. It closed with a snap. He considered James's words, his head shaking, "How can you do that? We don't even know if a planet exists, and how will you find it? It's crazy, James!"

Jerry was still working through the idea, so James focused on Harry. Harry, we have the technology to search for a planet." He raised a hand. "The key is Quinn, the first hybrid quantum classic AI. Quinn makes all this possible because of its ability to create and tune algorithms."

James made eye contact with Harry, "Controlling test scenarios is a milk run for Quinn. It's the algorithms that make this possible. I didn't see it until Quinn mapped the Earth. It took only five hours to do what I would have expected a supercomputer to take months or years."

James took a breath. "Quinn's forte is collecting data, incorporating new data into its processing and determining more efficient algorithms to do the work." Harry started to nod, and James smiled as he continued thinking. "To find planets will take time. But we can minimise data collection time by using miniature drones that flick back and forth, each a data point, each getting closer to a star, a solar system and, eventually, a planet."

James's eyes narrowed as he visualised the process: "We'll need to have larger drones ready to analyse a planet and determine its atmosphere, its position relative to the sun, and its mineral composition. Plus, anything else we need to determine if the world is habitable. Then, even larger drones will Step onto the world and test samples."

James laughed out loud. "After that? A rat!"

"A rat?" asked Harry.

Jerry was nodding and smiling. "Yes, a rat! A test pilot to breathe the air and ensure the world is safe for our type of life!"

James saw that Jerry was on board alongside Imogen, so he turned his attention to Harry, who was thinking it through. Harry was slowly getting there, though. "James, this is surreal. We've gone from a sideline look at an anomaly and found a technology that can Step anywhere on Earth instantly." He frowned and exclaimed, "That's a game-changer on its own." A pause. "And now we're looking to Step into the stars!" He looked at Imogen and the smile in her eyes, then at Jerry, whose mind was already working through various computational permutations. Then Harry turned back to James, eyes flashing. "It's shattering! Nothing will ever be the same again!"

James grabbed Harry's shoulder. "Harry, we don't have a choice. We have to try. It won't change if we don't make it happen." He calmed his energy, brow furrowed. "And, when we make it happen, we can't just spring the idea on an unsuspecting world. Imagine the carnage!" He shook his head, "No. We'll have to be very careful." He tilted his head. "I don't want to think about that now. Let's find a new home and get out of here first!"

With them all focused on the new goal, James brought them back to reality. "We can't make this happen with the resources we have. The three-point-four-centimetre Step to Canada was close to the diameter of Earth. To get to the sun would need a Step of close to thirty-eight kilometres. It won't happen with compressed air."

He leaned forward, eyes dark points. "We also need a vehicle, and I'm sure NASA isn't going to give us one of theirs!" They looked at each other and understood the challenges facing them. James's jaw tightened. "Harry, do we know anyone involved in the space programs? We need to get our hands on a couple of CubeSats. They're microsatellites that can be equipped with propulsion systems and solar collectors to recharge batteries, and they can be joined like click blocks to make more complex machines." He shrugged and smiled. "At a pinch, we could buy some, but it would use time we don't have to take delivery and get them ready for use."

Harry made a note. "I may have an idea; leave it with me."

James looked surprised. "Crikey! That was the hard one!" He smiled. "I also have an idea for a vehicle, but we'd have to find a used one for sale or build one." He paused, "We don't know what conditions are like when Stepped back; we need to do some specific analysis. We'll need air to breathe, which means a pressurised vehicle. The structure and entry hatch must be effectively sealed against leakages." He frowned at a scrap of paper in his hand, "I was thinking of an aircraft fuselage or a specially rigged bus, but they seemed too much of a stretch." He looked somewhat sheepish as he continued, "Then it came to me a small submarine may fit the bill."

Imogen pursed her lips and frowned, "Whatever it is, it'll need to fit in here, and it'll need propulsion."

Jerry looked at Harry and back to James. "If we want a vehicle in the short term, we may need to source it from someone with more resources."

Harry nodded, "I'm sure we can solve both problems." He looked at James and smiled. "You're going to have to trust me enough to trust the people I have in mind."

James shook his head slowly. He was still struggling with the need to involve other people and their motivations. He was especially cynical of the Department of Defence or anyone associated with the government. "Harry, I don't know; you're thinking of Defence?"

Harry folded his lips closed and nodded. He looked James in the eye. "Yes, I am."

James put his hand to his forehead and rubbed his temples. "Shit! I don't trust the bastards! Look at the submarine disaster and the helicopters that can't use weapons. Those are the ones we hear about! They're bloody corrupt and self-serving. How on earth would you find an honest person in there?"

Harry ducked a shoulder in acknowledgement and nodded. "I understand how it seems. But it's not the Defence Department that makes these stupid decisions; it's the politicians. And, when they do, they get outside contractors and consultants to deliver these projects." Harry snorted and shook his head, "In the end, Defence is stuck with having to make things work." He paused a moment. "I've been working with people in defence for a good five years now and, in the main, have found them competent and trustworthy despite the problems. In fact," he smiled brightly, "In fact, because of all the crap they operate in every day, they are remarkably innovative and resilient, two qualities we'll be needing every bit of if we're to get this done!"

James sat back, put his hands behind his head and let the cynicism fade while he thought objectively. Harry was right; they needed more support, and the military was an ideal resource for them. If they were going to succeed, they would need help. He laughed at himself as he realised he'd changed. "Let's do it!"

The four looked at each other, nodded in agreement and smiled. James took a deep breath. "Our autonomy is critical. We can't allow any of this technology to get out. If we can keep defence at arm's length, we do so. We can't have the tech get into the wrong hands." The others asserted their agreement. James finished with a grin. "If defence must have information that puts us at risk, make damn sure it is going to someone we all trust and who knows the danger associated with it."

James had changed, but he wasn't going to be hasty. He still had doubts, but he recognised that doubts stopped people from moving forward. "Harry, how do you want to play this?"

Chapter 24

Harper Caldwell was ruffled. It didn't happen often, but this situation took the cake. He could feel control slipping through his fingers as the seconds ticked away. He had to either act or forget about it altogether. He dialled the number from memory. There was a chime when it answered, followed by, "Roche".

"Roche, it's Harper Caldwell. I need your help."

"Where are you?"

"Home."

"Wait there. I'll send someone. Be ready."

The line chimed again and clicked off.

Harper hung up, poured a Laphroaig and collected his thoughts.

A knock at the door roused him from his angry rehash of events. He grabbed a briefcase, his notes and a jacket. He turned out the lights as he left his home and walked to the dark sedan waiting with an open door.

They drove to Sydney's Eastern Suburbs and pulled into the driveway of a harbour-side mansion. As the car stopped, a man opened the door and beckoned to Harper. The man took Harper's briefcase and coat before indicating that Harper should put his hands on the roof of the car for a personal search. Harper shrugged and complied; he wasn't the one calling the shots here.

Satisfied Harper was unarmed, the security aide escorted him into the home's entry foyer and handed both briefcase and coat to another man sitting at a desk.

The man smiled. "I'll bring these back to you shortly."

The first man pointed to a door towards the back of the foyer and gestured for Harper to follow him. The man reached the door and opened it silently. The room was warmly decorated, and as Harper entered, Robert Hickey-Roche rose from an armchair and greeted him with a smile and handshake. "Harper! What a wonderful surprise! I've been looking forward to getting to know you better."

Harper shook his hand. "Good evening, Roche. I've been looking forward to it, too." He frowned. "I wish the circumstances were better!"

Roche chuckled. "If everything worked out properly all the time, it would be a very boring life, don't you think?"

Harper sighed. "You have a point, but sometimes the trouble comes at the worst moment!"

Indicating one of the armchairs, Roche said, "Sit! Drink?"

Harper sat in the indicated chair. "Yes, thanks. Scotch, neat."

"A man after my own heart." Laughed Roche. "High or Low?"

"Highlands will be great, thanks." Roche poured a good measure of The Dalmore for both and handed a glass to Harper. After clinking glasses, both men took a good sip and allowed the flavours to develop before talking.

"That's an exceptionally nice whiskey, Roche!"

Roche smiled. "That it is. If I were honest, I'd say all whiskey is nice." They laughed together and discussed WestProtect for a few minutes.

There was a quiet knock on the door. "Yes!"

A man entered and placed Harper's briefcase on the floor beside his chair and his coat on a hanger by the door. He nodded to Roche and left, closing the door quietly.

Roche looked at Harper and cocked his head. "Now, how can I help you?"

Harper spent an hour explaining to Roche what he understood of the situation. He summarised, "If I am right, they have technology that can deliver a payload to any precise location on Earth."

He caught Roche's eye, and his brow puckered, "I'm guessing, but if you take it to the next logical step, they'll be able to deliver large payloads such as groups of people and goods." He tilted his head a fraction and raised an eyebrow. "It may be they will have the capability to do that anywhere in the galaxy. Perhaps, beyond." Harper sat back and picked up his glass. It was empty, and he put it back down.

Roche was silent as he looked over the photos and transcripts of the recordings Mo had taken. He sighed, rose, and went to the sideboard where the bottle was waiting. He poured a good double in both glasses and raised his glass to Harper. "I'm glad you brought this to me, Harper. If you're right," he waved his hand, "If you're right, and I think you are onto something, then this will make WestProtect one of the most powerful institutions on the planet." His eyes took on a faraway look, "Our civilisation will succeed where others have failed, and our place in history, as promised by God, will be achieved!"

They clinked glasses and had a good swallow. Roche looked at his desk. "I'll convene an extraordinary meeting with the leadership group. Many international members are still in Australia, so arranging shouldn't take more than a few days." He tapped his upper teeth with a forefinger. "In the meantime, I'll put Emanuel on alert and have him get local assets to gather intelligence on the site and the people."

Roche looked at Harper. "You have done well, Harper. I will discuss a conditional promotion to the Leadership Group for the duration of this campaign. If all goes well, you should achieve the goals you have set yourself."

Harper smiled, warmed by the acknowledgement, "Thank you, Roche! Yes, I believe I can contribute more at a higher level."

The ends of Roche's mouth lifted. "We shall see Harper, we shall see." His smile broadened, "Let's focus on this technology first, though. Go! Return to your home, and in the morning, I will call you when the place and time are known."

Roche pushed a button on his desk, and the door opened. A man stood to the side and accompanied the two men back to the front steps.

Roche was silent but shook Harper's hand and nodded as Harper got into the car. Roche thanked his guards and returned to his study as the car disappeared around the drive.

He poured another whiskey, and his brow knotted in thought.

Chapter 25

They sat around a table in a secure room at RAAF Williamtown, north of Newcastle. On one side were James, Harry, Jerry and Codie; on the other were Major General Macaulay Hancock and Colonel Leona MacPherson. General Hancock, known as 'Mac' to his friends, headed Australia's DDU (Digital Defence Unit). Colonel MacPherson was responsible for the Space Technologies branch of the DDU.

Harry, with a hint of determination in his voice, introduced his team to Hancock and MacPherson. "First of all, we deeply appreciate both of you for taking the time to hear us out." He paused, his brows furrowing. "I have asked you here under a shroud of secrecy, fully aware that this might not be an easy situation for either of you."

General Hancock turned to James. "Mr. Kentley, Harry told me about Imogen Matthew's abduction and subsequent return." He narrowed his eyes. "I'm glad she is safe now, and I want you to know that my staff will treat our relationship with the utmost respect, confidentiality, and security." He turned to Harry, "Don't worry about secrecy, Harry. It's well within our terms of reference to maintain confidence. There are limits, and I will let you know when we approach them. Until then, feel at ease. The trust we've built in our dealings over the years counts for a lot with us, Harry."

Harry smiled. "Thanks, General. What we talk about here may push those limits, though!"

Harry turned to James. "I've given the General an overview of the situation and your research. Tell him what you need and why."

James, his voice filled with a mix of excitement and awe, stood up. "Thanks, Harry." He nodded to the officers. "General. Colonel." He took a deep breath, "I stumbled upon something truly extraordinary while working on a miniaturised linear accelerator. Following up on what caused the anomaly, we found the conditions required to generate two electromagnetic fields. On their own, they are dormant. But when used together, they cause whatever is contained inside the merged field to 'Step' back in time. Stopping one field returns the contents to the present."

James, his voice steady and confident, checked to ensure they had no questions before continuing. "We also discovered we could move an object while 'Stepped' back. Doing this places the object in a slightly different physical location than where it started. In other words, we can move something from one place on Earth to another place on Earth with remarkable speed and precision."

The General raised a finger. "How large an object can you do this with?"

James turned to Harry with a frown but returned his eyes to the General, "Sir, to this date, we have used simple drones pushed by compressed air. My understanding of the fields and how they interact indicate we could, conceivably, move an object of any size, but we'd need different and more powerful propulsion."

The Colonel raised an eyebrow. "James, may I ask something?"

"Yes, Colonel, of course."

"You say you Step back to a different location on Earth. Is it possible to Step to a place in Earth's orbit? Or the moon's surface, for that matter?"

James raised his eyes in surprise, "We haven't looked at doing that, but there's no reason why we can't."

Colonel MacPherson looked at the General, raised her brow and cocked her head before turning back. "Thank you. Please go on."

James looked thoughtful and then tilted his head. "I can see the wheels turning, Colonel. From a military perspective, we've discovered an enormous opportunity." He sighed, "Frankly, it's the military, corporate, criminal and political spheres that concern me the most when it comes to this discovery being used in ways I can't agree to. I'd prefer to see the discovery lost rather than abused."

James held out a hand to forestall any response. "Don't get me wrong. I trust you on Harry's recommendation because I know he sees things like I do. As do Jerry and Imogen." He gave a slight shrug. "I am happy to help you find use cases for the technology within your areas of responsibility, but I cannot see it used for anything that makes life worse!"

The General stood, "James. Have no fear on that account. You have my word that knowledge of the discovery will not be released through the DDU, nor will we ask you to do anything unaligned with our common purpose." He gestured at the Colonel, "Colonel MacPherson has lost a satellite and thinks your tech may help her find it."

James looked at the Colonel, shook his head and smiled. "Anything we can do to help, Colonel, just ask." she inclined her head in acknowledgement.

James took a deep breath and raised his head. "We believe there is no reason we can't use this technology to explore, if not all of space, then certainly the Milky Way and the closer galaxies." He focused on the General, "With the right drone and propulsion system, we can, over time, look for, map and analyse planets."

He held the General's eyes as he dropped the bombshell, "With the view to populating them."

There was silence for a moment. Then the General looked from James to Harry, a question on his face. "Is he serious?"

Harry chuckled and sighed. "He certainly is. And I'll tell you now, we'll do it!"

The General looked back at James, compressed his lips and nodded slowly. "Very well! Let's get down to brass tacks. What do you need?"

James's body, face and head relaxed. Then, his shoulders and back. Regardless of all his worries, he hadn't realised how stressed he'd been or the degree to which he'd invested himself in this meeting. He rolled his shoulders, nodded thanks to Harry and gave the General his full attention. "For the exploration phase, we need something like a CubeSat. It needs to be small because the less the mass, the further back in time it will Step and the shorter the distance needed to travel. It also needs to have a good propulsion system."

He turned his attention to Colonel MacPherson. "They don't need to travel far. Our current drones would have to move around five kilometres to get to the nearest star, Alpha Centauri." He smiled. "Our nearest galaxy, Andromeda, is around three and a half million kilometres travel away!"

James raised his eyebrows. "I have looked into current CubeSat technology and believe chemical thrusters will keep mass down, perhaps using hydrazine. It would be a great help if you had someone familiar with the various thrusters."

The Colonel nodded and made notes on her phone as James was talking. "The key thing is that more mass equates to a shorter Step back, which results in a longer distance to travel once Stepped. But we need the mass so we can have the motor. There will be a trade-off, but it should be relatively easy to manage for the mapping project."

James smiled more easily. "Mapping will give us data about where to look for a habitable planet. Perhaps more. Once we find one, we move to the planet and continue experimenting and building the technology from a location out of harm's way."

James paused a moment and had a drink of water. The General smiled at him, "So, you'd have yourself a planet to call your own?" James smiled and continued the joke. "It's a big universe, General. I reckon we could all have one or two planets each." They laughed. Still, James felt they should lay a foundation for what they may do with a habitable planet when one was found.

James looked at each of the people in the room. They were good, honest people doing the things they enjoyed. Harry loved his company and the opportunity it gave his team. He lived to push the boundaries of computing and develop a fully operational quantum computer.

Jerry's imagination was fired by the promise of artificial intelligence to improve humanity's lot and reduce the cost of technology on the planet. He didn't view AI as a prelude to machine consciousness and laughed at the effort put into just that. What he did see with AI was the opportunity to interact more closely with the program and give it pathways to analyse results differently so it could rewrite itself to improve continuously. Jerry needed data, fast memory, and fast processes.

James's passion was miniaturisation and robotics. He lived for nanotechnologies and the quantum world, looking for ways to make technology smaller and simpler so they would use fewer resources and open new research pathways.

James looked across the table again. "General, Colonel. We do what we do because we love it, not for the salary. I have often thought I'd still do what I do even if I wasn't paid for it." He smiled a small, sad smile. "Naive, I know, and it won't ever happen. But I'm an idealist at heart."

He cocked his head, "I tell you this because I want to find a habitable planet or two, not for myself but for us. For humans." He shrugged, "We've broken this planet. We have spun a fable based on consumption and economics and warred for resources. Rich people get richer by farming the rest of their populations. Populations are kept in thrall by consumption, celebrity and sport. And a continual serving of 'them and us' propaganda so we have something to complain about." James sighed. "While we do all that, poorer nations fall to the wayside as we grub around their homes for resources."

James paused and shrugged, "I want to give a choice to the people who don't want to live the way they are now. It's simple."

He shook his head. "That's for the future. It won't happen unless we find a planet and get to it." James raised his eyebrows. "To get there, we need a vehicle to transport people."

The general nodded. "Well, I believe we can help with that."

James looked surprised, so the General pointed to Harry, "Harry mentioned it when he gave me an overview before this meeting. It jogged my memory about an item at a project briefing six months ago. The RAAF had canned a project about developing strong, environmentally secure, pressurised cans to deliver aid and supplies to disaster areas." He smiled. "It was the canned cans that jogged my memory." He got serious again. "They built a few prototypes before the project was terminated. The prototypes are stored in a warehouse at Richmond, and the RAAF is happy for DDU to take them off their hands if we want them."

James looked at the General with a delighted smile. "General, I'd be happy to look at their specifications and see if we can use the cans!"

After the formal meeting ended, James made his way over to Colonel MacPherson. "Colonel, could I ask one more thing?"

She smiled. "Call me Leona; we don't have to be overly formal these days. What's on your mind?"

"Thanks, Leona. As for my mind? I'm not sure what I need to be honest."

She grinned and shrugged. "Just start talking, and I'll ask questions where I need to. How's that?"

James raised his eyes in thanks and ploughed into his idea. "Well, the plan is to use the CubeSats to map reachable space. The mapping will provide data from which we can tune the search for suns with planets." She nodded understanding, and James went on. "When we are ready, we'll have a couple of CubeSats modified to gather detailed data about the solar systems we find. These will check for planets with atmosphere in the habitable zone."

Leona's eyes narrowed as her mind worked. She remained silent, so James ploughed on. "I need a purpose-built CubeSat or probe that will go to a planet and collect data on the planet's suitability to support human life."

Leona smiled, and her eyes crinkled. "James, I am so amazed by your confidence. It is a dream of mine to see another planet or, at least, set foot in an environment other than Earth." She laughed, "It's why I joined DDU and set up the Space Technology Unit."

James suddenly felt confident that they would be okay. "I'm relieved, Leona. Your energy and confidence are also infectious!"

Leona laughed. "Leave it with me. A few of our scientists have been dabbling with ideas about how to classify and explore exoplanets. I'll keep a CubeSat back for their use."

She cocked her head. "Is there anything else you can think of I may be able to help with?"

James went over the plan in his mind. They had CubeSats to map and collect the data needed to search. They had a vehicle that could Step people. Leona would look into a probe to collect planetary data.

Was he missing anything? "What about when we find a planet? We'll need to drop off supplies for building, power generation, and shelter." He frowned, "I am pretty sure I can get all the gear we'll need, but once we're out of Tumbi Umbi, we may not have a safe place on Earth to ferry equipment and goods back and forth."

Leona nodded in agreement, and her brows came together. "It will need to be secure. Leave it with me. I'll talk with General Hancock and figure something out. If Defence can't solve that problem, nobody can!"

"Thanks, Colonel. You're a great help!" She looked over her shoulder. "It'll cost you a seat on another world, Mr Kentley!"

James laughed and nodded.

Chapter 26

Hickey-Roche didn't waste any time; he needed to move hard and fast to get his hands on this new technology.

He called a number in the USA. "Kelly's Brick Yards. There's no one here to take your call right now. Please leave a message after the tone. When you're finished, dial zero or hang up... beep."

"Ainsley, Roche. Call me ASAP."

Ainsley van den Favel's phone vibrated, but he left it in his pocket. He was in a private room at his club, having an online meeting with three commanders of WestProtect's military arm.

The meeting wasn't going well. Two of his commanders were training militia groups in West Virginia and Alabama and had problems. The personnel being trained were continually argumentative, and having them acquire the required skills was proving difficult. The people paying for the training were dissatisfied with WestProtect's progress and threatened to pull the pin and take their business elsewhere.

Ainsley's commander in Alabama was finishing his report. "They aren't just stupid, Ainsley; they're convinced they are right." His voice rose a notch. "In everything! From attack formations to using cover! Everything. They don't want to learn." He raised his arms and shook his head, "Even simply cleaning their weapons calls for an argument. One went so far as to say his daddy's spirit was at rest in his pistol, and he only cleaned on the anniversary of his father's death! There's no reasoning with them!"

Ainsley shook his head. "The employer is a Congresswoman; she has a lot of influence with her GOP colleagues. We need to make this work," he thought for a moment. "Do any of them listen and learn?"

The commander nodded. "Well, yeah, there's a few who seem to get it!"

Ainsley frowned. "Okay, I want you to try this. Promote those who are learning into an advanced group. Have them train the others. Hopefully, they listen to their own, but if not, they'll fight each other rather than us!" The commanders smiled and shook their heads but shrugged okay.

Ainsley looked at the third commander. "Chas, how's your team recovering?"

"We're doing okay, sir. Another week or two, and we'll be at full strength." He winced. "My ribs still tickle though!"

They all laughed. "What you get for underestimating the opposition. Don't let it happen again."

Chas shook his head, "One of those things. You don't know you've done it till you've done it! And by then, it's too late." They had a chuckle and nodded in agreement.

Ainsley told them. "Take a break for five before we get onto the financials. I need a refill!" He keyed the lock and made sure to lock the door behind him. It was a secure conference facility provided by his club, and he was careful not to compromise his team.

He walked to a bar and poured himself a scotch before pulling out his phone. The message had been from one of his WestProtect colleagues in Australia, Robert Hickey-Roche.

Ainsley had a lot of time for Roche and decided to call him back.

"Ainsley! Thanks for getting back to me, mate!"

Ainsley chuckled and put on a broad Aussie accent. "Hay there, mate! How're you going?"

Roche laughed. "Good try, but no pass. You sound like a bearded dragon after being jumped on by a mad red roo!"

"Oh well, worth a try!" Ainsley got to business. "What's happening?"

"I've got a big problem and need help."

Ainsley stood. "Hold on a moment." He returned to his room, keyed the door and locked it behind him. He muted the Zoom meeting and held up a finger to his team, saying he'd be a minute. "Okay, Roche, what's the issue?"

Roche detailed the problem, the risks and the reward. Ainsley immediately saw how he and WestProtect would benefit from having the technology and how they'd lose out if they didn't.

He ended the call from Roche and got back to the Zoom meeting. "I have to end this early. He looked to Chas, "Chas, you stay on the line; I have something for you." He nodded to the other two, "You get on with the new strategy. Give it a try for a few weeks and see how we get on." He clicked them out of the meeting.

After Ainsley explained the situation and the technology, Chas raised his eyebrows. "Phew! That sounds awesome! It'd be an excellent weapon, for sure!"

Ainsley agreed. "They're holed up in a warehouse-cum-factory arrangement in a suburb called Tumbi Umbi; it's around an hour and a half north of Sydney." Chas nodded his understanding. Ainsley looked at his watch. "I can get you a flight out of Bali in six hours?"

Chas checked his watch and nodded. "We'll be there."

Ainsley looked at Chas. "I'll forward details to you, but this is a critical assignment. Luckily, we're getting in early before they lock down the place, so make the most of it. Will your team be fully functional? Do you need any other resources?"

Chas frowned and shook his head, "Clive and Dick are at eighty-five per cent. The other four are close to a hundred per cent fit. I believe the seven of us will be enough."

Ainsley smiled. "Don't underestimate them this time."

"I won't. If they've only got a few cops and internal security guards, we'll be able to get in and out, and they won't even notice the tech's gone!"

Ainsley agreed. Chas's team was one of their top outfits and had achieved their objective despite being bloodied from their encounter in the DRC.

* * *

Two days after their meeting with the DDU, a battered 4WD pulled up on the apron in front of the roller shutter.

James welcomed the driver, "G'day mate, what's up?"

The driver confirmed James was who he said he was before smiling. "Delivery from Colonel MacPherson. Orders say to 'unload inside'." He pointed to the shutter.

James told him to wait and went inside to open the warehouse. The driver backed the 4WD inside, and the shutter was lowered. The driver removed the tarp covering the tray to reveal twenty-four wooden crates.

They unloaded the crates into a vacant space. Once finished, the driver gave James an envelope and asked him to sign an app on his phone. The shutter was raised, and the 4WD drove off.

Harry had returned to Macquarie Park, so it was just the three scientists and security team at Tumbi. Imogen was asleep in the mezzanine, which left James and Jerry to see to the crates. James levered the top off the nearest box with a heavy-duty pry bar and carefully peeled off a thick, waterproof covering. Underneath, in all its glory, was a CubeSat. "Bloody Hell!" He turned to Jerry and asked, "How on earth did they come up with this?"

Jerry pointed to the envelope sticking out of James's shirt pocket. "Perhaps, read the letter?"

James laughed. "Of course! I do often leave the instructions till last!"

James opened the letter and read it out so Jerry could hear. '*James, These CubeSats were ordered for a project we're conducting in a few months. They are a standard configuration with attitude adjusters and chemical thrusters for propulsion. You can interface your AI with the main onboard computer to link to the star map and other sensors. You can have them for six weeks. After our project is complete, we expect to have four left you can hang on to. Good Luck! Col. L. MacPherson.*'

James looked at Jerry and grinned. "Six weeks isn't long, but it is long enough. Can you get Quinn interfaced with their onboard processor?"

Jerry nodded. "Should be straightforward. There's a circuit diagram and sensor chart included with the satellite."

"Great!" James considered waking Imogen but chose to let her rest a bit longer after her shake-up. He frowned at Jerry and shrugged. "I'll get on with the Step drives. By the looks of it, I'll be able to hook them into the onboard power supply and interface with Quinn via the CPU."

With that, they got to work. James put together twelve Step drives, one for each of the cube's edges. He figured twelve were overkill, but he knew Imogen would advise him to ensure a decent level of redundancy.

Jerry provided an interface port for the Step field generators to access the onboard power and an interface for Quinn. He'd also added a CPU for a Quinlet and a petabyte of storage for star data as needed.

They were ready for a test run by eleven that morning.

* * *

Imogen joined James and Jerry shortly before they set up the CubeSat tests. She assured them she felt much better, but they decided to break for lunch as it was close to noon and a sunny day.

Codie sent Matt with them and admonished him. "No funny business this time, Matt!"

Matt smiled and gave his boss the bird before driving them to the local cafe for lunch. They took their food to a picnic table on the lake's edge and were happy to enjoy each other's company and relax.

When asked again, Imogen related her capture and rescue: "Apart from being questioned by one of the men, nothing terrible happened." She recalled being confused by the questioning because AI4U came up, and her questioner asked, "Who is James Kentley really working for?"

She frowned. "He also wanted to know what you'd done with the materials. I told him I had no idea what you'd done for AI4U. I think he was frustrated. He told his associate they may need to 'have a word' with you, James."

James pondered her words and replied. "We're doing everything we can, within reason, to keep safe. I don't think they'll get another chance at us!"

When he heard this, Matt looked around the area and checked the time. He was about to say something but stopped, frowned and looked around the area again. He shrugged, grimaced, smiled and had another bite of his sandwich.

Nothing happened, and after another half hour, they packed up and returned to the warehouse, where Jerry, Imogen and James headed over to the test bench. James and Jerry brought Imogen up to date and explained that the first test of the CubeSat was a simple Step back and return.

Imogen asked if it included sensors for electromagnetic radiation. "Knowing what radiation there is in the Stepped back environment is worthwhile; If it's high, we'll need to protect some equipment. And ourselves, of course!"

It turned out that they already had what they needed since the CubeSat's onboard sensors recorded all wavelengths over time.

Jerry started the test. "Quinn, Systems test of CubeSat test module."

"CubeSat test module, all systems one hundred per cent."

Jerry explained what he was going to do. "Because the CubeSat is a new and more complex test vehicle, I will prepare for the test manually."

"Quinn, setup Step test."

"Step Test Setup Ready."

"Quinn set Potential at standard output."

"Potential Output Set."

"Quinn, Set Activate output at standard output and Set Activate Timing at Standard plus one second."

"Activate Output Set. Activate Timing Set."

"Quinn, Execute Step Test."

"Step Test starting in Five.. Four.. Three.. Two.. One.. Mark."

"Test complete."

The CubeSat remained where it was supposed to be.

"Quinn, Ready for setup of Step Test."

"Step Test Setup Ready."

"Quinn set Potential at standard output."

"Potential Output Set"

"Quinn, Set Activate output at standard output and Set Activate Timing at Standard plus fifteen seconds."

"Activate Output Set. Activate Timing Set."

"Quinn, Execute Step Test."

"Step Test starting in Five.. Four.. Three.. Two.. One.. Mark."

The CubeSat disappeared and, fifteen seconds later, reappeared.

"Test complete", said Quinn.

They smiled and congratulated each other. They hadn't expected any problems, but it was great to confirm that. They had preset further test parameters in a new series called Voyager. Voyager-zero-one was a simple Step and attitude change to check the thrusters. It had a timer set for ten seconds so they could observe the Step itself.

Jerry continued. "Quinn, Set parameters for Test Voyager-zero-one."

"Voyager-zero-one Parameters Set."

"Quinn, Execute Test Voyager-zero-one."

"Voyager-zero-one starting in Five.. Four.. Three.. Two.. One.. Mark."

The CubeSat disappeared. When it returned, it had switched end for end.

"Test complete."

Jerry held his thumb up. "Looking good. Now for the big test."

He explained to Imogen. "Voyager-zero-two is a Step followed by an attitude set towards Proxima Centauri. We then thrust at ten per cent for one second and reverse thrust at ten per cent for one second to stop. We follow that with a location check, a ten-second delay and an attitude set to get back home. Then we repeat the thrust sequence and check the location before Stepping home." He paused a moment. "It's a critical test and will give Quinn data it can use to fine-tune the modelling of thrust, acceleration and velocity. We expect the CubeSat to travel two centimetres, which we estimate will equate to the distance from the Earth to the sun or one Astronomical Unit."

Imogen nodded and smiled. "Sounds fantastic."

Jerry continued. "Quinn, Set parameters for Test Voyager-zero-two."

"Voyager-zero-two Parameters Set."

"Quinn, Execute Test Voyager-zero-two."

"Voyager-zero-two starting in Five.. Four.. Three.. Two.. One.. Mark."

The CubeSat disappeared. When it returned, they all took a breath in relief.

"Test complete."

Jerry smiled. "Quinn, check all test module systems and physical attributes."

"All test module systems are fully functional."

"All physical attributes are within normal ranges."

"Quinn, summarise test location data."

"Step return location positive. Identified as one Astronomical Unit from Home."

"Step home location positive. Adjustment before final Step home not necessary."

Jerry turned to James and Imogen. "Well, that's that! Quinn is calibrated to go!"

James shook his head. "How can it be so simple? I was expecting all kinds of trouble."

Jerry laughed, "James, we did the hard yards when we took the first Step and built Quinn. Nothing's changed except the vehicle and the distance it can go."

Imogen asked. "What about the radiation counts?"

Jerry smiled. "I checked them on the screen. We get no wavelength shorter than ultraviolet inside the field. Outside is a hot mix of Gamma, so I theorise that the Step field acts as a barrier. We'll add radiation to the list of experiments, but for now, radiation isn't an issue."

James grinned from ear to ear. "Okay. Now seems as good a time as any to go star hunting. I've set Voyager-one-zero for full thrust at 0.5 Newtons for seventy-five seconds, then reverse at the same rate to stop. That should have us move five and a half kilometres in total and should have us close to Proxima Centauri."

He smiled. "I have us stationary for a minute to take readings before reversing and returning home." He shrugged and raised an eyebrow, "I'm hoping Quinn gets enough data to work out a mapping strategy we can automate like we did for Earth."

Jerry grinned. "This is the big one!" He took a deep breath. "Quinn, Set parameters for Test Voyager-one-zero."

"Voyager-one-zero Parameters Set."

"Quinn, Execute Test Voyager-one-zero.

"Voyager-one-zero starting in Five.. Four.. Three.. Two.. One.. Mark."

The CubeSat disappeared, and the wait was interminable. The Step timer had started at six minutes and was winding down the last few seconds until Quinn finally announced, "Test Complete."

The three scientists spent the rest of the afternoon poring over the results and pictures Quinn had collected on its Step. Without a doubt, they were planet-hunting!

Chapter 27

The successful Voyager-one tests marked the beginning of a crucial planning session, which James, with a hint of humour, dubbed as an Orderly Survey of the Galaxy. The central point of contention in the planning discussion was the size of the Step and its efficiency, a matter that was eventually resolved through a compromise. Jerry's straightforward argument for a one light year Step prevailed over Imogen's 'quarter light year will yield more data' and James's 'five light years is the average interstellar distance'.

Jerry smiled, a twinkle in his eyes. "So, we are agreed. Thrusting at point-zero-two Newtons for four minutes and eighteen seconds will move a CubeSat close to one light year when it returns to the present. That means we'll be close to Proxima Centauri within twenty minutes." He pursed his lips and nodded. "One light year will also mean we collect valuable location data plus not miss the possibility of other objects like rogue planets or asteroids."

James smiled at Jerry's mention of rogues, but Jerry shrugged. "They're theoretically possible. If we don't keep an eye open, how will we know if we found one?" Jerry grinned. "We've also agreed that Imogen's idea of a 'Radial Tunnel' search pattern will be more efficient than an expanding sphere."

The three scientists had talked for some time about an appropriate search pattern. By returning home after each Step, they'd get an even spread of expansion, but once they were farther out, the time to return and set off to the next point would be inefficient. Imogen's idea was to

Step to a point and use it as the centre of a wheel by Stepping around its circumference and, when complete, step ahead to set a new point. That way, they would save on fuel and time.

Imogen had shrugged as she'd mentioned the idea. "It sounds complicated, but it is simple to program Quinn with the parameters and let the AI go from there. As more CubeSats are prepared, Quinn starts another tunnel."

After the planning was complete, Jerry set up the parameters for Voyager-two-zero. The first CubeSat would be headed towards Proxima Centauri, and Quinn was left to work out the other paths according to its algorithms. That left the three of them to get to work readying the rest.

By the end of the day, they had twenty CubeSats flying, and Quinn had already flagged solar systems that may contain useful planets.

* * *

Given the precarious state of their security, Imogen, Jerry and James were now restricted to the inside of the warehouse. James had originally planned to go to Richmond Air Base and look at the 'cans' General Hancock had mentioned. Instead, he called the General and explained the situation. The General said he'd handle it.

That conversation came to mind when James heard the wheeze of air brakes early the following morning.

Codie carefully checked and verified the delivery, the driver and his offsider. After a call to the General, they were given the go-ahead to unload.

James and Imogen watched as the shutters were raised. Two men jumped out of the prime mover and moved to the rear of the trailer, where they lowered a liftgate. As the gloom lifted, James could make out shapes. "Pressure containers!" He looked at Imogen and smiled. We have our vehicles!"

Imogen grinned back at him. "Look at the big one!" Her eyes went wide. "It must be ten metres long!"

Apart from helping point out various places to put the containers, James and Imogen kept out of the way. Jerry got up to have a look but, unimpressed, shrugged and went back to work.

Twenty minutes later, the shutters were down, the truck was gone, and warehouse space was at a premium. There were six pressure containers in all, the largest seven and a half metres long and two and a half metres in diameter. It was supported by a cradle at either end and had a loading hatch on one side. James looked at the containers with a slight frown on his face and nodded. "Let's set up the big one first."

Jerry rejoined the others once the truck left and nodded in agreement. "Mass isn't an issue because there's no gravity when Stepped back." He looked towards his bench. And we have enough thrust to handle the distance without a long delay."

Imogen walked around the various containers before heading to the mezzanine to change. She returned in well-used overalls and carrying a welding mask. "I'll reverse the hatch and replace the seal." She shrugged and smiled. "We'll need it when we have pressure, and it won't take long to sort out."

Jerry got to work installing thrusters at the front and rear of the container, and James secured nine Step field generators that would create more than enough field to cover the container.

Jerry helped Imogen when he finished, and by the end of the day, they had a test vehicle that could accommodate up to four people for a few hours. All the connections had been double-checked before being patched through to Quinn.

Jerry frowned slightly as he set the test protocol for a one-light-year Step and returned: "Quinn, status check Test Tincan-zero-zero."

"Tincan-zero-zero systems are ready; communications and circuits fully functional."

James was confident that the test would succeed but couldn't help being nervous. It must have shown on his face because Imogen and

Jerry moved closer in solidarity, Imogen with an arm around his waist. Jerry looked at his friends and nodded in appreciation.

"Quinn, Execute Test Tincan-zero-zero."

"Tincan-zero-zero starting in Five.. Four.. Three.. Two.. One.. Mark."

The container disappeared and returned within a minute.

"Test Complete."

James breathed a sigh of relief.

Jerry grinned at him. "Quinn, check all test module systems and physical attributes."

"All test module systems are fully functional."

"All physical attributes are within normal ranges."

"Pressure loss of zero point zero zero two detected."

"Quinn, summarise test location data."

"Step location positively identified and added to the database."

"Thrust directed in the direction of Proxima Centauri."

"Thrust timing extrapolated for one light-year."

"At-rest location positively identified and added to the database."

"At-rest distance travelled one point zero two five light-years."

"Step movement database updated."

"Thrust directed in the direction of Step home."

"Thrust timing extrapolated for one point zero two five light-years."

"Step home location positively identified."

"Step home distance travelled one point zero two five light-years."

James looked across at Jerry, and they both turned to Imogen. Imogen frowned, but the frown turned into a grudging nod and smile.

Jerry walked to a table and picked up a cage. In the cage was a rat. The rat was quiet; it had been fed and watered and appeared happy now it had had a day or two to calm down. The rat looked through the cage, whiskers waving, nose sniffing and ears twitching.

Jerry handed the cage to James, who frowned uncertainly. He squared his shoulders and placed the cage inside the pressure container. He closed the hatch and silently walked back to where Jerry and Imogen watched.

James took another deep breath. "Quinn, Execute Test Tincan-zero-one."

"Tincan-zero-one starting in Five.. Four.. Three.. Two.. One.. Mark."

The container disappeared and was back in ten minutes.

"Test Complete."

The ten minutes was difficult for all three of them. Nothing was said as they wandered off to do something else while the minutes and seconds counted down. When the test was complete, they met at the container. James reached out to open the hatch, his hand joined by two others. He nodded his acknowledgement of the shared responsibility, and they opened the hatch together.

The rat squeaked at the interruption before turning away from the three oddly smiling faces and moving to the far end of the cage.

James laughed. His relief bubbled from his belly, his chest and out his mouth. Imogen and Jerry quickly joined in; a few minutes later, the fuss caught Codie's attention, and he came to investigate.

"We can Step people," James pointed to the rat. We were not a hundred per cent sure, but we are now. If we find a planet, we can get there!"

"People?" Codie looked taken aback at the idea. "What in?"

James pointed to the pressurised container. "In that. It's a tinca.." He frowned and looked at Imogen. "We need a better name than Tincan. What should we call it?"

Imogen shrugged as if it was no big deal. Her mouth quirked. "It's a Personnel Transit Vehicle, of course!" She smiled. "A 'PTV' for short!"

James turned to Codie. "In the PTV over there. That's what we travel in."

Codie looked at the cylinder and raised his eyebrows. "If you say so!" He started back to the office, shaking his head when James called him back. "Codie, can you do something for us?"

Codie shrugged, "Sure. What do you need?"

"We need to return this little critter to the wild." He grinned. "Can you snap a photo of us with it and let it go in the scrub at the end of the drive?"

Codie chuckled and shook his head. He took photos of the rat and the three scientists before carefully releasing the rodent into the sparse shrub adjacent to the industrial block. "Bloody thing will likely be back in the warehouse before me!"

The best photo had the rat on the table, peering out of the cage at the camera, nose pushed through the mesh. Jerry's smiling face is on the left, Imogen is above the cage, and James is on the right. All four looked to be smiling happily. The photo was enlarged and taped to the office wall in honour of their little assistant.

* * *

James and Jerry were reviewing the mapping results and potential solar systems for planets when a 4WD pulled up in front. A bespectacled woman left the vehicle and went to the front door. All the doors were kept closed as part of security. Additionally, a security guard, John, was in the office looking at a camera feed of the front of the building.

The woman pressed the call button, and John asked, "Yes?"

The woman wasn't fazed. "I have a package for James Kentley and a note to explain it."

John buzzed the intercom. "Mr Kentley. There's a person here with a parcel for you and a note."

James looked at Jerry and smiled. "Let's go. This may be a good surprise!" The only package he expected would be from a certain Colonel in DDU. They checked the camera feed first but didn't recognise the person outside.

John pointed to her hand on his screen. "She says she has a note to explain; do you want me to get it?"

James ducked a shoulder and nodded. "Better safe than sorry, I guess. Besides, Codie would skin us alive if we made another mistake!"

John pressed the intercom button. "I'll need to check your credentials and the note. Is that okay?"

The woman smiled and nodded; she added another document from her pocket. The guard opened the door on a restraint and took the paperwork. "Hi. I'm John; I won't be a moment."

He gave the note to James, who opened it and saw the DDU logo and Colonel MacPherson's name at the bottom. The note was simple. *"Here's the planet sniffer and one of the inventors, Olivia Gilmour. She's a good friend of mine and very smart."*

James smiled. "She's fine, John. She'll have a box to come in. Can you help her with it, please?" John nodded, "Sure, James, no trouble."

Olivia was introduced to the team, "I'm assigned to you for as long as I'm needed. From what the Colonel tells me, I may be with you for some time."

James smiled enthusiastically, "Olivia, you are very welcome. You're going to be busy!" He cocked his head. "Colonel MacPherson mentioned 'Sniffer'?"

Olivia smiled. "That's the name we gave the Planetary Suitability System. Her eyes rose. "Sniffer was shorter and encapsulated what the PSS does."

The group, used to naming new things now, could understand and nodded approval of the name. Olivia looked around the warehouse.

"The Colonel also told me you were restricted to the warehouse due to security concerns." She hefted a bag. "Where should I drop this?"

Imogen pointed to the mezzanine. "The Ladies' lounge is up there. There's a couple of spare cots and a separate bathroom." She shrugged. "The cot's a bit to get used to, but it's not too bad."

Olivia pursed her lips. "I get no special treatment as a scientist. We still go out on exercises with the other members of the DDU, so I'm okay with roughing it when necessary." She smiled and shrugged. "I'd climb Everest if it meant I had a chance to find a habitable planet!"

"Let's get to it." James pointed to Jerry, "You and Jerry can get the system calibrated and hooked into our AI, Quinn." He thought for a moment and laughed. "Once it's automated, set it free and see what you can find. I want a mountainous place with a few nice ski runs!"

Olivia laughed. "If we can find anything humans can live on, I'll be surprised."

James's brow furrowed, "Don't you think we'll find one?"

She cocked her head. "Oh, we'll find one for sure! It's simply that I don't think it'll happen soon. There's a lot of ground to cover."

James smiled ruefully. "True. I'm an optimist, though, and we need one urgently!"

Chapter 28

After tweaking the parameters to save fuel, mapping the galaxy moved faster than expected. Eighteen of the twenty-four CubeSats are rigged for mapping; each one-light-year Step took six and a half minutes, and a sector, which included the Step away and eight Steps around the away point, took under an hour. Every five hours, they mapped another five-light-year-long volume of space. Multiplied by the eighteen CubeSats had them building up data at light speed!

As mapping progressed, Quinn filtered out a shortlist of systems based on gravity and light. It was this list Olivia's Sniffer would review.

Jerry asked Imogen and James to join him and Olivia for the Sniffer test. Olivia had settled into the team and environment very well, leading James to realise there were many more good people than bad. He still thought it unfortunate that the bad seemed to have the power and resources to keep a foot on the others' throats!

Olivia was a physicist but had chosen to work with large objects rather than quantum. When James talked with her about her career, she replied, "I just love the idea of gases swirling to the dance of gravity and forming planets and suns and galaxies." She sighed, "It's simply the world we live in. I want to explore it. I want to see it breathe."

James understood her passion and smiled as she continued. "I want to go to another planet and see how it fits in the scheme of things. With Hubble and the James Webb, we can see exoplanets and make good guesses about what they are like and whether or not we could live on them." She chuckled. "I jumped on this project when the Colonel asked. It's perfect for me and gives my ideas a chance."

Olivia worked closely with Jerry to design and build interfaces between Quinn's standard systems and the Sniffer hardware. It was Jerry who kicked off describing what they'd finished up with. The Sniffer was a comparatively large structure that looked like a rack that contained small blocks. "The module is quite different from the mapping probes." He smiled, "The sensor array Olivia has developed is small and fits into a 3D printed carrier that includes a power supply, a Quinlet and a single Step drive."

He held out a cube of around two centimetres per side. "These 'Sniffettes', for want of a better name, fit into the Sniffer's storage array where they remain secure until needed. We jump the Sniffer into the area identified by the mapping process. Once there, the onboard Quinlet jumps to a point above the system's plane and controls the sensing operation."

He pointed to the Sniffettes in the rack. "The Sniffer Steps the Sniffettes to the planet where they do the fine work. When finished, the Sniffettes return to the storage rack, and the Sniffer goes to the next system on the list."

He gave a slight shrug. "Once the onboard Quinlet's list of sites is finished, the Sniffer returns home for refuelling and a fresh list of targets. It also dumps the sensor results and star maps into our main digital storage."

He shrugged, "That's it for the mechanics." Jerry passed the floor to Olivia.

Olivia's obvious expertise and passion were evident. She was hopping with excitement at the prospect of actually testing the Sniffer. "The Sniffer consists of three sensing phases. After the jump above the plane, we use sensors in the CubeSat to check the atmosphere and temperature. If we get a rough match, we send a flock of planetary sensors, the Sniffettes, to take more detailed measurements of atmosphere composition, sun-side and dark-side temperatures, gravity and the like. We also look for signs of photosynthesis and analyse electromagnetic radiation to give us some idea of life, intelligent or otherwise. If we tick the boxes, the final phase will decide whether we should visit."

She pointed to the yellow-coloured cubes. "At the end of the storage array are two rows of yellow Sniffettes. These have a different range of sensors and are designed to get into the planet's atmosphere, swim in its oceans and burrow into its soil." She paused and lifted her chin, "If we can breathe the air, drink the water and eat the fish, we'll be onto something."

Imogen and James shook their heads, amazed. They just needed to find one!

James found himself getting impatient. He felt like events were bearing down on them, and time was running out. Much to his delight, James heard that Jerry and Olivia had picked out Trappist-one for their test. This star had seven planets discovered over the years, and despite slim chances of one being suitable, the test would give the Sniffer system a good workout.

Jerry gave Olivia the kudos for the test. She smiled broadly. "Quinn, Execute Test Gaia-Trappist-one."

"Test Gaia-Trappist-one executing."

The Sniffer disappeared, and they looked at each other. Jerry smiled, "Now we wait for a machine to ping!"

There was nothing to do until the test finished, so they got on with helping Imogen prep the PTV.

* * *

Imogen rested on her haunches and pushed the welding helmet back to check her work. She pulled a cloth from her hip pocket and wiped her forehead before shutting down the welding equipment and getting out of the container. James saw her come out of the hatch and walked over to relieve her of the welder and helmet so she could review their progress.

Imogen smiled as she wiped her face again. "Thanks, James." She looked to where Olivia and Jerry propped sheets of plywood against the side of another container and frowned. "Looks like they've collected enough timber for the floor." She looked back at James. "Did you get enough steel for the support frame?"

James smiled and pointed to the lengths of steel laid out lengthwise by his bench. "Codie brought in the last length a few minutes ago." James shrugged. "There is more if we need it."

Imogen wiped her brow with the back of her hand. The plan was simple. The steel would be bolted onto the anchor points she'd welded onto the curved floor of the cylinder. The anchors' heights were designed to provide a level surface for the steel frame and five-ply timber flooring. The steel would also allow for securing seating for travellers.

The four workers came together to review their next steps. All were happy with the physical nature of the activity as it gave welcome relief from mental tension.

Imogen grinned. "You all look like you're enjoying yourselves!" She chuckled as Jerry worried at a splinter in his palm and finally got enough of a grip to pull it out.

He grinned back at Imogen and shook his head. "Good fun!"

Imogen got serious. "Okay, we should be able to pair up and bolt on the frame." She looked across at Olivia. "Livie, you and Jerry take port while James and I take starboard." She frowned and looked at the timber. "Once we have the steel in place, we'll screw on the flooring and mark out the spacing for seating."

They manoeuvred the rails into the cylinder and prepared their equipment before starting to secure the steel rails. Apart from an occasional grunt as steel was moved and spanners turned, they were quiet as they worked.

"Ping."

"What was that?" asked Jerry as he looked up to see Olivia and James trying to get out of the hatch together. He looked at Imogen and then back to the hatch as James had the good manners to step back and let Olivia through first.

Imogen smiled. "I do believe the Sniffer is back from its test!"

Jerry dropped his spanner on the deck and made his way out of the canister. After he'd gone, Imogen picked up the various dropped tools and bolts and calmly exited. She looked at the test area; the Sniffer was back and looked perfect.

Jerry looked at Imogen, a sense of urgency on his face. "Come on!" She smiled broadly as she put the tools in a safe place and joined her friends.

Jerry grinned. "Quinn, Provide a summary of Test Gaia-Trappist-one."

"Test Gaia-Trappist-one summary: Test module Sniffer Stepped to Trappist-one followed by Step above plane; Phase One analysis result: Nine planets orbiting the sun. Zero planets with atmosphere; Initiated test scenario override for zero count; Launched Sniffette modules to Trappist-f; Phase Two analysis result: Nil atmosphere; Gravity sixty per cent Earth normal; Nil life signs; Temperature extreme on both light and dark sides. Result Negative.

Olivia looked at the others and shrugged. "Cheer up! We didn't expect to get a winner on the first attempt! The test worked. Let's get Quinn to run the plan, and we can finish off the PTV."

James had a fire in his eyes. "Well said, Olivia." Nobody moved for a moment, so he added. "Well, get on with it!"

Jerry laughed. "Quinn, Execute Gaia-one-zero and ping on finding an acceptable planet."

"Test Gaia-one-zero executing."

* * *

Leigh's brow was knitted in worry as he reread the report he'd received from the surveillance team he had monitoring Harper Caldwell after he met with Mo Banks. The news wasn't good, although only a few people would know. The team following Caldwell had seen him picked up and taken to Robert Hickey-Roche's home in the East. Hickey-Roche was known to be a senior figure in the conservative think tank WestProtect. Roche was a multi-billionaire and had significant influence with politicians, industry leaders and the press.

Leigh was aware of situations where AFP leadership influenced investigations that got too close to several organisations, including WestProtect. The interference wasn't overt, but it shifted a policy here, or a focus there, or something went wrong with a chain of custody. If Leigh passed his new information up the chain, it would eventually be seen by someone who would compromise his position.

He shook his head and made a decision. Once outside the office, Leigh called Harry Barnes and asked for a meeting.

A short while later, Harry and Leigh walked around the grounds of Hyde Park while Leigh talked. "It's a big step up, Harry. WestProtect is a powerful group with extreme beliefs. They see themselves as the people chosen to lead the world into a glorious and peaceful future - under their rules." He shook his head, "I don't know why someone thinks they're right and differing opinions are wrong." He shrugged, "Regardless, Hickey-Roche is a big gun in WestProtect in Australia, and it would mean trouble if Harper was there to tell him about the discovery at Tumbi Umbi." He scratched his head. "I am almost certain that's the case because Harper called Roche after he met with Mohamed Banks." He looked at Harry, "If I had to hazard a guess, Hickey-Roche knows all about your discovery and what the next steps could be."

Leigh stopped and grabbed Harry by the shoulder, eyes wide with concern. "Hickey-Roche will be after the technology and your people. He'll transfer knowledge to his people and disappear you and yours." He squeezed Harry's shoulder to emphasise his point. "You have to get out of there! Get somewhere where you are not known. And get out soon!"

* * *

Harry called Codie as soon as he finished with Leigh. "Codie, we've got a problem. I'm on my way. Be on your toes." He disconnected the call and concentrated on his driving.

Codie, for his part, heard the urgency in Harry's voice. He understood a threat was inbound but didn't know what form it would take. He checked in with his team to ensure the electronic surveillance was set to maximum sensitivity. He bit his lip with worry and considered various independent operators he had worked with in the past. He shook his head. While some were good at their work, he couldn't trust them to the level he needed to. The idea of trust brought another possibility to mind, Ken Hayden. Ken was tough, strong and highly trained. Codie tilted his head in thought. He and Ken had been good friends, but Ken wanted to keep his distance after an operation that went wrong in Afghanistan. Codie shuddered at the memory. He could easily be dead if 'Sarge' hadn't saved him and the rest of his team after a betrayal. The trouble was the betrayer had been one of Sarge's closest friends, and Sarge had had to kill him or be killed himself.

He pulled the name on his phone and considered what he was about to do. The contact's name was 'Sarge'. He dialled, and the phone rang a long time before it answered. "Codie, what's up?"

Codie chuckled. "Hey, Sarge. I wasn't sure I could expect a welcome."

Sarge grunted. "I've had enough of chasing my tail. In the end, the bloke I called a friend was an enemy. Nothing for it but to move on."

Codie smiled. "I'm glad to hear it, Sarge. I need your help."

"Call me Ken, Codie. The Sarge has gone. I'm smarter now."

"Roger that, Ken. Where are you located? Still in Sydney?"

"I headed to the Sunshine State a year back. Bought a place in the bush out from Coolangatta."

"That'll work; you can fly into Newcastle." Codie paused. "Ken, I'm not sure what we're up against yet, but it could get nasty. We may encounter some of the old crew if they've taken the job."

Ken chuckled. "Codie, are you still on the good side?"

Codie smiled to himself. "No idea what side's good and bad nowadays, Ken. The best I can say is the bloke I'm working for is honest. He made something good, and the other mob want to take it from him."

Ken nodded to himself. "Okay. I'll be there on the first available. Text me the address." With that, they hung up.

Codie smiled to himself. Sarge, or Ken, was the smartest, toughest infiltration expert he'd met. The guy had single-handedly saved Codie and his squad after they'd been conned into an ambush by a man they'd considered a friend for a year. Ken had seen the trap sprung and wiped out the ambushing force alone. The last of the attackers was his best mate.

Ken had been devastated, he would have given his life for this bloke. Ken stood over him at the end and asked, "Why?"

The bloke spat in Ken's face. Ken was streaming tears as he quietly broke his friend's neck.

Ken asked us not to speak the bloke's name afterwards, and we never did. He returned to Australia after his rotation and was given an honourable discharge three months later. Codie kept a distant eye on Ken via text but knew the disloyalty had hurt.

Chapter 29

Chas and his team booked into a motel at Chittaway Bay, acting the part of husbands out for a week's fishing and carousing. They kicked off with an enthusiastic session at the local pub. The men had worked together for almost two years and were a close-knit team. Frank Clappers was the oldest at thirty-four. He'd served in the US Marines in several conflicts in deserts and jungles. He was a tough nut and stood as Chas's second in command.

Clive Halliday was the youngest at twenty-five. He and Richard 'Dick' Colton were the quiet boys. They could move like shadows and were often sent to surprise the enemy from the rear. They had well-honed skills with sharp things such as knives and nails.

They were carrying minor injuries after their scrape in the DRC. Clive and Dick had made a successful entry into the opposition leader's home in Kinshasa but were surprised by a maid using a concealed servant's door. She got off a partial screech before being taken care of. This meant they'd had to ask Chas for help when pinned against the wall outside the back door. They were just fifteen metres from the cover of the garden and the boundary wall to the road.

As luck would have it, their target appeared on a balcony, presumably to check out the noise below. Chas's sniper, Kelly Marks, shot the opposition leader before his security team could hustle him back inside. That had been enough to divert attention from Clive and Dick for a few minutes, which gave them the chance to make good their escape. They weren't unscathed, however. Clive received a bullet wound to the right shoulder, and Dick gashed his calf on a "damned big hunk of steel sticking out of the ground in the garden!" Both men were still on the mend.

Their escape still had a twist. The ex-opposition leader's security team wasn't skilled, but they made up for that with numbers.

Chas's team regrouped at their van and were hightailing their way down Ave Benseke towards the Airport when a jeep screeched onto the road behind them. They played cat and mouse on the main roads while their technical guru, Steve Garibaldi, prepped one of his special drones.

When it was ready, he yelled. "Jock, Give me five seconds of straight when you can!"

Jock Matthews yelled back. "Wait, one!"

Jock was coming up on the Basoko River crossing on the way to N'Dolo Airport. He shouted. "Five seconds after we cross the bridge... Go!"

Steve launched the drone through a hatch in the rear of the van. It immediately shot up one hundred metres and oriented above their vehicle. He used the drone's camera to lock onto the chasing vehicle. "Got him." They took the right onto Sergent Moke, and Jock hit the gas. Steve dropped the drone to the road; as the racing jeep moved over the drone, he detonated the charge. The jeep jumped and swerved off the road, smoking.

Jock checked the rear vision mirror. "They're out!" He slowed to a more normal speed and continued as though heading for N'Dolo, but instead of going into the airport, he turned onto Lumumba, and they made their way to Ndjili International. Dumping the van in the public car park, they entered the airport and walked to a private terminal where the company jet waited. Half an hour later, they were in the air and on their way to Indonesia for a much-needed rest.

Now, they were in a pub in Australia with an open order to retrieve some technology from a partially hidden enterprise in Tumbi Umbi!

Chas had a map of the area on a table at the back of the pub's main lounge. It was a Tuesday evening, so it wasn't busy, and they almost had the place to themselves.

Chas put a finger on the map and drew a circle. "There's no good high ground for kilometres, Kelly; it's either too public or the distances are not good. Looks like you're with the ground troops for this one."

Kelly grimaced, disappointed. He wasn't as fit as the others and preferred a good spot with a view of the action from afar. Kelly's aim was legendary, and he'd often been an essential asset to the team. That said, he was a tough barrel of a man with a short cover of thin white hair and horrible feet.

They talked about what they had to do and decided on a strategy. The first step was an initial look around by Kelly.

* * *

The Gaia-one-zero ping came a little after half past four the following morning.

Despite the early hour, the whole team was assembled at the test bench within ten minutes.

Olivia did the hard yards and worked her way through the sensor results. Jerry reviewed the location of the discovery while Imogen reviewed the Sniffer and Sniffettes to be sure they were all at one hundred per cent capacity.

That left James to look at visuals. The first few were of the solar system itself. It looked much like Earth's: a type G star and five planets he could see. As the probe moved closer, he could pick out the world being targeted. It started as a blue-green blob, details of the landmass becoming more apparent as the Sniffettes approached.

There was a moment when the Sniffettes Stepped to positions around the planet, and James could see it from multiple views. He noticed the dark side showed no sign of artificial light. He was relieved at that; he didn't want to think about what they'd do if they found actual intelligent aliens.

The view changed to one much closer to the planet. These images were from the last phase of the analysis and showed the yellow Sniffettes at work, sampling air, water and soil. James watched as they flew through clouds and made their way to the surface, collecting atmospheric data as they moved.

He zoomed in on one view as the probe approached an ocean. It smashed into the surface in a spray of water before turning towards the depths. It was pretty shallow initially, and he could see what looked like weeds and fish-like organisms. The probe moved deeper and deeper, showing strange but familiar life. James considered what he saw strange because the shape and form of the fish looked familiar, but the colours were different, and the shapes weren't quite right especially the fins. He didn't see anything like a whale in the views of that Sniffette.

He switched to another Sniffette as it approached land. It looked like a large continent, and the probe headed for a decent-looking valley hemmed in by mountains on one side and low hills on the other. A river ran through the valley. It was greyish green and flowed like a river on Earth, fast in places and slow in others. As the probe got closer, he saw trees and shrubs and grass. The plant life was familiar as plant life, but the differences made James think they were exotic. He couldn't articulate what the differences were apart from being woodier. The Sniffette eased onto the ground. Then, it was below the surface. After that, the view was dark.

James sat back and noticed the others looking over his shoulder. Their faces looked like he felt - absolutely stunned! He couldn't wait to go there!

James smiled, "Well, the visuals pass inspection." He gave a thumbs-up and asked Olivia, "How about the rest?"

Olivia's eyes brimmed, and her smile was indescribable, "They are all excellent. We've found a habitable planet!"

The group jumped around like mad and made enough noise to stir Codie. "What's going on?"

James smiled and gripped him by the shoulders. "We've found a planet, Codie! We've found one!"

Codie's eyes widened as his mouth opened, and his jaw dropped. "A planet?"

James nodded and grinned.

Codie swallowed. "One we can live on?"

James nodded again.

"Bloody Hell!" Codie shook his head and repeated himself. "Bloody Hell!" He started laughing. "Who'd have bloody thought it! That's amazing!"

James watched Codie and saw his expression turn from amazement to worry. "Shit! I better get security beefed up again. If anyone finds out about this, we'll have armies trying to get in!" Little did he know how prophetic that would be.

While Codie checked in with his team and considered security options, the rest of the group sat around a table and discussed the discovery and their research options.

James started. "This planet may well save us. If we can relocate there and minimise contact with Earth, we should be safe from discovery." He looked at his colleagues and could see both excitement and anxiety. "I know. It's breathtaking." James compressed his lips, looked up, and smiled. "The fact is, against all odds, we have found a habitable planet, and the only people who will see it in the short term are us." He shrugged his shoulders. "It's a big responsibility and a big step for all of us. It's a bit like stepping off a cliff into the unknown. It'll be exciting, frightening and wonderful all at the same time." He looked at them. "We found this world! For whatever reason, we've built enough good luck, so our work and effort have come up with something fantastic!"

The mood settled as their excitement, fear and uncertainty were gradually replaced with a sense of achievement and the beginnings of something new. James looked up cheekily and asked, "So, what shall we call our new planet?"

There was a general sense of fun at picking a name and the odd murmur but no suggestions.

James had been thinking along the lines of 'Second Chance' and was going to suggest it when Olivia suddenly smiled. "How about 'Karma'?" She looked at James, "You said it earlier. In a way, the work we do and the way we think has led to this result. It creates Karma!"

James sat back and thought about it. "I like it! 'Karma'. It has a good feel to it!"

Imogen smiled and nodded her agreement. "I've always been fond of 'What goes around, comes around! Karma works for me."

They all turned to Jerry, who laughed. "I have trouble naming pet fish! Karma sounds like an excellent name to me!"

With that, Karma was found.

James suddenly laughed. He looked at his friends as he chewed on his bottom lip, "I better give Harry a call!"

* * *

With the discovery of Karma, the team was so excited and wound up that their focus splintered. There was too much to think about, too much emotion and too many new concepts. In the end, Codie brought them back to Earth. They were having a round-table discussion about where to go on Karma and what to do next when Codie, who had listened quietly, interrupted. "Who is checking Karma out?"

James looked at him. "What? What do you mean?"

"I mean," he mooned his eyes, "Who is going to make sure nothing is going to eat you when you land in their territory?"

James looked around the table and shrugged. "Like bears? And dinosaurs and stuff?"

Codie nodded. "Just because you didn't see anything nasty doesn't mean they aren't there. If Karma has evolved like Earth, there are sure to be predators of some kind."

James shook his head and sighed to himself. "You're right. We can't go to Karma until we know it's safe and have a secure site. We have no understanding of what we could run into."

And, just like that, they were back on track. James rubbed his face. "What do we need to do?"

Codie eyeballed James. "First of all, we'll need trained people. Then we'll need to get them there along with equipment."

James watched the excitement of immediate travel drain out of the others and put his head in his hands. "Where on earth will we find the people? How can we trust them when we do?"

Codie shrugged, "I can't help with that. The only people I know are good, but they're individuals and already doing what they want to do." He looked up at James. I'd suggest you contact General Hancock and see if he has any ideas. The military is your best chance, and the Australian military has some standards, at least!"

James stood. "Okay. I'll call the General now. Imogen, can you check out what we need to get people and equipment to Karma? A container would do fine if it's all within the Step field. Jerry, can you and Olivia look at automating Step drive production? We'll need lots of the little blighters at the rate we're going!"

With everyone busy again, James called General Hancock. "Hancock, who's this?"

"Oh, hello, General. It's James Kentley."

"Kentley! How are you going? I hear all our help is working out alright for you."

"Yes, it is General. We couldn't have got where we've got without you."

The General laughed. "It's our pleasure. So? What can I do for you?"

James scratched his head. He didn't know how to ask, so he just came up with it: "General, hypothetically speaking, if we found a place nobody had been to before, we'd be stupid to go there as a mob of scientists without knowing it was safe, wouldn't we?"

"Hmm?"

"I need a team of trained people to secure the area and, if necessary, engage with any predators that may be about."

"I see."

"The team of people must have the same commitment to security as you. I would also suggest they have no emotional ties and don't mind being away from home for an extended period."

The General was quiet. "Timing?"

"ASAP!"

"Will advise," he said and hung up.

James smiled to himself. He enjoyed dealing with Hancock!

Just two hours later, James's phone rang. "Hello. James Kentley."

A gruff voice replied. "Mr Kentley, this is Major Stan Moreton. General Hancock has asked me to bring you a team. Depending on connections, we will arrive by bus in two to three hours. I want to keep my men in the dark as much as possible, so please tell your people to keep their mouths shut."

James smiled delightedly, fist clenched in the air. "How many men, Major?"

"There are twenty-one of us."

"Thanks, Major, see you soon."

"Goodbye, Mr. Kentley."

James went looking for Codie, but he was outside the building where James couldn't go.

One of his men called him on the two-way, and he entered the warehouse ten minutes later. "Sorry, James, one of the lookouts thought he saw something in the scrub out the back. We've looked and can't see anything out of place, but I'm installing another heat-sensing camera tomorrow morning." He looked around nervously. "I wish Ken would get here. I could do with his eyes sooner rather than later!"

They sat, and James updated Codie about his conversation with Major Moreton. "I plan to Step the men through to the valley on Karma in two lots using the PTV." They had settled on the valley they'd seen a few hours previously as it had access to water and different terrains if required.

Codie went off to brief his team on the upcoming disruption and how they'd handle it while James sat in the PTV with Imogen to discuss logistics. By now, all the flooring was installed and secured. Seating was arranged as six rows of three seats. The PTV would be cramped but not too tight if all the seats were occupied. They should be able to get Major, his men and minimal supplies to Karma in two, perhaps three Steps. They still had to source a container, and James suddenly remembered Marty mentioning a container somewhere along the way.

James called Marty's number, and Marty greeted him cheerfully. "James, how are you? No more crazy moments, I hope!"

James heard the humour in Marty's voice and the clatter of crockery in the background. "Always having fun out here, Marty. Can you talk? Sounds busy wherever you are!"

"No problems, James. I'm at the club having a cold beer and a bit of linguine. Do you want to join me?"

James laughed out loud, "I'd love to, but I can't at the moment."

Marty chuckled. "I understand, mate. What can I do you for?"

James shook his head at Marty's no-questions-asked support. Where are these people coming from? "Marty, I need a container. Do you recall mentioning one earlier?"

"That's right. I keep equipment in one at the back of my property; it's a bit like a storage locker! Hmm.. Let me think." He was quiet for ten seconds or so before asking. "How good a condition do you need?"

James considered and replied, "Nothing perfect, that's for sure. I want to put supplies in it and transport it elsewhere."

Marty hummed tunelessly as he thought about what he had. "I have an old one I can empty; it's a bit battered, and there's some rust on the outside. Inside is reasonable, if I recall. Perhaps some dusty corners."

James shrugged and chuckled. "Beggars can't be choosers at the moment, Marty. Can I hire it from you for a while? At least, until I get one for myself?"

Marty laughed, "You can hire, buy, or take it on loan. I don't need it anymore, and you'll save me a few bob for getting rid of it."

James shook his head. "Deal, Marty! Can you get it to me, or will I need to send in a crane?"

"Nah, I can get it to you. Not till tomorrow morning, though. I need my beauty sleep!"

James laughed again. "Thanks again, Marty; I owe you one!"

"Don't you forget it!" Marty fired in as he hung up.

Chapter 30

James dropped a screwdriver as his focus was interrupted by a shout and scuffle from outside. The roller shutter crashed as something banged into it, and all was silent. He and Imogen had crouched by the PTV when the crash sounded and, now, slowly stood, wondering what was happening.

James put his finger to his mouth and signed for Imogen to stay where she was. He wasn't brave but wasn't one to stand around in an emergency. He carefully walked to the office door and was about to open it when Codie came through with Matt supported on his shoulder.

Codie lay Matt on the floor. "Get him something for his head to rest on; I'll get the first aid kit."

Imogen heard Codie and brought a folded towel from the workbench. As she put it under Matt's head, he let out a groan.

Olivia and Jerry joined them outside the office. "What's going on?" asked Olivia.

James shook his head, "I don't know. We heard a scuffle, and then Codie brought Matt in. He's injured, but I don't know where."

Jerry bent over Matt. "Matt, what's the problem?"

Matt shook his head. "Bastard got me with a knife. Right-hand side. Ribs."

Jerry nodded and looked at James, "Can we clear one of the benches and get him onto it? It'll make it easier for me to check him out."

James looked at the benches and shook his head; too much equipment was hobbled together. He frowned. "How about the office table?"

Matt shook his head. "Not secure enough." James cleared his miniaturisation research off his bench. Hopefully, that work was far enough along to see them through the move to Karma anyway. They carefully moved Matt to the bench and secured the office door again.

The lights were off in the warehouse, so James held a torch for Jerry to see Matt's injury. "How come you know what you're doing, Jerry?"

He chuckled. "I'm in the State Emergency Services! I did a field medic's course a few years back." He shrugged. "I found patching people up satisfying, so I enrolled in Nursing at the University of Technology Sydney." He smiled more broadly still. "SplitQC paid for the course and gave me time off to study! It was a great program!"

Matt groaned. "Enough with the chit-chat! Can we get on with it?"

Imogen returned with the first aid kit from the PTV and held it open for Jerry to see what was in it.

He nodded and focused. "No worries, Matt. This'll hurt a bit!" Jerry proceeded to remove Matt's jacket and shirt and check the wound. "The cut's pretty deep and may have scored a rib or two, but you'll live." He cleaned the wound and used butterfly strips to hold the deepest part together before wrapping a bandage around Matt's torso.

Matt winced as he shrugged into his shirt. Jerry admonished him. "Those strips aren't stitches! If you pull them, they'll come unstuck, and you'll bleed again. Try to keep it still until we get you patched up properly."

Matt nodded. "I'll try and thanks for your help, Jerry. It's been too quiet out there, and I need to help if I can."

James and Jerry helped him into his jacket, and he pulled out his walkie-talkie. Before he did anything, he put his finger on his lips. "Shh..".

Matt pressed the talk button twice and waited. A few seconds later, Codie spoke softly, "Just on the final sweep. Have them all, we think. Wait Five."

They waited quietly in the dark until they heard voices and some grunts. The office door opened again, and Codie entered with another man they hadn't seen before. They were followed by a group of six individuals whom Mary and two others from Codie's security team escorted into the warehouse.

"That's the lot," Mary said, pushing the last man face down onto the floor, where he was trussed with duct tape and ignored.

Codie nodded his head. "Well done! Anyone injured apart from Matt?" They all indicated no, and Codie smiled. "Good."

He put his arm around the stranger's shoulders and grinned. "This is my good friend Ken Hayden. Ken is going to help us with security."

Codie nodded at the six on the floor, "These blokes are amateurs, but they could have surprised us and done more damage before we got the better of them." He looked at Ken and shook his hand. "Thanks, Ken; I'm glad you showed up when you did."

Ken smiled, "Pure luck, mate. I had the taxi drop me off a kilometre down the road where I could get a feel for the area and some exercise after the flight. As I approached the industrial park, I noticed a couple of blokes moving towards your warehouse." He shrugged, "I figured they were your people, so I followed behind." He smiled at Matt. "As things went, I was near enough to get the blighter who blind-sided Matt, and then it was a simple bash and scoot."

Codie snorted, "At least you left us a couple to deal with ourselves!"

Ken looked sideways at Codie. "Well, they were around the back where I couldn't see them!"

They laughed, and Codie gave Ken a solid hug. "It's good to see you, mate!"

Ken smiled. "Likewise, Codie. It's been too long."

Codie called Leigh at the AFP, and an hour or so later, a car and van pulled into the drive.

Leigh looked over the captives and shook his head. "Mo Banks! What a surprise!"

Mo, who had been silent until then, sighed deeply. "Leigh Buchanan. Shit!"

Leigh called Imogen over. "This is the bloke who kidnapped you. Looks like he wanted the technology for himself!"

Imogen looked at Mo and grunted. That was it. She grunted her disdain, turned and walked to join her colleagues. She turned and looked back at Mo and shook her head. Mo and his group were formally arrested and secured in the van. In time, Mo would go to trial and be sentenced to ten years for kidnapping, amongst other charges.

* * *

Despite Mo and his goons' attack, they all still had an enormous amount of work to do, and the night was getting well underway.

Ken Hayden talked with each of the team to get to know them and understand what they were doing. Codie briefed Ken about their research and the challenging security situation, but he was stunned when James told him they'd already found a planet and their current plan to move there. He also looked concerned. "We don't have enough men to hold off a determined attack from a trained force." He called Codie to join them. "I'm very concerned. That mob just now were amateurs! We'd be in deep trouble if a decent force attacked us!"

The tension in Codie's voice was obvious. "We need to know and have absolute confidence in the people we bring in. We also have to trust them enough to bring in people we don't personally know. It's a bloody difficult task! One whisper of this to the wrong people could ignite a war! It's not just important; it's a matter of life and death to get off this planet as soon as possible. Once we reach Karma, nobody can follow us. Yet!"

James looked at Codie. "Yet? What do you mean?"

Codie grimaced. "From my experience, secrets rarely remain hidden indefinitely; it's simply a question of time before others become aware of it."

James shook his head. "Not in this case, Codie. This was a fluke find in the first place, and everyone with anything to do with the fluke is on this team."

Codie's eyes widened as he spoke, his voice filled with a mix of fear and resignation. "James, you'll be astounded at the resources and pressure powerful, wealthy people can apply to uncover a secret. Right now, they're sifting through your university projects, AI4U's digital assets and personnel, any interactions with SplitQC, Mo Banks's surveillance data and what he was able to collect before we bolstered our security. He definitely knew something! There's a wealth of data and people peripherally involved who can all contribute a piece of the puzzle." He sighed, "They'll inevitably unravel the secret. It might not be next week or a year from now, but they will, without a doubt, crack it eventually."

James sighed, "Then what hope is there? If a bad actor gets the tech, we've all had it!"

Ken put a hand on his shoulder. "It's not hopeless - we need to keep a step ahead." His eyes bored into James's "That's your job!" He eased back a little, "We have the tech, and we know they're looking for it; there's a lot we can do to minimise the risks until we're ready." He looked at Codie. "There are also things that can be done to obfuscate knowledge or isolate it from prying eyes."

Codie considered the situation and raised his hands. "All we can do is all we can do. Let's make sure we do it! We have Major Moreton to worry about for now, and he'll be here in less than an hour." With that, they got back to work.

They had the PTV ready by the time the Major's bus arrived.

Codie and Ken met the Major and discussed the situation locally and on Karma. The Major acknowledged their lack of personnel at the warehouse and agreed to consider splitting his force once he knew what Karma had waiting for them.

Security discussion finished, the three men moved to the front of the warehouse to prepare the troops. The Major introduced his men to the warehouse team but referred to the technology as new without mentioning what it did. He addressed the scientists, "These men and women with me are volunteers. They are part of an elite group who have trained to operate effectively in unknown circumstances." He looked over his troops with pride. "They know they are heading somewhere new, possibly hostile and certainly different to anything they've seen before." He paused. "Their mission is to assess the environment, set up a perimeter and build a base of operations. They know civilians will be using the base and that you will be protected from all threats." He smiled. "We expect the mission to be a challenge."

Looking at James, he said. "Mr Kentley, would you be kind enough to outline our transportation arrangements?"

James joined the Major at the front of the room. "First of all, thank you all for undertaking this job. We have studied the area carefully and have not been able to identify anything or anyone that could be considered hostile. But we don't know for certain."

James pointed to the PTV. "That is a Personnel Transport Vehicle or PTV. It is a pressurised vehicle and has no view of the exterior. The trip will take approximately twenty minutes, and you must strap into your seats. The trip is called a Step. A Step is controlled by an artificial intelligence called Quinn. You shouldn't feel much of anything during the trip, though you will experience acceleration and periods of weightlessness." James shrugged. "We only have one PTV at this stage, so you'll need to make two trips."

James turned to the Major. "You need to decide how to split the force given the unknowns at the other end."

James turned back to the faces in front of him. "We can send any supplies you need with subsequent PTV trips. We will also receive a container in the morning for further supplies."

He pointed to his colleagues and the security team. "We are a small team. That team has now grown to include you. You are part of the team, and we trust you with our lives." He frowned. "You don't know this now, but you are also entrusting your lives to us." He looked at the calm, serious faces in front of him. "I look forward to getting to know you all and working with you over the upcoming months." He smiled broadly. "I can guarantee they'll be very bloody interesting!"

The Major thanked James and called his two team leaders over. "Let's get fifteen into the first trip. Cover off all forms of fire and ensure they have plenty of weapons and ammo. I want you both there, and I'll bring the remainder. Your job is to set up an initial perimeter and clear the space around where the PTV lands. Once away from the PTV, tell the AI to return. It'll come back here, and we'll load up for the second trip."

The men nodded. "Yes, Sir!"

Imogen helped the two team leaders and their thirteen troops into the PTV and showed them where to store their gear. Once loaded, she exited and sealed the hatch from outside.

Jerry spoke to those waiting in the warehouse and those in the PTV. "We're ready for the Step. Quinn, Execute Karma-deployment-one."

"Karma-deployment-one executing."

Jerry looked around and smiled, "Now we wait. The PTV should be back in around forty minutes."

Chapter 31

Quinn had been programmed to keep the PTV passengers informed of their progress. The troops experienced weightlessness and low acceleration whilst travelling in the Step, but they were well buckled in and most took the experience in their stride. If any were concerned about the low acceleration of half a metre per second squared, they kept quiet. They reached the halfway point in under twenty minutes and Quinn informed them when five minutes remained so they could get ready to exit and send the PTV back.

Quinn said. "Karma-deployment-one complete."

The men readied themselves to exit the PTV. The two lieutenants stood at the hatch. Marcus McGrath and Hugh Sharp had known each other since joining the SAS. They were best mates and lived for moments like these.

Marcus spoke above the rattle of gear. "Righto, here we are. You all know what to do. Alternate left and right. Form a perimeter. No weapons fire unless at death's door." He looked at the calm faces before him and grinned. "Let's go!"

With that, he pulled the hatch release, jumped through the opening onto the grass, and moved ten metres to the front. He took a deep breath and relished the clean air. He turned as the troops exited the PTV and formed a circle ten metres from the vehicle and all around it.

Hugh was the last man out and shouted. "Last out! Sitrep?" He waited for fifteen men to respond with "All Clear!" and said. "Quinn, egress complete. Return for next group." Quinn actuated the locking mechanism, and the hatch closed and sealed. A minute later, the PTV disappeared.

Hugh and Marcus looked at each other, eyes raised in astonishment when the vehicle vanished. They looked at their force, and Hugh walked towards Marcus. "It looks peaceful. Thoughts?"

"I haven't seen anything threatening." He pointed. "Some birds circling over that hill. It looks to be about five kilometres."

Hugh chucked his head back. "Let's stand down, set a watch and organise patrols to check the surrounding area."

Marcus nodded in agreement and broke the communication silence. "It looks like we're on a holiday, but don't let it fool you. Anyone got any ideas as to where we are?"

"Sir, I believe I know where we are not. Is that of any help?"

Marcus chuckled. "Dexter! You surprise me, my man. Tell me what you think."

"Yes, Sir! We're not on planet Earth, sir!"

Marcus heard the murmurs and laughed. "Don't you play 'Sir' games with me, Dexter, or I'll have you digging trenches! Now, why do you say we're not on planet Earth?"

Dexter laughed, "Well, the two moons in the sky are a clue; I also feel a bit heavier." He paused a moment. "But the main thing is it's bloody quiet and smells good!"

The murmurs had grown into more excited chatter as the group realised Dexter was right. Marcus said. "Okay, calm down. It may look like a good place, but we could have hungry critters come and chew on us if it's another bloody world and we are not careful!"

He narrowed his eyes. "From my position, every third man holds fast; the rest come to me."

When the group had formed, he said. "We'll do a terrain check. Form into two teams of five. Hugh will take the first squad, and Sergeant Carmody will take the second. I'll hold the fort here." He frowned at his team. "We are here because we're good at what we do and want to be here. That can cock you up if you get overconfident. Don't be! I want you to go slow, always in sight of the other team and watching each step." He smiled softly, "I don't want a broken foot or a disappearance!"

The assembled team laughed. They knew what they had to do. Marcus looked at Hugh and pointed towards the hills. Hugh nodded, and Marcus said. "Just one hundred metres. Turn towards the other team and go another twenty metres before coming back in. It should take a good while to do it properly. I want details of what you come across, so don't miss anything!"

Hugh and Layton Carmody headed out in different directions. They set up in line abreast, two metres apart, and walked onto new ground.

They were back from their patrol when the PTV reappeared, and the Major came out with the rest of the group, weapons ready. They relaxed on a signal from Marcus and, after a quick discussion, agreed to set up camp where they were. They returned Quinn with a note asking for command and personnel tents, perimeter wire, kitchen equipment and waste disposal systems.

The Major selected two members of each of the terrain patrols to start a walking perimeter guard. One pair walked clockwise and the other counterclockwise around the camp at a range of fifty metres. The rest of the group discussed the terrain patrol's findings.

Hugh shook his head. "There wasn't much to find. I didn't see any insects or rabbit holes. There were smaller holes big enough for large mice, but we didn't see any animals or their traces."

Layton nodded in agreement. "Nothing from us either, sir. I was surprised there wasn't more diversity in the grasses, and there's not a lot of weeds either."

Moreton shrugged and cocked his head. "I'm happy with not being eaten straight away! Let's get set up and then plan our exploration campaign."

* * *

Codie was on edge following the previous night's raid by Mohamed Banks and his thugs.

He watched suspiciously as an old man walked along the driveway. He wore a black t-shirt with a dinosaur on the front and faded black footy shorts. His gut hung over the front of his shorts. He was carrying a plastic supermarket shopping bag stuffed with rags. He wore black thongs. Codie also noticed the man had terrible feet. The toenails were thick, discoloured and poorly cut, and he had scratches and scabs on his ankles.

As far as Codie could see, the man paid no attention to the warehouse as he passed. He glanced at the number over the dock with a short-sighted squint, curled his nose and continued to the next unit.

Codie waited a half hour, but the old man hadn't returned, so he decided to check on him. He walked up the driveway and, at the last unit, found the man lying on the concrete in the shade. His head lay on the bag of rags. Codie shook his head. He reached to shake the man awake and, at the last moment, held back. The bloke smelled of piss and probably needed a sleep. He decided to leave him alone for the time being and check on him later in the day.

When Codie went back later with Ken, the man had disappeared. They looked for the old man as they walked to the warehouse but caught no sign of him. Ken frowned. "Let's check the CCTV."

They watched as the old man made his way back down the road. Ken's eyes narrowed when the man stubbed his toe, but he didn't say anything as the man slowly made his way out of the frame.

Ken shook his head. "It's probably nothing, but I don't like it anyway. What's the chance there's more than the six last night? Or another group?"

Codie's nose wrinkled as though he'd caught the scent of rotting meat. "The bloke was a mess. If he's a player, he's leagues ahead of the mob last night!"

Ken shook his head and grimaced. "Call me paranoid if you like, but I'll never forget the beggar in a shop front in Istanbul. He'd pissed himself and was so disgusting nobody would go near him. He was the bloody assassin who shot the Russian oligarch back in '08." Ken shook his head, "He didn't even move from his bloody step! When all the hue and cry moved down the block from the shooting, he got up and staggered away. Nobody was the wiser until the following day when CCTV footage from the shop showed what happened!"

Codie shrugged and nodded. "That's why I wanted you with us, Ken. We'll double the guard and set up outer perimeter sensors."

Ken nodded. "I'll do a few patrols myself over the next night or two." He frowned, "I have my stealth kit, so I can lay up outside the fence at the back until we get sorted on Karma."

* * *

After the security guy had left him alone, Kelly waited another fifteen minutes before stirring himself. He stood and looked around before rummaging in his bag of rags. As he did, he palmed a sensor resembling an odd-shaped stone. He'd seen the security in place was well-hidden and appeared effective, so he wasn't sure he'd be able to place the device anywhere it was helpful. Knowing the CCTV cameras were active, he kept on with the persona of a hobo. He was also careful in case the bloke from the warehouse showed up again.

He passed the warehouse on the far side of the road and stubbed his toe on a rock. "Ah Shit!" He swore as he hopped around before getting on one knee and pulling a rag from the bag to treat his toe. He spat on the rag and wrapped it around the toe with his hand while blowing it as hard as he could; mummery, of course.

As he played the act out, he placed the sensor in the rubble by the side of the road. After a short while, he removed the rag and stood. Limping a few steps, he started to the warehouse door as though to ask for help. He scowled and sneered and looked down the road. A last hopeless look, and he set off hobbling along the road again.

Once on the main road and out of sight, he pulled off his smelly clothing and called Chas. The van collected him minutes later, and they returned to the motel.

* * *

Kelly shook his head as he bit his lower lip. "These blokes are good Chas. The camera system and heat detectors are top-of-the-line. They were small; you wouldn't know they were there unless you knew what to look for. Even then, they were hard to spot."

Chas nodded. "Well, we wouldn't be here if it was easy."

Kelly shook his head. "They're really on their toes as well. I got the sense they'd had trouble recently and were ready for more."

Chas cricked his neck. "We'll have to be more careful and smarter than they are. As things stand, we count the techs at four or five and security at six. We only need to get inside. Once there, our strength will overcome them quickly. Discounting the scientists, our numbers are the same. If half of their guys have our experience and expertise, we're still well on top."

Chas leaned forward. "We'll go in with a simple choreography." He frowned as he played it out in his mind. "Kelly. You'll get us in the door; that's all you need to do." He side-eyed Kelly and smiled. "Wear your smelly stuff again and kick things off by scratching around the unit and its door like you're muddled in the head." He smiled again. "Should be a piece of piss for you." His face became serious again. "They have already seen you, so it'll take the edge off. We need the door opened."

Kelly crossed his arms and sat back in disgust. He'd much prefer to be somewhere high with his sniper rifle.

Chas grinned at Kelly's displeasure and turned to his team. "Once you've got the door open, get in the face of whoever is there. Steve and I will be behind you and can push on whoever else is nearby." He set his eyes on Clive and Dick, who stood together. "I want you two to come in from another angle. Start at the shutter if it's open. Otherwise, come up behind us through the office." He didn't like the idea of a bottleneck but expected to be well into the warehouse within a minute or two. "We should be clear of the office and in the process of clearing the mezzanine and warehouse. Finish off anyone we've left operational and check with me."

Clive and Dick exchanged a look and nodded.

Chas turned to Steve Garibaldi. "Steve, as soon as we're secure, start sorting out the technology; Jock will be on the way with the van, and we can start loading it."

Turning to his number two, Chas cocked his head. "What do you think, Frank?"

Frank Clappers was a seasoned fighter who had led operations for WestProtect and others. He furrowed his brow and sighed. "If our assumptions are right, it should work as planned." He tightened his lips in distaste. "I'd still prefer to be there than stuck as Comms in the motel, though."

Chas chuckled. "It's your turn, Frank." He grinned and shook his head. "And it's your schedule!"

Frank looked like he'd chewed on a lemon. He shook his head because backup Comms had been his idea following missions that went sideways, and nobody ever knew why. The idea was that they agreed on the timing and other operational parameters. If any of those limits were breached, the Comms backup assumed the operation had failed and made his way out of the area with as much intel as possible. The backup was also available to organise a response to unexpected circumstances if required.

Frank grunted and shook his head again.

Chapter 32

There was the wheeze of an air brake, and a minute later, Mary came in and motioned James over to the office.

Marty stood by the door and smiled broadly. "G'day James! How are you, mate?"

James looked over Marty's shoulder and saw a trailer with an old container sitting on it. He laughed and slapped Marty on the back. "Marty, you do know how to deliver. This will be a big help! Thank you so much!"

Marty grinned. "It's my pleasure, James. I'm happy to help." He looked into the office. "How's Imogen? Is she here? I'd like to say hello."

"Of course. She'll be happy to see you, I'm sure. Sit down, and I'll go get her."

James walked into the warehouse and told Imogen that Marty had brought a container and wanted a word. She smiled in delight, and they went back to the office together. Imogen immediately called out. "Marty! It's good to see you." She gave him a big hug. "How is my saviour?"

Marty chuckled, "All quiet now that the excitement with you folks has died down."

James could see something was on Marty's mind as he looked sheepish and unsettled. "Come on, Marty, out with it! What's up?"

Marty looked from James to Imogen and back again. His face opened a little. "I've been working for myself for a long time." He shrugged, "I thought it was for the best, given my inability to accept corporate and social rules." He paused and took a deep breath. "But meeting Imogen and the rest of your group, plus hearing about the technology you're developing, got me thinking." He paused before plunging on. "I want to work with you. I'm good at solving problems, acquiring, connecting, and innovating. Do you need someone like that?"

James's eyebrows shot up in surprise. He looked at Marty again and saw the man's genuine sincerity like an aura. James looked at Imogen and knew Marty had her trust as well. James decided then and there to include him in the team. "Marty. Welcome!" James chuckled. I'm not exactly sure what we are, but you're now an official part!"

Marty's eyes lit up. "Thank you! I'll get that container unloaded. Where do you want it?"

Imogen introduced Marty to security as they arranged to have the shutter raised and the ram protection bollards lowered. Marty's eyebrows raised in appreciation. "Wow! You've certainly beefed up your protection out here!"

Imogen smiled grimly, "You better believe it! We don't open this unless we have to, and we all live inside now."

Marty paused and whistled. "Inside? Really?"

Imogen shrugged. "We have to if we want to keep what we're doing secure." She looked around the site. "We've already had two attempted break-ins, one of them with the gangster who kidnapped me!"

Marty's jaw dropped. "Mo Banks? Here?"

Codie heard the discussion and joined them. "That's right, Marty. Some people want what we've got here and are serious about getting their hands on it. Mo thought he'd get in first!"

Marty shook his head, "I had no idea the Step engine was so special."

Codie smiled. "Just wait a few hours, and you'll get a first-hand look. Once you're up to speed, we can discuss what we need and how you'll best fit in."

Marty pursed his lips and nodded, "Sounds like a plan, Codie. Get me when you're ready."

Marty turned back to Imogen, "Where shall we dump this?"

Imogen laughed. "Dump? Not dump! We'll place this important item over by the side wall there." She frowned. "It would be best to leave it on the trailer for access; if not, I'll make a cradle."

Marty shrugged. "You can have the trailer if you like. I don't have anything else to cart around at the moment."

They manoeuvred the trailer against the wall and began cleaning its outer edges, which were not in as bad condition as Marty had said. He helped Imogen place the Step field strips along the cleaned edges, and Imogen explained as they went along. "The Step field generators are manufactured using an automated process." She pointed to a workbench in a well-lit area at the back of the warehouse. "When it comes off the production line, it's incorporated into a graphene strip rolled onto a spool in ten-metre lengths."

Marty nodded as Imogen pointed to the strips they were placing on the container. "The strips are connected in series and protected by a coating of flexible epoxy resin."

They finished off the last strip, and Marty asked. "How do you control the operation of the Step field?"

Imogen smiled, "Good question! The individual generators incorporate power rails, actuator circuits for each field, and a communications circuit," she pointed to the server rack on the opposite wall. "The AI we use for Stepping, also known as Quinn, is connected to all our Step drives via the communications WiFi."

She smiled and raised her hands. "Simple!"

Marty shook his head. "So, you can send large objects anywhere in the world as well; that's great!"

Imogen laughed. "Marty, you don't know the half of it!" She saw Codie and James walking towards them. "I'll let these two take you on a different tour. See you later!"

James waved as Imogen went to join Olivia and turned to Marty. "You ready for a trip, Marty?"

Marty chuckled. "I sure am. You've made a lot of progress in a short time!"

James and Codie looked at each other and back at Marty. "You ain't seen nothing yet, mate! Come with us."

They walked to the PTV, James explaining what it was as they climbed through the hatch and settled on the seats.

Marty was thinking he was in for a trip somewhere else on Earth, which would be incredible.

James said. "Quinn, Karma base, if you please."

"Karma base, Executing"

* * *

The PTV arrived on Karma with its new visitors.

James stuck his head out of the hatch and smiled. He stepped onto Karma for the very first time and breathed deeply of the clean, cool air. He was followed closely by Codie and Marty, who looked around suspiciously at first, then with eyes widening as he took in the temporary camp and soldiers.

"Welcome!" Said Major Moreton. He had a large smile of his own as he laughed. "Couldn't keep you away for long, could we?"

James shook his head, "I wish it were that simple, but you couldn't be more correct! I've been busting to get here!"

Codie grinned and nodded his head, "It's amazing! I'm lost for words. It's just amazing!"

James introduced Marty as an occasional assistant to the project now turned full time.

Marty smiled his beaming smile. "A pleasure to meet you, Major Moreton. Let me know if you need anything, and I'll see what I can do!" He looked around. "Nice place you've got here!"

Major Moreton laughed appreciatively. "You get used to it after a while. Then you notice something else you haven't seen before! Come to the tent, and we can catch up on where we are and what we're planning."

As they neared the tent, he waved to one of his troops. "Corporal, can you let Marcus know the PTV is here and can be unloaded?"

She replied with a brisk. "Yes, Sir."

Marty looked around, "Where are we? I don't recognise the area."

Major Moreton looked across to James. "You didn't tell him?"

James smiled at Marty. "No. Thought we'd surprise him!"

The Major laughed out loud. "You bastards!" He laughed some more and got his breath. "Well, you'd better tell him!"

Marty looked at the Major like he was mad, then turned to James. "What does he mean? Tell me what?"

James and Codie laughed as well until James got some wind. "I'm sorry, Marty, it just seemed like such a good joke."

Marty pleaded. "What joke?"

James shook his head. "Look around, smell the air, look at the sky. This isn't Earth!"

Marty finally understood. "Not Earth?" He looked around, the others joining him.

Codie smiled. "It's the first Earth-like planet we found. We call it Karma."

Marty looked at Codie and closed his mouth. He looked at James and the Major, eyes wide. "Karma?"

James grinned and placed a hand on Marty's shoulder. "Don't feel too put out. It's Codie's and my first Step here also." He smiled. "It's beautiful, isn't it?"

Marty was lost for words and shook his head. "Karma." He took a deep breath, "Have you found any more, or is this it?"

James looked at him with a broad grin. "No, it's not the only one. So far, we've found six planets that are very much like Earth and can support life like Karma can." He looked more serious. There are another twenty that have small variations to gravity or the atmosphere but are close enough to populate, plus another hundred or so that are borderline survivable in particular areas or with additional equipment."

Codie added. "We've scanned less than a thousand possibilities, a fraction of what we can reach." He shook his head. "There are probably hundreds of thousands of Earth-like planets waiting to be discovered."

They entered the tent and sat in canvas chairs around a table. The Major asked. "Can I get you anything? We've got plenty of water and tea if you like."

James shrugged. "Local water?" At the Major's nod, he chuckled. "Then count me in! I'd be more than happy to try the local bugs!"

Moreton cocked his head, "Funnily enough, the locals are easygoing on us; ours don't seem to cause any trouble for the locals either, that we can see. Early days yet, but all the analysis looks fine."

James took the proffered cup and had a healthy swallow. "It tastes nice, sweet almost. Very refreshing."

Codie made sure James didn't keel over and had a taste of his own. His eyebrows lifted, and he nodded. "Very nice. We could be onto something here. Bottling plant!" He smiled. "Distillery!"

The Major laughed. "That's been suggested a few times since we've been here! We'll have to find a peat bog to make the good stuff, though!"

Marty cocked his head and started to think about it.

Codie noticed and grinned. "Not now, Marty! Put it on the list, though!" They laughed good-naturedly.

The Major's face turned serious. "To work! We've patrolled the immediate area in minute detail and found no problems or threats. I've had the men reconnoitring further out to get a representative appraisal of the area with the same result. We're happy to call the valley floor and surrounding hills safe for use, and don't expect surprises." He smiled and shrugged, "We've sampled the river and the top of a few hills to the west. So far, all good."

James smiled and started to say something, but the Major raised a hand. "I know you want to get here as soon as possible, but we need another week or two to check further. It's better safe than sorry."

James sighed. "You're right. One more week! If everything is okay, I'm going to start the move."

The Major nodded. "You're on."

Codie looked at the Major. "Stan, would we be able to take back a small contingent to help out with security? We've already had trouble and have intel there's something in the wind. The attacks are getting stronger, and I think another will follow when whoever is after us gets their act together."

The Major frowned. "You blokes are experienced. If you sense something's not right, then it probably isn't. I can spare a team of six. Hang on." He stuck his head out of the tent and saw Marcus approaching. "Ah. Marcus! Just the man."

"PTV's all clear, Major." Marcus cocked his head. "What's up?"

"Come inside."

Marcus nodded greetings as he sat, and the Major continued. "Codie's got wind of the possibility of trouble back at the warehouse. He wants some men to help out. Can you get a team of five and go back for a few weeks?" he looked at Codie.

Codie looked pensive. "No more than that, I should think. If we get your okay, we'll all be out of there within two weeks anyway."

The Major tilted his head and looked at Codie. "We'll have the group Step back to Earth the day after tomorrow." He checked with Marcus, who nodded. "That will be fine, Sir."

Codie's smile was tight, "Thanks, Major, it will make a big difference."

Chapter 33

Codie woke to a shake of his shoulder by the guard from the front office. "We've got company." Codie rose, pulled on his boots and checked his equipment before going to the CCTV monitor at the front desk. He watched the live feed as the hobo from the other day shuffled around as though looking for something.

Codie checked his mike was on. "Ken? You seeing this?"

"Yep. I have three unknowns. One at your position and two more out of your line of sight."

Ken was looking through night vision binoculars and turned full circle, looking for any more intruders. "Hold while I change viewpoint."

Codie frowned and spoke to the guard. "Get the others. I want the civilians behind the barricade at the rear." He held out a hand before the guard left. "Also, tell Matt to come back here with Mary, and then go and set yourself by the roller shutter." The guard nodded and moved off.

There was a loud scratching at the office door as the hobo shuffled and banged about.

Ken called back in with an update. "Codie. We've another two in the scrub beside the unit over the road from you. They're laying up in a dip and watching proceedings through scopes. I'd say they are back-up."

Codie grinned. "Just the six then? I'll get my guys to stand down, and you can sort them out!"

Ken snorted quietly. "I'll get around the back of the two waiting in the scrub; give me two minutes, and I'll be ready to take their place. From what I can see, they plan to have you open the door and then surprise you."

Codie grunted. "Roger. Out."

Ken silently made his way to the rear of the units on the other side of the driveway. He went to ground and closed to under ten metres of the men in the dip. He watched them for a half-minute. They were well-drilled but too confident; they didn't watch their backs. Assuming no external security personnel, they focused on the immediate task: a fatal mistake in any situation.

Ken considered his options. Although the unknowns had weapons, this was a non-military engagement. He decided to wait for Codie to give him a distraction.

Suddenly, the warehouse door opened, and the exterior lights went on. There were sounds of a scuffle, and the two men in front of Ken started to rise. Ken let the first one move off before giving the laggard a crack on the back of the head with a cosh. The man grunted and fell in a boneless heap. The first man turned at the sound of his friend falling, but all he saw was a giant fist swinging out of the shadows. He fell and joined his friend.

Meanwhile, Kelly shuffled through the open door and came face to face with Codie, who had a taser pointed at him. Regardless of what Kelly wanted to do at that point, he was pushed forward by Chas and Steve, who had been waiting out of sight of the cameras. Codie fired the taser, but its prongs got caught in the many folds of Kelly's smelly suit. Kelly grunted as Codie jabbed him on the chin but kept moving into the room. When he was close enough, he grabbed Codie in a bear hug and held him close. Codie couldn't do much more than beat on Kelly's head.

Matt and the guard were waiting behind Codie, and they moved towards Chas and Steve. Matt punched Kelly in the ribs. When that didn't do anything, he tried again. Codie felt the hold ease off and had space to force his hands down Kelly's face and under his chin. He heaved and broke Kelly's hold. Both men staggered slightly, but Codie recovered quicker and landed a few good shots on Kelly. At least it was enough to give Codie a more even contest.

Chas saw the two men coming at him and wondered what was keeping Clive and Dick. He called into his mike, "Dick! Now would be good." He didn't get an answer and looked behind to see what was happening. He was shocked when he saw a stranger moving on Steve. That was all he saw before he was grabbed and punched by one of the two men who had been heading his way. Chas, an accomplished fighter, landed a good right to his attacker's face, sending him sprawling to the ground. He didn't have much time to react when the second man put two quick jabs into his gut, but he turned to soften the blow and got a surprise hit to the guy's head. He was about to pull his knife when he heard a click and felt cold metal behind his ear. "I wouldn't do that, mate." Chas brought his hand away from the knife and turned slowly.

Ken smiled. "That's very smart. Do you have anyone else apart from you three and the two over the road there?"

Chas looked back with a grimace and shook his head. "Nope! We're it. Fuck!"

Ken closed his lips and nodded. He looked at Codie. "I don't believe him. I'll have a look around. Send someone over the road and collect the two in the gully before they come to their senses." As Ken moved off, Matt and the guard secured Chas and Kelly with duct tape. Codie told Matt to get Mary to help wrap up the two in the trees while he and the guard finished with Kelly and dragged all three into the warehouse.

Matt and Mary secured the men's hands behind their backs before they regained their senses. Once secure, they slapped them awake and pushed them towards the warehouse. They were joined by Ken, who had his hand around the back of the neck of another struggling person.

Chas shook his head when Jock was brought into the warehouse with the others. "Oh Shit!" he muttered.

Ken smiled at Chas and looked at Codie, "He was waiting in a van parked back from the driveway." He grinned. "I think that's all of them. Best fun I've had in a long while!"

Codie shook his head and sighed. "I hope that's it! I've had enough of these surprises."

James and the others walked up as the discussion quietened. James asked. "Do we know who they are or where they're from?"

Codie shook his head. "They're not talking, and they've nothing on them. Leigh's on the way to take them back to AFP HQ. I reckon he'll find out and let us know." In the meantime, we've got to keep our guard up."

Back at the motel, Frank looked at his watch again. It was five minutes past the scheduled check-in call. "Shit!" He packed their gear and checked out.

Once he returned to Sydney, he called the number Chas had given him, and a voice asked. "Yes?"

Frank replied. "It was a bust, Sir."

The voice on the other end of the line swore and was silent for a minute. "Your name?"

"Clappers, Sir."

"Clappers. Okay, Clappers, take this number down and call me when you return to the States."

Frank wrote the number into his notes app and hung up.

* * *

Leigh Buchanan and Callie Stubbs left for Tumbi as soon as they heard about the attack. Following them were two secure vans and six officers to collect the attackers.

Before checking on the prisoners, they spoke quickly with Codie and Ken, who explained how the situation had unfolded. Leigh frowned. "So, you don't recognise any of them?"

Codie shook his head. "Apart from the bloke who stinks, I've never seen them before."

Leigh turned a questioning look to Ken, who shook his head. "No idea who they are." He tightened his lips and shrugged. "Only thing I can add is that the little I heard spoken during the fight sounded American."

"American." Leigh looked at Callie. "WestProtect?"

Callie took a deep breath and let it out slowly. "From the intelligence we've received since Caldwell went to Hickey-Roche, I'd have to say so." She shook her head. "We've seen no movement from the States to here, so they must have been based elsewhere, and we didn't pick up on their entry."

Leigh shook his head, and his eyebrows knotted. "If it is WestProtect, they'll be back again - stronger and wiser." He looked at Codie. "Keep an eye open, and we'll do the same."

They entered the warehouse, where the prisoners were secured to the wall. Leigh turned to Callie, "Recognise any of them?"

Callie peered at their faces and shook her head. "Nothing I've seen on any of the Interpol bulletins." She frowned at Steve Garibaldi as though there was something familiar but shook her head. "No. Nothing I can recall." She looked up and grinned. "Facial recognition should get a hit somewhere, though."

Codie shrugged. "Their weapons are on the bench, there. Nothing unusual and nothing you couldn't pick up in Australia with the right connections."

As they spoke, the two AFP vans arrived.

Leigh briefed the officers. "Treat them carefully and make sure they are secure. Three in each van, hands and legs restrained." He made sure he had their attention. "These blokes are not local thugs; they are professionals. Treat them carefully!"

The officers nodded and went about securing the prisoners one by one. There was no chance for trouble, so the prisoners didn't try anything and were soon on their way to cells in Sydney.

Leigh reiterated his concern. "These people are a big step up from Mo Banks and his lackeys." He frowned. "They look like professional soldiers; you were lucky this time."

Codie nodded, "If it hadn't been for Ken's paranoia, we'd have been toast! There would have been too many for us." He nodded towards Ken, "We're going to need more people if we're going to hold out."

Leigh offered. "I can get one of our tactical response teams up here." He looked doubtful, "It's just that I don't know how secure they are."

Codie frowned, "It's no good if we can't trust them. An enemy appearing from your side in a time of trouble is worse than a hoard of enemies when you know where they are." He nodded to Leigh, "Thanks all the same, though, Leigh. We should keep it as tight as possible." He grinned. "Things seem to keep getting done here, so don't worry too much about it!"

Leigh promised to update Codie if they learned anything new about the assailants. Then he and Callie headed back to Sydney again.

* * *

Leigh and Callie sat with their boss, Jacko Dunne, at AFP's office in Goulburn Street. They had identified the members of the captured assault team from Tumbi Umbi via Interpol's facial recognition system and were discussing how they should proceed.

Leigh's arms were raised to emphasise his point. "Unless there's a bloody good reason, these guys aren't going to talk. They're known mercenaries, and their credentials would be stained for years if they were known to give out who their employer was for this action."

Jackson Dunne reclined in his chair, his hands folded across his flat stomach. "We know who they're working for already." He paused, his eyes narrowing. "And, we know what they were doing there. They're after the Step Drive."

Callie piped up, "If we already know what we need to know, why question them? Let's just lock them up!"

Leigh's voice was firm as he raised his hands. "No, No, No... We don't know who they're working for, and we don't know what they know about the tech." He held his hand up to forestall the others, his eyes darting between them. "Sure! We know they're working for WestProtect. But, we don't know who in WestProtect has them on this operation." He kept a hand raised. "We also don't know how much they know about the Step Drive. It has to be worthwhile getting that intel if we can."

He paused a moment and lifted his head. "Surely we have to go after the WestProtect connection! That organisation is getting more extreme by the day!"

The three of them sat back to think about how to get some information out of this crew they'd caught.

Jacko was the first to speak. "Would you agree these guys are reasonable but not top-tier?" Callie shrugged, and Leigh gave a little shake of his head. Jacko took that as agreement. He wasn't sure where he was going with his thinking but ploughed on. "So, if we lose them and they scurry back to the States or wherever they base themselves, we haven't lost much?"

Leigh's mouth turned down. "They were overconfident. Professional, but used to overwhelming force rather than highly trained and practised skills." He shook his head, "Not a big loss, no. There's plenty more of their ilk."

Callie was puzzled by Jacko's thinking but agreed. "No big loss."

Jacko sighed. "It goes against the grain, but nobody was hurt by the attack apart from them! And nothing was damaged. And nobody is pressing charges."

Leigh suddenly looked at Jacko with a smile on his face. "What you're saying is, if they give us a good reason to, we'll give them a slap on the wrist and send them packing!"

Jackson smiled. "That's the gist of it, yes."

Callie was open to the idea. "Will they go for it, do you think?"

Leigh scratched his head. "They haven't got anything else. They must expect a few years in Long Bay to come up regardless."

Jacko cracked his neck. "It's worth a shot! Play it any way you like. Let's see if we can learn more."

In the end, it worked. They didn't do the 'Good cop, Bad cop' routine, but Callie played bored and unattached to why we were bothering to get new information. She built up the potential sentence, conditions in Australian gaols and the lousy food; Leigh focused on a deal for reduced sentences and better conditions if they gave over useful information. After two days of individual questioning, they started to see cracks in Chas's reticence when he was given the idea his accomplices were weakening.

Leigh and Callie discussed it, and Callie hit the nail on the head: "He's the one who was in charge; it was his operation."

Leigh nodded. "Go on."

"Well, look at the type of organisation WestProtect is! You could almost guarantee Chas' life will be forfeit when they get their hands on him again."

Leigh shrugged. "May as well give it a go! How do you want to approach it?"

Callie considered an approach. "How about we get Jacko in? The Boss! The bloke who can make things happen!"

As Jacko entered the room, he switched off the recorders. "Hi Chas, my name is Jackson Dunne. I head Organised Crime in New South Wales for the Australian Federal Police." Chas looked at Jacko but didn't say anything. "I have been hearing some of the things one or two of your colleagues have been saying, and my team suggested I make you a one-time offer." He looked at Chas. "Do you understand what that means?"

Chas looked at his feet, then back at Jacko and nodded.

Jacko leaned onto the chair across from Chas. "If you tell us what you know of WestProtect, your boss there and the contents of the warehouse at Tumbi Umbi," Jacko left it hanging and looked at Chas, who sighed and nodded. Jacko continued, "Then we are prepared to drop you off at a location of your choice with fifteen hundred in Australian currency."

He checked that Chas was on board so far. "Moreover, we will release each of your ex-teammates individually in an unspecified foreign country." Jacko shrugged. "At least you'll be alive, and you should have time to bury yourself before anyone comes looking."

Chas nodded and was about to speak, but Jacko held up a hand. "Don't forget, this is a one-time offer. Any gaps or bullshit, and the deal is off the table! Understood?"

Chas sighed deeply and nodded. "I'll cooperate. It's more of a chance than I'd have given you in the same situation!"

Jacko turned on the recording devices and left the room. As he left, Callie and Leigh entered with smiles on their faces.

Chas told them everything he knew about WestProtect and Ainsley van den Favel and the technology they had been looking for. Fortunately, WestProtect didn't know how far they'd been able to push the Step Drive and still viewed it as a form of instantaneous movement of a weapon such as a bomb or a communications device. When pressed on the comms idea, Chas shook his head and shrugged.

The AFP kept their promise, and neither Chas nor his team were heard from again.

Chapter 34

Leigh called Codie to update him on the result of their arrest of Chas and his team. One thing they agreed on was that Codie had been lucky; the situation could have worked out a lot differently if Ken hadn't been around and they hadn't been paranoid.

Codie's interest was sparked when Leigh mentioned something about Step field communications. "What was that?"

Leigh said, "When he talked about what they'd do with the tech, he mentioned weapons and communications."

Codie grunted, "Did he mention how it would work?"

Leigh shook his head. "No. He said it was one of the ideas someone at WestProtect had about how transportation could be used." He frowned. "I got the feeling it was small objects that came and went with communication data. Does that make any sense to you?"

Codie laughed. "Not to me, Leigh, but you never know; there may be someone here who will see something in it."

They agreed to catch up in more detail in a few days and left it at that.

Codie went looking for Jerry. "Hey, Jerry? Got a minute?"

"Sure, Codie, what's on your mind?"

Codie shook his head and shrugged. "When the AFP questioned the guys who attacked us, one of them mentioned there was interest in using the Step tech for communications."

Jerry looked thoughtful. "Anything else?"

Codie nodded. "He said something about using small objects that came and went with data." He shook his head, "That's it! It may be nothing, but I thought I'd let you know."

Jerry's eyes went distant as his mind worked. He came back with a start, "Oh. Ah, thanks, Codie! That may be useful! Thanks."

Codie smiled to himself and shook his head as he watched Jerry wander over to Olivia's bench.

Olivia looked up as Jerry approached. She could see the concentration on his face and waited quietly.

When ready, Jerry cocked his head. "We can't communicate with Karma in real-time, so we update systems via Quinlets when we Step somewhere."

Olivia nodded in agreement and waited.

"What if we had communication nodes in Step space for active presents such as Earth and Karma? The node could have some", he frowned, "bugs?" He nodded to himself. "Yes, bugs that flit back and forth. The nodes themselves can have tight beam connectivity." He looked at Olivia and shrugged, "Earth and Karma are only 143 kilometres apart in Step space."

Olivia smiled at Jerry, "It's a good idea! Let's set up tests and see if it works!"

* * *

Frank Clappers sat across from Ainsley van den Favel. The office space was large and easily accommodated a heavy mahogany desk on a

Persian rug. Behind the desk was a matching credenza with a computer screen, clock and mouse, surrounded by thick books and sports trophies in the various glass-panelled cupboards and open nooks.

Frank briefed Ainsley on the fiasco in Australia, and Ainsley reviewed Chas's notes and other digital records. He looked up and held Frank's eyes. "What's your assessment of getting into that warehouse and recovering the technology it contains?"

Frank compressed his lips and nodded. "Stealth hasn't worked. They are top-notch, experienced professionals." He shook his head. "We've been out-smarted and out-muscled in every interaction. They learn from us each time and improve their capability to counter further attempts."

Ainsley nodded. "So, how do you think we should proceed?"

Frank's eyes narrowed as he lifted his head. "With overwhelming force! We prepare well and go in fast from multiple vectors." His teeth bared, and his eyes darkened as he made each point. "A team to blow the wall at the back. A team through the roof. A team to blow through the side wall of the adjacent unit. A team through the front office door. And a team in a reinforced 4WD through the shutter!" He gave a tight-lipped smile, "They couldn't possibly prepare for an engagement like that and won't know what hit them!"

Ainsley sat back, fingers steepled under his nose. "What about police?"

"What about them? Tumbi Umbi is a good ten minutes away from any local police response. And that's if any cars are available. Another ten minutes at best from larger stations." He frowned. "Police are not an issue, and neither is extraction."

Ainsley nodded. "About extraction, what's your plan there?"

"We have multiple road, rail and water routes available. I'll have teams use separate routes to minimise the size of any one group." He cocked his head and looked again at Ainsley, "I'd split the tech and any digital records amongst different groups to ensure retrieval. Any technology would be allocated to the strongest group who would be directed to the best escape route at the time." He grinned. "There's even an air route via a local airfield if we want to cover all the bases."

Ainsley looked at the desk as he played a mental run through Frank's plan. After a few minutes, he took a deep breath, sat back and smiled grimly. "Frank, I want you to make it happen! You can have all the resources you need." Frank nodded as Ainsley continued. "I'll assign the two teams from the training exercise in Alabama and give Marsh Bellamy a call to supply us with two squads from his ground troops."

Frank raised his eyes in appreciation. "That'll give me close to sixty people; Marsh's men are top of the line."

Ainsley looked into the distance. "How long will you need to put this together, Frank? Frank glanced up as he considered the training and travel. "We should have all our ducks in a row in two weeks at the earliest. Let's say three weeks to be safe." Frank smiled broadly, "We'll begin the assault at three thirty on a Sunday afternoon. They won't expect that!"

Ainsley cocked his head and frowned. "Why is that? I thought you'd go at dawn?"

Frank shrugged, "The folks on the coast like their Rugby League. They'll be at a club or home watching their heroes slug it out with their most hated enemies!"

Later in the day, Frank made a call to Brogan McDonnell. Brogan ran an independent surveillance team he'd used previously and who had proven effective.

The call was answered with a curt, "Hang on, Frank" There was the sound of raised voices and silence. "Frank. What's up?"

Frank smiled to himself. "This a good time to call?"

"Depends on whether you're going to give me grief!"

Frank laughed. "Not likely, Brogan." He paused before continuing, "I need your help. Starting as soon as possible. Roughly three weeks."

Brogan grunted. "Well, as it happens, I may have time. Where?"

"In Australia. A place called Tumbi Umbi, north of Sydney."

"Tumbi, what?"

"Don't worry about the name. It's a suburb in the boonies around an hour and a half north of Sydney."

Brogan muttered to himself for a few seconds. "Yep. Okay. I can have the team there in a couple of days. It'll take a half day to check it out and work a schedule, but we've got all the gear available." He talked with someone in the background for a half minute before talking to Frank. "What are you after?"

Frank groaned. "It's a long, sad story I won't burden you with. The address is one of those business warehouse units in an industrial park. I'm planning a raid to retrieve something on the premises."

"Why do you need me?"

Frank shook his head. "You don't want to know! We've already had a go, and they were too strong. We lost the team."

"Chas?"

"Yep!"

"Shit! Who are they?"

Frank chuckled. "Damned if I know. We thought they were high-level corporate security, but they're way more than that. I'd have to say they're ex-military. Plus, they have top-grade technology."

Brogan was quiet as he considered what Frank had told him. He'd been in operations with Chas and found it hard to believe amateurs had beaten him. "Frank?"

"Yes?"

"We'll do it. Fifty per cent now and fifty on completion."

"Thanks, Brogan. See you in Tumbi Umbi."

Brogan chuckled. "If I can find the place!" He closed the call.

Chapter 35

Leigh knocked on Jacko Dunne's door. "You wanted to see me, Jacko?"

"Ah, Leigh. Yes. Come in. Callie with you?"

"I'm here," Callie said as she entered behind Leigh. "I wouldn't let him out on his own now, would I?" They laughed and sat around Jacko's desk.

Jacko looked at them with a frown. "I've heard from Interpol that there's been a movement of military types, known to be associated with WestProtect, from the US to the local region."

Leigh cocked his head and looked at Callie as Jacko went on. "A few small groups and a larger contingent in a Hercules made their way to the Philippines. They were tracked, again in groups, as they made their way south, through Indonesia and into West Papua." He looked up and shrugged. "They lost them in the islands. Interpol has no idea what they are doing there or what equipment they have." He shrugged, "They only kept a distant eye on them at our request."

Leigh nodded and compressed his lips, "Thank your mates there for the heads-up! My money's on them getting ready for another assault on Tumbi Umbi." He chewed his lower lip. "Any word on numbers?"

Jacko shook his head. "Nothing concrete, a minimum of forty, possibly eighty or more."

"Shit! That's a small army!"

Jacko nodded in agreement. "I hope your friends are getting out of there soon. If these blokes are coming together to attack Tumbi, I'd expect them in two or three weeks."

Callie looked at Leigh and nodded. "They're working as hard as possible to get out of there ASAP. They're looking at two weeks, so it'll be a near-run thing."

Jacko looked grim, "You know we can't help them except to watch and advise if we're to keep them secure. We can't even involve the local police."

Callie's puckered forehead turned to Leigh's tight-lipped smile, and they nodded. Jacko sighed. "Okay. Keep them briefed. I'll let you know when I get more information."

"Thanks, Jacko," said Leigh as he and Callie left to call Harry.

* * *

On one side of a cobbled-together table in the warehouse were James, Harry, Jerry, Imogen and Olivia. Ken, Codie, Marty and Colonel Leona MacPherson were opposite.

Major Stan Moreton applied another overlay to the image on the main screen. "The area marked in green is suitable for your laboratories and other work areas." He indicated a rectangular area of a hundred metres by fifty metres east of the PTV site. "They'll need to be tents until we get building resources on site, but the surface is firm, and the weather is mild enough given it is early autumn in the valley."

The displayed geography consisted of the low hills ten kilometres north of the original landing area. The site for their base camp had been relocated after they discovered the valley could flood and, although elevated, they could get wet. The new site covered a gentle slope overlooking the valley and gave an appreciation of the area's beauty and potential.

Stan looked at James. "I'll hand it over to James now."

James picked up the laser pointer and indicated the green zone. "As you can see, there's plenty of space to set up different project areas. As we expand, we will have a growing group of researchers and need to develop different disciplines."

He pointed to an area covering ten hectares, coloured light pink. "The planned Step vehicle area starts less than five hundred metres down the slope, and we expect to have Step Transport Vehicles rigged well before we utilise space farther out. The terrain there is rocky and unsuitable for food production, making it ideal for SVs (Step Vehicles)."

He indicated an area on a flat hill five kilometres to the northwest. "This space will be reserved for SVs in case there is flooding in the valley."

Harry raised a finger in question. "What thought have you given to ground vehicles? I'd expect we'll need them sooner rather than later."

James nodded. "That's true, Harry. However, we don't want to build infrastructure like roads because we don't know how events will pan out in the longer term." He looked at Harry with a frown. "To be honest, I'd prefer we find another means of transport altogether. If we can use SVs to get around, we don't need cars, trucks, planes, or boats unless needed for a specific task." His eyes narrowed. "We also don't want to use fossil fuels. That leaves vehicles powered by battery or hydrogen fuel cells when we do need them." His brow furrowed as he continued. "One of our fundamental principles is minimising our impact on the planet. Transport is one of the most impactful technologies on Earth; we have to find a better way, and SVs are the answer." James shrugged. "In the interim, any movement of people and materials will be conducted using SV's. Quinn has already mapped all of Karma and can even drop the larger PTVs wherever we need to go."

James looked at Harry, who nodded in acceptance of James's points. James looked around the table. "We are fortunate Karma is such a good match with Earth. But that raises other challenges. We need people with skills to join our team. We need to produce food and calories to drive us. We have water. We need to know what resources are available and how easily we can or cannot get to them."

He shrugged. "Earth still works on cash. To acquire items, we'll need to generate income through trade. We need to achieve a lot before they can even know about us, but when we tell them we're here, we'll need raw materials to trade. Firstly, we need to keep going and, secondly, to grow ourselves into self-sufficiency.

"We all know our priority is food production." James looked at each person for any comments. "To achieve this production, we need people and resources." He lifted his head. "On people, we are simply human life and respect that. None of us is special or better than anyone else. We have a unique gift in that we have a brain and are aware. That awareness allows us to make decisions that can affect the planet and other life on it. We have to respect all life."

James looked around the table again and couldn't see any disagreement. "Any new people who join us will have as much input as we do. We'll work out a system of government as we grow, but all our people will be equal. In the long term, people can choose what to do with their lives. They can be scientists, artists, fighters, landscapers, teachers, students, whatever they want. They can choose to do nothing except enjoy Karma and its beauty if that is what they want to do." James raised his eyebrows, "I don't believe many people will choose to do nothing, but you never know." He grinned. "But I'll bet there's not many of them!"

There was a general chuckle and murmur at the table. Due to their individual experiences with people, the principle of equality had been interesting to them. In the end, none of them could deny that a full hundred per cent of the team freely gave themselves to the project and, to a person, wouldn't give up their part for all the tea in China.

James grinned, "It has been suggested that we kick-start our population growth with people who are disadvantaged or displaced. That remains an excellent strategy, but politics, logistics and security issues make it too complicated at present. We will work something out once we are better set up."

James frowned. "That still leaves us with a problem. We need manpower and know-how. We've all been thinking about it - has anyone got an idea that may work?"

The group looked around at each other, shaking their heads. James sighed. "We can't expect to have everything we need straight away. We still need to review what crops we can import successfully and what native plants will be usable. It will take a few months before the situation becomes urgent; perhaps we can find an answer by then. One area of research we'll be following through is automated production techniques. If successful, that alone will significantly reduce our need for skilled labour."

James chuckled and searched the room. "While focused on fundamental principles, I may as well put this on the record. We've discussed this previously, and it is close to my heart that we use technology and automate as much as possible. This will free human brains to explore new ideas and create new opportunities and understanding."

He smiled again. "Our second priority, after food, is to explore and document this world. The Defence team will do the bulk of the exploration using four-person PTVs. Quinn will record all findings and make them available to anyone who wants to review what we've found and what opportunities they may deliver." He pulled at an ear lobe. "Any non-military personnel are advised to leave exploration to the professionals; we don't want to have to mount rescue missions!"

He shrugged. "And that leads to our third priority. Energy. We have a portable solar array planned, so we don't need to send batteries back to Marty for recharge. What I'd like to see is a hydro or a space-based solution. Keep your eyes peeled and brains working!"

There was a chuckle; in recent days, they'd talked about energy a lot. Some preferred solar, some wind, and others had different options. In the end, they all realised the need to use renewables. James's favourite solution was the clean simplicity of hydro, but whatever they could find would play a big part in where they eventually settled.

"Those are the current priorities. Others will come to the fore when we have learned from these top three. So, let's keep that focus laser sharp until we know how to feed ourselves and get energy."

James spread his hands, "Has anyone got anything to add?"

Leona looked agitated and was biting her lip as she raised a hand.

James smiled. "Colonel? What's up? I know you haven't had the chance to talk about these issues. Is something bothering you?"

She frowned and gave a grin. "No, James, nothing bothering me about what you've said. It all makes perfect sense." The group quietened and waited for her to continue. "My brother-in-law's family have had to sell their five-hundred-hectare farm on the Darling Downs in Queensland as part of the Condamine buy-back scheme. The family's association with the farm goes back generations, and the loss is devastating."

She brushed a tear from her cheek. "Sorry. It breaks me up to see them trying to rebuild. They only know farming, and they were very good at it!" She sat straight. "Over the years, they have built a great store of knowledge and farming skills for wheat, barley and cotton. They've bred strains that are resistant to drought and disease and return a balanced yield."

James frowned and nodded with interest.

"They also farmed sheep and cattle in a part of the property that did less well with crops." She smiled, "It was my sister's idea. She called it a hedge against a rainy day." She sniffed. "The rainy day came, and the hedge didn't help."

She wiped her eyes again. "They would jump at the chance to come here and put their experience to work with local grains."

James looked at Codie, Stan and the others, "It sounds like a win-win to me. What do you think?"

Codie answered, "If Leona vouches for them, it's good enough for me! Let's get them here as soon as we can." The others did not disagree.

James grinned and smiled. "Leona, it looks like you've got family here if they want to come. Can you talk with them discreetly and, if they seem positive, be upfront about the dangers and difficult conditions over the next few months." James smiled, "If they still want in, let Codie know, and he'll arrange transport."

Leona beamed. "I'll get onto them as soon as I get back. This has been a worry for me for the last six months, and I never thought Karma would have a solution!"

Imogen looked thoughtful. "The situation with Leona's sister is one we can all consider." She looked around at her colleagues. If you have friends or family who you can be sure of, it may be worthwhile talking with them about the possibility." She looked at James and shrugged. What do you think?"

He shrugged. "Remember, it'll be a big step for people who don't know anything about us or what's happened." He shook his head. "It comes down to remembering your life is in their hands. If you trust them with your life and ours, it's a good idea."

Once the room was quiet, Marty looked around before raising an arm and asking, "What about housing? It sounds like we'll get more civilians joining us over time, and I'm not sure how used they are to tent living."

There was a murmur of agreement, and James ducked his head in acknowledgement. "That's true, Marty. We've been living rough on Karma and sleeping on pallets at the warehouse for a few weeks, so I didn't even consider it! More than happy for you to look into it."

Marty smiled. "No problem. I'll get onto it." He shrugged and cocked his head. "How are we funding all the purchasing I'm doing? The Government doesn't even know we're here, so Defence can't fund us beyond the interactions we have already had." He raised his eyebrows and shrugged. "If we're going to source resources and equipment from Earth, we'll need to pay for them, and we can't trade in resources without raising questions." That bought a moment's silence before various discussions started amongst the team.

Marty frowned. "Could we have a business that uses the capability of the Step Drive but doesn't expose the technology itself?"

That started a discussion that ranged over several possibilities but, in the end, failed to resolve the issue. The most viable idea was Leona's idea about recovering satellites for repair, such as Starlink satellites. The problem was that someone would try to militarise the ability to get to a satellite in the first place. In the end, it went back to the drawing board, awaiting ideas.

James ended the discussion. "We have challenges, but they are not insurmountable. Given time, we'll be able to find a business model that suits our needs without risk. For now, let's focus on food, housing and exploration. We need Karma ready so that we can reside there within two or three weeks. Let's aim for two!"

He looked around the room. "Is there anything else we've not yet addressed?"

Harry stood, a frown on his face. "I've had a call from Leigh and Callie. Mercenaries affiliated with WestProtect have been seen moving into the waters northwest of Papua New Guinea." He folded his lips and shook his head. "The risks to my staff are too great given SplitQC's association with our discovery and WestProtect's increasing interest." He took a breath. "I am going to shut down SplitQC."

James looked up, frowned and cocked his head. SplitQC was Harry's brainchild, and he'd invested much of himself in its success. Harry smiled. "I've given it deep consideration and can't see any alternative." He smiled more broadly. "I will propose to my staff that we all relocate to Karma." That sparked a buzz of conversation, and Harry spoke slightly louder to be heard above the noise. "I believe most people in the company will want to 'migrate' and continue their work here. That will help bring in skilled people." He held a hand out and went on. "Many people have extended family members who could also be at risk, and if you're all agreeable, I want to extend them an invitation. I can't know their skills, but hopefully, they will include a hairdresser."

He looked across and caught Marty's eye. "On funding, I'll talk with my lawyers and have them start a fund with SplitQC's remaining cash." He smiled. "It won't last indefinitely but will be enough to get us going."

There were a few chuckles at that. Harry sat again, and the talk gradually subsided when James stood. "Major? Do you have anything we should think about regarding this idea?"

Major Moreton smiled and shook his head. "Nothing to worry about on our side, James. There's plenty of space out there!"

James looked over the crowd to see if there was any more input. When none was forthcoming, he grinned at Harry. "Looking forward to our first population influx, Harry! This is great news!"

The meeting ended, and groups formed to discuss developments and the future before James and his earthbound buddies made their way home.

* * *

Jerry walked to the bench, where James stared at a computer screen that flashed changing numbers. The bench was littered with bits of silicon, small screws, glue, burned-out capacitors and all types of other electronic detritus. He put his hand on James's shoulder. "How's it going, mate? Need anything?"

James sat back and blinked up at Jerry. "I think we've got it, Jerry! Quinn's running through the final figures so we can track any movement at the ends." He smiled. "Wouldn't do to have the transceivers on the loose."

Jerry grinned and nodded. "I knew you'd work it out. Which way did you go after our brainstorming?"

James shrugged. "I ended with a compromise. I took the Quinlet off the transceivers and placed a single Quinlet with each node. The Quinlet adds a control data packet to the message stream, and I save a few grams of controller weight on the transceivers. It makes the transceivers smaller and Step back further to reduce transit time."

Jerry pursed his lips and nodded. "Sounds reasonable. How about thrust?"

James snorted. "I'm using a modified Step field generator without the target. The distance required to travel when Stepped back was so small that a short burst of particles was sufficient. There's a port on either side of the transceiver along the axis of movement."

Jerry chuckled. "Ha! Now that hadn't occurred to me!"

James shrugged, "I got the idea from Olivia. She asked me if a laser could provide thrust, and it dawned on me that I had the answer in hand all the time."

Jerry shook his head in amazement. "How easy things do seem on occasion!" He cocked his head. "So, how do you see it working?"

James got a gleam in his eye. "This is the first time I've tried to put it in words, so let's see how we go." He took a breath. "I'm thinking of it as an Interplanetary Communications System. It's a cloud of transceivers that, under Quinn's control, Step to different nodes in the communication array." He nodded to himself. "The end, or planetary, nodes are what we'll use on the ground. They provide a contained area for the routing of the transceivers. We'll want a contained area we can see because the movement in and out of individual transceivers is visually stunning." He shrugged. "Communication is achieved in near real-time through interactions with Quinn. Quinn posts data packets to the swarm of transceivers. Transceivers Step to the next node after spending a short time in the present. The constant movement of transceivers through nodes allows Quinn to recombine an unbroken stream of information and relay it to wherever it needs to go."

Jerry grinned. "That makes sense! Can I see it working?"

James checked his computer screen and saw that Quinn had completed the analysis. "Sure. I've set up a node in low orbit at Karma and a planetary node defined here." He pointed to an empty lava lamp on the bench top. "Quinn, start ICS using Karma-visual-test."

"Karma-visual-test executing."

A window opened up on James's screen, and an image of the area on Karma where the base had been established started to appear. Jerry noticed that the lava lamp had come to life and, on closer inspection, could see bee-sized objects come and go within. "What causes the glow in the contained area?"

James shook his head. "I don't know for sure. It looks like photons being generated by a release of energy as the transceivers come and go."

They looked back at the image of Karma and watched the cloud cover slowly change as the image updated. James looked at Jerry and smiled. "I'll prepare nodes for Marty, Colonel McPherson and Jacko Dunne so we can talk with them when we move out to Karma."

Chapter 36

It was late afternoon, and a light breeze waved in the tops of the grasses. Leona sat with her sister, Selina, outside a large tent in the foothills near the valley. Selina looked at Leona, her eyes brimming with emotion. "Leo, I can't thank you enough. You've saved us."

Leona smiled back and laughed softly. "Perhaps. But, in the end, you are perfect for what we need here, and you were available to come." She looked out over the valley and noticed movement. "Here come Coby and Dennis. By the look of it, they have grains to test."

Coby Crossing waved as they walked up from the valley, a massive smile on his face. They were accompanied by four of the Major's men and two of their old hands who opted to come with them on this adventure.

When they were closer, Coby held up a bag and Dennis another. "They look great to the eye. They are very similar to wheat and barley. We'll have to wait and see, but I'm confident we'll be able to work with both."

Dennis, Coby's father, added, "And there's more! About a kilometre away, we saw taller grasses that looked heavy with grain." Leona thought how wonderful it was to see them laugh and talk excitedly about the various things they'd seen while collecting samples. It had been years since she'd seen them this engaged and animated.

Coby gave Selina a huge hug whilst kissing her happily. He pulled a plastic bag from the side pocket of his overalls and smiled. "I have a present for you, Sel."

Selina cocked her head, wondering what he could have found. She took the bag and looked at the contents. Her brow creased before smoothing, and she quickly opened the zip lock to smell the contents. "Poo!" She smiled with delight. "It's old but smells good." She looked some more, "Round like sheep? Roos?" She looked up to see her family watching her inspection of old animal poo, and they all laughed loudly.

Selina's face beamed with joy. "Oh, my goodness! Wouldn't it be wonderful to find local fauna we could work with!" She looked out over the valley, a different light in her eyes now she had a new mission.

Harvey Bell and Nate Stoner were almost family, having worked with the Crossings since their early twenties. Neither had blood family to speak of. Harvey had an estranged cousin living in Adelaide who he hadn't had any contact with for nearly twenty years, and Nate was an only child whose parents had died in a bus crash when holidaying in Indonesia. Both men carried samples of soil and moisture readings from various depths.

The Crossings had been sampling across the nearer reaches of the valley for the last few days and were close to making decisions about the viability of the grains they'd come across.

* * *

Marty scratched his head. His experience building cheap housing was helpful, but he still had to choose an appropriate technology for the different circumstances of Karma. They didn't have the resources to supply manual labour as people were limited. He had discussed various technologies with the others and shortlisted gantry-style 3D printing and automated bricklaying. 3D technology had been around for a few years, so the equipment was available. Unfortunately, they weren't ready because they couldn't produce the needed materials until they had production facilities. It was a classic chicken and egg situation.

Another promising alternative that Marty explored was mud bricks. After considering the logistics of transporting the bricks, they turned their attention to an automated mud brick maker and bricklayer. One particularly intriguing tool was a Chinese brick-making machine that could be adapted to make mud bricks using soil and grass from the valley, and water from the river. The team, especially Jerry, was enthusiastic about the concept of an AI controlling the brick build and working with Quinn to transport racks of drying bricks to a storage site. As the bricks cured, they would be racked and ready for use. Marty then delved into bricklaying technology, and the best solution he found was a Semi-Automated Mason or SAM. The SAM could be modified to use the mud bricks and slurry he had devised, further fueling the team's optimism.

Despite his efforts, Marty ended up at a dead end because he couldn't produce a roof! He could make a round mud brick enclosure, but a conical roof required a different technology. He considered thatched roofs, but the process was too complex to automate. He even considered a building with a slope onto which a flat sheet could be attached but there were too many variables including sourcing the materials and the weather.

In the end, he decided to source caravans. As he explained to the team later, "Houses are fine when we know where we'll settle and when we can manufacture the required building materials. We need transportable accommodation with four walls, a roof and some comforts!" He shrugged. "Being transportable is another obvious bonus!"

He started buying simple caravans in his local area and, in a short time, had a fleet of six two-berth caravans the sellers delivered to the warehouse. After a structural checkup and good cleanout, they rigged it with Step drives and sent it to Karma.

Marty also picked up a special delivery for the Crossings. He came across the equipment on an online marketplace and thought they'd get a kick out of it. He packed it into a container and went to the office to chat with Codie.

Codie looked up as Marty came into the office. He'd been talking with Ken and Marcus, the leader of the five men sent back from Karma to help with security. Codie smiled. "Ah, Marty! Come on in. We were talking about you!"

Marty smiled uncertainly and took a place at the table. "Talking? What about?"

Codie cocked his head and raised his eyebrows. "All I ever talk about these days! Bloody security!"

The others laughed ruefully, and Marty shook his head. "I believe it! It's got to be a huge problem with WestProtect knowing where we are and wanting what we're doing!"

"Exactly!" nodded Ken. "That's why we wanted to discuss an idea with you."

Marty shrugged. "I'm all ears, mate. What are you thinking?"

Ken looked to Codie, who continued. "Well, there are two things that have come to mind. First is your work with getting equipment and housing for Karma."

Marty nodded and cocked his head for more.

"There's a lot of activity with stuff coming and going. If you get my drift?"

Marty nodded. "Yep. I see where you're coming from. It's harder to manage security with so much action, creating more vulnerabilities."

Ken chuckled to himself and looked at Codie and Marcus. "He's got it in one." He looked back at Marty and winked. "If you ever want a job, come and see me, mate!"

Marty shrugged. "Nothing special. Comes with the life I lead!" He raised his eyebrows. "What's your suggestion?"

Codie sat back. "How would it be if you moved your acquisition program to your acreage? Do you think it would work?"

Marty pursed his lips and grinned. "Well, nobody knows much about me. Certainly not the mob who are after us here." He scratched his head and muttered to himself. "I'll need a copy of Quinn and a few rolls of Step field generators." He nodded. "I reckon that'll work. Once I'm set up with Quinn, I can relay stuff back to me if and when I need it."

Marcus raised his eyes and nodded. "Good. Neither my men nor Codie's have found anyone interested in our suppliers or outside contacts beyond normal business connections. It's probably the best time to get you out so that you and your activity are out of the loop. I'll have two of my team go with you to check security over a few days. Is that alright with you?"

"No problem at all. They can be relatives in for a holiday if anyone asks." Marty got a cheeky grin, "Can they cook?"

Marcus paused for a moment, then snorted. "As good as you can, Marty, but no better!"

They discussed logistics before Codie caught Marty's eye and tapped the table. "We have another idea that we want to run by you."

Marty could tell that Codie was a bit unsure how to broach whatever was on his mind. He looked resigned and chuckled. "I know what you're after. Don't let it worry you. I'll stay!" He smiled ruefully. "I always knew that we'd need someone here who was under the radar and could keep an eye on things. I'm ideal for the job."

Codie let out a breath. "Thanks, Marty, And you're right! You are ideal for the job."

Marty folded his lips tight. He was disappointed that he'd have to wait to get to Karma but knew that having someone on Earth who could do things that needed doing and could keep an ear to the ground for news was a critical asset to the operation. Marty stood slowly. "Well, I better get going. I have a few things to sort out." Ken and Codie thanked him profusely. It was a sacrifice but an important one.

As Marty was walking back into the warehouse, he turned back to them. "Almost forgot. The blue container has a package for the Crossings." With that, Marty returned to the warehouse to organise his return to the property.

* * *

The building was clearly outlined in the failing light. Frank, fully aware of the significance of the upcoming operation, slid back down the embankment and called his group leaders for a final briefing.

He had split his men into five groups of twelve. Each group was allocated a callsign of Alpha through Echo, with group leaders designated callsign one and their seconds, callsign two. He had a total of sixty men to work with.

The training since they'd arrived at the Biak site had been rigorous. Team members, now well-acquainted with each other, were improving their knowledge and skills with the newer weapons that WestProtect had supplied.

Frank pulled out a drawing of the training site. "Listen up!" His group leaders and their seconds gathered closer. "This exercise is designed to familiarise you with the nature of the target site and our roles. I want us to try alternative approaches to the target building and how we engage their security. Our objective is to get samples of the technology they have developed. If we get the chance and it doesn't impede the main objective, we'll grab any scientists and technical experts."

He regarded his men grimly. "Any means of entry into the building is acceptable so long as the technology within isn't destroyed. Whatever force is necessary to meet that objective is acceptable." His face took on a determined expression. "If you go down during the operation, we will try to recover you, but there are no guarantees."

He nodded to them. "Let's go! We attack in five minutes."

The building used for the exercise was fitted with movement and heat sensors. The sensors were connected through automated paintball weapons managed by artificial intelligence. The assault team assumed the security at the building included detection technology and a security team with a mix of skills.

While they had limited information from Chas's attempt, they knew his assumption of the defenders being six average men was wrong. For this exercise, they increased the capability of the electronics to equal military specifications. They also assumed their opposing force would consist of men equivalent to special forces.

Unbeknown to the group leaders, Frank had placed sensors and weapons in the forest around the objective. If any of the men were careless, they'd be finding out soon enough.

At the end of the exercise, the group had performed reasonably well. Losses were just over fifty per cent. That was a high cost, but they had infiltrated the building and captured the technology markers as required. Only eight men had fallen to the booby traps in the forest. They'd be in a better standing when they made the actual assault.

"Well done! That was a reasonable result for an initial training run." Frank looked at the men in front of him. "Any questions or ideas?"

One of the men raised his hand. "Sir. Are we expecting booby traps around the actual target like we had here?"

Frank frowned and shook his head. "Not as such. It's a civilian area. However, they have top operators; the first team didn't make first base." He scowled. "Be prepared for some highly trained men who can move in silence and kill quickly." Frank looked around the men, a smile on his lips. "If I were you, I'd expect someone to be waiting behind every tree or buried under every square inch of sod."

Frank took in his team and growled. "Understood?"

"Yes, Sir!" shouted back the men.

Frank smiled. "Have a break. We'll work on more training and another exercise at the end of the week."

He looked at the sky and back to his men. "I want to get on the way to Australia by next Monday. That will give us six days to get to the Central Coast and set ourselves for the Sunday assault."

With that, the men broke into their groups, and their group leaders took them back to the operations area for a briefing and planning session.

* * *

Coby finished digging another row and stopped to wipe the sweat off his forehead with a towel stuck into the pocket of his overalls. He looked at the line and smiled. It wasn't perfect, but it would do. He heard a shout and looked up as one of the Major's men scrambled over the field, waving an arm. He set his mattock to one side and walked towards the man. As he got closer, he recognised Terry Jones, one of the Major's men assigned to logistics. "Morning, Terry; what brings you down here?"

Terry smiled. "Hiya Coby. You've got a parcel from Marty, and I need to know where you want it delivered?"

"I wonder what Marty's got for me? I can't recall asking for anything." He scratched his head, his curiosity piqued. "I guess I can come over and pick it up later today."

Terry laughed. "You'll need a few more blokes to help if you do, mate. Can I have it transferred here somewhere?"

Coby was puzzled. "Down here? Just how big is this parcel, Terry?"

Terry snorted. "I don't know for sure as I've not looked in the container. I've no time for that. If it's in a container, it's big!"

Coby scratched his chin and shrugged. "Okay. Can you have it dropped on the flat area over there?"

Terry looked where Coby pointed and nodded. "No problem, mate." He switched on his microphone and gave some instructions. Suddenly, a blue container appeared. Terry spoke into the microphone again and turned to Coby. "Give me a shout when you want the container removed, mate."

Coby looked at Terry, then at the container. "No worries, Terry. Thanks."

Coby yelped when he opened the container. The first thing he saw was a tractor. It wasn't a large vehicle, but looked solid enough to make a big difference in their farming effort. Farm implements were stored in a rack at the rear of the container, and a stack of solar panels was strapped tight to one side. He walked back to the tractor and climbed into the cab. The basic controls were familiar enough, so he turned the key. There was a whirring noise, and the display screen lit up, showing a view of the tractor and battery capacity. A broad smile spread across his face as he backed the electric tractor out of the container and drove the few hundred metres to where Harvey and Nate worked. Once they noticed Coby coming towards them, they downed tools and stared.

"Hey boys!" Coby shouted excitedly. "Look at this!"

Harvey and Nate joined Coby in walking around the machine and discussing its capabilities. They all hopped on, and Coby drove back to the container.

The three men got to work unloading and soon had a variety of implements spaced out on the ground beside the container. The implements included tools for cultivating the field, planting, harvesting, and performing other tasks.

When the tractor and its attachments were unloaded, they moved on to the solar panels. They'd unloaded around half of them when Nate shouted. "Bloody Heck!"

Coby jerked back from tidying the unloaded panels, "Are you okay, mate?"

Nate was shaking his head. "Come and look at this!" Coby and Harvey joined him, and all three stared silently.

There, at the side of the container, stood three battery-powered trikes. Coby scratched the back of his head and whistled. "Well! Blow my bloody socks off!" He looked at the others. "How does he get this stuff? These will be invaluable in getting us around the place to find seeds, plants and good soil." He smiled hugely. "We'll need a shed for this lot; I wonder if Marty can source a prefab for us?"

Chapter 37

Brogan paid off the cab and joined his team in the lobby of the Menzies Hotel in Sydney. He looked at his watch. "Get yourselves settled in, then join me. We'll go over the job one more time." There were a few good-natured comments from his team. They'd already been over the plan many times; Brogan was a stickler for detail. The fact he and his team were still alive backed him up. They'd go along with it.

Brogan McDonnell had learned his trade with the CIA. He wanted to supplement his skills with more hands-on experience and applied for a two-year unit swap with an elite reconnaissance unit in Israel's IDF. He got his chance to work hands-on in Syria and Gaza and returned to the States when the swap ended.

He retired from the CIA eighteen months later after picking up a shrapnel wound during a mission in Afghanistan. Not one to watch TV, he'd been freelancing ever since and gained a reputation for covert actions and surveillance. Brogan and Frank Clappers developed a deep respect for each other's skills during a WestProtect-sponsored mission in Africa, and they'd worked together in various operations since.

Frank emphasised that this mission was more challenging than it looked despite the apparent lack of opposition. As a result, Brogan organised an independent company to provide satellite coverage of the area. The service was expensive but worth every penny, and after some haggling, a surveillance satellite was moved into place. It had been monitoring the industrial park for the past twenty-four hours.

Brogan gathered his team for the briefing. "Okay, listen up. I've checked the first day's satellite coverage. During the day, there is a lot of movement inside and around the unit. Security patrols are active during the night. They are random and competently managed and executed." He cocked his head slightly. "It looks simple, but, as you know, I've been given the heads-up that it's not. There are elite personnel involved. That means you need to be elite personnel for this mission."

He eyeballed each of them. "Got it?" The men nodded and agreed.

"Good. Our task is surveillance only. We'll do it from a distance, and all tech must be stealthy, so we need low power settings and minimum microsecond exposure times."

He looked at one individual. "Kobi, I want you to focus on electronics. Same stealth constraints, but I'll need to know what they've got and where it's located."

Kobi nodded. "I'll have to move around, but it should be relatively safe with the satellite coverage."

Brogan grinned but shook his head. "Don't depend on the satellite. It's our friend for sure, but it's not going to save our butts from carelessness." He paused to emphasise what he was going to say next. "I repeat! There are elite players on the other team! Do not underestimate them or their capabilities."

He gave each of his team a stern look and continued. "I expect to see our employer in six days. We'll need round-the-clock logs of activity, personnel and tech. Kobi, you're free to work up your own schedule. Liaise with me so we don't cross paths." He waved a finger at the others. "That leaves the four of us to pair up and work six hours on, six off." He grinned. "We've done this before in worse conditions. You know what to do, so let's do it, and then we'll find somewhere nice on the Gold Coast to let off steam." There was general, good-natured agreement on that idea.

Brogan grinned. "We've got two days to sort out gear and jet lag. We drive up there Tuesday morning."

* * *

A truck pulled into the warehouse's loading dock, and two men jumped out of the cab. The area was quiet and looked deserted. The driver lifted his cap and scratched behind an ear. "I hope there's someone here. Go check the office door." His mate tried the knob and, finding it locked, knocked on the door. He heard a sound from inside and gave a thumbs-up to the driver as the door opened.

Codie's security man looked the delivery bloke over. "What's up, mate?"

"Delivery for..." He looked at the driver. "Hey, Bill, who's this lot for?"

The driver looked at the delivery instructions. "Coby Crossing. It's a prefab shed."

The security guard shrugged and nodded. "Okay. Hang on a tick!"

He shut the door and went into the warehouse. "We've got a delivery for Coby—a prefab shed. Should I send him over to Marty or take it here?"

Jerry stopped packing various computer bits and pieces and shook his head. "No. We can send it from here; I'll set it up."

Ken, trying to catch up on sleep, looked from his bunk. He'd been patrolling the area at night to make sure they weren't surprised again. "Does the delivery check out?"

The security guard checked the order logs and nodded. "Yep. No problem. It looks like it was ordered not long before Marty moved out."

Ken stood and pulled on his boots before walking to check with Jerry. "Sounds okay to me. Give me a moment to get the others ready."

He turned on his mike and called. "Codie?"

"Yes, Ken. What's up?"

"Nothing to worry about. Can you send some of our blokes to the warehouse? We have a delivery. It checks out okay, but I want to be sure we're ready if there's a surprise."

Codie chuckled lightly, "No problem. They'll be with you shortly; we're doing a perimeter check."

"Roger that. Thanks."

Ken nodded to Jerry. "Give us a minute to get backup, and you can get going."

Jerry nodded and made his way out of the office to see what they had.

"It's a prefab shed." The driver pointed at flat-pack boxes on pallets in the back of the truck. "Not too heavy but a bit cumbersome."

Jerry chuckled. "No worries, mate. We have a forklift to do the work!" He turned back to the roller shutter. "We need a minute for security to get here and open it."

The driver pointed at the ram bollards and shook his head. "It's a shame we need so much security nowadays. Bloody thieves are everywhere!"

As the driver spoke, Ken and three others from the security detail walked out of the office. The bollards started to retract, and the roller shutter whirred into motion. As the bollards were retracting, they stopped and moved up an inch before retracting again.

Jerry cocked his head. "Better get them cleaned or greased!"

Ken frowned and looked around before he nodded in agreement. "Let me know if you find anything." He looked to the three men with him. "Keep an eye open. I'm going inside."

While the pallets were unloaded into the warehouse, Ken quietly went to his bunk and pulled out a portable scanning device. He looked at the screen and turned in a circle before turning the scanner off and returning it to his pack. The scanner didn't detect anything unusual, but Ken felt uneasy regardless. Back in the warehouse, he made his way to Jerry. "Best to keep inside, Jerry, if that's okay."

Jerry picked up on Ken's unease and nodded. "No trouble, Ken. I shouldn't have gone out just now." He shrugged, "Forgot in the moment."

Ken placed a big hand on Jerry's shoulder before leaving the building to sweep the area again.

Chapter 38

SplitQC's thirty staff sat in the auditorium and wondered what their boss had in store for them. Harry stood on an elevated stage and looked over the familiar faces. Those faces looked back at him with expressions varying from concern to positive expectation. He smiled and started talking. "I won't beat about the bush. The news I have is as wonderful as it will be frightening. The first thing is that it means change. For some of you that will be welcome." He looked over his team. "But, for others, it will be the worst news you could hear." He straightened his back and lifted his chin before making eye contact with each expectant face. "I am closing down SplitQC."

There were a few seconds of shocked silence before everyone simultaneously started talking and asking questions.

Harry raised a hand for silence. "Okay. That's the worst of the news over with." He grinned. "Wasn't so bad, was it?" There were a few chuckles, and some shouted questions. Harry raised his hand again. "For reasons I can't go into, I have to wind up SplitQC. In the end, it comes down to safety. Your safety, my safety and the safety of our friends and families."

Expressions moved from expectation to fear and concern. "Don't be afraid! You need more information before you panic and run off into hiding!" He said the last with a laugh that most staff recognised from prior discussions with Harry.

The mood quietened. "You and I know that without all of you, there wouldn't be a SplitQC. You are all important to our success. Not just your knowledge and its application but also your attitude - to yourself, your colleagues and your communities." He raised his hands, palms upturned. "In a general sense, we all know situations change, and we just have to go with the change and make the most of it." He frowned. "Sometimes, it is us who begin that change. We begin the process that will change things for others, and then they must cope and make the best of it."

Harry looked into every pair of eyes, his own bright and wide. "SplitQC is part of a change that will impact our world and how we live." The mood in the room was hushed. People looked questioningly at each other and back to Harry. "I can't tell you what the change is." He held up a hand to forestall questions. "But, I believe the change is a good one. Not just 'good' but bloody fantastic." As he said 'bloody fantastic', his voice rose in volume, and he smiled broadly.

The team took a few moments to regain their senses before turning their full attention back on Harry. "Change is almost always a two-sided coin. Some people do not want this change to happen unless they control it." He paused and cocked his head. "These are powerful people. People who are used to getting their way."

Harry's employees were now entirely focused on his words. "SplitQC's part in this change has been significant. Most of you don't know about this because of the need for security. Despite that security, when people look, our part is obvious. And, the people who want to control it will look!" He nodded seriously. "When push comes to shove, we are at risk of being threatened by these people." He shrugged a shoulder. "I would have preferred events happen differently, but we can't predict the future, and I certainly didn't expect the future we now have."

His face lightened. "So. We have decisions to make."

He held up one finger. "First, I have to shut down the company. It has to cease to exist. No assets, liabilities, people, addresses. No anything." He paused to let that sink in. "That means none of us will be employed by SplitQC." The group looked at each other with a variety of expressions. They had each found their way to SplitQC by different pathways, but all of them had found meaningful work, a share in the company's success, respect for each other and the chance to make something of their lives.

Harry waved to get their attention. "It's not all doom and gloom! It's time to reveal the second decision we must make. This will be easy for some of you and more difficult for others."

He took a deep breath. "I will be restarting company operations almost immediately. BUT..." He held out a hand to silence the sudden activity his comment had sparked. "... BUT, it won't be located here! It will be located somewhere safe. A place where the people searching for us can't go."

He smiled. "That's got you thinking, hasn't it?"

Before his people could get too far off-track, Harry continued. "To help your decision-making, know this. Except to say it is a safe location, I can't tell you where it is. It has no internet connectivity. No mobile phone coverage. No way to get out once you are there until it's safe to do so." He smiled grimly. "There's no television, no restaurants, no footy matches, no shopping malls." He looked at the faces of his people and nodded. "There will be plenty of work, however!"

That got a few chuckles, and Harry smiled before getting serious again. "That's the situation. I have decided to close the business, relocate to a safe, undisclosed location and reopen our work under a different business plan."

He looked at his employees again. "You know me. This decision is not made lightly, and I know it will affect all of you. Given the nature of the discovery, this is the only course of action available to me to protect the discovery and to protect us." Harry felt his emotions rise. "Your decision is simple - do you come with me?" His eyes narrowed. "Do you take a chance to, let's say, move to a secret base on the dark side of the moon? Do you take a chance?" He leaned forward, brow furrowed. "I know it's a lot to ask you to take in. It's a lot to ask you to trust me because I can't tell you what's happening until we're out of harm's way. Do you take a chance?"

Harry pulled in a deep breath. "Before we get onto questions," he looked at his watch. As of ten minutes ago, SplitQC was deregistered. Jerry Bos and Imogen Matthews have packed and moved the company's equipment to the new site. Imogen is ready to move in the next few days; a third party is managing her local affairs. Jerry and the others in the technical team will move as soon as possible."

He held up a wagging finger. "One more thing. Jerry's mother and her pet cat are also making the move."

Harry shrugged. "That's enough from me. Over to you for questions."

There was a clamouring of voices and raised hands. Harry pointed to a man in the front row on the left. "Jimmy, I'll start with you and take questions from front to back, left to right. Hopefully, many of your questions will be answered on the way!"

Jimmy looked concerned as he rose from his seat. "Harry, I have a young family. We've got three under five. What will life be like for them? Is there a school?"

Harry nodded as Jimmy sat. "Thanks for the question, Jimmy. I expect a few of you to have similar concerns. We haven't set up a school yet, but we will. There are already a couple of kids at the site, and we're sure there will be lots more." He tapped a nearby table with his fingers. "In looking at this, think of it as a frontier. We have to do things for ourselves until we get organised. If we help each other out, it'll be easier to handle situations, and," he smiled, "it will probably be fun as well." He paused and cocked his head. "The same goes for elderly parents, families needing healthcare and the like. We don't have a hospital, nor do we have specialist healthcare practitioners. At least, I don't know of any as we speak. That said, it won't be long before we do. Also, the further removed the family members, the less likely they'll be in danger. Also, you may not have anything to worry about without direct contact with the project. My concern is to have zero risk for all of you." He looked back to Jimmy. "Did I answer you well enough, Jimmy?"

Jimmy smiled and nodded. "Yes, Harry, thank you."

Harry smiled and noticed half the raised hands had gone. He picked the next "Phil. What's on your mind?"

Phil, SplitQC's maintenance man, stood slowly. He was in his late seventies and had a couple of bee hives as a hobby. "Ah, Harry, sir, what about me? And my hives?"

Harry shrugged. "Phil, you are as welcome and needed as anyone." He frowned uncertainly. "I'm pretty sure the hives are out, but I'll check on it. If they're a no, will you be able to find someone to keep them for you?"

Phil winced, his lips pressed together in disappointment. "It'll be sad not to have them around, but I have a friend who will look after them."

Harry smiled and nodded. "Don't think it's the end of your bee-keeping, though; I'd be surprised if there weren't plenty of local bees for you to work with. It could be a project if you like?"

Phil sat, looking thoughtful, and Harry pointed to the next hand. "Ezra? What's your question?"

Ezra worked as a technician in the clean room, building specialised circuit boards. "What is the risk if I don't come with you?"

Harry rubbed his eyes. He looked at Ezra and the others. "Honestly? I don't know." He frowned and shook his head. "I believe it is extreme, and my actions should back that up. There have already been incidents of listening devices, secret cameras, a kidnapping, burglary and two assaults, one with guns." The group was shocked at this element of news. "I don't want to cause a panic. I believe, and the people outside of SplitQC believe, that we're in for a serious attempt to steal what's been developed along with any of the developers if they can get them. It's a major objective of these people." He lifted his chin. "To be perfectly frank with you, they scare me. I have complete faith in the people helping us with security, but they can't cover everyone and everything. That's why we have to disappear and disappear soon." Harry looked squarely at Ezra. "Ezra, the only lead these people have, if they fail to catch us soon, is SplitQC. There have been others who are peripherally aware of where the discovery was made; people like delivery contractors or accommodation staff who have no information of value." His eyes narrowed. "SplitQC is going to be their fallback when they think about it. You may be able to keep a low profile and evade them, but they're professionals, and I wouldn't like your chances."

Harry looked across the group in general, "That's why I'm being guarded with what I tell you. If you elect not to come with us you won't have any information of use to them." He frowned and swallowed. "It's for my protection, not yours. If you elect to stay, that's your choice. I've never lied to you guys about anything, and we've always run an open business. You've probably guessed that Jerry and Imogen have been involved. Already, digital traces have been deleted from phone and mail servers, chat apps, and the like. There wasn't anything useful there, but we had to make sure. The fact we've been able to do that should give you insight into the capabilities of the people helping us." He lifted his head, and his eyes narrowed. "They're no slouches!"

"Ezra, all of you, I urge you to take the chance and come with me. If you don't, you'll be at risk, but I don't know how dangerous it will be. Based on what's already happened, my gut tells me it could be extreme. I can't tell you more than that for the moment."

As Harry spoke, hands lowered until one was left. "Alice?"

Alice was the office manager and kept things organised for everyone. "When would we have to decide? And, when would we be leaving?"

Harry chuckled and shook his head, smiling at Alice. He suddenly felt exhausted. "We have to decide as soon as possible. Now won't be too soon. For the laggards, you have until mid-morning tomorrow. I've arranged transport to take us to the next stage of the move. Those buses will leave the old office car park at midday tomorrow."

The group started to talk amongst themselves, and Harry raised his voice to cut them off. "This change is happening right now, for all of us and for those we love. I want you all to join me and the others who are coming. You don't have to worry about details; I have people to look after everything! Don't worry about what's in the fridge or an outstanding debt or anything else. Tell me," he looked at Alice, and she nodded. "Tell Alice you're coming and how many, gender and ages. Leave the rest to us. Get those you love to the car park before noon. Then sit back and enjoy the ride!" He said the last with a smile of relief. He'd done all he could.

Soon, Alice was swamped, and a line formed for people to leave their details. Eventually, everyone agreed to take the chance and make the move.

* * *

Imogen decided she'd procrastinated long enough. She'd finished packing and stowing her gear and instruments a half hour previously and was ready to head off to Karma.

She walked to where James and Jerry tinkered with improvements to the comms system and held out her hand.

James folded her a big hug instead and smiled. "We're going to miss you, Imogen." He looked at his watch and laughed. "For all of a week or two if we last that long."

Jerry shook her hand and chuckled. "It won't be long, and we'll be back in action together again." He looked at her more seriously. "Let's see if you can find interesting metals before we get there!"

Imogen laughed. "Will do!"

She raised her voice a bit. "See you all soon." She waved back to various security personnel around the warehouse and walked with James to the PTV.

James held Imogen in a tight embrace. "I'll miss you. You know that, don't you?"

Imogen's face softened, and she smiled. "I know. It's been hard to find time just for us, but we'll make up for that on Karma."

James swallowed as he looked deep into Imogen's eyes. "I love you already, you know?"

Imogen's face lit up, and her eyes twinkled. "Of course, I know." Her smile softened, and she leaned forward to kiss James softly on his lips. The kiss lingered, but Imogen pushed them apart, eyes still on James. "I love you too, so don't be long!"

Their arms fell apart slowly, fingers last to separate. Imogen entered the PTV, and the hatch closed.

Shortly after, Quinn Stepped her to Karma.

Chapter 39

Frank Clappers and Marsh Bellamy sat at a portable table in a clearing inside the perimeter of their training camp on Biak. They'd been working hard for a week and a half, and the men were coming together well. They were putting the final touches on their planned assault before setting up a training exercise incorporating the main elements of the plan and the resistance they expected to encounter.

Frank sat back and regarded Marsh. "I think you're right. Your guys have more experience with explosives and a better general appreciation of an operation of this scale. To get into the building, we have the protected roller shutter, the main office entry, the concrete block wall shared by the adjoining unit, the roof and, perhaps, the back wall and rear entry."

Marsh nodded. "We'll need input from your surveillance team about the adjoining unit and shared wall. They should also look at the ram protection bollards. If we can get rid of them, it'll make surprise and entry much simpler." He scratched his neck. "The office door will be easy to break down, but I expect strong resistance at that point unless they concentrate their defence inside the main warehouse." He frowned. "I think we should keep the roof and rear as red herrings; Make some noise and, perhaps, blow a hole but not use them for entry." He nodded to himself as he imagined the battle playing out. "If we hit the roller door and unattached side wall hard, we'll have a field of fire that forces them against the office and into the mezzanine. A hole in the back wall would give us an ideal location for one or two men to provide suppression fire to keep their heads down." He pursed his lips, "A few men with automatics can cover the front, so we'll leave that alone."

Frank nodded. "That sounds good to me. Keeps it simpler than four or five entries and the mayhem that would create." He looked back to their diagram of the site. "Between us, we've got sixty men. We can use three of your guys to cover the front and two to snipe from the back. That'll leave fifteen of yours to split between the front and side assaults."

Marsh frowned. "Let's hold five back; they can clear the adjacent unit if required and provide backup if either assault falters."

Frank nodded in agreement. "Okay. So, I'll take fifteen of my guys for each entry point. They'll be led in by five of your team who'll make the initial blast through roller and wall."

Marsh nodded and cocked his head. Frank grinned. "My remaining ten men will join the entry that shows the most promise. They will have the additional task of recovering the tech and the scientists." He sat back on his chair. "I can't see them getting out of this even though they have six more people than your last attempt. We'll have overwhelming force. If we're lucky, we'll get the job done without casualties."

Marsh chuckled. "It does look simple, but that's when my gut starts making itself known." He grimaced. "Let's go with this, but make sure we don't underestimate them. Always on guard!"

Frank shrugged. "I can't argue with that, especially with Chas' failure. Let's get the men sorted out, and we'll go through a simulation."

The training exercise went well. WestProtect had arranged access to an abandoned industrial area east of Wardo, away from prying eyes and ears. The teams went through several scenarios, and while they made minor changes to the plan over two days of rehearsals, the essentials remained the same.

At a final briefing, the men were given relevant documentation and travel instructions to get into Australia. They would hold a final operation meeting in Newcastle on Australia's east coast in three days, on the coming Friday morning.

* * *

Leigh Buchanan was sorting through administrative emails when he took a call from his boss, Jacko Dunne. "Yeah, Jacko? What's the news?"

Jacko didn't beat around the bush. "Got a minute?"

Leigh laughed. "Sure do! Anything to get away from email! On my way."

As he rose, he called out to his partner. "Hey Callie. Jacko wants a word."

Callie grabbed her jacket and joined Leigh as he walked down the corridor to Jacko's office. The door was open, so they walked in.

Jacko pointed to the chairs and perched on the corner of his desk. "I've had word out of Papua New Guinea about slightly unusual numbers showing for people passing through and into Australia." He scratched an ear and shrugged. "It may be the mob we lost a few weeks ago."

Leigh leaned forward. "What details have we got?"

Jacko shook his head. "Not much, I'm afraid. Just a note from Moresby that three lots of two men have shipped out for Australia in the last six hours or so. Going to different locations in Queensland and New South Wales. Nothing threatening. Just unusual."

Callie frowned. "Can you get me the movement data out of Papua New Guinea and into all Australian ports over the last week?"

Jacko pursed his lips. "Shouldn't be a problem; I'll get a dump of the real-time feeds. Do you just want air?"

Callie's brow furrowed. "No. Let's have it all. That way, I can cover other bases if needed."

Jacko nodded and made a call. "You'll have the compressed files on the cloud in ten minutes." He rubbed his chin. "I've got a bad feeling about this; the timing is too much of a coincidence. Check that data, Callie. If we get even a sniff that this is related to the Central Coast, we have to warn them. People coming in means they are ready to try something."

Callie imported the files from the cloud server into her reporting tool and quickly extracted the numbers relating to Papua New Guinea outgoing and Australia incoming. An analysis of the aggregated land, air and sea data showed an increase in the arrival of males in general over the last eighteen hours. The movements were spread across origins and destinations and wouldn't be noticed under normal circumstances. Air accounted for seventy per cent of the total, and sea accounted for the rest. Interestingly, the sea arrivals originated at Merauke, Saumlaki, and Kupang, and they arrived in Weipa and Darwin, making them short journeys. Callie flagged it as an attempt to diffuse the data enough for it to go unnoticed. She told Leigh they were lucky to pick up on it.

Two hours after leaving, they were back in Jacko's office, and Callie was summing up. "Fifty to sixty people have come onshore in twelve to eighteen hours. No arrivals landed south of Sydney, and about half entered via regional airports." She looked worried. "By the look of it, they could all come together on the Coast by Thursday night or Friday at the latest."

Jacko nodded in agreement. "Leigh, get in touch with your friend Codie and tell him what we've got. I expect they won't have more than a few days before someone comes sniffing around there again."

Leigh frowned and shook his head. "I hope they're ready for a sizeable sniff!"

Chapter 40

With the field freshly ploughed and planted, the Crossings were enjoying a mid-morning planning session. Their peaceful discussion was interrupted by a commotion out back at the tractor shed. They looked questioningly at each other to see if anyone knew what was going on, and, as none did, they all stood and made their way outside. What greeted them was both mayhem and amazement.

Three men moved a cage into one of the shed's vacant bays. The cage contained an animal vaguely resembling a deer. It was well-trussed so that it couldn't hurt itself, but the noise it made was loud and shrill enough to shatter glass.

"Bloody Hell!" said Coby as he dashed to a nearby supply cupboard. He pulled out a handful of ear protectors, which he distributed to his family. The men moving the cage smiled and pointed to their ears into which they'd already placed earplugs.

Once able to talk, Coby looked at the men, shook his head and shrugged. "Where on earth did this come from?"

The men chuckled, and one held out a hand. "Hi, Coby. I'm George Steel, and these are Bobby Park and Renee Kennedy." The two groups greeted each other and introduced themselves.

George shrugged and raised a brow. "We're one of the exploration teams. We were checking out the woodlands adjacent to the big prairie to the southwest and came across a herd of these." They looked again at the animal in the cage. It had calmed and, mercifully, stopped bleating. It didn't look like any animal on Earth but was similar enough to make it familiar. George smiled. "We call it a 'Tubsheer' given its wide girth, deer-like body and sheepish face!"

Coby chuckled. "Tubsheer? Good enough name if you ask me!"

George displayed a map and pointed out where they'd found the herd.

Selina looked interested. "The terrain a couple of hundred kilometres south of here is not too different from where you spotted the herd. Now we've got the crop in, I'd say it's time to get on the road and see about finding a few local herds."

Coby nodded in agreement. "I'll talk it through with the Major. In the meantime, how about you butcher this tubby and see how it pans out." He smiled and added. "Pardon the pun!"

Coby and George headed to the Major's HQ, where they outlined their idea. The Major agreed it was a good one. "But, why send people? We need manpower here. Can't we use technology?"

Coby shrugged. "I don't know what technology we have. Can we make something?"

The Major frowned. "If the communications solution is anything to go by, then it shouldn't be too hard, should it?"

He walked over to his computer. "Quinn, ICS to Jerry Bos."

"Major. How are things up there?"

"Hello, Jerry. All is excellent up here. We've had nice rain in the last few days, which has pleased the Crossings. Other than that, no trouble, which has me pleased!"

Jerry laughed. "What can we do for you, Major?"

"One of the exploration teams found a herd beast. It looks like it will be edible, and the Crossings want to look for a herd closer to hand with the idea of managing domestication and development." He shrugged. "I'm happy with the idea but wanted to see if you could sort out a technical search rather than us using manpower."

Jerry snorted. "A great idea, Major, and simple to do. We already scan for life when we find a new planet. I can modify the search parameters and reassign a planetary probe to do the job." He paused, and they could hear chatter in the background. "I'll add it as another process for Quinn and include it in the new planet protocols." There was more chatter in the background. "That was Codie telling me to hurry up. We have to get our equipment packed up and ready to move. There's certainly a sense of urgency here at the moment." Another pause. "Okay, done! You should start getting results in around ten minutes."

With that, the call ended.

The Major looked up with eyebrows raised. "Well! Sounds like we'll be having more guests soon!" He scratched his chin and raised his eyes. "Jerry said Quinn will record its results in ten minutes; you'll pick them up on the network." He cocked his head. "I need to get out and check our preparations for the new arrivals. They may be here sooner than we thought."

Coby grinned. "Thanks, major. I'll head back to the farm."

He looked at George, who shook his head. "I'll stay with the Major for the moment. See if he needs the help. Can you send Bobby and Renee back here when you get back?"

Coby noted the worried change in tone portrayed by the military men and nodded. "Will do. Thanks to you both." As he returned to the farm, Coby realised they'd have to increase their efforts. Manpower was the key.

While Coby was with George at the headquarters tent, Selina and Harvey killed the tubsheer and got to work. They recorded details of weight, blood volume, organs and the like. Samples were set aside for analysis in the lab they'd recently started to fit out, and the various cuts of meat were bagged and refrigerated. The hide was set aside in a barrel of salted water until they got the materials they needed for tanning.

Coby gave them the news about the search program Jerry had programmed and left them to their work while he went and checked his computer screen. Quinn's search pattern worked through the grassy areas around the settlement and gradually expanded. Displayed on a map, areas were shaded with different colours relating to the size of animals and herd numbers. When Coby looked, there were only a few small patches on the screen, so he left it and went to help with the tubsheer.

By late afternoon, they had enough data on the composition and nutrient value of the meat to pronounce it safe for consumption. The smile on Selina's face was beyond wide. She had been bubbling since she and Harvey started the butchering; the final results were all she could have hoped for. "I was so disappointed when we had to give up the herds back on Earth."

Harvey nodded in agreement; it had been a distressing time for them all. Selina's face became more serious. "That work wasn't in vain. What we learned will stand us in good stead now." She took a deep, satisfying breath, and her eyes hardened. "We'll make it work this time, and this time, we won't use land that will go underwater!" Selina laughed and hugged Harvey. "Let's go see if anyone else wants a BBQ tonight!"

That evening, as the sun set behind the mountains to the west, the Crossings and their friends, Harvey and Nate, sat around the BBQ with grilled tubby steaks on their laps. After some general talk, Coby sat back with a sigh and smiled. "I don't know about you folks, but that was delicious!" He smiled as the others agreed and pursed his lips. "But, we're going to have a big problem, and it'll be with us sooner than we think." Intrigued, the family and their friends waited for Coby to clarify.

"In the next day or two, we have close to a hundred people coming from the SplitQC group. That's a lot of food we have to produce and process. How can we achieve this? We need ideas." He took a drink of water and smiled. "I've been thinking about it and want to run some ideas by you and see what you think."

The family leaned closer as Coby started to talk. "The first thing we have to realise is that we can't do it all on our own; we're not even feeding ourselves, let alone the Major's men and another hundred coming in. What we do have is a lot of fertile ground, and grain-producing grasses as well as these tubbies for meat." He smiled. "And milk!"

Selina looked up at her father and nodded understanding. "What are you thinking, Dad?"

"We'll have to stop depending on Stepping food from Earth soon, or Marty will come under scrutiny. The WestProtect people will be looking hard for any leads back to us. That means we have to add to our stores as much as possible in the next few days to give us time to train the newcomers." He chuckled at the looks on his family's faces. "We need market gardeners, butchers, tanners. We'll need people who can handle a tractor to plough, sow and reap. We'll need to grind grains, make bread, compost scraps." He paused to let it sink in. "We'll need to work out farming methods and training processes that can be replicated as more people arrive in the future and, perhaps, as more worlds are settled."

The family chewed over Coby's words for a good hour. Dennis had pulled out a notebook and jotted different ideas down as they were aired. As the discussion slowed, he summarised topics on a fresh page. The rest of the family were smiling and awaiting his presentation.

Dennis growled at them and chuckled. "Don't look at me like that, you blighters! I'm not too old just yet!" There was a good bit of laughter at that. Dennis was certainly capable despite his years and was probably the best of them at planning. He had handed Coby the running of their property ten years previously when he was seventy. At the time, he'd had a heart scare, which resulted in a stent and a warning to take things easy from his doctor. The changing climate and self-serving politics were a step too far, and he'd moved aside to let Coby take the headwinds. Despite everything Coby could do, in the end, he was beaten by both weather and politicians.

Dennis raised his eyes. "Selina's volunteered for the animal husbandry. She and Nate will focus on building a herd of tubbies. Nate's a decent enough butcher and has volunteered to train new folks willing to get their hands bloody." He looked at Selina and Nate, and they both agreed.

"Next is Coby and Harvey, who will focus on the grains. There's a lot of ground involved, but the mechanics are not too difficult for a new hand to get on top of. The other advantage we have is the climate here.

It's different from Earth's but in a nice way. We look like we'll have two good growing seasons." Coby and Harvey looked at each other and nodded.

"Last of all is me. I'll need the tractor to get started, but I'll get going on a market garden. I'd be surprised if there weren't one or two of the SplitQC family members who would like to lend a hand. For that matter, I'd say both your groups will have a good few volunteers before you know it."

With the foundations set in place, the Crossings enjoyed the rest of the evening discussing past, present and future. At one point, Selina went to the computer display to see if the probe had found anything concrete yet. Her eyes widened, and a smile broke out. "Hey! Come look at this!" When the rest of the family joined her, she pointed out two areas in particular. "There is a good-sized herd of Tubbies, and they're less than twenty kilometres away. "Her smile broadened as she pointed to a small highlighted area a few kilometres further. "Quinn's found another herd, but they aren't tubbies." She paused for the drama of the moment. "These look more like horses!"

"Horses?" exclaimed Dennis, Coby, Nate and Harvey as one.

Selina shrugged and displayed a picture of what looked like a camel without humps or a horse with longish legs and a camel's face. "Well, almost horses by the look of them, but they'll do!"

The Crossings hit the sack early. They had a lot to do!

* * *

Brogan and his team reviewed the satellite data from the last three days. They had made a motel north of Gosford their base for the upcoming week.

Brogan's brow furrowed as he studied the heat signature that mysteriously appeared outside the warehouse each night. "This bloke is a puzzle. He's clearly equipped with advanced technology and his experience is hard-earned, likely from navigating treacherous situations." The green shape, almost motionless, seemed to taunt them by appearing in different locations each night. "His routine is unpredictable. He emerges at any time before four in the afternoon, surveys the site, and then disappears into the night, choosing a new hiding spot each time."

Brogan's voice was firm. "We can afford to lose a few hours. Our plan is solid. We'll withdraw from the area by three in the afternoon and return once he's settled and we've pinpointed his location. Our priority is to gather information on their numbers, strength, and habits. Let's stick to the plan."

They went as a group to conduct an initial visual inspection of the area and the people they were up against. They were looking for any line of sight from a distance of not less than two hundred metres. The distance would keep their general surveillance well out of the way of electronics and any eagle-eyed security men. They reviewed all access roads and walkways around the site and cross-matched them with the visuals from the satellite. They found an excellent long-range view of the front of the unit from an adjacent hill. The hill had a children's play area and a couple of picnic tables with tin roofs to keep the rain and sun off. Moving back into the trees at the park's edge made it easy to set up a scope on a tripod and get a good view while out of sight.

Closer work was more difficult as the perimeter was inconveniently fenced. At the rear of the unit, the fence was ten metres from the building, and the scrub behind it provided reasonable cover, but the location wouldn't get them much information apart from electronics. The fencing at the front was forty metres from the building. Between the chain link mesh and the warehouse were car parking, a service road and ten metres of scrubby garden. Various angles between tree trunks and shrubs gave limited but acceptable views, but using the front posed a greater risk of detection by the lab's electronics or security sweeps.

Brogan checked his watch and signed for his team to move back quietly. They returned to the motel and discussed options over an early lunch. "The last thing we want is to be compromised, so we'll stick with one man on the hill and one in the scrub at the front. The hill is far enough away to avoid running into whoever our night owl is, but whoever is out front needs to evacuate the area by three in the afternoon. We can't get back in there for visuals until the owl is set for the night."

He looked at Kobi, "You'll have to be at the top of your game. We'll need you to let us know if we're missing anything and get the frequencies of any remotes, such as the ram bollards."

Kobi frowned and nodded. "Will do, boss."

"Any questions?" asked Brogan. "Okay. I'll take the next couple of hours at the front. I want to get a better sense of what we're up against. Mike, you can take the hill. Kobi, you're on your own."

He looked at the other two. "You two get some rest. You'll be on deck tonight."

Chapter 41

The atmosphere in the car park was charged with anticipation. People had gathered since mid-morning, their curiosity piqued by the element of surprise. The wait was a mix of excitement and wonder, with every sound causing a stir and children's eyes wide with anticipation of the unknown.

Harry moved amongst his employees, offering encouragement where needed but mostly being a calming influence. Not long before eleven, a bus pulled into the car park. It was shiny dark green, had no markings, and had opaque windows.

The bus driver and another person came out of the bus and were greeted by Harry, who hugged the other person. "It's Imogen!" Someone called. Suddenly the gathered people moved closer with questions and smiles.

Imogen put her hands in the air. "It's okay. We'll explain everything as soon as we can. Let's get you guys onto the bus." Her smile had an immediate calming effect.

As people got onto the bus, their bags were stored in the luggage bay, and Alice ticked their names off a list. When the last of them had gotten on, Harry checked the list with her; there were still a few more staff members plus their families to come. With half an hour until midday, Harry decided to send the bus on its way; he'd use the second for the rest of his people.

He climbed into the front of the bus and used the speaker system to address his staff. "First and foremost, I want to express my deep gratitude for your trust. I am confident that this surprise trip will be a memorable experience for all of us! We still have a few dozen people to pick up and will use the second bus to bring them. Imogen and I will be with them, ensuring a smooth journey."

He pointed to the driver beside him. "This is Matt Wallace." There were a couple of hellos from people who knew him, and Matt gave a wave. "For those who may not have recognised him, Matt is one of SplitQC's security team, led by Codie Maxwell. They have been our protectors since we discovered someone trying to steal our work. Once you arrive at where the bus is taking you, Matt will guide you to the second phase of the trip. Once again, he cannot reveal the final destination until you arrive." He smiled. "So don't give him too hard a time when he doesn't spill the beans!" There were a few chuckles at this.

Harry continued. "I also want you to know that everyone involved in this operation has my full trust. I trust them with my life. I trust them with all our lives." His face became serious. "By the same token, all our lives depend on each of you. You know the situation is dangerous, and this move is to protect you. It also protects all of us who are involved." He paused and gave them a small smile. "Please bear with us for the next few hours. When you are asked to do something, don't hesitate; do it how you are asked to. There's nothing to fear, and you'll soon know everything."

Harry looked over their heads and saw the second bus entering the parking lot. "It's time for you to go. Good luck, and I'll see you all in a few hours."

Mary Harding drove the second bus and arrived in time to join the group waving off the first bus. Alice gave her an update on the relocation numbers as they waited for the rest of the employees to arrive. There was still one family missing when noon passed. Alice tried calling on her mobile, but it rang out, so she left a message. A minute or two later, she received a call from a breathless Sid Towers. "Alice! Sid here. I had a flat tyre! It's my first flat in bloody years, and I had trouble changing it."

Alice looked concerned. "Are you alright? Do you need help?"

Sid laughed. "No, it's all okay. Between us, my wife Sarah and I got the bloody thing done. We're about five minutes away."

Alice smiled. "Don't rush, we'll wait for you!" She heard a hurried "Thanks!" and the line went dead.

* * *

Mary turned into Marty's drive and slowed down as she drove on the dirt road for two hundred metres, pulled in beside the first bus and opened the doors. Imogen left Harry and Mary to organise the group while she went to the shed where the PTVs were operating. "Hi Jerry, how's it all going?"

Jerry looked at Imogen and smiled. "Like a well-oiled machine. We've got one more trip after this, and the first busload is done."

"Excellent! I'll join the next group and help Major Moreton settle the new arrivals into their new home." She pointed back the way she'd come. "All passengers are present and accounted for, so we can say phase one has been successful!"

Jerry smiled, "Harry will be relaxing a bit, I hope! He's been wound pretty tight these last few days."

Imogen chuckled. "Yep. He was a lot more relaxed in the bus coming up. It's been a load for him to move the entire company and their families." She looked up as Harry entered the shed, "Speak of the devil, here he is."

Harry greeted Jerry and got an update on their progress. He was relieved it was all going so well. "I'll wait and go with the last Step. How many more trips are there?"

Jerry checked the lists. "Three more trips after this one."

There was a ping, and Quinn's voice came over a speaker. "Step commencing in Five.. Four.. Three.. Two.. One.."

"Step Complete."

Matt and Mary took their leave as they left to return the buses.

Harry was the last to board the PTV for the final Step to Karma. Before closing the hatch, he shook Marty's hand. "That's it for the moment, Marty. Thanks for all your effort, and I hope to see you on Karma soon."

Marty smiled. "No problem, Harry. I'm not sure I'll be out there anytime soon, but hopefully, in a year or so."

Marty saw the PTV off and closed the shed.

All was quiet for the moment.

* * *

Marty checked his list even though he had it well memorised. He was expecting three prefab sheds to be used as labs on Karma until they had more enduring building methods. The fleet of caravans had grown to fifty, and he'd send another ten or so over the coming week, depending on their condition when he received them. He'd also got hold of a source of second-hand solar panels from a local installer who was upgrading to more efficient technology. On average, the panels were five years old and had a good fifteen to twenty years of generation left. He figured using them was better than having them go to landfill.

The Karma settlement didn't have the resources to use concrete for building, so they opted for wooden piers and timber floors. As a result, Marty had issued a standing order for second-hand timber from the contacts he'd made in connection with his low-cost housing projects. Every few days, he sent a load, which the Major's men stored under a tarp off to the side of the PTV landing zone.

Amidst the ongoing logistics, there was also a request for a second tractor and a list of smaller items such as bee hives, kitchen utensils, fishing nets and other assorted bits and pieces. Marty, always ready to adapt, took on the challenge. Some of the items had been ticked and labelled if he had been able to procure them from his network. The others he'd have to find elsewhere. He scratched his head and logged into his favourite online shopping sites, where he got to work. He was interrupted when a horn sounded out front. He checked the manifest and saw it was the prefab sheds he'd ordered for the labs.

He pointed to the blue container twenty metres away. "Can you drop them in there?"

The driver smiled. "No problem, mate." He set to work with the loading ramp and delivery forklift.

When he'd finished, Marty asked him if he'd like water or to use the toilet. The driver was delighted and took him up on both offers. "Thanks, mate," he said, "people rarely ask these days."

Marty smiled and shrugged. "Yeah, it seems like things are different now. We do the best we can, though."

The driver jinked his chin at the container. "What are you doing with the sheds?"

Marty sighed. "I'm thinking of growing fruit and vegetables in the back paddock and figuring out how to store stuff there. Perhaps strike seeds and stuff like that." He sighed again and rolled his eyes. "Been thinking about it for a while now, so I'm hoping to get it going this time!"

The driver laughed. "I understand how you feel, mate. Well, good luck with it."

Marty smiled and shook his hand. "You too, mate. Thanks again."

Once the driver had left, Marty closed the container and returned to the office. "Quinn, Container delivery to Karma."

"Container to Karma, executing."

The container disappeared, and Marty went back to his screen.

After a half hour, Marty stood from his desk and went outside into the fresh air. He was feeling unsettled, as though he'd forgotten to do something. He walked back and forth, trying to work out what it was. He only had one problem that he worried about - housing. He wasn't happy with caravans as a solution for much more than a few hundred people. He shook his head in frustration and wandered around his home site.

He spent fifteen minutes wandering through a potting shed, compost area and garage and found himself on the way to his main storage shed. He pushed the door open and looked inside. The shed was well organised, with a clear space at the front and various, occasionally used, tools stacked neatly at the back and sides. He looked around without getting any inspiration and turned for the door to go back to his office. He noticed the old red cement mixer and paused. He looked at it for a while and frowned before closing up and heading to his desk.

He sat and thought for a moment, then cocked his head. "Quinn, I need to talk with Jerry on the comms system."

Quinn replied, "Acknowledged."

A moment later, Jerry's voice came across the speakers. "Hi, Marty. First time on the ICS! What can I do for you?"

Marty smiled. "Hi, Jerry. I have an idea, but I don't know if it will work. I'm worried about housing and reckon we need to move beyond caravans sooner rather than later."

"I agree with you, Marty. Especially now SplitQC is coming over. What do you have in mind?"

"The issue we have is digging foundations and pouring concrete. I was wondering if we could use the Step drive for both?"

Jerry was silent as he thought about it. "I'm shaking my head, Marty. I can't see a way it would help. Did you have something in mind?"

Marty sighed and pursed his lips. "Not anything I can put words to, no."

Jerry chuckled. "Don't let that stop you thinking about it. You may be on the way to solving the problem, so keep at it!"

Marty laughed ruefully. "I will, Jerry." He paused a moment, thinking. "Jerry? Am I able to work with Quinn to try things? How much does it understand?"

Jerry grunted. "Huh! No reason why you can't. Hang on a tick."

Marty heard mumbling, and Jerry talked again. "I've opened Quinn up so you can use its solution code. You'll have access to problem-solving and analysis, which will let you discuss new ideas with Quinn and find new solutions. I have restricted your access to ensure one hundred per cent safety. This means you can't break anything or hurt anyone!" He chuckled. "Call if you get into strife, and I'll help."

Marty laughed again. "Thanks, Jerry! I've never had an AI working for me before. I'll be careful."

"No worries, Marty. Good luck!"

Marty sat back and considered for a moment. "Quinn, Marty here. Can you help me with an idea?"

Quinn replied. "Yes, Marty. What do you need?"

It took a while for Marty to get the hang of asking the right questions, but he got there in the end. The first part of his idea, excavation, was achieved with a shaped Step field that fit tightly to the test device. Marty used a beetroot can from his recycling bin as the device and placed a set of field generators under general instruction from Quinn. When the device was Stepped into a pile of earth and then returned to a position outside the pile, the can was full of dirt. Trying the same action inside a sandstone block destroyed the can. After analysis, Quinn applied more power and hardened the field to the degree that it vaporised the stone around the device. This returned a smooth chunk of stone the size of the inside of the new can. Marty ran a few experiments in his back paddock and was able to dig holes and trenches.

The second part, 'pouring' concrete into the excavations, proved simpler; Quinn suggested they use two devices. It involved a poly tube and a cover plate. The cover plate was placed on the ground, and the tube was set lengthwise onto it. The plate had four electronically controlled clips to retain it in place. Marty mixed a batch of concrete and filled the tube. When ready, Quinn Stepped it to the rim of an excavated foundation hole and removed the cover plate, allowing the concrete to fall into the hole.

Marty scratched his head. "Well, Quinn, it's not the most elegant solution, but it does work and should do until we work out something better."

Quinn replied with a simple, "Yes, Marty."

The idea for housing foundations never came to fruition due to the cost of Stepping concrete. However, the techniques weren't wasted, as the core ideas were used in irrigation, composting and mining.

Chapter 42

The morning after Quinn found the herd of tubsheer, Selina talked with Coby and Dennis. "I'll go with Nate on the trikes and find the herd, but I'll need a fenced pasture to put them in when we round them up and bring them in," she grinned. "We'll probably need some help encouraging them to go in when the time comes."

Dennis laughed out loud. "I'd say there will be a bit of new learning going on around here for both man and beast when the time comes. Wild animals are not quite as accommodating as our domesticated mobs." He grinned. "That said, I can get a couple of Stan's men to help, so we should have a good paddock ready for you by tomorrow afternoon." He took off his hat and looked around the nearby area. "Have you any particular place where you want them?"

Selina thought for a moment. "There's some nice grazing land southwest of the grain field."

Dennis nodded. "I know where you mean. How about the big loop in the river? We could fence off the neck, and you'll have around a hundred and fifty hectares bounded by the river and a hundred metres of fence?"

Selina smiled. "That sounds perfect! Thanks, Dennis!"

While Dennis went to get help with the fence, Selina and Nate took an e-trike each, packed supplies for the night, just in case, and headed south. After an uneventful but scenic hour of easy travelling over the undulating terrain, they noticed a small cloud of dust ahead and to their right. They slowed and made their way towards a low hill that would give them a view of whatever was causing the dust. They dismounted from the trikes when they arrived and crawled up the easy slope.

Selina smiled. Not more than three hundred metres away was a herd of fifty or so tubsheer; it looked like they were headed for a stream two or three kilometres distant.

They slid back down the slope to the trikes. Nate opened a storage saddle and pulled out two whips. He handed one to Selina. "I didn't think we'd get to crack a whip again, but I couldn't chuck them out!"

Selina took hers. It had been a gift from Dennis when she'd started to work with cattle a few years before the floods. She looked at Nate, a tear in her eye, "Thank you, Nate! I regretted leaving it after we left. This is such a wonderful surprise". She cocked her head. "What made you keep them?"

Nate smiled and shrugged his shoulders. "Simply as a reminder of good times. I never guessed we'd get the chance to live that life again, and I wanted to keep a part of it alive."

Selina grinned. "Well, let's see how a tubsheer responds to a bit of coercion. I wish we had a dog to help!"

Nate laughed. "Old Dolly would even be a help now!"

Selina snorted as she remembered. Dolly was the pick of the litter and ended up a hopeless sheepdog. She became the family pet and never rounded up a beast in her long life. Selina hopped on her trike. "Let's go get them, Nate. We'll play them easy to start and see how we go."

The tubsheer didn't know what hit them! Harried by these strange animals with cracking whips, toots, hoots and whistles, they took the easy path north. After six hours of travel at a comfortable tubsheer walk, they brought the herd into sight of the newly fenced paddock and were quickly joined by the rest of the family, plus eight of the Major's men. The cheering and hat-waving that followed encouraged the herd through the opening, and once inside, the gate was closed and secured.

The tubbies milled about restlessly for ten minutes but gradually wandered off to look at their new home.

Selina thanked the soldiers and promised them a steak as they returned to their duties. She took Coby by the arm and hugged him. All was right with the world - this one, at least!

* * *

James raised his arms for quiet, and the chatter in the community tent stilled.

"My friends from SplitQC, you have been on Karma for a few days now, and I know you've had both fun and difficulty settling in. These changes have been a surprise and a shock for us all, and I commend you for your ability to come to terms with our new lives as quickly as you have. I also thank you for the trust you have shown in Harry. I am sure it wasn't easy to come all this way before finding out you'd come all this way!"

He looked at the crowded tent and smiled at them. "The first thing I want to say is I'm one of the people responsible for your being here. I was 'lucky' enough to notice something odd, and with the help of Harry and SplitQC, we were able to work out the technology that got us here." He frowned, and his face drooped. "It's sad we had to leave so preemptively because other people wanted to control the Step drive for wealth and power." His eyes narrowed, "Those people are still hunting us, and in a few short hours, we'll all have left Earth so we can continue our work in peace.

"Our task now is to invent and build technologies that will help us move from the temporary accommodations of caravan and tent into something a bit more 'civilised'."

There were a few yells of agreement and cheers. "Our priorities are clear. Food, Energy and Automation." He grinned. "The Crossings and those of you who have volunteered to help them and learn new skills have food covered." He shrugged. "I haven't tried one yet, but I've heard tubby steaks are delicious!"

There were calls for more steaks, and James laughed as Coby Crossing stood and bowed. James shrugged. "We need energy. Not just to cook steaks but also to power our homes and Quinn's central processors on Karma.

"My focus, and that of Imogen, Jerry and Olivia, is automation. We aim to automate as many tasks as possible using Step technology and our AIs. The reason for this is simple: our goal is for people to be able to choose what they want to do with their lives. I'd certainly choose nanotechnology over servicing composting toilets!"

Once again, the hoots indicated the crowd's general good mood and understanding of what was needed.

James lifted his head. "We have moved here under pressure. The thing is, we're here now, and we have what we have. As I see it, we've got a beautiful world that has welcomed us with open arms." There were many shouts and agreement with this sentiment, and James waited, a tear in his eye. "As importantly, we have good people with great minds who can work on the things that need to be done." There was a murmur of agreement and cheering.

James put a hand to still them and smiled broadly. "We don't need roads or cars. We can move around the planet using Step Vehicles." He cocked his head. "We have a solar array to recharge batteries and power our computers and essential services. We've also gotten a good start on exploring our new planet, and Quinn is building a database of potential resources.

"If I had a priority, it would be energy production. What do you see? If you see something you can get involved in or an initiative you want to start, get onto it. Talk with Harry or Alice and see what resources are available." He held his arms at chest level, palms up. "This is your world as much as it is mine. Love it and build it!"

He paused a few seconds. "Thank you all. Welcome to Karma, and I look forward to joining you soon."

With that, James walked around the tent with Harry and offered his heartfelt thanks to everyone there.

When he was ready, he said a quick goodbye to Imogen before he jumped into the PTV and Quinn Stepped him back to the lab at Tumbi Umbi.

* * *

Dennis slapped Imogen on the back. "Perfect!"

He was looking at lengths of six by four hardwood in the 'timber yard' Marty was creating.

Imogen grunted as she regained her balance and turned to Dennis. "You don't have to bowl me over, Dennis." Looking at the timber, she frowned. "What's got you so excited?"

Dennis looked a bit sheepishly at Imogen. "Sorry about that. I forget you're an office worker sometimes!"

"Office worker!" Imogen snorted. "I'll have you know," her composure cracked, and she laughed. Dennis joined in, and they chuckled for a minute or two. Once their humour was under control, she looked again at the timber. "What's on your mind?"

Dennis slapped a rough palm on one of the six-by-fours. "There's a method I've used previously called skid foundations. It works well on flat, level surfaces." He drew a picture with his hands as he explained. "The six by fours, the skids, are inserted into trenches and the floor frame built on top of them." He shrugged. "It's an easy process and very durable. It'll certainly be much better than a few boards on the ground."

Imogen, having been informed about the pending arrival of the prefabs for the three scientific laboratories, was filled with a sense of anticipation. She had volunteered to oversee their erection. After a thorough discussion with Major Moreton, they agreed a grassy knoll a half kilometre to the east of the main settlement would be the perfect location, far enough away for any safety concerns and well within the defensible perimeter.

Since manpower was at a premium, she asked if she could borrow the Crossing's tractor to help level the three building sites, and Dennis offered to do the tractor work. Once the sites were level, he'd asked about the prefabs and the floor, and, in a short while, they were looking through the timber yard.

Dennis selected the timber they needed for the first shed and, with the help of one of the Major's men, loaded it onto the tractor and dropped it near the chosen site. He smiled at Imogen and pointed to the topsoil he'd pushed whilst levelling the area. "I'll get tools for the trenching and drop this lot in the market garden."

Imogen went along as a passenger in case help was needed as Dennis ferried the excavated topsoil to the 'farm', as he called it, and dumped it in a pile by the market garden. Then he drove them to a shed where he collected trenching shovels and a couple of mattocks. Imogen helped as they dug the trenches, set the skids in place and built the floor frame. By the end of the day, they'd completed the prep work for the first laboratory.

Imogen leaned back and stretched her back. "Ow." She chuckled and shook her head. "Thanks for your help, Dennis. I'm not sure I could have got anyone else, and I certainly wouldn't have ended up with a floor like this to work on."

Dennis smiled warmly. "It was my pleasure, Imogen. I got some good topsoil, and I'm always happy to give science a chance to improve life." He pointed to Imogen's back. "I may have some horse liniment." His face broke into a cheeky grin. "It may sting a bit, but.."

"Horse liniment!" Imogen snorted. "I'll have you know," again, they broke into guffaws of laughter—a situation they often found themselves in during their efforts.

They finished the preparation in good time. The following day, a blue container was on the knoll and being unloaded by one of the Major's patrols. Imogen smiled as she watched them work. These were some of the most highly trained men in the Australian armed forces, and they happily worked as labourers and builders in a new world. She walked up to the Sergeant in charge of the patrol. "Sergeant Booth. Good morning to you."

Arnie Booth smiled and wiped his brow. "Morning, ma'am." He watched his men unpack the first shed and lay out the various pieces.

Imogen smiled back. "Imogen is fine, Sergeant. I'm not used to ma'am and marm."

Arnie chuckled. "I suppose not, ma'am.. I mean, Imogen." His eyes crinkled in a smile. "You and Dennis did a good job getting the site ready; I may have a job for you if you find some spare time!"

Imogen looked at her hands and gave a rueful laugh. "I don't think I'm cut out for too much of this heavy work! My hands have blisters and splinters, and my lower back's none too happy!"

The sergeant laughed. "Nothing a bit of hard training won't put right, ma'am."

Imogen started to laugh but suddenly stopped short, a quizzical look on her face. "You know what? I think that's a good idea!"

Arnie jerked his attention back to Imogen and cocked his head. "Say what?"

Imogen shrugged. "I think some training is a good idea." She cocked her head. "We've got a lot of people coming to the settlement, and we'll be on our own for a while. It would be good to have exercise classes to help get and keep fit!"

Arnie pursed his lips and nodded. "You may be onto something. I'll talk with the Major and see what he thinks."

Imogen watched as Sgt. Booth and his squad erected the shed in quick time. She was working out where to put stores and equipment a few hours later. Arnie popped into the shed as she was mulling it over and smiled. "I had a word with the Major, and he agrees that exercise sessions for the civvies are a good idea. He will set a schedule that fits in with the exploration teams as they come in for briefings and R&R time between gigs."

"That's great. I look forward to it. Thanks, Sergeant."

"Arnie, if you like, ma'am." They laughed in good spirits. "One other thing. We've prepped the other two sheds after seeing how you and

Dennis set out the foundations. We should have one more done today, and we'll finish the third tomorrow morning."

Imogen looked at him in surprise and looked at her hands. "That's even greater news, Arnie! I wondered how my hands would cope with another bout of digging!"

Arnie smiled and took his leave to return to work while Imogen continued moving into her new lab.

Chapter 43

Ken shrugged into his body armour and checked his weapon.

Codie raised an eye as Ken exited the office. "You're like a cat on a hot tin roof, mate. What are you sensing?"

Ken shrugged and frowned as his eyes scanned the area. "I can't say for sure, Codie; it's been building over the last few days. Something's spooking me. I can only think of small things that don't register in the conscious." He shook his head. "It doesn't make them any less real, but it's frustrating not to be able to identify them."

Codie looked around the area as well. "They're almost done with the packing. Not more than another day, and we'll be off."

Ken snorted with disdain. "I hope it's soon enough, mate. I'll do a circuit. If nothing else, it'll burn off the tension."

Codie walked back into the office and locked the door. Mary was at the security station. "Keep a good lookout, Mary. Something's got Ken on edge."

Mary grinned through her own tension. "Will do Codie. I'll be glad to get out of here, though!"

"Won't we all," said Codie with a grunt as he headed into the warehouse.

Jerry was taping a box.

Codie looked at the workbench and shook his head. "All those boxes packed, and your bench is still chockers! Bloody hell!"

Jerry chuckled. "Don't let the mess fool you, Codie. I know where every bit goes, and it'll only take a half hour or so to pack it."

Codie sighed and made his way to James's area. James wasn't there, but the bench was clear. Seeing movement at the PTV, he looked in time to see James disappear inside with a box over his shoulder.

James smiled when Codie popped his head through the hatch. "Hiya Codie. How's your end going?"

Codie smiled at James's good spirits. "We're not sure, James. The Sooner we get the hell out of here, the better. Ken's wound up like a spring, and he's not easy to spook!"

James frowned. "Okay. I reckon we're far enough along to move the schedule up anyway. Quinn's got most of the CubeSats back now, and Marty has them stacked and ready to send to Karma when we want them." He thought for a moment. "I'll check with Jerry. By rights, we should be able to have Quinn send the next couple of loads and then shut down. Marty's got another Quinn operational at his place, and I believe it can handle the last Step rather than a Quinlet as I'd first thought."

Codie raised his eyebrows and rubbed his chin. "If we could do that, when can we take the last Step?"

James looked at the boxes and gear yet to go and estimated it would take another three Steps to clear the place. He looked at Codie. "Hang on a sec." He walked over to where Jerry was packing another box." Jerry, if we had to leave ASAP, can we have Quinn transfer control to Marty's Quinn to manage the transfers?"

Jerry shrugged. "Easy to do." He smiled evilly. "They're of a like mind!"

James sighed and dropped his head into his hands before chuckling. "Let's do it, mate. Security is getting agitated; we should listen to them."

Jerry looked at Codie. "Will do, James. Won't be before time anyway if you ask me!"

Codie called Marcus. "Marcus, can you spare one man to help pack in here? I want to get out of here ASAP."

Marcus acknowledged. "Wait, one." There was a short pause while he checked in with his squad. "I talked with Ken, and he reckons I can give you two if he stays out here. He agrees with getting out."

Codie snorted. "Not surprising, given he's stressed. Send them in; there are boxes to load."

James worked with the Major's men, Phil Butler and Charlie Hogg, to load the PTV. While James and his friends loaded the PTV, Jerry called Marty to explain their plans.

"The security team is spooked, Marty, and we've decided to bring forward our Step out."

Marty frowned to himself. "Okay, I understand. Is my position here still secure?"

"Yes. You are fine. Nobody except us locals knows you even exist. We'll keep it that way!"

"Roger that. What do you need me to do?"

"Nothing. I am going to transfer the main AI operations to your Quinn. Once that's done, it will manage ICS and any Steps we take from here. You won't notice anything."

"Okay. What if the power goes out?"

"Good question. Once again, there is nothing to worry about. Quinlets can make decisions autonomously if there is a problem mid-Step. Otherwise, the Quinn on Karma will keep the ICS going from that end. There's nothing to worry about."

"Okay. Enjoy the trip, and good luck!"

Jerry could hear the smile in Marty's voice. "Thanks, Marty! And good luck to you. And thanks for taking on this job. It's important!"

"No worries, Jerry. Give my best to Imogen and the others, and I look forward to joining you all sometime in the future."

"Will do Marty. Jerry out!"

"Bye."

Jerry shook his head. They were lucky to have Marty as a resource on Earth. After testing Marty's Quinn was fully connected, Jerry shut down the system and got it ready for transport.

As Jerry cleared off the last of his bench, James joined him and asked about Marty. Jerry smiled. "He's handling it all without any problems. Wishes us all good luck and looks forward to joining us sometime."

James smiled ruefully. "I hope it's not too long before he can. We just have to get the basics organised." His eyes shot open. "Hang on! I had something I wanted to ask him." James grabbed his phone and opened his notes app. "Here we go; I want him to look out for a power turbine." He shook his head at Jerry. "Remind me when we get back, will you?"

Jerry laughed. "No problem, mate." He pointed at his boxes. "These are ready, and that's all for me. Where do you want them?"

"Let's put them in the next load; this one is ready to go." He looked around the space. "I'd say we have two more after this. We should be out in an hour or two."

* * *

Brogan frowned as the reports came in. "Kobi! What's happening inside?"

"There's a lot of electromagnetic activity, Brogan. Heat shows twelve people, down from seventeen a couple of hours ago."

"Shit! Where are they going? We haven't seen anything out here."

"I don't know Brogan." Kobi sounded stressed. "I haven't seen anything like it."

"Keep on it, all of you! I'll get onto the boss."

Brogan shook his head. "I can't figure it out, Frank. The only thing that makes sense is they have some kind of shield or electronics that confuses their footprint." He was trying to explain to Frank and Marsh that there had been increased activity at the site over the last few hours, and it looked like the occupants were leaving, but he couldn't say how.

Frank furrowed his brow. "These blokes have shown an uncanny knack for thwarting our efforts, so I'm not surprised something is going on." He looked at Marsh. "Have you any ideas, Marsh?"

Marsh shrugged. "They may have a shielding technology we're not aware of. Given that you say at least twenty people were there this morning, and they're down to twelve now?" He chewed his lip. "Has there been any sign of digging? Perhaps a tunnel? Or a basement?"

Brogan shook his head. "Nothing. And they have no idea we're watching them." He frowned. "Unless they're much better than we planned for, and they've known all along and not been concerned about it."

Frank growled. "Fuck it!" He looked at Marsh. "We have to go in there anyway, and we'll have the element of surprise regardless of whether they have a shield or not." He thought a moment. "We go now! It's Friday afternoon, so our risk is increased, but we can't afford to wait."

Marsh cricked his neck but remained silent as Frank focused on Brogan. "You've seen no heavy weapons?"

Brogan shook his head. "No. Only small arms, knives, that sort of thing. There is a team of six who look like special forces. They're equipped with automatics, and we've seen one, presumably a sniper, with a rifle and scope. The security group itself consists of eight plus their leader. At least one is female. They appear competent but not special forces. That does not apply to their extremely capable leader." He paused and frowned before continuing. "The last bloke is another matter entirely. He moves like a cat and can stay motionless for a night if necessary." He scratched his head as he remembered his mistrust of the satellite images. "If they know we are out here, he's the bloke that would spot us. But I can't figure out how he'd have done so! He's a bloody dangerous bastard, that's for sure."

Frank signalled for the men to deploy from the buses they'd parked in front of a vacant warehouse two units away from the one they were interested in. Fortunately, the adjacent unit was closed for the weekend, and they could move about freely. He turned to Brogan. "Anything on the satellite at the moment?"

Brogan glanced at his tablet's display and shook his head. "Clear." He frowned. "Just three people left in the unit!"

Marsh nodded. "Brogan, can you get the ram bollards to retract?"

Brogan nodded and handed over a remote-control device. "They're operated via a remote. We scanned the coded frequency and now have a copy of the key."

Marsh raised an eye. "Tested?"

Brogan laughed. "Yep. We stopped them lowering and restarted them when a delivery came in a few days ago. They put the odd performance down to a glitch or dirt in the mechanism."

Frank sighed and looked at the sky as a mob of kookaburras laughed in the evening light. "What do those bastards know that we don't?" He turned to Marsh. "The men are ready; let's get this job done."

Marsh nodded and approached the team waiting in the shadows across from the roller shutter.

Frank's voice came over their comms. "Ready to go on my mark." Ten seconds went by. "Mark!"

A reinforced 4WD vehicle started to accelerate on the 'Mark'. It was fifty metres from the shutter when the ram bollards began to retract, and the vehicle increased speed. With thirty metres to go, two pairs of men jogged silently into position at the rear and side walls, where they placed explosives and moved clear. With ten metres to go, the 4WD travelled at nearly seventy kilometres per hour.

The 4WD suddenly swerved and rammed the roller shutter. As it did so, a large explosion was heard at the side of the building and two smaller at the back and on the roof. Men rushed into the unit through the damaged roller shutter and the side wall, their weapons raised and shouting. Dust from the ceiling glittered as the lights on their helmets and guns slashed the air.

The shouts and their echoes slowly subsided, and all that could be heard was a circular piece of steel dislodged when the PTV Stepped out. The men watched as it slowed and spun down to the concrete floor with a hollow clatter.

Marsh signalled to two of his men. He pointed to one and then the office. He pointed to the other and the stairs to the mezzanine. They each took two men and cleared those areas. There was nothing there. There was nothing in the whole unit.

"Shit!" Frank looked around in dismay. "Let's get out of here."

About the Author

Keith Brady was born in Melbourne, Australia. His family moved to Hong Kong when he was five, and he grew up in both Hong Kong and Sydney.

Keith discovered a passion for writing short anecdotes about his football team's games. He expanded into poetry about people on his walking soccer team, incorporating humour and insights into the lives of those involved. He then read the poetry over a coffee or beer post-match. He has not published the aforementioned beyond his team.

His enjoyment of penning poetry led him to write a novella, 'Walkers in Space,' a sci-fi adventure story about Keith and his teammates. These writing experiences sparked the desire to write stories for his grandchildren and short stories for competitions.

'First Step' is Keith's debut book and first publication in the StepWorld series. The series has provided Keith with the platform to combine his love of science and space exploration with his concerns about planetary health and global power relationships.

Keith's goal is to explore different genres and writing styles, including fantasy, litRPG as a serial, and children's books for his grandkids

Keith's website is www.keithbrady.me, and he encourages readers to register for an occasional update on his progress or to ask a question about his writing.